The Kiss That Consumes

"David, David," she murmured, drawing her lips away. She grazed his cheek with hers, moving her hand up his shoulder to the back of his head. She ruffled his hair with her fingers. Then she tilted her head to one side and put pressure on the back of his head, urging him to lower his mouth to her bare neck. . . .

"Do it, David," she said in an urgent whisper. "Drink from me."

Possession

Berkley Books by Lori Herter

OBSESSION
POSSESSION

POSSESSION

LORI HERTER

B
BERKLEY BOOKS, NEW YORK

POSSESSION

A Berkley Book / published by arrangement with
Goddard and Kamin, Inc.

PRINTING HISTORY
Berkley edition / February 1992

ISBN: 0-425-13133-5

A BERKLEY BOOK® TM 757,375
Berkley Books are published by The Berkley Publishing Group,
200 Madison Avenue, New York, New York 10016.
The name "BERKLEY" and the "B" logo
are trademarks belonging to Berkley Publishing Corporation.

PRINTED IN THE UNITED STATES OF AMERICA

10 9 8 7 6 5 4 3 2 1

This book is dedicated to
Dana, Liz, and Laura. They
know why. And to my husband,
Jerry, for his patience.

Prologue

A Letter

A CENTURY OLD edition of Shakespeare's Sonnets sat on a small shelf within the rolltop desk in David de Morrissey's mansion. A letter had been slipped between the book's pages at the place where Sonnet 120 began, "That you were once unkind, befriends me now . . ."

The handwritten letter read as follows:

David,

I found the note you left for me as you rested in your coffin. Your handsome face looked so serene in your deep sleep, finding an envelope beside you with my name on it took me off guard. Even more unsettling were your words saying how much you love me, yet so full of stern advice about getting on with my life without you. I thought you loved me because I was shy and innocent. Yet you advise me to "live a rich and varied decade on my own as a mortal." You even tell me to take a lover! As if I could ever want anyone but you.

So you discovered that I still use the keys you gave me to visit you. I'd often wondered if you would guess. How did you know? Did you find my tear stains on your shirt? When you rose in the evening did you recall my voice too vividly for it to have been a dream? I often spoke to you as if you could hear me and give me comfort, the way you used to do.

Yes, I'm guilty, David. I have disobeyed you. I've broken our agreement—what you call our "pact"—to separate for ten years. But in my defense, I can only ask you again, How

1

do you expect me to go on without you? Just because your marks on my neck have healed doesn't mean our bond is dormant. At least, it isn't for me. Maybe you've been able to put me out of your mind, but I can't overcome my constant desire to be with you. Can't we please forget this pact? Transform me into a vampiress now, not ten years from now.

You say I need a decade to make the decision between mortality or immortality, that I'm too young to know my own mind. But I'm not too young to know that I love you and I always will. Now or ten years from now, my decision will be the same—I would choose to live forever with you.

I wonder why I'm bothering to write this. I know you won't listen. Trying to make you see my point of view is a waste of time. But then, I have ten years to waste, don't I? You will always think you know best and will make me abide by this miserable pact no matter what I think or how much it makes me suffer. I remember the last night we spent together. I tried logic, I pleaded, I wept, I promised I would hate you if you made me leave you. Nothing I said then mattered. You were going to be noble and do what you believed to be morally correct, even if it crushed me. By the tone of your letter, I can tell you haven't changed.

I do hate you, David. I'm so upset with you as I write this, I can barely see for the tears in my eyes. My hand is scribbling so fast, I wonder if you'll be able to read my words. What else is left for me to do? You've closed every door that could give me comfort.

All right then. Fine! I'll do as you say! You won't have to change your locks on my account. As for getting on with my life—well, I'll take your advice about that, too. You want me to take a lover? Then I'll start with Rob Green-field. He follows me around like a puppy at work, and I know he won't hesitate a second this evening when I tell him I'll sleep with him. In fact, at the very moment you wake and find this note in your hand, I may be in bed with him!

This news, I hope, makes you happy? Just remember, I'll be doing it for you only—giving myself to a man I don't love so I can gain all the worldly experience you think I lack. You see how willing I am to do anything for you, David. Even prostitute myself.

So this is my final goodbye. For ten years anyway. Or will it be forever? Because I can't believe you really love me as much as you say, or you would never put me through this. I've survived these past months only because I went against your wishes and visited you while you slept. Now you won't allow me even that. No one has ever been as cruel to me as you.

I won't close as you did by saying I still love you and always will. Because right now I despise you.

Veronica

1

No, I'm not into vampires

ALEXANDRA PETERS sat at her worktable scrutinizing the thin, pale, delicately molded piece of wood she'd shaped into a violin top. The soundboard felt satiny smooth to the touch. Using finger-sized planes and scrapers, she'd painstakingly carved it from a block of two-century-old imported spruce. The soft wood looked almost white, its grain exquisite in its refinement. She reached over to pick up a tiny, keyhole saw from the tool chest at her side.

"Are you going to cut the f-holes now?" an eager voice asked, startling her a bit.

Alexandra smiled, keeping her patience. "Yes. You may watch if you like. But if you have to talk, do it softly?"

"Sure," Susan said, putting down the small plane she was using. She'd been sitting at another worktable on the other side of the cluttered room, doing the preliminary shaping of the back of a viola. As she walked toward Alexandra, she brushed feathery wood shavings off of her denim shorts, then flicked her long black hair behind her ears.

Alexandra turned for a moment to look into the college girl's intelligent, quick, hazel eyes. "It's just that I'm used to working alone," she tried to explain.

Susan nodded, her straight, thick hair falling forward again from behind her ears. "I'll be quiet. I just want to see how you do it."

"Okay," Alexandra said and began carefully to cut into the wood.

Alexandra had met Susan last year when the girl's parents commissioned her to make a violin for their daughter. Susan

4

had shown great promise in high school as a violinist, and her parents wanted her to have a good instrument when she went on to college.

As she usually did with clients, Alexandra had consulted with Susan and her parents about precisely what type of sound they wanted the instrument to have and what color it should be. She'd helped Susan select the blocks of wood from which the various parts would be carved. The student became so interested in the process that Alexandra invited her to help make her own violin. Finding her a careful and reliable, if talkative, young woman, Alexandra offered to pay her by the hour to continue helping out after her own instrument had been finished. So, during college break times Susan had come a few days a week to work under Alexandra's constant direction.

In June, Alexandra had been glad to see Susan return for the summer, because she needed the help. But she quickly found that having someone else in her private workshop for more than a week was an intrusion, especially since her workshop was in her home. Alexandra played violin in the Chicago Philharmonic, and the orchestra was all the social outlet she wanted in her life. She liked Susan and could appreciate her talent. But she also liked a quiet house with no one else in it.

When Alexandra put down the keyhole saw for a moment to brush off the wood, Susan asked, "How do you know how wide to cut the f-holes?"

"Experience."

"So it makes a difference how big they are?"

"It's critical," Alexandra said. "If the f-hole is narrow, the sound will be dark and full. If it's wide, then the violin will sound bright and sharp."

"That was going to be Mr. Ponzini's violin, wasn't it?"

"Yes," Alexandra said with a sigh. Mr. Ponzini, a man in his seventies, had been a first violinist in the Chicago Philharmonic. He'd commissioned Alexandra to make him a violin, but had died of a heart attack only two days ago. So Alexandra was left with a half-finished, custom-carved violin that was not paid for.

"What will you do with it?" Susan asked.

"My friend had a good suggestion. Edith's a member of the

Friends of the Soames Library. You know, on the North Side?"

Susan nodded.

"Well, there's an institution in England that's selling its Shakespeare collection. The Friends of the Library decided to have a fund-raising auction to buy the collection. Edith's on the auction committee, and she suggested I donate this violin."

"That's a wonderful idea!" Susan said. "Then it would go to a good cause. That's so giving of you."

Alexandra scratched her eyebrow. "Before you endow me with sainthood, I'm not doing it to be noble. As Edith pointed out, it would be good publicity for my instruments. She's expecting this auction to be a gala event with lots of media attention. They're getting a lot of local big-name people to donate expensive items and attend."

"Like who?"

"Who?" Growing a trifle irritated by the girl's constant questions, Alexandra paused to remember. "Oh, Edith mentioned a few TV and radio personalities. Some bluebloods from Chicago's social register. Oh, yes, our conductor is donating a chance to conduct the Philharmonic. Bet you'd like that."

Susan's eyes grew big. "Can I come and bid on it?"

"I could bring you as my guest, I suppose," Alexandra said. "But you probably wouldn't be able to outbid all those Gold Coast types."

Susan nodded with resignation. "Who else is coming? Any movie stars?"

"I don't think many movie stars would fly to Chicago at their own expense," Alexandra said, amused at the question. "Although there will be some local theater people attending. Edith said she even wrote to David de Morrissey. She heard a rumor that he's a Shakespeare devotee. But then, there are all kinds of rumors about *him.*"

"Did he reply?" Susan's eyes grew lively.

"I haven't heard. I don't think he would, do you? He's a recluse. The papers said he didn't even attend the opening night of his last play. Maybe down deep he knew it would get all those horrible reviews."

"Did you see *Street Shadows* a few years ago?"

"His vampire play? No, I'm not into vampires. I'm too grounded in reality to sit through that kind of thing. Why, did you see it?"

"Yeah. I thought that one was great." Susan pointed to her slim neck and grinned. "In fact, his Vampire can come bite me anytime!"

"But I thought your secret pleasure was watching those sugary old musicals. Fred and Ginger. Nelson and Jeanette. How could you jump from that to vampires?"

Susan shrugged. "I have eclectic tastes. I like Madonna, too."

"Yes, well . . . ," Alexandra muttered in disapproval as she went back to her work. She didn't see what there was to admire about a blonde strutting across a stage in her underwear. But then, at age thirty-eight, maybe she shouldn't expect to understand.

"That reminds, me," Susan said. "My boyfriend's taking me to a rock concert tonight. I have to go get ready."

"I hope you're going to stuff some cotton in your ears."

Susan laughed. "Why?"

"All that loud noise will ruin your hearing. Hands and ears are a violinist's most valuable possessions."

"I already have a mother at home," Susan said in a nurturing tone, as if Alexandra were the younger of the two. "But I appreciate your worrying about me." She wrapped an arm around Alexandra's shoulders and gave her a quick hug and a "Bye!" The next second she was out the door.

Alexandra sat in her chair for a moment, slightly stunned. Why the hug? She wasn't the type who usually brought out that sort of behavior in other people, and she wondered what she'd done to prompt it from Susan. The girl merely worked for her and all Alexandra had done was to give her a piece of advice.

Well, Susan was young and impetuous. Alexandra chuckled. For some reason she found herself feeling something like a grandmother. And she wasn't even a mother! Was she getting so out of touch from living alone for so long that the young were starting to be condescending toward her?

Of course, she might not understand youth because she'd never felt young herself. Her father hadn't let her. If only her mother had lived. Things might have been different.

She put away the small saw, into its proper slot in her wooden tool case, which she'd made years ago. There was nothing wrong with living alone, she reminded herself. She was her own mistress, she could keep her life orderly because there wasn't anyone to interfere in it, and she could devote herself to her craft without the worry of taking time away from family or close friends who might expect her company. She could work without distraction toward her life's goal: to make a perfect violin, flawless in sound and form.

With her demanding, artistic temperament, she didn't believe in maintaining close emotional involvements. Too draining and disappointing. That was the beauty of being a member of an orchestra—it gave her a sense of belonging to a group of people, and yet no emotional expectations were ever had of her. Once she packed up her violin and left the rehearsal hall, she was on her own again and didn't have to answer to anyone.

Alexandra rubbed her nose as she amused herself with a new thought. She ought to get a personalized license plate holder for her car, saying, "Happiness is being with me, myself, and I."

At dusk, David de Morrissey lay in his narrow chamber, awakening from his deep vampiric sleep. But an image would not leave his mind as he came to full consciousness: Veronica. As in a fresh dream, he saw her beautiful brown eyes flowing with tears and heard her soft voice calling to him, pleading with him. Resisting her had taken all his will. And now he felt a remnant of sorrow, a longing that the dream could have ended differently.

Was she using their mental bond to call to him while he rested? Or was it only his profound desire to be with her again that created these visions? A decade apart from her was too long, even for a man who had lived centuries. Their ten years of separation were far from over and he was much too lonely already. This wouldn't do.

Work. That was the cure, he told himself. Work was the only thing keeping him going.

He sprang out of his coffin in the musty blackness of the secret room and made his way by instinct to the door. After unbolting the lock, he felt for the candle and matches on the small table outside the door and lit a flame. He made his way by candlelight along the winding path that led him through his expansive basement filled with priceless, mildewing, antique furniture. The frayed satin couches, carved writing desks, armoires, and so on, were interspersed with trunks and crates, and all were netted together by the dusty threads of thick cobwebs. The crates were filled with a cornucopia of items once important to David in other lives in other centuries, all uncatalogued and mostly forgotten.

When he reached the steps, he found the switch for the hall light, blew out the candle, and climbed to the ground floor. He turned down a short hallway and entered through another locked door into the elegant, cream-colored, oval entryway of his home. His polished black shoes sank into a colorful Oriental rug as he crossed to the spiral staircase. After climbing two flights to the third floor, he entered his living room with its flower-and-insect-patterned drapes and upholstery and walked to the small adjoining room which served as his office.

Sitting down at his rolltop desk, he pulled out a tablet of yellow, lined paper. The night before he'd begun the task of reworking the lyrics of a song. To get back into the mood quickly, he put on a set of headphones and turned on a tape of music already in his cassette player. He had a deadline to worry about, and the deadline was yesterday.

David was working on a musical, which presented both a departure and a challenge for him. He'd always written plays, and most had been highly successful. *Street Shadows,* for instance, his best-known one, was still running on Broadway. Its star, Sam Taglia, had won a Tony for his performance as the Vampire, and the play had also secured David his second Tony award. He'd received his first award for the first play he'd written after moving to the United States almost a decade and a half ago. Taken all together, the half-dozen plays he'd completed in America had been highly successful, earning him a lucrative income as well as critical acclaim.

Until *Miseries. Miseries* had been a dreadful flop. It lasted all of three weeks in Chicago before it closed, giving David his first theatrical failure not only in America, but in his previous four centuries of playwriting under various pseudonyms in Europe and in England.

His producer, a gray-haired man with a crew cut who

chewed gum to keep from smoking too much, had warned
David he had bad feelings about the project. "Maybe you
should stick to writing about ghosts or vampires," Merle
Larson had said. He was still unaware after working with
David for several years that David *was* one of these supernatural creatures.

Miseries had been David's first attempt in many decades to
write a play about normal, everyday mortals, without any hint
of the supernatural, his theatrical trademark. His *Miseries*
characters were obsessed with tragic loves, and David felt he'd
written something brimming with deep meaning and angst.
The theater critics, however, called it "self-indulgent, maudlin, soap opera drivel" and "worse than watching a steamroller mow down your pet cat."

The comments had stung David. But the disaster made him
realize how low he'd sunk into depression after forcing himself
to separate from the greatest love of his existence. Veronica's
angry letter had sent him into an overwhelming despair. He
was sure he'd lost her forever. Trying to work out his anxiety
and grief through his work, he'd produced a play that was
literally too painful for theatergoers to watch, even those who
had been his loyal fans.

David stopped writing for over a year. He passed the time
rereading Shakespeare and other classics, and playing and
replaying his collection of tapes of Gene Kelly musicals. Kelly
was his modern-day idol. For recreation he tried to analyze
and imitate all the famous dancer's choreography.

Meanwhile, Darienne had stayed by him almost constantly,
urging him out of his low morale in her blithe, relentless
manner. It was Darienne who had suggested that he start
writing again and try a new type of project. "How about a
musical?" she'd said. "Something with a happy ending to
boost your spirits, like those old movies you love." When
David had impatiently reminded her he knew little about
writing music, she'd suggested he write lyrics and find a composer to create melodies for them.

And that was the beginning of *The Scarlet Shadow,* the
David de Morrissey musical extravaganza that was to open in
Chicago in five weeks.

Five weeks! Whenever David thought of the amount of
work that remained to be done, and the dwindling number of

days in which to do it all, he panicked. In fact, everyone was
in a panic. Leonard Southfield, the young, unknown composer David had selected to write his music, was swamped
with revisions and orchestrations. He'd had to visit his doctor
for a bad case of writer's cramp from drawing endless stanzas
of sixteenth notes. Merle had begun drinking milk to soothe
a new case of ulcers; his career as a producer and his finances
couldn't tolerate another failure. The director, who'd been
flown in from Los Angeles for the job and who was also going
through a divorce, made it through each day on a self-devised
combination of Yoga and Valium. The set designer argued
with the lighting director, the computer which ran the stage
effects had a mind of its own, the costumes were weeks behind
schedule, and Elaine, the show's very talented but very young
leading lady, had bouts of stage fright. The only one who
didn't complain, who remained calm, cooperative and dedicated to his job was the show's star, Matthew McDowall.
Thank God for Matthew, David had thought again and
again, his one oasis of hope and sanity in a production that
seemed to be evolving into a masterpiece of chaos.

As Leonard's wistful, melodic refrain played in his ears
through the headphones, David pulled his straying mind back
to the task at hand—revising the lyrics to the show's major
love song. It was Matthew's principal song in the first half,
and David wanted it to be a hit for the actor's sake as well as
the show's.

At that moment, in the darkness outside, Darienne Victoire
contemplated David's three-story Oak Street home from the
narrow alley behind it. Almost a year had gone by since she
had last seen the mansion. And it looked as splendid as ever
with its dormers and gables, its arches and bays, and its massive sandstone walls.

Some of the windows on the third floor were lit. She knew
David was home. Was he alone? Most likely, knowing him.

Should she be polite and walk around to the front door? His
doorbell never worked, so she would have to use the heavy
brass knocker nailed to the thick, wooden door and hope that
he heard. But there was a much simpler way to get in. Just
because she'd been overseas so long didn't mean she shouldn't
take up her old, informal ways with him. The huge sandstone

blocks that formed the mansion's walls were fun to climb, and
she also preferred to peek into his window first, just to be sure
he was alone. If by some miracle Veronica was with him, she
wouldn't want to disturb them.

Darienne easily climbed over the high, iron fence and
walked around to the side of the building in the dark. Pushing
the long strap of her shoulder bag over her head, she set her
sandaled foot into the first wide, deep crack between the
rough-hewn blocks. She grasped onto a higher crevice with
her strong fingers. She remembered then that in the past
climbing up to David's living room had sometimes marred her
nail polish. Oh, well, it was a small price to pay. An adventur-
ous vampiress had more to exist for than maintaining a perfect manicure!

David was in the midst of trying to think of a fresh new
phrase to rhyme with "belong to me" when all at once his
office went black. David's head was forcibly tilted back by two
hands covering his eyes. He smelled spicy, exotic perfume, and
his head, he noticed, now rested against something soft, sensual, and warm. And instantly he knew: Darienne had finally
returned.

All at once he could see his desk light again, but the headphones were being pulled from his ears. And then a throaty,
delighted, feminine voice purred, *"Bonsoir, cheri.* Guess who's
come back to you!"

"Lucrezia Borgia?"

She slapped his cheek lightly and then pushed his swivel
chair around to make him face her. She wore coral-colored
shorts and a matching halter top, both revealing every lush
curve of her spectacular body. Her long, waved, honey-blond
hair hung gloriously about her shoulders. She looked down at
David, her bright green eyes impish and sparkling. "Happy to
see me?"

David didn't like to admit that he was. It was never wise to
give Darienne ammunition. "Where have you been?" he
asked, looking her over in surprise. It wasn't her sudden reap-
pearance that took him off-guard. She always returned without warning, usually climbing in through one of his windows.
It was her clothes that surprised him, though they were certainly appropriate for the heat of a humid, late August eve-

ning in Chicago. "I've never seen you so casual. No furs? No diamonds? You don't even have high heels on."

Darienne glanced down at her sandals. "I bought them when I visited my estate in Italy. *Charmant, n'est-ce pas?*" She turned her leg stylishly, showing off her shoes' delicate straps and graceful, one-inch heel. "The shorts and top I bought on the ship."

"Ship?"

"I cruised South America this summer. A marvelous way to travel. Those Latin men were *so* handsome."

"How did you manage it?" David asked. "Your coffin—"

"That's the beauty of it. Once it's on the ship, there are no more problems. The ship goes from one port to another, so you can travel without having to worry about transporting it. It's always right there with you."

"Ingenious," David, who hated to travel, mumbled. "You've been gone a year. Where else have you been?"

She made a Gallic shrug. "Home to Paris for a few months at my château. Switzerland, Germany . . ." She paused airily. "I can't even remember all the places I've been." Running her fingers down David's cheek, she asked, "Why, did you miss me?"

"Miss you?" he said in an arch tone.

"You'd better say yes after I invested all that money in your musical," she warned him while sensually running her forefinger down his neck and beneath his open shirt collar. She sat on his lap then, ran her fingers along his chin, and kissed him on the mouth.

David made no objection. He had to admit she'd rescued his project for him. Merle had found it extremely difficult to procure backers willing to invest money in a musical production written by a playwright who had no track record for doing musicals and whose last play had flopped. The fact that the composer was unknown and, worse, just out of college did not help matters. But most of all, the basic premise of putting a vampire hero into the *The Scarlet Pimpernel* storyline and setting it to music was what made potential investors keep a grip on their checkbooks. "Preposterous" was the reply they'd received most often.

David, who had already lost money on *Miseries,* had poured all he could into the show, as had the producer. But

The Scarlet Shadow needed highly expensive set designs and stage effects if it was to be produced successfully. When they still fell far short of the needed finances, David realized he had to do something drastic. He believed in the project, and after working on it for two years with his young composer-collaborator, he couldn't let it die. But was it worth selling his home? It was that thought that had made him turn, with some misgivings, to Darienne.

Darienne had cheerfully said, *"Mais oui,"* apparently relieved to see David interested and committed to something after his long depression over Veronica. She quickly sold dozens of her older diamonds, ones she said she didn't wear anymore, and presented him with a huge sum of money. Before accepting the check, David had dutifully suggested that she ought to read the working libretto first, so she'd know exactly what she was investing in. She'd smiled patiently and spent all of ten minutes glancing through the manuscript. "It's wonderful," she'd told him, then tossed it aside to begin coaxing him into sex as her reward for rescuing his show.

And by the subtle fires in her green eyes as she kissed and caressed him, David knew she had sex on her mind now. Again, no surprise. Sex was what had always brought her back to him, decade after decade, century after century, since they'd first known each other as adolescent mortals in Paris in the late 1500s.

"I've missed you," she said, her voice like honey.

"What about all those Latin men?"

"No one does it like you, David." She began unbuttoning his shirt. "I'm starved for you."

David took a breath and grabbed her roving hand. "One thing you'll never be accused of is subtlety. Gone nearly a year, you're back not even five minutes and already you're pulling at my clothes! You haven't even bothered to ask how or what I'm doing."

She made a French pout. "How are you?"

"Fine, thank you. But I'm busy. I'm rewriting a song for the show that they needed yesterday for rehearsal."

"How tedious. When does the show open?"

"In five weeks."

She nodded with mild interest. "I remember you saying you booked the theater for early fall. That's another reason I came

back. It occurred to me that I ought to check on my investment."

"Yes, that's wise." David twisted his mouth in a wry smile.

"Don't humor me," she chided, mussing his hair. "Just
because I don't think about work all the time like you . . ."

"You mean, you do think about it sometimes? What work
do you actually do?"

"I take care of you," she said, poking a finger into his ribs.
"That seems to be my job. Until you let Veronica come back
to you, anyway. I suppose you haven't seen her."

"No."

"How do you know the poor, sweet creature hasn't died of
a broken heart?"

David reached out to run his finger down the leather-bound
spine of Shakespeare's Sonnets, where he kept the letter she'd
written him. "I can still feel her with me. If she were gone, I
would sense it. The bond between us doesn't disappear. I
didn't know for sure. I thought it might"

"She loves you. That's what doesn't disappear."

"But in her letter she said she despised me. I still can't get
that out of my mind. I've tried."

"David, did I explain nothing before I left?" Darienne
sighed. "I told you, she wrote that in a moment of despair.
Time has passed and you can't know what's in her heart now.
Though you could if you'd attune your mind to hers."

"Our separation must be total," David said with finality.
"She needs years and the wisdom that comes from maturity to
make the irreversible choice between mortality and immortality. If she continued to see me, she would think only of me
instead of what's best for her. God help her."

Darienne merely shook her head. David knew her feelings.
She had expressed them often enough. Darienne had always
thought the ten-year separation he'd imposed on himself and
Veronica was a needless agony for them both. But Darienne
had always taken vampirism and immortality lightly, a choice
she herself had made on a Sunday afternoon after a glass of
red wine. She never thought deeply about morality, God,
eternity, damnation, or the universe. Darienne believed in
having fun.

As she glanced over his shoulder, she seemed to become
distracted with something on his desk. She reached over him

to pick it up. David saw it was a letter he'd received regarding the Soames Library Auction. He took a long breath, anticipating the inevitable.

"Who is Edith Cornwall?" she asked, reading the return address. "A new woman in your life?"

"Hardly. She's running a fund-raising auction."

Darienne perused the letter. "You donated a manuscript?" she asked, looking up at him in surprise.

"They're raising money to acquire a Shakespeare collection."

"Oh, she wants you to attend," Darienne said, reading further. "Look at the list of people who'll be there!"

"She only wants me to lend my name to the event to get publicity. I don't think she really expects me to come."

"But you ought to. And take me as your guest!"

"Darienne—"

"Well, look, David," she said, showing him the letter, "opera stars, politicians, radio and television people . . ."

"I've read it. Put it out of your mind, Darienne. I hate being in the public eye. Not only do I hate it, I think it's dangerous for us. I've decided to write Mrs. Cornwall to give her permission to tell the media I might attend, since she thinks it may help the cause. But—and get this straight," he said, tapping Darienne's temple with his forefinger, "I'm not going to attend."

"Oh, David."

"Oh, David," he mimicked. "Not another word!"

She draped her arms around his neck and brought her mouth close to his. "If you won't take me to that, then you must do something to make up for it. Or I'll be very put out with you."

He placed his hands on her shoulders to keep her at bay. "I have lyrics to rewrite tonight. I should go to the theater, too, to look in on the rehearsal."

"Doesn't the producer or director or someone like that oversee rehearsals?"

"Yes, but they want my input, since I wrote the damn thing. And I have a big financial investment in it, too, as you do."

Darienne grew thoughtful for a moment. "I have even more money invested in it than you, don't I?"

David nodded. "Actually, your chunk of the pie is the

biggest of anyone's. So, you see, by allowing me to work tonight, you'd be protecting your share." Darienne wasn't methodical in her approach to anything, especially money, but he hoped this reasoning might work. Otherwise, he'd lose the whole night.

Darienne's expression was a puzzle to him. She seemed to be mulling over what he'd told her, and her mouth took on a firm set that he could only describe as businesslike, a word he'd never have applied to her before. "What are you thinking?" he asked, getting an odd feeling in his stomach that he'd made a mistake here somehow.

"You're right," she said. "I ought to protect my investment."

"Then you'll let me work?"

Darienne hesitated, seemed torn between two altogether different desires. "How long will it take you to finish the lyrics?"

"It's hard to tell. I'd almost finished last night, but dawn came. Maybe an hour. I need to get it to the theater."

"Yes, I see." She paused, thinking again. "Can I help?"

"With the lyrics? You're not a writer."

"What about the rest of the play? How's it going?"

Some instinct made David reluctant to confide in her how chaotic things were. "Every show has its ups and downs. I'm sure we'll get everything ironed out in time," he said, hoping he wasn't lying. "We've got a great actor for the lead, that's for certain."

Darienne's eyes perked up. "Really? Who?"

"Matthew McDowall."

"Never heard of him."

"To tell you the truth, I hadn't either. That's because neither of us watches much TV. But he's well known in America. He's done two very popular sitcoms and a few Hollywood movies, as well as theater."

"TV *comedies?* What about his movies?"

"They're comedies, too, mainly."

Darienne looked aghast. "You haven't turned your musical into a farce, have you?"

"Of course not. Would you like to read the current version?"

"I'd better," she muttered. "But this actor—why did you

choose an American comedian to play a romantic English
vampire?"

"He's a multitalented man, Darienne. He can play anything. He can affect a perfect English accent. And he's got an
outstanding singing voice. Here, get up so I can show you."

Darienne stood up and David got a tape off a nearby shelf.
He switched cassettes in his tape player, pulled out the head-
phone cord, and turned it on.

The pure, vibrant sound of a tenor voice filled the small
room. Every word sung was cleanly enunciated in the British
manner and rich with emotion. The words of the song expressed the anguish of the show's vampire hero, who felt he
could not allow himself the love of a mortal woman. David
had spent long hours on the lyrics, and he thought Matthew
sang them with as much conviction and understanding as
David felt when he wrote them. Leonard had composed music
that was plaintive and moving, but which demanded a voice
with a wide vocal range. Matthew sang every note, from bari-
tone to falsetto, with remarkable strength and ease.

David switched off the player when the song was finished.
"What do you think?"

Darienne looked pleasantly surprised. "The music's lovely
and he does have a beautiful voice. I liked his slow, eerie
quality. Is that his interpretation of how a vampire would
sing?"

David couldn't help but smile as he nodded.

"The audience ought to relish that," Darienne said, also
amused. "Mortals have all those odd notions about what
we're like. What does McDowall look like?"

"I have photos here somewhere," David said, rummaging
through some file folders on his desk. He pulled one folder out
and opened it. Inside was a composite sheet showing several
small photos of Matthew in various poses as well as two 8 ×
10 glossies. There were also Xeroxes of some magazine articles
Merle had given him. He layed them out on his desk so
Darienne could see.

First she picked up the Xeroxed pages and fingered through
them quickly. *"Time* and *People,"* she said, sounding impressed. "Can I take these with me and read them later?"

"Sure. Take the photos, too, if you want."

She slipped the magazine articles into her shoulder bag,

then bent to look at the pictures with interest. Soon her expression grew perplexed and disappointed. "He barely looks like the same person in each photo."

"He's a versatile man," David explained, wondering what Darienne could be finding wrong.

"He's mildly handsome in this one and that one." She pointed at the pictures. "He only looks good from certain angles, I think. His face is—I don't know—surprising. It doesn't match his voice. I suppose he looks like a comedian. Has he gained and lost weight? In this one he appears robust, barrel-chested, while over here he looks thin. Here he seems gregarious, but in these others he looks like the quiet, reflective sort. Exactly what have you got here? I can't see why you chose him, when it's so hard to determine what type of man he is. Your stage vampire must be very definitive, David. Like Sam Taglia was in *Street Shadows*. Powerful. Overwhelming. And, most of all, sexy. This man is not sexy."

David felt dismayed. "How can you tell from a few photos?"

"I can tell," she said with a knowing chuckle. "Any woman worth her libido can tell you that! I can't think why you chose him. Because of his voice?"

"It's casting against type," David tried to explain. "If you take an actor with a given personality and allow him to tap into that opposing part of himself he never shows, you can get a very powerful performance. Matthew is a congenial, soft-spoken man. And, yes, most of his experience is in comedy. But when he allows the dark side of himself to come out, believe me, he's an overwhelming presence on stage. I've seen him in rehearsal."

"But what about sensual?" Darienne reiterated. "He doesn't look the least bit sensual in these photos. He looks like someone's next-door neighbor out in the suburbs, ready to mow his lawn." She pointed to a large, full-length photo of the actor, dressed in a sweater and jeans. "He doesn't look terribly tall. His hair's starting to gray. I think he's too old. Look, there are deep lines around his eyes. He does have a nice rise under his zipper, but that's not enough."

"Really?" David said with asperity as he gathered up the pictures to put them back into the folder. "I thought that was always enough for you."

"I'll ignore that." She raised her blond eyebrows as she spoke, taking the photos out of his hands and slipping them into her shoulder bag. "This is business, and I won't let your stuffy self-righteousness miff me. Now let's be sensible about this."

"Sensible! You'll have to look that up in one of my dictionaries first."

"Now listen carefully, David." She spoke with unexpected authority now, her eyes steady and determined. "This play is romantic. Therefore the majority of your audience is going to be women. Women expect a handsome, romantic leading man. More particularly, a *sexy* man. Besides that, this leading man is a vampire. Mortals think of us as larger than life, so that's what he has to be. This casting-against-type idea is ridiculous. I say we need a Frank Langella who can sing."

"But you haven't even seen Matthew perform yet! On stage he'll wear a wig and heavy makeup. In fact, he's insisted on it. He's worked long hours with the makeup people precisely because he doesn't want to look like himself. He knows his familiarity as a comic actor is a drawback."

Darienne's beautiful eyes hardened with impatience. "I repeat, he has to have a sensual presence, David. He has to exude sex from every pore out across that audience, all the way up into the second balcony. You think a little makeup is enough to fool women?"

David grew angry. "Must I remind you that you know absolutely nothing about the theater or about acting?"

"May I remind you that you're only a man?" she shot back. "In fact, you're all men creating this show—writer, producer, director, composer—every one of you is male. How can any of you claim to understand what makes a man alluring to women? How do you know what a male actor needs to mesmerize the female audience? Unless you want this show to bomb, you'd better listen to a feminine point of view, and quickly! *And,* as you aptly pointed out, it's *my* money that's keeping this show afloat. You have no choice but to listen to me!" She paused, looking calmly at David, as if allowing all that to sink in. In a quieter voice she added, "I think I'd better accompany you to the theater tonight to see for myself what's going on."

David felt his head swim. Where had he gone wrong? Why

were women so damned unpredictable? God, he wished he could read their minds the way he could men's! He'd better find some way to nip this in the bud or Darienne could cause a mountain of trouble, and they had enough of that already.

Fortunately, he knew just the way to derail her. "Darienne," he said in a soft tone, slipping his hands around her waist, "I thought you had another reason for coming all the way here to see me."

She gave him a coy look. "I did. And if you think you can use your body to distract me—well, you can." She moved closer and ran her hands over his chest. "For a while anyway. Mmm, maybe even a few nights."

Till the show opened, David thought, if he could manage it. He bent his head to kiss her. As he tasted her warm, eager mouth, he realized he was in an odd position. Usually, it was Darienne doing the seducing. Now their roles seemed to have reversed. He hated being so obvious. Worse, he didn't want to look like an easy mark. She'd turn him into her sex toy, if he'd let her. He needed to employ a little psychology here.

She leaned up and bit his earlobe. "You ought to star in the musical yourself, David. You're just right for it."

"I don't sing."

"You could learn. You have the presence, the looks," she said, running her fingers through his dark brown hair, "the body . . . oh, especially the body." She pressed her pelvis against his. "Oh yes, keep me from the theater tonight, David. Distract me. Seduce me."

"If you *want* to be seduced, how can I seduce you?" he asked in a dry tone.

"Oh, don't be so technical about words! I've traveled halfway around the world just to be with you again. I've thought of you often while I was away."

"In between Latin lovers?"

"In between and during," she whispered. "My memories of you enhance all other men I'm with. They're only feeble mortals. But you . . . oh, you know how I need you. You're the only one who has the strength to satisfy me the way I like to be satisfied."

David nodded. He felt used, which, oddly, was just how he wanted to feel right now to get their relationship back to normal. "So then it's only my anatomy you want."

She sighed and tilted her chin sideways, looking sweet and patient. "What do you want me to say? That I love you the way Veronica loved you? I don't think you'd *want* me to be in love with you. What would you do with me if I were? I'd drive you up a wall."

"That's true."

"But I do admire you. You're all I have left from the old days when we were mortals. We enjoyed each other then. Why shouldn't we now?" She stroked his cheek. "It's not as though you don't enjoy our couplings, too."

"I enjoy them," he admitted. "I wish I didn't."

"Silly man. Why? When I make you forget your problems."

"Sometimes you are the problem."

"Me? When?"

"Now. Look at me standing here, playing up to you. It's only to keep you away from the theater, as you've already guessed. There, I've admitted it. I hate lies. I can't stand to be in one for longer than two minutes, even with you."

She lifted her smooth, bare shoulder with sensuous umbrage. "What do you mean, 'even with me'? I don't deserve the same treatment as everyone else?"

David exhaled. "You deserve respect, all right. You're a handful. I'm tempted to use devious methods just to keep you in line. Besides that, all your talk about men not knowing anything about female sexuality makes me want to teach you a good lesson!"

Darienne's eyes ignited with an inner fire, their green hue growing deeper and more luminous. "Oh, teach me, David. Any lesson you want."

He folded his arms across his chest. "No. I don't want to now. I've admitted my ulterior motives. Your self-respect should make you angry. Besides, I need to get back to work." He began to turn away.

She grabbed him by the shoulders. "When it comes to pleasures of the flesh, I have no self-respect. Use me, teach me, distract me, employ any underhanded, ulterior motive you want! The choice is all yours. Only let's do it! Please?" She reached down and ran her fingertips along his zipper. "Let's forget about the theater for now. I'll get that straightened out in good time. Let's enjoy ourselves. You've been working too hard, I can tell. You need recreation. Use me, David. Be angry with me, be contemptuous, be impatient. Be anything. Only give me what I crave. Please, David? My beautiful David. Please?" she whispered. Her large breasts pressed warmly against his chest as she kissed him, the soft, aggressive femininity of her compelling.

David's breaths were coming faster and he could feel the stirrings in his groin. There was no question, Darienne understood her area of expertise.

And maybe, all things considered—or not considered—she was right. Recreation sounded good to him right now. He'd been alone too long.

2

Your way or mine?

CIRCLING HIS hands around her waist, David lifted her to him and kissed her hard on the mouth. He inserted his tongue, explored the recesses of her mouth, then allowed her to do the same to him. Already she was whimpering with pleasure and eagerness, tearing open his shirt as her mouth clung to his. Darienne could become aroused as quickly, faster perhaps, than most men. And David had always found himself following *her* lead.

Well, this time it would be different, he decided, burying his fingers in her thick hair as he pushed her head back and bent over her in a dominating manner. If she was going to come to him begging, demanding his services, then he would be the one to command the pace of their lovemaking. He would show her a thing or two about male sexuality!

"Oh, David," she breathed when he ended the intense kiss. "You see, you do need me tonight." She began unbuckling his belt. "Hurry."

"No," he said, stopping her. "I want to take it slowly."

Her emerald eyes, radiant with desire, took on a shocked expression. "Slow? Why?"

"I'm keeping you from the theater, remember? We have all night."

"But we can do it so many more times when we go fast."

"But the feeling can be so much more intense if we build up to it."

"The way mortals do it?" she said. "We can have the intensity without all the preliminary rigmarole. It's one of the benefits of being a vampire, *cheri.*" She pulled his shirt out of his trousers and ran her fingers over his nipples.

24

David closed his eyes at her tantalizing touch. "I like the preliminary rigmarole, as you put it." His tone was firm, but his hands gentle as he reached beneath the inner slit of her halter to caress her breasts.

Her dazzling eyes winced with pleasure. "All right," she whispered hotly. "If you must. But don't waste too much time!"

He chuckled and bent over her to kiss the lush, inner curves of her cleavage. After several long moments enjoying the feel of her flesh, sliding his mouth over her skin, he moved back up to her mouth. He lightly chewed and then bit her lip, his sharp incisor drawing blood. The taste of it shot arousal through him, but he kept control. Darienne, however, gasped with rising pleasure and turned her head to bite him just beneath his collar. It was taboo for vampires to drink from one another, but the simple pleasure of biting flesh and drawing blood aligned itself with sexual gratification for their kind.

Feeling her teeth sink into his flesh gave David an acute sensation, sending pulsing electricity through his system, making him long for satiation as urgently as she. But he was determined to make Darienne wait for it. She was such a flaunting, know-it-all little beggar.

While she moved down his bared chest, licking and biting his skin, he reached beneath her hair and unbuttoned the top of the halter behind her neck. The cotton material floated downward over each smooth, swollen mound, one side falling off completely, the other side coming to precarious rest at her large, upturned nipple. Her breasts, one barely covered, the other free, jutted toward him at a tilted, inviting angle.

She smiled at him with a knowingness in her eyes that David believed came from her long experience with many men over the centuries. She understood perfectly just how desirable her body was. Winding her arms around his neck, she edged toward him until her bared nipple brushed his chest. The contact made the halter fall off the other breast as well, and she pressed herself against him. Her breasts flattened a bit, like firm, luxurious pillows, and he felt their heat and softness seep through him like liquid fire.

"Do you want this body, David?" she purred, pronouncing his name in the French way as she always did, *Dahveed*. "It's yours. Take your pain and your frustration and make them disappear—inside me. Use me all you want. Use me up. Now," she said, pressing the lower part of her body against him.

He knew she could feel his arousal by the change in the expression of her eyes. Triumph flickered in their green depths and then demand. She stepped back a bit and reached behind to undo the bottom part of the halter top. In a moment it fell from her smooth, slender rib cage to the floor. Next, she unfastened her shorts and let them fall to the floor. She wore nothing beneath. Her rounded hips and long, lean thighs framed the blond center of pubic hair. She touched it provocatively with her pink-polished fingertips.

"I'm ready for you," she said in a breathy tone, moving close to him again and reaching for his belt buckle.

"I know you are," he said, stopping her. "But I want to wait yet."

"No, David," she pouted as he pushed her hands away from his trousers. He took both her wrists in one hand and held them over her head. She might be three times as strong as a mortal woman, but David was stronger still and had no trouble controlling her with minor force. Stepping forward, he made her step back toward the wall next to the desk, until her heels came against the baseboard. He pressed her hands up against the cream-painted plaster above her hair and bent to lick, kiss, and then suck her nipples. Soon she was writhing and moaning with ever-rising ecstasy, rubbing one thigh against the other as if trying to assuage her pulsing need.

"Please, David," she gasped. "I don't like frustration. Take me!"

"When I'm ready."

"You are ready!" Her tone grew angry, fire in her eyes. "No more, David," she objected with painful ardor as he lowered his head to her breasts again and bit into her downy, heated flesh. Soon little rivulets of blood ran down her skin while her breasts grew more swollen and her nipples hard with peaking desire.

She raised one knee and wound her leg around him, her inner thigh rubbing against his hip. As she pressed her pubic area against his hardness, he could feel her throbbing heat and moisture seep through the material of his pants.

"Why are you torturing me?" she asked, her eyes pleading.

"Because you need a little male domination for a change."

"Chauvinist!"

He smiled. "The pot calling the kettle black. If ever there was a female chauvinist, it's you!"

"Me? I just want to be free."

"You enjoy manipulating us. You think you're smarter than us."

"Men behave the same way with women. It's just the old battle of the sexes. What's wrong with that?"

He shrugged, still keeping her wrists braced against the wall above her head. "Nothing. I feel like being the dominant one tonight, that's all. And you'll have to adjust to *my* pace for a change."

"You're making me angry!" She jutted her pelvis against him with a sudden, strong move meant to create discomfort.

He backed away a bit, avoiding the sharp blow without letting go of her hands. "You try that and you may ruin the satisfaction you're looking for!"

The anger left her eyes, replaced instantly by a contrite look. "All right, David, I'll go along with whatever you want. You can be boss. But hurry!"

"Not much longer," he said softly as his hand trailed down her stomach, pausing at the indentation of her navel, then further on. He teased her blond hairs with his fingertips.

"Yes, David," she breathed, her breasts moving up and down with her quick intake of air. "Touch me. Please . . . Ohhh!" she cried out as he slid his fingers into her heated moistness. Slipping two fingers inside her, he stroked the striving center of her desire with his thumb until she screamed with need.

"Learn to enjoy the pleasure of this by itself," he whispered, kissing her perspiring forehead. "Don't be in such a rush."

Her face contorted with pleasure and pain. "You don't know what agony this is for me."

"Other women enjoy foreplay."

"I'm not like other women! I've never behaved the way society said a woman should."

"Yet you wear your femininity like a rich perfume." His voice rose with temper. "You tease men, and then all you want us to be is an efficient machine!"

Her eyes widened. "Why are you so angry with me?"

"You told me to use you," David said, not sure himself what his emotions were anymore. "That's what I'm doing. My way."

"But you're torturing me!" She tilted her head back against the wall in sensual agony, a tear spilling from her eye, as he continued working his fingers within her. "Please, David, I can't stand anymore—"

"All right," he said, relenting. Perhaps her needs were different than other women's. He let go of her hands and removed his clothing.

"David," she said with relief, reaching for his swollen member. Before she could, he picked her up beneath her arms, lifting her and pressing her against the wall.

"Here?" she asked, taking in panting breaths, already spreading her thighs.

"Here!" he said. He thrust himself into her savagely and she screamed with joy.

"Yes! More!" she cried, almost incoherent, as he rammed her repeatedly against the wall. She wound her arms around his neck and her legs around his body. "Harder," she told him, her voice aching. "You can't hurt me. Harder!"

He did as she asked, taking a savage, beastly pleasure in the coupling, driving himself deeper and deeper into her hot, pulsing flesh, biting her shoulders and breasts as he did so. Yes, Darienne was different from other women. She could withstand any violence to her body. In fact, she craved such treatment. Even when she was a mortal, she liked rough play. She was so unlike Veronica—

Oh, God, don't think of Veronica now, he told himself, the emotional pain at the thought of her almost making him lose his drive.

David had Darienne for comfort. *Enjoy her, use her,* he told himself. *It's what she wants.* He bit her shoulder as he thrust again, forgetting everything in her throbbing, overheated body, in her vampiric stamina and strength. He couldn't have this brand of fierce, primitive sex with any other female. A mortal woman wouldn't survive it. And if Darienne demanded a night of climax after climax, forgetting tenderness and loveplay, so what? Darienne could make him forget Veronica for a while. She was Woman to the nth degree. And tonight she was all his.

He could sense her peaking. Her breathing was shallow, coming in spasms. Her eyes had grown vivid, iridescent with vampiric passion, just as his eyes, he'd been told, radiated cobalt blue. He drew back his full length and thrust into her one last swift, savage time. She was already climaxing. He could feel her contractions as he slid into her. She threw her head back and arched her spine, silently at first as her body was wracked by larger contractions. Then she screamed as the final pulse whipped through her body, just as David allowed his own release, shooting searing stars into her.

She collapsed onto him, resting her cheek on his shoulder. He supported her, as he had through their coupling, her legs still wound around him, his maleness, growing limp now, still within her.

"David," she said, her voice husky from her screams. She lifted her head to look at him. Her eyes were soft now, worshipful as she gazed at him. "You were right. It's better with foreplay. I'm sorry I argued."

David felt guilty. "I don't know why I wanted to be so domineering with you."

She pushed the damp hair off his brow. "You miss Veronica so much, *cheri.* You're worried about your musical, too. You took it all out on me. It's all right." She nodded, her tone reassuring. "I asked you to. I didn't realize you could be that way and it took me by surprise. I understand now." She swallowed and then her lips parted languidly. "But at the heat of the moment . . . what you were doing to me . . . oh, David, do it again!"

"Your way or mine?" He watched her smile as he grew large within her once more.

"I don't care. Yours," she said as he pressed her back against the wall, biting her collarbone. "No," she said with a throaty moan as he began slow, rhythmic thrusts within her. "Mine! My way this time. Oh, yes, David. Harder. Don't be gentle. Harder! Yes! Yes—"

A few days later at the Philharmonic's Michigan Avenue concert hall, Alexandra stood by a table packing up her violin after rehearsal. She was downstairs in the musician's locker room along with other members of the orchestra. Everyone was dressed in casual clothes and in a convivial mood. Alexandra wore a comfortable pair of old slacks and a T-shirt. That morning she'd pulled her blond hair up at the back of her head in a verticle fluff, securing it with a long hair clip.

As Alexandra wiped rosin dust off the top of her violin with a soft cloth, Edith Cornwall came up to her carrying her flute case. She was dressed in a turquoise summer jumpsuit which made her red hair look even more vibrant. The trim, middle-aged wife of a prominent lawyer and also a recent grandmother, Edith had more energy and social ease than anyone else Alexandra knew.

"Go for some iced tea?" Edith asked.

"Sorry, not today," Alexandra said with regret. She didn't quite know why Edith had taken a shine to her over the years. But she liked having her as a friend, even if Edith did tend to talk her ear off. "If I don't spend every spare minute in my shop getting that violin finished, you won't have it for the auction."

"I didn't realize." Edith's expression changed to one of concern. "How long does it take to make a violin?"

"A hundred fifty to two hundred hours. And I'm usually working on more than one instrument at a time, so it can take up to six months."

"Really." Edith looked impressed, her green eyes staring. "I'm sorry if my suggestion's put you under pressure."

"No, don't apologize. It's a perfect solution. But I wasn't planning to have it finished for Mr. Ponzini until October. With the auction coming in a few weeks, it puts me in a bind. But I'll get it done. I'll just put my other work on hold."

"I hope your customers won't be upset."

"They're pretty understanding," Alexandra said, carefully setting her violin into its velvet-lined case and putting the cloth into a small compartment at one end. "How are the plans going? Is the mayor coming?"

"You bet!" Edith replied, the excitement in her voice reappearing. Alexandra always marveled at the way Edith could jump on her charity bandwagon at the drop of a word or two. "And David de Morrissey sent us the original manuscript from his first play to auction off. You should see it! It'll get lots of attention because it's entirely handwritten by him."

"No kidding. How'd you get him to donate it?"

"I know his producer," Edith replied, eager to tell the story, "and he told me Mr. de Morrissey just might be pursuaded if I took time to mention the specific books and Shakespearean artifacts that the Soames Library is hoping to acquire. The producer said Mr. de Morrissey is like a walking encyclopedia on Shakespeare and he'd be most impressed if I took a scholarly tack in my letter." She shrugged happily. "I guess it worked."

"Congratulations!" Alexandra said.

"I'm not giving up on getting him to come to the auction, either," Edith continued. "In my thank-you letter, I asked him if I could announce to the media that Mr. de Morrissey *might* attend. You know, to get publicity? His last play didn't do well, but now he's got that new musical opening in a month that everyone's talking about. If people thought he might be there, we'd really get everyone out that night. And the more rich people that come hoping to meet him, the more money will flood in from the auction. We'll see what happens." She chuckled. "Of course, it'd be wonderful if he actually would attend!" She was almost girlish in her enthusiasm, drawing out the word "wonderful" to twice its natural length.

"I agree." Alexandra picked up her case and they began to walk out together. "But he has such a reputation as a recluse. Getting a manuscript from him must be a first."

"It may be," Edith said with pride.

"Which play was his first one? I can't remember."

"*A Tale at Twilight.* It won several awards."

"That's right," Alexandra said. "I vaguely remember seeing it years ago. It began with an old man telling a story to his grandson. And when the play was finished, you couldn't tell if the old man was alive or a ghost or what."

"Yes, that's the one. His plays always have a supernatural bent to them. Except for his last one. He seemed to have gotten off-track with that one."

"Too bad he's going downhill. I read he's back to vampires again with his new musical."

Edith looked at her in surprise. "Did you see *Street Shadows?*"

Alexandra felt a trifle annoyed at being asked the same question two days in a row. "No, I decided not to bother."

"Well, you should have. It was remarkably well done. Not at all like those old horror movies. That play had a sense of realism and poignancy about it." She smiled. "And romance."

Alexandra shrugged. There was no accounting for people's tastes. They had reached the front doors and were walking out onto Michigan Avenue. North of them, on the other side of the street, stood the Art Institute, its two huge, sculptured lions guarding the building beneath bright flags hanging from its roof. Beyond it were many of the city's towering skyscrapers, including the Prudential Building and the Standard Oil Building. Behind them the black, tapered John Hancock Building stood outlined against the blue sky.

As the heat of the streets and the bright sun began to be oppressive, Alexandra thought of her poor violin, having to adjust from the air-conditioned building they'd rehearsed in and then to the ovenlike temperature outside. Such climatic changes weren't good for the instrument.

"Going straight home, then?" Edith asked as they came to the street corner.

" 'Fraid so."

"You spend too much time alone."

"I don't mind. Anyway, Susan's working with me for the summer."

"That's good," Edith said, as if she felt better now, having been reassured. "You shouldn't be alone all the time."

"I always have the Philharmonic."

"But that's not the same," Edith said, as if correcting her.

"It isn't?"

"It's not a husband or family. Or even really close friends, the kind that you can call on if you've got a problem."

Alexandra shrugged. "It's enough for me. I actually like being alone."

Edith's thin brows drew together in a perplexed expression. Then she tilted her head to one side and smiled. "Well, as long as you're happy. I'm so family oriented, maybe I only see things one way. Take care." She pointed a delicate finger and shook it at Alexandra. "Don't work too hard, now."

"I won't," Alexandra said with a grin. "See you next rehearsal." As she walked on toward where her car was parked, she told herself it was sweet of Edith to want to mother her. Having had two children, now grown, Edith probably couldn't help it.

The incident reminded Alexandra to feel relieved that she

would never have children. She wouldn't want to wind up in that perpetual mothering mode, as so many women who were mothers seemed to. The style didn't appeal to her, went against her grain. She wouldn't want to grow unable to relate to people in any other than a nurturing way, to wind up speaking even to adults as if they were children in need of care and guidance. To Alexandra, there was something nonintellectual and self-indulgent about such behavior, however well meant.

Indeed, Alexandra felt quite fortunate that she could not have children. A medical problem had taken away that option a few years ago. Fate had reaffirmed the fact that she just wasn't cut out for motherhood. Not having to worry about getting pregnant was an added bonus. It made sex, when she bothered with it, a much more pleasant diversion. And even she needed a little diversion every now and then.

3

For the first time in centuries

SOMEWHERE THROUGH the shining mist of her erotic bliss, Darienne realized how much her strength was waning. Nevertheless her body's intense drive carried her mercilessly toward what she knew must be her final fulfillment tonight with David. The night would soon vanish into morning.

For two nights in succession, she'd allowed David to keep her from the theater. While she enjoyed the distraction, she wondered all the more what was happening at the theater that made him go to this length to scotch her interference.

As they writhed together on the living room floor, cushioned by the plush Aubusson rug, she sat astride him, his thick, engorged masculinity urgent within her, driving deep. She used her thigh muscles to accentuate the rhythmic pull and push. His hands were on her buttocks, pressing her hard onto him with each plunge. She supported herself as she leaned over him, her hands making indentations in the thick wool rug on either side of his shoulders. Her breasts hung pendulous between them, swollen from passion and use, her nipples grazing his powerful chest.

Every nerve of her body shivered with supercharged electricity that was about to explode. She gazed down at him through her thick blond hair that fell in disheveled tangles around her face. She found him looking up at her, his translucent cobalt eyes afire with such vampiric radiance that their intensity startled even her. Intelligence, hedonism, wolfish lust, and love—all these were in his eyes as he looked at her in such a compelling way that he might have hypnotized her into being his forever if she let him. No wonder he had

changed poor little Veronica irrevocably. How could a weak
mortal ever withstand him?

The tension centered below her stomach and radiating
through her was building to a peak with each sensual clash of
their bodies. She was riding the crest of a huge wave, building
with might and certainty, racing headlong toward shore. Soon
her body would explode into ecstatic froth and she would float
like sea foam over land and water into another realm. She
took each new height that David brought her to as a challenge, and, for tonight, this would be the last and most delicious hurdle to conquer.

By the pleasure mixed with pain in his eyes, and the rigid
pulsing of his strong neck muscles, she knew that even David,
with his marvelous stamina, couldn't last much longer. She
smiled at him with delirious, panting delight as he surged into
her again. He rose up to bite her breast and then her shoulder
while squeezing her buttocks to drive his powerful, pulsing
need home. She felt him reach the furthest depths within her.
As searing liquid poured through her, she arched her head
back and tried to scream, but couldn't. The intensity was too
big and her voice had left her. She gasped as if she couldn't get
enough air and felt her eyes glaze with passion. She'd reached
the plateau of no return and was hurtling through some dark
endless space, weightless, waiting each fraction of a moment
until . . . at last . . . the joyous end came. Her body convulsed
in glorious release, energizing every nerve ending, making her
float through the clouds of another galaxy, where stars like
diamonds shattered in shimmering array all over her, shower-
ing her skin and hair and making her shiver with the beauty
and the ecstasy of the sensation.

She felt the strength and warmth of David's hands as they
rose up her back, pulling her toward him. The heat of his
palms, the tenderness of his touch, dispelled like a vapor the
rarified atmosphere he'd taken her to, replacing it with familiar, earthly warmth. For a moment she didn't know which she
preferred. But as he pulled her to him and she collapsed onto
his chest, she knew where she wanted to be: here in his arms,
cradled by his body, all warm and appeased, like a baby who'd
just been fed milk and honey.

Darienne had never felt so exhausted or so deliriously

happy. David lifted her by the shoulders and began to sit up, looking at her with indulgent, curious eyes.

"Why are you smiling so much?"

"I'm in such a euphoria, David." She reached up to brush a bead of perspiration from the side of his forehead. "Being with you is so satisfying. I could melt with the happiness you've given me. No one is like you," she told him in a heartfelt whisper. "No one in the universe."

He held her softly, stroking her arms, her back, her breasts in an affectionate way. He tugged at her hair. "I feel good, too. But damned tired."

"Oh, so am I." She raised her arms to stretch. The movement made her breasts rise and he bent to kiss each nipple. "You've worn me out," she said, digging her fingers into his hair, gently pushing his head up from her breasts. "But don't do that or I'll want you again."

His eyes widened slightly. "You're insatiable."

"I know." She slid her hands around his neck, pressing her chest to his again just to feel him once more. "When I'm with you, my body can't keep up with my desire. Oh," she whispered, kissing him below his chin, "I do want you again. But I'm too tired and it's too late."

"Dawn will be here in less than an hour," he warned.

"Yes," she said, straightening, taking her hands from his body. "I must go."

He pulled her toward him a bit. "You don't have to. Stay. You can share my resting place. I don't want you to go."

The offer surprised her; he seemed to have forgotten his confessed ulterior motive. To lie on his glorious, masculine body through the day in his coffin was indeed a temptation. But she'd better not. She didn't want to set a precedent, especially not with David. As she looked in his eyes she could see his longing, his chronic loneliness. He wanted a woman's companionship so much, sometimes she wondered if it really mattered to him who that woman was. Especially if he'd settle for her. Wasn't it only yesterday that they were arguing even while in the midst of coupling? Poor David. If only he'd forget his pact with Veronica. Veronica would be loyal and true to him throughout the ages, if he'd only let her. And Darienne was almost certain that Veronica would allow her the right to enjoy David from time to time, too. Yes, Veronica was the one

and only perfect companion for him. What could be done to
bring them together again, to obliterate their pact? Should she
interfere?

"So, will you stay?" David asked, disrupting her contemplation.

"Stay?"

"Share my resting place. Where are you?" He looked deep
into her eyes, as if trying to read her thoughts.

"Here."

"Where's your brain?" he asked with humor.

"Oh, you know me. Juggling a hundred ideas at once."

"Name one."

"That I don't want to disappoint you, but I must leave."

His eyes did grow disappointed, but then seemed to steel
themselves for the inevitable. "It would spoil your independence to stay with me through one little day?"

"I might like it too much, and then you'd be stuck with me
for eternity."

"Well, that's a thought to weigh seriously," he said with
mock gravity.

She rose to her feet. "I'll leave you to weigh it, then," she
said as he stood beside her. She looked down at her body,
covered with already healing bite marks and dried rivulets of
blood. "I'll need to wash up."

"Of course." He walked with her behind the wet bar, where
he opened a drawer and pulled out a clean towel.

As she took the towel and turned on the faucet, she eyed his
refrigerator. "David, do you have any bags to spare? I just got
in from traveling and haven't acquired a supply yet."

"Sure." He opened the small refrigerator door and pulled
out two bags filled with garnet-colored liquid. "I went to the
blood bank last week."

"How do you do it?" she asked, curious.

"I put on old clothes, a baseball cap, and dark glasses—"

"What?" she said, beginning to laugh. "I can't imagine how
you must look!"

He smiled, continuing, "I come in after the nightly cleaning
crew has been there and say I forgot a sack of dirty cloths. In
the middle of the night, there's only one person on duty and
they don't care about the cleaning crew, so they just nod and
let me pass. I go into the back rooms, into the walk-in refriger-

ator, pull out a trash bag I have stashed under my jacket and fill it with a month's supply. I nod as I walk out. Nine times out of ten the person's on the phone or asleep."

"It's that easy? Don't they notice the blood is missing the next morning?"

"Sometimes in a day or two an article will appear in the newspaper about the theft indicating the police were notified," David replied. "An officer is quoted saying he's questioning employees and the cleaning crew. But nothing more has ever happened. With all the assaults, murders, and rapes being committed, the police probably don't have much time to spend tracking down some missing pints of blood. But I worry the blood banks may tighten their security and begin checking everyone who comes in more closely."

"They won't," Darienne said with a shrug. She never worried about what occurred in the natural world because she felt superior to it. Though she reminded herself that she needed to attend to her investment in David's musical. She still had to do something about the actor they'd selected.

"David," she said, running her hands up his chest. "The past two nights have been lovely, but tomorrow we have to go to the theater."

"We do?" he said, his tone of voice falling.

"Well, I'm going. And you haven't been there yourself. What about that song you were to send them?"

He smiled grimly. "I finished it before you came over tonight and dictated the lyrics over the phone. I said I was sick."

"I knew you were too conscientious to forget your work."

"I'd hoped I'd managed to make you forget the theater," he said, massaging his temple.

"You made a valiant effort, *cheri,* and I adored every minute. But I won't let our musical be ruined by bad casting."

"Our?"

"I own most of it," she reminded him.

"I created it!"

"Yes, but it's always the one with the money who has the strongest voice, *n'est-ce pas?* I'll meet you at the theater tomorrow. You will tell them all exactly who I am, please. I don't want any trouble with security people or anyone else questioning the propriety of my being there. Not that anyone could stop me."

David nodded with resignation. "I'll inform everyone. You won't be embarrassed. Unless you embarrass yourself. You're out of your element, Darienne."

"Embarrass myself?" She chuckled. "I don't blush, David. And I learn quickly. We'll see about this . . . what was his name?"

"Matthew McDowall."

"Yes, him. You'd better be prepared to find someone new. But don't worry. I'll help you select a proper replacement."

"No," David said with dry gallows humor, "why should I worry? It's only two years of work and several careers you're about to destroy."

Darienne ignored that and put on her clothes quickly. David helped her button her halter top at the back. She picked up the two blood bags he'd given her and put them in the stylish leather bag she'd brought in with her. Slinging the strap over her shoulder, she headed for the window.

"I'll walk you down to the door," David said, objecting.

"No time for proprieties," she said as she sat on the open window's ledge and slung her legs over it.

"Where are you staying?"

"I have a place."

"Why won't you ever tell me?" he asked, his tone irritated, hurt. "You've spent an entire night pulling me into your belly, but you won't let me know where you live. Why is it always such a secret with you?"

"Now, David. This is how it must be, or I won't be happy." He was too desirable and too possessive for her to keep him in her life on anything but her terms. Darienne owned herself, and no one, not even David, would ever take her independence from her. "Rest well," she said in a caring tone. "See you at the theater."

With one last, adoring look at his beautiful physique and the blue eyes that both accused and indulged her, she gripped the ledge with her hands and pushed herself off. She jumped three floors to the grass below and walked along the iron fence to the back of David's house, wanting no stray passersby to see her.

As she walked in the chilled air, she felt light-headed and weak. How David had sapped her strength tonight! she thought, feeling warm and smug. As she reached the back gate, she grasped it for a moment, almost dizzy with the rekindled electricity of her hours with him. Giving in to her euphoric feeling wasn't wise. She had perhaps twenty minutes to get to her apartment in the John Hancock Building. Her place was less than a mile away. If she ran, she'd be there in five minutes. But she was quickly realizing she no longer had the strength to run any distance.

She needed sustenance. How fortunate she'd had the foresight to ask him for a supply, she thought, opening her purse and taking out one of the blood bags he'd just given her. Holding it carefully so as not to spill any on her clothes, she punctured the plastic with her sharp incisors. Quickly she put it to her lips and drank down the contents.

When she finished, she was already feeling stronger. She climbed the locked gate, dropped softly to the other side, and ran down the alley on her way toward North Michigan Avenue.

When she reached "Big John," she rushed in only slightly out of breath. Nodding to the middle-aged, uniformed doorman, who'd grown used to seeing her come in at unusual hours over the years, she headed for the elevator that would take her to the ninety-first floor.

As she sped upward to her condo apartment, she leaned against the elevator wall. Though the ride was fast and smooth, the quick acceleration upward always made her lightheaded, the same physical reaction she experienced on airplanes. She'd gotten used to it, expected it, but didn't like the feeling. The dizziness was caused by distancing herself from the earth. She was supposed to have returned to the soil when she died in 1617.

She'd found that holding the packet of soil from France that she always carried eased the sensation and helped her body become accustomed to the great height. Taking it out of her purse, a small, earth-filled satin pillow bordered with lace, like a sachet, she closed it in her fist and immediately the dizziness began to ebb.

When the elevator doors opened, she felt almost normal and dropped the packet back into her purse. Taking out her key, she walked down the corridor to her condo, unlocked the door, and entered. Looking out her living room window to her spectacular view over the city, she noted that the sky was growing the thick charcoal shade that indicated the first rays of the sun were only minutes away.

She took the remaining blood bag from her purse and walked into the kitchen to store it in the refrigerator. Coming back into the living room, she tossed her purse on the modern white couch, kicked off her sandals, and walked barefoot over her textured white wool rug toward the adjoining room. Inside, on the carpet, lay the white enameled coffin she'd bought for this apartment.

Darienne owned a number of homes in different parts of the world, and each had its matching coffin. Her ancestral château in France, the source of her family's vast fortune, contained her ancient coffin carved from oak. It looked somewhat like David's, though more delicate in design. In her Swiss chalet, she kept a simple coffin of varnished pine. For her Mexico City apartment, she'd had a coffin specially made with Aztec designs ornamenting it. In Rome, she felt especially pampered resting in her casket of Italian marble.

In addition to these and others, she could not do without the coffin she used for travel. Sturdy, made of metal with inside locks, it looked like a trunk that files might be stored in. When she traveled she simply made arrangements to have her trunk shipped, with herself in it, to one of her homes or to a storage facility, as she did in Chicago. Her condo here was too small to stash the trunk away. Besides, she didn't want her white rugs soiled from any dirt picked up en route.

She opened the white casket and reclined on its luxuriant emerald velvet lining. She'd chosen the material, which covered a thin layer of French soil, to remind her of her second favorite jewel. Diamonds were her favorite, but they, of course, had no color.

As she pulled the lid shut over her, she regretted not having had a chance tonight to linger over the view of the city through her spacious windows. The view was one of the reasons she'd chosen the John Hancock as her home in Chicago, shortly after David had moved here. The other reason, of course, was its location close to David's home. Through the centuries she'd always followed David as he moved from place to place every few decades. It was one reason she had so many homes. When he left Italy during the last century, for example, she hated to give up the hilltop estate she'd acquired, so she kept it. The same with her ancient stone farmhouse near Strat-ford-on-Avon, though she hadn't returned to it for some time and wondered if she should sell it. She preferred London now.

She promised herself she would have a chance to enjoy the view tomorrow for a little while before she left for the theater. Closing her eyes, she thought of David again. She almost wished he didn't have the ability to pleasure her so thoroughly. Craving anyone or anything made her less than totally free. Actually, she was a slave to her own sensuality, not to David. Though perhaps if she'd never known David, she wouldn't have learned to crave sex.

Ah, well, she thought as the deep lethargic sleep began to creep over her with the dawning of the sun's rays outside her protective coffin. Why question her desires? Why not simply enjoy?

The next evening, David waited for Darienne by the stage door. He'd decided it best to walk in with her to make her entry into the theater world smoother for all involved. She showed up about a half hour after dusk wearing, of all things, a suit. He'd never seen her dressed like a business woman before, and it surprised him to know she even owned such clothing. Her suit was beige, chicly conservative and summery. With her blond hair gathered in smooth elegance at the back of her neck, she reminded him of Eva Peron. The diamonds in her earlobes and on her watch provided subtle evidence of her underlying passion, like Eva, for riches and glamor.

She said, *"Bonsoir, cheri,"* in her honeyed voice and took his arm demurely as they entered the theater. Most of the cast had gone home, having been rehearsing since early morning. David hoped that Matthew had also left. Putting off a meeting between him and Darienne might buy a little time, during which he might get some idea to stop her from interfering before she did any damage. But knowing Matthew's dedication, the actor would probably still be there.

They entered the auditorium by a door close to the stage. The orchestra pit was dark and empty. The pianist hired for rehearsals had apparently been dismissed for the day. Several men were busy working overtime hammering out a set that looked like a historic Parisian street. Others were laying some wire. The stage lighting altered in hue and intensity as adjustments were made. A guillotine stood at one side of the stage, where a crew member was testing it to see how smoothly the blade moved up and down.

David spotted Merle in the third row of the empty theater audience, a pint carton of milk in his hand. He'd apparently gotten his crewcut trimmed since David last saw him. His round gray head had a fuzzy look. Next to him sat the show's designer, Loni Gustafson, who oversaw the creation of the sets and the costumes. A svelte brunette in her fifties, Loni looked much younger, particularly in her jeans and comfortable, colorful gauze top.

David walked up to them and introduced Darienne. "She's the 'angel' who saved us," he added, both to remind them and to puff Darienne's psyche. He hoped, in vain probably, that if they made a fuss over her, she might somehow be charmed away from getting involved in the mechanics of the production.

Merle and Loni greeted her warmly, though Merle eyed David with a hint of anxiety at Darienne's arrival.

"How are you feeling?" he asked David.

David was reminded of his lie that he'd been ill. "Fine, now," he replied, experiencing a twinge of guilt. He and Merle had worked compatibly together for several years. Merle had long ago adjusted to David's eccentricities—particularly the fact that David was available only in the evenings. David claimed he kept to a strict personal writing schedule during the day. Merle always accepted the excuse without question, perhaps because he'd known many theater people with offbeat habits and superstitions. If a person had talent and a professional attitude, that seemed to be enough for Merle.

"The lighting crew's trying different effects to see how it looks with Sir Percy's costume and makeup," Loni said. She was referring to Matthew's character. Matthew, Loni, and the makeup expert had spent months working out how the play's vampire hero, Sir Percy Blackeney, should look. She pointed to the director, a tall, very thin man who stood by the rail of the orchestra pit, supervising what was happening. "Charlie's in a daze," she confided to David. "One too many Valiums today, I think. I heard his wife's lawyer called with new demands."

"I'm surprised he's coherent," David muttered, taking a seat next to her. Darienne sat beside him.

Everyone looked up at the stage then as the director said, "All right, let's try it again. Lights? Begin . . ."

And then, all at once, out of the shadowed doorway of one of the stage buildings, came a silent figure dressed in black breeches and high, shining black boots. A long black cape hung from his broad shoulders over his short-waisted black satin coat. Beneath it a dark red waistcoat fit snugly across his chest. A wide-brimmed hat that kept his face partly hidden completed the costume. When his face showed beneath the shadow of his hat, his skin looked pale and smooth. There was a glimpse of blond hair at his ear.

He moved with a slow, stealthy dancer's precision toward a raven-haired actress who had also come on stage, dressed in a long cloak and eighteenth-century dress. He approached her with eerie, mesmerizing grace, an ominous silhouette, his fingers tautly extended. When he surprised her, she showed fear and tried to back away. But he loomed over her, touched her face with hesitance at first, then deliberately ran his fingertips along the side of her throat, slowly, sensuously, until she grew compliant. She tilted her chin to one side, exposing her neck more fully.

Shoulders lifted in a batlike stance, he hovered over her, his mouth drawing closer and closer to her bared throat. But then he turned his head away from her, his face contorted with anguish. As if stabbed by guilt, he backed away. He moved around her as she stood transfixed, eyes wide. Each step he took seemed a reflection of his inner torment. He grasped a nearby lamppost, clung to it, eyes closed, head tilted at a poignant angle. His chest visibly shuddered with each breath, the scarlet waistcoat expanding and contracting. His ragged gasps were audible to the several viewers in the audience.

Ah, Matthew, David thought, watching the actor. He played his vampire character so convincingly he didn't even need the music and lyrics to express himself. Matthew could show huge feeling with his body language alone. His emotion was so inspired, David wondered how he could understand the vampiric point of view, the power, the bloodlust, the sorrow, and guilt, so well. The actor empathized with his character so perfectly, David had occasionally wondered if

Matthew could possibly *be* a vampire himself. But when he heard from everyone how many daylight hours Matthew put in at the theater, there could be no question but that Matthew was mortal. Yet, he displayed such deep perception, such love, such humanity, all conveyed through his craft, that David had come to think of him almost as a brother. In reality, however, they barely knew each other.

David smiled with complete satisfaction as he watched. Remembering Darienne, he turned to glance at her. His heart rate picked up with anticipation: Darienne's bright green eyes were riveted to the actor. She appeared more than impressed; she looked awestruck! Just as David had hoped—even Darienne couldn't be blind to Matthew's profound talents.

Darienne couldn't believe what she was seeing. The man in the cape possessed such incredible sensuality! The undulations of his body as his stomach compressed and his chest expanded with each breath, the broad-shouldered power of his physique in his tight-fitting clothes, the lean muscularity of his thighs as he moved . . . Darienne had to catch her breath. Her nerve endings were all in a dither and her pulse was starting to jump. How she would love to replace the mesmerized actress on stage! Only she wouldn't have played the part the same way. She'd throw out the script and seduce him right then and there! End of musical!

Where on earth did they find him? Who was he? Some stand-in for McDowall? Darienne's mind stopped thinking rationally as she watched him approach the actress again from behind. After a bated pause, he suddenly enveloped her in his arms. She leaned back against him, her long, flowing cloak covering her from head to toe. Without truly touching her, his hands moved with deft, fluid strokes over her feminine contours, showing his deep desire to possess her. I've never seen anything like him! Darienne thought. Her heart began beating erratically and warmth flushed her cheeks.

In her imagination, she saw herself in the actress's place. Only she let the cloak slip from her shoulders to the floor, so he could caress her unimpeded. Without thinking, Darienne touched her own bosom, then realized with a start what she was doing and that her hands were shaking. Embarrassed for the first time in centuries, she folded her fingers together in her lap and tried to calm herself.

All at once, on stage, the actress whirled about and kissed the actor on the mouth. His shoulders lifted again and his body shuddered. Slowly, as if in agony, he drew his mouth away. With tenderness, he cupped her face in his large hands and gazed at her with huge sorrow. He turned from her then, swiftly leapt over a cart in his path and bounded off stage, leaving the actress looking after him with genuine tears shimmering in her eyes.

Well! Darienne thought, caught up in his emotion as well as his sensuality. This man can act, too! He even had athletic prowess. Was he McDowall's understudy? Maybe he could sing, as well. If so, she'd see to it he got the part!

The director muttered that the lighting still wasn't right and tiredly dismissed the crew, warning they'd better have it properly adjusted by tomorrow night. Darienne turned to David.

"What do you think?" David asked in a bright tone before she could say anything.

"Obviously they've got to get that lighting together." She repeated what she'd heard as if she knew what she was talking about. "As for the rest, I haven't seen enough to make any firm judgment." She maintained a cool manner, wanting to keep her own counsel a while longer. David sounded too eager for her approval. "By the way," Darienne added in an afterthought, "the costumes aren't accurate historically." She was surprised David hadn't noticed that the stage vampire's apparel would never have been accepted in the eighteenth century. But then David had never been a devoted student of fashion in any century she'd known him.

"It's to be taken as romantic fantasy," he explained in a hushed voice. "It's not meant to be *that* authentic."

Darienne smiled to herself. Yes, she was nitpicking. The red vest and tight breeches looked fine to her! She enjoyed being in a position of influence, though, and wanted to make the most of it.

"Would you like a tour of the theater?" Merle asked.

Darienne eagerly accepted the offer and the four of them spent the next half hour exploring. They showed her the computer that ran the intricate stage and lighting effects. She didn't understand the technical jargon, but did read between the lines that they'd been having a lot of trouble getting the complex system to function properly. Next they pointed out the trapdoor, the twelve-foot drop down which Sir Percy disappeared from the stage in a cloud of dry ice. They also showed her the forty-foot ladder he climbed off stage in order to appear at the top of the proscenium arch, from which he swung to the stage floor on a rope.

At last they wound up backstage in a hallway lined with dressing room doors, most of them closed because the actors had left. While they stood around a portable costume rack filled with elaborate clothing, Loni showed Darienne the various laces and rich, imported materials used to re-create the refined gaudiness of the era.

As she listened, Darienne noticed that at some point they'd been joined by another person. It took a moment before she recognized him from the photos David had shown her. Matthew McDowall stood quietly between David and Loni, curly hair falling over his wide forehead, silver tendrils mixed with brown. He might charitably be described as tall. A large T-shirt with a cartoon cat on it hung from his angular shoulders and fit snugly across his chest. Old jeans that bagged at the knee and puckered over his chunky Nikes covered his lean legs. She could understand now why the photos had confused her. With his barrel chest and sturdy neck, he looked stout from the rib cage up. But full-length photos took in his narrow hips and long legs, making him look thin, which was his general body type.

Deep laugh lines creased the corners of his eyes and the outer tops of his cheeks, yet his face appeared youthful. His skin had a high color, as if it had been rubbed with a towel. His deep rib cage stood out in an imposing manner due to his straight posture and seemed at odds with his quiet demeanor. All in all, he looked and dressed like a comic, Darienne decided.

Hands in his jeans' pockets, he glanced in turn at each person in the small group, apparently more interested in studying the personalities about him than in Loni's on-the-spot lecture. Loni's voice had grown noticeably higher and more feminine with Matthew standing beside her, but this didn't seem to faze the actor. He seemed conditioned to it.

All at once his round eyes settled on Darienne. They were

a misty gray-green, calm, intelligent, and a trifle droll. He kept up his steady stare as if measuring her, delving into her character, her mind, and he showed only the barest hint of the usual admiration she expected from men. She saw little sensuality in those alert eyes, only curiosity and perception. Yet his gaze felt so penetrating, she grew uncharacteristically rattled and confused.

She broke the eye contact and looked back at Loni, who was still speaking. In a moment, however, her eyes were drawn to the actor again as the young woman who had worn the long cloak on stage approached him. Out of costume, she looked unexpectedly small, fragile, and young in her shorts and blouse. Her own long, straight, auburn hair had replaced the elaborate wig she'd worn, but her ingenuous face looked the same. Her upturned nose had freckles.

She took his arm briefly as she said good-night, looking up at him with a sincere smile and warm brown eyes that bordered on adoration. Matthew turned to her, murmured "Good-night, Elaine," and patted her hand with quiet affection. Then she left. Darienne's gaze followed the actress as she walked alone down the hall toward the stage door. Darienne wondered if Elaine was the show's leading lady or a stand-in for her, as the man in the black cape and hat must have been a stand-in for McDowall.

Meanwhile, Loni finished and David took over the conversation. "Matthew, I'm glad you've joined us. Let me introduce you to Darienne Victoire. She has a large investment in the show."

Darienne felt obligated to look at Matthew directly. He smiled—a broad smile, revealing white teeth not quite perfectly aligned. "I've heard your name mentioned," he said. His voice was soft, musical, mysterious somehow. "It's a pleasure to meet you."

Darienne merely nodded and looked away. She didn't like him. She couldn't think of a logical reason why, but she instantly didn't like him. David claimed she had no logic anyway, so why should she worry about a reason? She knew her instincts were usually correct. McDowall wasn't right for the part of Sir Percy Blackeney, and that was all there was to it. She'd save David's musical from the hands of this washed-up comedian whether David liked it or not!

* * *

David winced and glanced painfully at Merle. Fortunately, Darienne had waited to begin her tirade until after Matthew and Loni had left. ·

"He's too soft-spoken, too rumpled, not tall enough, and certainly not sexy!" she continued. "You think women are going to pay good money to see *him?* You need someone dynamic. Like that stand-in who performed for the lighting crew. Now *there* you have a man women will die for! Can he sing?"

"Of course he can sing!" David replied. "That was Matthew!"

Merle chimed in. "Yeah, that was Matthew. He doesn't have a stand-in. Matthew would never let anyone else try out his makeup."

Darienne looked almost hostile. "How can you tell me that was McDowall? There's absolutely no resemblance."

"That's the wonder of makeup and Matthew's acting ability," Merle said. "He gets himself so deeply into character, he becomes Sir Percy."

Darienne listened with what appeared to be tethered patience, then turned her bright, stubborn gaze to David. He felt the heat of her glare. What on earth was the matter with her? David wondered. Was this fun-loving Darienne, who never troubled herself about anything? "We're telling you the truth," David told her, sensing she was thinking they were trying to pull some trick on her. "That man on stage was Matthew. He's the one who sent your pulses racing." David had noticed her tremulous hands as she'd watched. "I know Matthew is different in real life, but what matters is what he projects on stage. And if other women react as I saw you react, I'd say we have a new sex symbol in the making."

Merle chuckled, no doubt enjoying the prospect of lines of women at the box office.

"Never!" Darienne said. "That man simply doesn't have what it takes."

"But he just demonstrated that he does!" David retorted. He'd hoped he'd gotten through to her. "What difference does it make if he looks rumpled offstage? He's been meticulous about his costume. Loni says he's driving her crazy having it tailored and adjusted so that it fits exactly the way he wants it to. Look at the finished stage product, not the raw ingredients." David was trying to find a way to make Darienne think rationally. That was always difficult, but in this case, he didn't have a clue what her problem with Matthew stemmed from.

Darienne angled her chin, her mouth set. Merle looked on with an expression of increasing foreboding.

"I'll think further about this and let you know my decision tomorrow," Darienne said in a tight, superior tone. "But if my requests, whatever they may be, aren't met, I'll withdraw my finances from the show. Good-night, gentlemen. I'll find my own way out."

As she walked off, Merle began to run after her. David held him by the shoulders and stopped him. "Let her go. She's in a mood. I'll talk to her."

Merle pressed his hand to his stomach and grumbled, "Okay, you talk to her. Better than that, find some way to keep her away from here. At least till opening night. Or better yet, let her take her money out. I'd rather go deeper in debt than have her around messing things up!"

"We need her finances," David said, stating the simple truth in as quiet a tone as possible.

Merle shook his head, looking more and more pale. "I'd also rather die a pauper than from a bleeding ulcer."

David inhaled sharply in reaction to the word *bleeding*. With self-loathing, he pushed the vivid image of blood from his mind. He hated to see Merle in such a state. "I'll set her right," David tried to reassure him. "Don't worry."

4

I want to see the transformation

USING HIDE glue made from animal skins and hoofs, Alexandra carefully fixed the violin's top onto the sides. As she deftly wiped away excess glue, Susan walked in.

"Hi," she said, looking cool in the hot weather in her short shorts and tank top.

"Hi, Susan." Alexandra's cordial tone covered her usual ambivalence about having company while she worked. She was getting uncomfortably behind on her other commissioned instruments while finishing this violin for the auction. She needed Susan's help badly. But, oh, how she'd grown tired of the duty of making conversation with her.

"Wow, you've got it glued already!"

"How about that," Alexandra said, smiling.

"Are you going to get out your cauldron now and start making the varnish?"

"You make me sound like a witch."

"Well, you do look like a sorceress when you do it, standing over your double boiler. The smell of the alcohol and all those crystals and liquids. And those funny roots."

"Funny?" Alexandra said. "Your mother probably has turmeric in her kitchen."

"What about dragon's tooth?"

"Dragon's *blood*. That's a tree sap from South America."

"Oh, yeah, blood. Because it makes the brownish red color. So what shade are you going to make this violin?"

"I'll have to wait till the glue is dry. Then I'll see how it taps," Alexandra said, lightly tapping the top with her finger-

51

tips to indicate the procedure. "I can tell by the sound and feel of it what kind of varnish to make."

"That's amazing. *How* can you tell?"

"Experience," Alexandra said, using her standard reply for what was far too complex to explain.

"Bet you'll be glad when it's finished."

"You can say that again!" Alexandra wiped glue from her hands with a rag. "I'll be glad when the auction's over, too. By the way," she said, turning to Susan. "Edith thinks someone ought to play the violin briefly at the auction to show it off. Would you want to do it?"

"Me?" Susan said excitedly. "What night is it again?"

"The last Saturday of September."

"Oh." Susan's smile faded. "My parents' twenty-fifth anniversary party is that night. The invitations have been sent and everything."

"That's right," Alexandra said with a sigh. "I'd forgotten you've been planning it for them. That's too bad."

"I'm disappointed, too. Darn! So, what'll you do about the auction?"

Alexandra inhaled, pursed her lips and blew the air out, puffing her cheeks. "Looks like I'll have to play something myself."

"You don't like soloing?"

"Nope."

"Didn't you do recitals?"

"A hundred years ago when I was your age. I'm a team player in the orchestra, Susan. Competent, but no virtuoso. I don't even know what to play for them."

" 'Meditation' from *Thais?*"

"That old workhorse? It's too long anyway. I think Edith wants something short and flashy."

Susan chuckled. "A hoedown jig?"

Tongue in cheek, Alexandra said, "Actually, I've been considering 'Love in Bloom.' Then if I make a mistake, everyone will think I did it for a laugh."

Susan stared at her blankly. "What's 'Love in Bloom?' "

"Jack Benny's old theme."

"Oh. He was—"

"Before your time, I know." Alexandra lifted her eyes to the ceiling.

"You'll think of something," Susan said. "What are you going to wear?"

"Oh, God, that's another problem I hate to think about. All I have are my everyday clothes," Alexandra said, lifting the soft blue cotton skirt and top she was wearing. "Or my long black dress that I wear for concerts."

"No, you've got to have something with panache, something that makes a real statement," Susan said, eyes dancing. "Low-cut with sequins. Scarlet red."

Alexandra laughed. "A real statement, huh? You want to go find this fantasy dress for me?"

"I'll go shopping with you, if you want."

Alexandra paused. "That's an idea. Let me think about it," she said, taken off-guard by the offer. "Right now we'd better get to work. I've got pegs to carve and you've got that viola back to work on."

"Okay. Just one more thing. A friend of mine from college will be dropping over in about a half hour."

"A friend?" Alexandra didn't hide her irritation. "Susan, this is a workplace, not the college cafeteria."

"She's a music student," Susan quickly explained. "Another violinist. She loves my violin and wants you to make one for her. Her parents can afford it. Don't worry."

Alexandra felt a quick, unpleasant sensation of embarrassment. It didn't occur to her Susan might bring in new business, and she felt guilty for jumping to conclusions. "That's great!" she said, covering her discomfiture. "What's her name?"

"But Darienne," David said, trying to keep a reasoning tone of voice in the face of her implacable demeanor. "You've got to see Matthew in more scenes, see him singing, before you make up your mind."

"I *haven't* made up my mind yet," she said as they walked up Michigan Avenue toward the theater.

"You said you'd give us your decision tonight."

Darienne looked momentarily startled, as if she'd forgotten her ultimatum of the night before. "And I will," she said smoothly. After a moment she added in a more hesitant manner, "I watched a rerun episode of "Rick and Rosie" late last night. I saw it listed in the newspaper television guide."

David raised his eyebrows in surprise. He'd heard Matthew's popular old sitcom was showing weeknights on some cable station, but he had never watched it. "What did you think?"

Again, she paused. "Well . . . he does have a knack for comedy. His face is very expressive. It surprised me. Last night he was so quiet, so contained. Nothing dynamic or remarkable about him at all. Yet on TV he showed such quickness, such a strong inner spark. Through his eyes especially." She left off, as though distracted. Then she glanced at David, as if suddenly aware he was still listening, waiting for her to finish. "So, as I say," she continued with more dispatch, "he's fine for comedy. But comedy isn't what we're looking for in *The Scarlet Shadow.*"

"There are spots of humor in the show. Sir Percy disguises his identity by playing a fop."

"Yes, but the main thrust—to use a delightfully appropriate word—should be his sexuality, David."

"But you saw last night—"

"I'm not sure what I saw last night," she replied, her tone sharp.

"You could have fooled me."

"I often do! Don't pretend you understand women, David. Even innocent little Veronica surprised you at times."

David's jaw tightened. Why at the most incongruous moments did she always throw Veronica into the conversation? Keeping his anger to himself, he said, "Let me remind you what hangs in the balance here. Millions of dollars of your money and others' have been invested in this show. Several careers, including mine, are at stake. Opening night is only a month away. To change the lead actor at this stage is foolhardy, especially when you're the only one who finds anything wrong with him!"

Darienne looked a trifle chastened. "I know, David. I'm not so insensitive I don't see the obvious. But if something is wrong, then it needs to be changed, or you could face a worse disaster if the show flops."

They reached the theater's stage entrance, and David gave up arguing for the time being. When they entered the auditorium, Matthew and Elaine, his leading lady, were onstage in costume singing a duet to a piano accompaniment as they enacted a long scene. David selected seats several rows back, hoping to keep Darienne at some distance from the producer, director, choreographer, and designer who were sitting together in the front row. Darienne didn't object. In fact, she seemed to want to settle herself as quickly as possible so as not to be distracted from viewing the rehearsal in progress.

Matthew was singing exquisitely, creating himself into a charismatic figure in his blond wig and black costume as he slowly glided around Elaine. He moved with the controlled smoothness of a figure skater on ice, his physical exertion seeming to have no impeding effect on his singing. David had heard what long hours Matthew spent doing dance exercises to increase his strength. And Merle had once mentioned that he'd seen Matthew spend over an hour singing one phrase over and over trying to get a certain vocal effect, sometimes throwing sheet music to the floor in frustration when he could not sing it to his own satisfaction.

The results of Matthew's efforts could be seen daily, for excellent as he was already, he improved each day, coming up with new, inventive ideas to reveal character, to play a scene, to sing a lyric. By opening night his performance, David felt sure, would be nothing short of sublime. And if Darienne couldn't see the treasure they had up there on stage, then she was more shallow than David had ever imagined.

With that thought, he glanced at Darienne. She was sitting absolutely still, her eyes unblinking, as vampires are apt to do, her gaze glued to Matthew. Her expression surprised him a bit. She looked—and David wasn't sure if he was choosing the right word to describe her—apprehensive. It struck him as odd. Darienne never feared or worried about anything that he knew of.

"Something wrong?" he whispered.

The disquiet in her eyes vanished, replaced by her usual aplomb. "No. In fact, I have to admit you're right. Matthew is . . . He's uniquely talented," she said.

"Then you accept him in the role?"

Her back straightened and she looked up at the man on the stage again. "I'll let you know before I leave tonight," she replied coolly.

David sank back into his seat. For a half second there, he'd hoped everything had been settled.

When the rehearsal finished and the director dismissed everyone, Darienne jumped out of her seat without a word, walked down the aisle and out the door closest to the stage. As David hurried to catch up with her, Merle caught up with him.

"David! Where's she going?"

"Don't know," David replied as Merle fell in step with him.

They reached the backstage area, where David guessed she'd headed. After turning a corner, they stopped short when they found her talking to Matthew. The actor looked as if he'd been accosted mid-stride.

Merle's forehead contorted with worry, while David tried to guess what Darienne was up to. From his position a few yards away, David could hear what they were saying.

"What do you think about," Darienne was asking Matthew, "when you move toward her, while you sing to her?"

Matthew, whose makeup was beaded with sweat, peered directly into Darienne's face as though he had difficulty seeing through his dark blue contact lenses. "I think," he replied, his voice quiet and out of breath, "how much I love her."

Darienne's eyes widened. "You love her?"

"Sir Percy loves her. Sorry. When I talk about my character, sometimes I say 'I' instead of 'he.'" He paused to catch his breath. "I think how much he loves Marguerite, but he feels he can't touch her because he's a vampire."

David lowered his eyes as he listened to their conversation. Matthew gave himself wholeheartedly to enact what he thought was a fable, never realizing the play's creator was such a night creature who experienced such feelings.

"Why are you out of breath?" Darienne asked Matthew.

"Because," he replied as he unfastened his black cape from his shoulders, "I need to move slowly to create the vampirish effect. Like fog. I try to creep across the stage like fog over water. To move that slowly and sing long, sustained notes at the same time takes a lot of energy. But I'm working up to it. By opening night, I'll have the strength I need to keep it up for the whole two-hour show."

David noted the tiny gleam of hidden knowledge in Darienne's eyes and wondered if she was thinking what he was—that if Matthew actually were a vampire, he would easily possess several times the strength he needed to do what he was working so hard to achieve.

"Excuse me," Matthew said, moving away, "I'd like to get my makeup off. It feels claustrophobic."

"Can I watch?" Darienne asked brightly.

"Darienne," David chided, stepping forward. "Matthew is entitled to some privacy."

"It's okay," Matthew called back as he walked toward his dressing room. "Just give me a chance to change out of my costume and then you can come in."

Darienne grinned and turned to David. "See? You needn't be so protective of him."

"Why do you want to bother him?" David asked.

"Why, David," she whispered, leaning close. "You know me. I love to bother men."

"I thought you didn't like him."

"Did I ever say that? He looks admirable enough in his costume. I want to see the transformation back to his real self. I don't understand how he does it."

"Why do you need to understand?" David asked as Merle, who had hung back, edged up to them. "All you need to know is that he *can* become Sir Percy. Better than any other actor could, I might add."

"Chalk it up to feminine curiosity," she replied, straightening David's collar.

"Have you made any decisions, Miss Victoire?" Merle asked in a deferential tone.

"That should be *Ms*," she corrected; then with a smile she added, "but you may call me Darienne." She walked off toward Matthew's dressing room without answering the question.

Merle looked at David. "What's going on?"

"I wish I knew. But . . . ," David said, watching Darienne's confident stroll, the full skirt of her sleeveless white dress swaying as she moved. "I have a feeling she's beginning to like Matthew better."

"So she won't make trouble?" Merle asked, new hope in his voice.

"I wouldn't say that."

"Why not?"

"She may start to like him too much."

"Oh . . ." Merle nodded as he, too, watched Darienne.

"How does Matthew deal with women?"

The producer raised his shoulders. "I only know what I hear. He's a private man, however friendly he seems on the surface. There was gossip about him and his co-star when he was doing "Rick and Rosie." And there was an incident with some other woman who claimed he'd gotten her pregnant, but it turned out not to be true. I haven't heard his name connected with any women lately. Probably more careful now about his relationships. He may even have a wife somewhere, for all I know."

"We'd better see what happens in the dressing room," David said, getting nervous.

They walked up just as Darienne, who had waited by the door, was invited in by Wendy, an attractive young redhead in a T-shirt and short denim skirt, who was Matthew's makeup artist.

Matthew's dressing room was actually comprised of two small rooms. The room in which they stood had a large mirror with lights around it and a counter below, a chair facing the mirror, and some shelves along one wall. Among books, cards, and odds and ends sat a framed photo of a boy about the age of fourteen.

David had no time to observe further, for the mirror posed an immediate problem. For Darienne, too. For a moment he thought she had forgotten, since she walked in without hesitation. But she took a position against the wall to one side of the mirror. David entered quickly and walked to the other side of the mirror before any of the mortals around him could notice that his body did not reflect. Still, he didn't like the situation.

Merle walked in and stood behind the chair. The door to the inner room was closed. Wendy explained that Mr. McDowall, as she called him, was still changing. Just as she finished speaking, the door opened and Matthew walked in. He wore a white undershirt and jeans and carried his costume over his arm. The blue contact lenses were gone. His natural gray-green eyes seemed bright against the pale makeup. He stepped to the hall door and handed the costume pieces to a young woman who worked in wardrobe.

Meanwhile, Darienne leaned forward to peek into the room he'd just come from. The lighting in the rectangular inner room was subdued. All David could see from his position was a long couch and a large green candle burning with a strong flame on a small table. The couch worried him. He wondered what plans Darienne might be envisioning for the unsuspecting actor. Though, perhaps, once Matthew got his makeup off, she might lose interest again.

Matthew sat in the chair, which resembled a barber's chair, in the center of the mirror room. All eyes fixed upon him as Wendy helped him peel off his blond wig and the skullcap beneath. His own silver-streaked tendrils, damp from perspiration, sprung free. Wendy handed him a black makeup cape, sewn like a loose coat. It looked as though he were putting it on backward as he slipped his hands into the cuffed sleeves. The heavy material draped over his chest and pants. Wendy went to work on his face with a brush dipped in some liquid. On the counter below the mirror were small bowls filled with liquids and small, yellow sponges.

"Here for the unveiling?" Matthew said to those curiously gathered around him.

"You don't use cold cream?" Darienne asked.

"The makeup is a rubber latex and has to be scrubbed off with mineral oil," Matthew explained while Wendy began to pull away a soft, flesh-colored foam piece glued high on his cheek. "It's all to give me cheekbones and an aristocratic nose. I couldn't go on stage looking like me. Everybody'd expect me to do a pratfall."

"You did some beauts on 'Rick and Rosie,'" Merle said with amusement. "You must've tripped, slipped, gotten your fingers stuck or goo on your face more times than Dick Van Dyke or Lucy or anyone."

"I've probably had more scars and broken bones, anyway," Matthew said. "The problem is, I really *am* clumsy."

David chuckled with the others but didn't believe Matthew's self-effacing humor for a moment. A man who moved with such fluid precision couldn't have a clumsy bone in his body.

Wendy had carefully removed the cheekbones and nose. Matthew picked up a sponge himself then and began dabbing mineral oil over his face. Wendy went to work with a cloth, rubbing off the pale-colored latex, which rolled off in tiny balls. Matthew's natural features and ruddy complexion began to come through. His eyes still looked unusually bright due to the eye makeup that remained.

While Merle talked more about Matthew's old TV show, David glanced at Darienne, who remained on the other side of Matthew and the mirror. She was looking down at him, as if fascinated to see the true man emerging. Fascinated, and yet, increasingly disappointed. Matthew wasn't nearly so elegant looking and suave as Sir Percy, David supposed she was thinking. Well, David hoped for the musical's sake that she would find him appealing enough to keep in the show, but not appealing enough to seduce.

When the makeup had been removed, Matthew pulled off the makeup cape and stood to one side of his chair, near Darienne. Her eyes never left him. She studied him as a student would study a map for a geography test. All at once she grabbed the sponge Wendy had set down. She walked up to him—in her high heels, she was the same height as he—and dabbed at his chin.

"You still have little balls of makeup clinging to your face," she said.

"It's okay," he told her, gracious, yet stepping away so she couldn't continue. "I'm going to take a shower now anyway. Good-night everyone. See you tomorrow." With a quick, dazzling smile, he disappeared into the subdued lighting of the other room and shut the door.

Darienne stared at the door for a moment, still holding the sponge, her expression both miffed and mystified. She covered this quickly, tossing the sponge nonchalantly back onto the counter. She and David followed Merle out into the hall, leaving Wendy behind to put away the sponges and bowls.

At the end of the hall stood the stage door out of the theater. Here the three stopped, Merle and David eyeing Darienne, waiting for her final word.

"What?" she asked, looking at them, perplexed.

David pinched the bridge of his nose. "What's your decision about Matthew?"

"Oh, that. Well, of course I don't want him replaced," she said blithely. "I never meant that seriously. Obviously he's the only man for the role." As David and Merle exhaled their relief, she chattered on. "But what about the computer? It still isn't working right, is it? The costumes aren't all in yet. Marguerite's wig looked ratty. Did you ever get the lighting straightened out? And I noticed the buildings in the scenes shake. Nobody's going to believe they're made of stone if they wobble every time somebody moves through a doorway!"

Merle raised his hands, palms out, in a defensive gesture. "We know, Darienne. We know. We're working day and night on all that stuff. It'll come together. Promise."

Darienne smiled prettily and squeezed one of Merle's uplifted hands. "I have every confidence in you. But I'll be back tomorrow evening, just to keep an eye on things. Goodnight, gentlemen." She blew them a kiss and was out the door.

David hoped to follow her out and catch up with her, but Merle held him back. "We've gotta do something about her. My ulcer can't take her, whether she likes Matthew or not."

"You have a suggestion?" David asked in a dry tone.

Merle paused and slanted his eyes in a secretive manner. "I might. If it would work."

"What?"

"I've gotten the drift that she enjoys the company of men?"

"That's the understatement of the year."

"Well . . . I have a nephew. Chad Hollinger is his name." He pulled out his wallet. "My sister gave me a photo of him and her."

David looked at the photo and saw a young, very handsome, athletic, blond man. He even looked a bit like Matthew did in his Sir Percy makeup.

"I got him a job as a financial assistant with another show in town," Merle went on. "Chad aims to be a producer, too. Looks up to me and all. Anyway, as you see, he's very good looking. Not only that, he has a knack with women. I mean I've seen him operate at parties. He's in his late twenties, so he may be a little young."

"That won't bother Darienne," David said, catching on to the plan. "But why would he—"

"Because the show he's connected with needs money, too. If I mention how much Darienne invested in our show, I think he'd be interested even if she looked like King Kong. You think if I can get him to sidetrack her, keep her occupied, it might solve our problem?"

David pondered the idea. Darienne liked young men and she liked to be courted. Whenever she visited Chicago, she spent a lot of time combing Rush Street for the choicest of the current crop. But to distract her from anything she'd truly set her mind to—well, that was a tougher question to call.

David shrugged. "I don't know. How would we manage it without her suspecting? She's very clever."

"Chad's going to be at that Soames Library Auction. You're going, right? You donated your manuscript."

"Yes, but I wasn't planning—"

"Matthew's going. Be good for our show if you went, too. Free publicity in the papers. You should go and take Darienne. I'll drop all the pertinent info in my nephew's ear and make sure he finds her. I say it's worth a try. Anything to get her out of our hair."

David exhaled slowly. He hated being in the public eye. "What about your nephew? Can he take care of himself? Darienne is . . ." What could he say? "A woman of much experience."

"Oh, yeah. If I know Chad, he'll relish the opportunity— and her. He's a hell of a lot more experienced than I was at his age. Or any age, for that matter," Merle said with a chuckle.

"Well," David replied with a grim half smile, "he may get more experience than he ever wanted."

Later that night Darienne walked down Michigan Avenue to the John Hancock. It was about midnight and she walked slowly, in no hurry. She carried a videotape of an old movie and a large, thick envelope. She'd stopped at the Chicago Public Library before going to the theater to pick up some research materials she'd requested. Later, after leaving the theater, she'd decided to visit Veronica, and on the way had passed a video store that kept evening hours. She'd gone in and asked if they had any old movies featuring Matthew McDowall. The proprietor came up with one called *The Boy from Savannah*.

She'd been curious to see it, but she'd gotten distracted with her visit to Veronica. Darienne had managed to maintain her sisterlike friendship with the shy writer, who knew Darienne was a vampiress. But the fact that their close friendship had continued was unknown to David. It had been about a year, since before Darienne had left on her travels, that she'd gone without seeing the dusky-haired young woman who'd been and still was David's beloved.

Veronica had been thrilled to find Darienne at her door and greeted her with a tearful smile and a hug. After a few minutes of conversation, Darienne had sensed that Veronica felt isolated, pining for David, counting the years and months until their pact was to end and she could see him again. She looked thin and pale, and more mature than when Darienne had first met her.

Veronica had been living with Rob Greenfield, who was in love with her. But their relationship had ended during the past year, Darienne learned. Veronica told her the story as they sat in the living room of Veronica's small apartment.

"I still love David. But I can't have him. And I can't love anyone else, because I only want him. Rob wanted to marry me," Veronica confided, dry-eyed but sad. "David told me once I should marry if I want to. But I don't want to. So I refused Rob, said I'd just like to continue living together. Though, really, I didn't care. He couldn't take my ambivalence anymore and moved out. It was nice having someone around who cared about me, but I'm glad I'm alone again. Honestly. It's easier to think about David when I'm by myself. That's all I want to do. Remember my time with David."

Darienne had tried to cheer her with reassurances that David still loved her. Veronica's anxious expression showed that she wanted to believe he hadn't forsaken her, but she wasn't sure if she should.

"He's worried that you've forgotten *him*," Darienne had assured her. "He remembers your letter."

"I was torn apart when I wrote that," Veronica told her, tears glazing her brown eyes. "I must have sounded so spiteful. I wish I could tell him I didn't mean it. But he'd be angry if I tried to contact him again."

"You only wrote what you felt," Darienne replied, touching her shoulder. "If David is going to put you through this ridiculous pact of his, then he deserves to suffer!"

Veronica had smiled at Darienne's brash pronouncement and Darienne felt relieved. Veronica was in a more uplifted mood by the time Darienne left, and she promised to visit again.

But now as she entered the Hancock building's lobby, Darienne wished she could do more than just act as a comforter to Veronica and David. She wondered how either would manage any more years of separation without one or both doing something foolish out of loneliness or grief. Neither seemed sure of the other's abiding love, however much Darienne reassured them. Both were pessimists at heart.

Not my problem, Darienne decided as she left the elevator on the ninety-first floor and got out her key. She wasn't going to let herself get depressed just because they were. Besides, everything would eventually work out.

Darienne always fell back into her comfortable, optimist's point of view. She felt at home in that frame of mind, and if others couldn't buy her philosophy, it wasn't her fault. She did her best to convince them. Still, Veronica was such a sweet creature, caught in a heartbreaking situation she hadn't created, that Darienne couldn't help but be concerned.

Darienne made an effort to dispel the stubborn worry from her mind as she threw her handbag and the large envelope onto her white couch. She had a movie to see. She picked up the cassette and inserted it into her machine, then sat on the floor in front of her television set.

She soon found herself immersed in a movie filmed in Georgia over twenty-five years ago. Matthew was in it all right, though she could barely recognize him. He spoke with a thick Southern drawl and looked about eighteen years old. His eyes were wide and ingenuous, dewy with youth, his hair sun-bleached. More cute than handsome with his boyish face and skinny legs, he nevertheless possessed an underlying energy, a quiet alertness that kept him the focal point of the easy-paced comedy with its folksy humor. He even sang in a scene where he was by himself, rowing a rowboat on a pond, and his voice was soothing and clear.

Darienne wondered how he grew from the naive youth in this film to his present self. She was intrigued particularly with his Southern accent. Being from France, she was no expert in American dialects, but the way he spoke in the movie sounded totally natural to him. She'd noticed at the theater that his manner of speech seemed rather precise for an American and slow, yet with no trace of a regional accent. And when he performed in *The Scarlet Shadow* he sounded like a genuine

Englishman. Where did he come from and how did he talk when he was a child?

When the movie ended, she glanced at her watch and realized "Rick and Rosie" would be in progress on the cable channel. She switched stations and found herself watching a much older Matthew, though he was still young enough to have brown hair with no hint of gray and fewer lines in his face. His physique, while still thin, was somewhat more filled out, too. The barrel chest had appeared. The clothing styles showed that the sitcom was about a decade old. He and the actress who portrayed Rosie played bumbling IRS agents investigating a new case of tax evasion each week and stumbling into trouble along the way. Trouble included the many pratfalls Merle had mentioned.

The show also included an ongoing shy romance between Rick and Rosie. Matthew portrayed Rick as an endearing but hopelessly tongue-tied would-be boyfriend. After seeing him in this, how anyone had thought to cast him as the overpowering, sensual vampire/lover in *The Scarlet Shadow* was beyond Darienne's imagination.

She watched him on the TV screen making comic faces while trying to yank his hand out of a computer disk drive where it had gotten stuck. Even as he slipped off the rolling chair he'd been sitting on, landing on his rear with legs sprawling, Darienne had to admit there was something fascinating about him. At times, in flashes, from certain angles, she could even call him handsome. Not sexy, but yet . . . stimulating, intriguing somehow. There was an energy. Something in his eyes.

Darienne remembered the envelope from the library. She reached back to pick it up from the couch and began leafing through the copies it contained.

A few days ago she had read the two magazine articles David had given her. The one from *Time,* written eleven years ago, discussed the huge popularity of "Rick and Rosie" and named Matthew the nation's top comic actor. It briefly mentioned a rumor that the married actress who played Rosie had fallen in love with Matthew. Though Matthew was quoted as saying that he believed his co-star to be "very happily married."

The other article, from a nine-year-old issue of *People,*

which featured Matthew on its cover, was about a movie comedy he was currently starring in. By then "Rick and Rosie" had ended and Matthew was planning to do theater work. The article mentioned a false paternity claim from which he'd recently escaped. Naturally, the paternity issue and the possible romance with his married co-star had piqued Darienne's interest, so she'd asked the library to do further research.

She spent over half an hour skimming the new copies. Two of the articles turned out to be the two she already had. The others contained much about the various injuries Matthew had sustained while playing his comic roles and how respected he was in the entertainment world for his professionalism and dedication, but there was little about his personal life.

Finally, she came across another *People* article which pre-dated the one she'd gotten from David. This one featured a photo of Matthew attending the opening of a movie with a stunning, young blond woman. The article said she was a model he'd met at a party and with whom he'd had a brief affair. After he broke off the relationship, she named him as the father of her unborn child and claimed he had promised to marry her. Matthew not only categorically denied this, but continued to refuse to marry her even when the model tear-fully told reporters she could forgive him for deserting her if only he would keep his promise. Eventually, the model admit-ted that she wasn't pregnant, but had claimed to be in a vain effort to get Matthew back.

As for Matthew's TV series co-star, Darienne could find only one further hint about the actress's reported infatuation. This was in an *US* magazine article that covered the show's unexpected demise after three years of nationwide popularity. "Rick and Rosie" was ending, it reported, because the actress who portrayed Rosie had decided to leave the show for "per-sonal reasons." The magazine noted that she and her husband were divorcing. Matthew had also chosen not to continue on the show, saying he feared being typecast and wished to do other roles. Both stars firmly denied rumors that there had been a romance between them. Nevertheless, the actress's hus-band reportedly blamed the breakup of his marriage on his wife's "worship" of her co-star, Matthew McDowall.

Darienne finished the last article and sat still for a moment, puzzled and intrigued. She pulled out the photos David had given her and studied them again. She couldn't put together how this quiet, average-looking man could have women so infatuated with him. What did they see in him? She'd observed with her own eyes a sophisticated woman like Loni on the verge of behaving like a teenager around a rock star. And Elaine had looked at him with blind adoration. Meanwhile Matthew had been nothing more than polite and congenial toward either of them. He had behaved the same way toward Darienne. In fact, he'd avoided even letting her wipe a little bead of makeup off his chin. Darienne paused to ask herself why she'd attempted to do that. She couldn't find an answer and dismissed the question as unimportant.

Another woman currently in his entourage was Wendy, his makeup artist. Wendy was quite an attractive girl, yet he behaved in a strictly workaday manner with her, too. Darienne put down a photo she'd been holding as her mind wandered. What an unusual way to make a living, applying and removing makeup from someone's face every day. For an artistic person, the job seemed a tedious, unlauded use of talent. But there was an intimacy about it. As the show went on Wendy would get to know him, understand his ways, all his habits and idiosyncracies. She might eventually know Matthew better than anyone.

Darienne caught herself. Why was she dwelling so much on Matthew? Why did he make her so curious about him that she was even doing research? She'd considered him long enough now. She had seen his photos, one old movie, two episodes of his silly sitcom, and most of all she had seen him in person. And he hadn't impressed her. What sexuality he could muster he seemed to save, like a miser, for the stage alone. What these other women found to admire in him she couldn't imagine. To Darienne he seemed like an effective stage prop who could sing. Offstage he wasn't worth a second glance.

Having settled on that conclusion, Darienne slipped the articles back into the envelope, put the photos away, then glanced at her watch. It was growing late, but maybe she should go check out Rush Street, see how this year's smorgasbord looked. It certainly made a better way to spend the night than watching old movies and reading yesterday's gossip.

5

The mysterious and spendthrift Number 101

DAVID GLANCED up briefly from his newspaper as he heard someone climbing in through his side window. Right on time, he thought, feeling a smug anticipation. Whether Merle's plan worked or not, David was going to enjoy the challenge of trying to manipulate a born manipulator.

Darienne jutted her head and shoulders through the open window, pushing aside the sheer drapery with her hands, then swung her legs over the sill. Her blond hair fluffed out in fat ringlets from the confines of a diamond clip at the top of her head. She wore a full-skirted taffeta dress, black with large white polkadots and a white sashlike top that hugged her upper arms and breasts and left her shoulders bare. A big red flower exploded gloriously from the center of the white top.

David made a show of shoving his newspaper to one side. "Can't you ever phone ahead? Do you always have to literally 'drop in'?"

"What sort of friendly tone is that?" she asked, bending to check her sheer black nylons for snags.

How she managed to climb up stone walls without ever getting rips in her stockings was beyond David. Something only a woman could do. She was carrying her shiny black shoes and dropped them to the floor.

"*Cheri,* you're not dressed!" she said, looking up at him for the first time, balancing as she stepped into her high heels.

"What do you mean, not dressed?" he said. "I've got a shirt and pants on."

"For the auction!"

"Good grief," David muttered. He got up from the loveseat

68

and began to pace, pretending to be on the brink of a tantrum. "I told you I had no intention to go."

"But it's been in the papers that you'd be there. Even tonight's," she said, picking up the newspaper he'd put aside.

She leafed through to the society section and pointed to a long article. It was accompanied by a photo of Edith Cornwall and a blond woman holding a violin. The article was headlined with the words, "David de Morrissey among guests expected to attend Soames Auction."

"I told them they could use my name," David said. "I don't think even Mrs. Cornwall really expects me to show up."

"Did she send you tickets?"

"I don't have to use them."

"But, David, I want to go."

"Fine. You take the tickets. Pick up some gigolo on Rush Street and go, if you like."

She slipped her arm through his. "I want to go with you. This is a high society event. I don't want to be seen there with just anyone."

"Go on your own and attach yourself to some muscle-bound celebrity."

"I just may! But I don't want to walk in alone."

"Too bad."

"David, this is for your sake, too. Being seen in public once in a while will counteract the bad publicity you've gotten in the past from living like . . . like a vampire."

"But what about the photographers who will surely be there?" he said, voicing a genuine worry. "We can't have them photographing us."

"Turn away if you see a camera pointed at you."

"But even if they photograph my back, or yours, our images will come out bluish."

She lifted her shoulders, making her collarbone protrude sensually. "So the photographer will think there was something wrong with his film, or he didn't set his camera correctly. He's not going to think, A blue person—my goodness, it must be a vampire! Who takes photos of vampires enough to know such a thing?"

David nodded. "That's true." He took a long breath and exhaled it slowly through his nose, making the most of keeping her waiting. "I hate parties," he muttered.

"Ah, now we have the real reason you don't want to go. Getting out with people for a change will be good for you."

"But all the mindless chitchat . . ."

"Maybe you'll find someone interesting. There may be others there who also admire Shakespeare. Think what a wonderful conversation you might have."

"Okay, okay. I'll go." He sighed again for effect. "I suppose I have to wear a tux."

"*Mais oui,*" Darienne purred, running a finger down his chest. "You look devastating in a tuxedo, *cheri.* I may not find another man there as appealing as you."

"Oh, I imagine you will," David mumbled, smiling inside as he left her to change his clothes. She'd *better* find Merle's nephew attractive. It was the only plan they had to rescue Merle from his ulcer and Matthew from being the possible target of her impossible lust.

Holding a slim glass of champagne, Alexandra paused between cloth-covered display tables, where a knot of people blocked her way. The crowd had steadily increased, guaranteeing the auction was going to be a success, and even Alexandra felt the excitement. The elegant Hilton Hotel meeting room shimmered with a rarified atmosphere as well-heeled art patrons and local celebrities milled about in their tuxes and vivid summer evening dresses. Across the room she spotted Edith buzzing about like a friendly bee, totally in her element, shaking hands, greeting people, encouraging everyone to bid.

Alexandra, by contrast, wished she could sit in a corner and observe it all, instead of feeling the duty to mix in and meet important people. She'd taught herself to be adept at small talk—oh, she could be downright charming when necessary. But she was an introvert at heart, and a room brimming with a swarm of people made a daunting environment for her.

Her violin, finished only two nights ago, stood propped up in a glass display case at the far end of the room. The instrument would be bid upon later, after dinner, during the live auction. Among other things to be auctioned off at that time and also on display were: a full-length Russian sable coat, tickets for a cruise for two to the Orient, a man's diamond ring, and an emerald broach. Each had been donated by some elite Chicago business. In a category all its own, of course, was the de Morrissey manuscript, displayed next to her violin. Her fiddle certainly had good company!

For the moment, everyone was participating in the silent auction, made up of less expensive donated items. Each person had been given a number as they arrived. Now they meandered about, looking over the merchandise and choosing which objects to spend their money on for a worthwhile cause.

The knot of people in her way shifted and Alexandra was able to edge forward. As she did so, a tall, hefty man pushed his way past her. His bulk crushed the large, puffed, elbow-length sleeve of her icy pink taffeta dress. The calf-length evening dress was flattering—it even made her waist look like it measured twenty-one inches again!—but difficult to wear. She puffed the sleeve out with her fingers, wishing there were a wall mirror nearby, but there wasn't.

Moving forward again, Alexandra reminded herself that she ought to participate and bid for something. Unfortunately, so far she hadn't seen anything there she wanted, or more to the point, could afford. She stopped a moment to peek around a few people still gathered in front of an enlarged photo of the Philharmonic. Beneath lay the bid sheet that offered a chance to conduct the orchestra. This marked the popular spot where the knot had formed a few minutes ago.

"Excuse me," she said to a gray-haired woman in a white silk suit and ostrich-feathered hat who was hovering nearby like a hawk. "How high have the bids gotten?"

"Six hundred dollars," the lady replied with a rueful smile. "There are five of us bidding against each other." She picked up the pen lying next to the sheet as an elderly man walked away from it. "I'm going to win it, though, if I have to stay by this table all night to be sure I have the final bid!"

"Hope you get it," Alexandra said and moved on. She might have bid on it herself, to give to Susan, but it was already well beyond her pocketbook range. With five people vying for it, the price was liable to go past a thousand dollars. Amazing how envy and one-up-manship could be channeled to earn money for a good cause!

She walked past people contemplating bids on gourmet dinners at well-known Chicago restaurants, bottles of rare wines, paintings, silver serving pieces, choice opera tickets, and so on. The sumptuous merchandise seemed to flow together before Alexandra's eyes. She found herself growing picky over whether the sterling silver pitcher was more attractive than the leaded crystal candy dish next to it, when in truth she couldn't afford either. The dress she was wearing, from a chic Water Tower Place shop Susan had sleuthed out for her, had broken her budget for the next five months.

Finding herself at the end of the room where her violin was displayed, she noticed a dark-haired, rather good-looking man—at least in profile—bending forward for a closer gaze at her instrument through the glass. His rapt studiousness struck Alexandra, especially since a stunning blonde in a black-and-white dress stood beside him, clinging to his arm. The blonde's attention, however, seemed to be focused on a tall, incredibly handsome blond man who was approaching them. Alexandra watched, curious, as the dark-haired man turned, observed the other man's approach, and then eagerly greeted him. The two blondes immediately fixed gazes on one another; they looked rather like a matched set, with their sensational physiques and obvious sense of flash. Within half a minute, the woman had switched male arms and clung to the new man with as much of a feline, proprietary air as she'd clung to her first escort.

The situation had created a fascinating little scene for Alexandra to speculate about, when suddenly Edith rushed to her elbow. "Come on, Alexandra, I'll introduce you to some of the single men here."

Alexandra gave her an arched look. "Did I say I wanted to meet any?"

Edith grinned. "Of course, you do. There are some prize catches in the room."

"Thanks, but no thanks. I'm not here to meet men."

"Now how can I play matchmaker if you have that attitude?" Edith said, adjusting the aquamarine choker at her neck, which matched her lace dress. "Such a grand selection of charming men, and you look so beautiful tonight, too! You expect me to just pass this opportunity by?"

"Pass it by—please!" Alexandra said, with a smile. With her solo later on to worry about, she didn't want to be paired off with a stranger, have to be witty, make conversation, and so forth.

"You're impossible!" Edith said, humor in her voice. "Say,

do you know if David de Morrissey is here? If he is, I'd like to speak to him."

Alexandra shook her head. "Does anybody know what he looks like?"

"No. That's the problem." Edith fretted. "It'd be dreadful if he actually showed up and no one noticed. I'll go ask at our registration desk and find out if he's picked up his number yet. If he's here, I'll find him."

"I don't doubt that! Good luck."

Edith began to move away, but as she turned she said, "If you change your mind about meeting someone—"

"I won't."

Edith disappeared into the crowd looking momentarily peeved. Alexandra chuckled as she glanced back at her violin. She noticed the same man still looking it over, his hands behind his back. Alexandra knew she ought to go over and talk to him about her instrument, in case he was thinking of bidding on it. But the crowded room oppressed her. She just wasn't up to doing a sales pitch right now. She'd never been good at that sort of thing anyway.

Instead she decided to head back to the table with all the restaurant tickets. Perhaps she could buy Susan a dinner for two somewhere. Susan had spent an entire afternoon shopping with her—pointing out every dress that was either mini-skirted or low-cut or both. Even so, Susan had led her to the shop where Alexandra finally found the dress she'd bought for tonight. More than that, Susan had brought her a new client. She felt she owed the young woman something more than just her hourly pay for these favors. But when she reached the table, she saw that even the restaurant dinners were bringing in bids escalating well past the hundred dollar mark.

Alexandra turned away from the table in disappointment. Then her eye caught sight of something she'd missed before. Or perhaps it had been brought in late. At another display table set against the wall stood an old movie poster, mounted and framed, for *Singin' in the Rain*. Below the title, Gene Kelly, wearing a hat and gray suit in the pouring rain, was hanging onto a lampost with one arm and leaning out from it, his mouth open as if in song.

Alexandra's mind clicked: Susan liked old musicals. And this item ought to be less expensive than most anything else here. She walked up and looked at the bid sheet. It was empty! Either no one wanted it, or it *had* been brought in late. A card tucked into the corner of the simple metal frame indicated the poster had been donated by a Hollywood memorabilia store in Old Town. The bid sheet stated that the opening bid should be at least fifty dollars and could be increased in increments as low as five dollars.

Alexandra wasted no time grabbing the pen next to the sheet. This was probably the most lowly item in the room, but it suited her needs and her pocketbook and she was thrilled to find it! She wrote down fifty dollars in the bid column, and the personal bidding number she'd been given when she came in, 77, in the column alongside it.

Feeling good, as if she'd accomplished something, she set the pen down and walked away. After getting herself a fresh glass of champagne and speaking for a while with a few other Philharmonic people who'd arrived, Alexandra went back to the movie poster to see if anyone else had bid on it.

Unfortunately, they had. Someone with number 28 had put the bid up to fifty-five dollars. And whoever held number 101 had further raised the bid to seventy dollars. Damn! Alexandra thought. She took the pen and wrote in seventy-five and her number on the line below.

As she began to move away, from the corner of her eye she noticed a man come up behind her. He grabbed the pen she'd put down. She turned slightly to get a better look. To her surprise, she found it was the same man who'd been apprais-ing her violin. He bent over the sheet and wrote in a new bid beneath hers. She turned away, not wanting him to see that she'd seen him.

What should she do now? she wondered as she sipped her champagne, her back to him. He'd already observed her bid-ding on the movie poster. If she returned immediately to top his bid, he might come right back and top hers. The price of the poster could go up to a hundred dollars, which she consid-ered her limit, in less than five minutes! No, she'd better bide her time a bit, play it cool. The trouble was, according to the rules announced at the beginning of the evening, the silent auction was to be cut off suddenly when a bell was rung. The big suspense was no one knew exactly when they would sound the bell. After it was rung, the room was to be cleared of people. Whoever had the last bid on each item was the one who would go home with the item.

Alexandra glanced at her watch. It was nearing 8 P.M., when they were to serve dinner. Would they cut off the bidding before or after dinner? Darn, she should have asked Edith. Though it would have been unethical for Edith to tell her, even if she knew.

With a sharp sigh, Alexandra turned to go back to the table. Better get her number last on the list. The bell might sound any moment. The dark-haired man apparently had moved away. At least she didn't see him in the vicinity. She walked up to the bid sheet. Number 101's last bid was ninety dollars. Alexandra wrote ninety-five dollars on the line below.

But just as she set down the pen, she saw a man's long fingers reaching for it. Forced to step to the side to get out of his way, she looked up at him.

Number 101 met her gaze with assertiveness in his pale blue eyes. The half smile on his lips made a vertical line in one cheek. "About finished?" he asked in a low, accented voice.

"I'd hoped you were."

He smiled again, lowered his eyes mysteriously and turned to write on the bid sheet. When he put the pen down, he stepped back so she could read it.

He'd raised his bid to two hundred dollars.

Alexandra looked up at him, a little shocked and angry. "Nice of you to raise the stakes so high! You must really want this thing."

"Indeed, I do," he said in a serious, quiet tone.

"Why? It's only a movie poster. There must be duplicates for sale."

He furrowed one dark eyebrow and pointed his forefinger toward the light gray of Gene Kelly's buttoned suit jacket. "This one's autographed by Kelly himself."

"It is?" She leaned forward to look closer. There it was, the famed dancer's signature in ballpoint pen. "How do you like that?" she said, laughing at herself. "I never noticed."

At that moment a colorfully dressed woman of about sixty, hair dyed a dramatic black, a long flowing scarf around her neck, came up between them to look at the poster's bid sheet. She moved with style and lithe flexibility, as if she were a dancer herself.

"My heavens!" she said, looking at the sheet. "This has sure gone up fast!"

"Are you Number 28?" Alexandra asked.

"Yes."

"I'm 77 and he's 101," she said, motioning toward the dark-haired gentleman whose expression had become watchful again.

"I see," the older woman said, turning toward him. "You must be a Kelly fan, too."

"Quite so."

"I danced with him in a movie years ago," she said.

"Really?" he said, his eyes widening and growing strangely bright. "Which one?"

"An American in Paris," the lady said. "I was only one of the chorus people behind him, but he's someone I'll never forget. A taskmaster, but brilliant!"

"How fortunate you are," the man said. "I've never had the privilege of even meeting him."

"Are you a dancer?" the woman asked.

The man appeared slightly self-conscious, Alexandra noticed, though it was almost hidden beneath the careful, refined exterior she was beginning to see was natural for him.

"I'm not a professional dancer. It's a hobby, you might say."

"I'm a dance instructor," the woman said, leaning forward to pick up the pen. "My studio is on Ohio Street, if you're interested in taking a class. It's coed. I have day and evening classes."

He paused, as if thinking. "Do you ever come to a person's home and give private lessons?"

"Yes, I've done that."

"How convenient," he said with interest, though a muscle in his jaw twitched as she wrote in a new bid beneath his.

When she'd finished, she took a card out of her purse. "Here," she said, handing it to him. "My name is Lotte Leone. Drop by to observe a class if you like."

"Thank you, I will," he said, taking it, reading it, then inserting it in his inner breast pocket. "It's been a pleasure meeting you, Miss Leone." He shook her hand. His eyes took on a look of sympathy and guilt then, like a charming thief.

"I'm truly very sorry that I have to do this." He let go of her hand and reached for the pen on the table.

Alexandra leaned to one side so she could see what he wrote as he bent over the bid sheet. The dance instructor had raised the bid to two hundred and twenty-five dollars. Alexandra couldn't believe her eyes as she saw him write in one thousand dollars just below it.

He stood to one side and let the older woman look.

Lotte's mouth dropped open. "Well, that's not very sporting of you!" she said to him, then cast her mascara-lined eyes to Alexandra in astonishment.

"I know," Alexandra agreed. "He obliterated me at two hundred dollars."

"I wanted to hang that poster in my studio!" Lotte exclaimed.

"I wanted to give it to a friend," Alexandra said. She and the dance instructor, as if of one mind, both looked at the mysterious and spendthrift Number 101.

"I just want it," he told them, spreading his hands in a simple, seemingly artless gesture. Along with it came a slow smile that brought back the attractive crease in his cheek, while his blue eyes seemed to deepen in hue, if that was possible.

God, this man is devastating, Alexandra found herself thinking. Not just his looks, but his whole bearing and manner exuded an effortless, cultured masculinity. He wasn't a piece of polished male fluff like so many men she'd met, but someone who possessed charm born of experience and sensitivity. As this insight bubbled into her consciousness like the teasing fizz of freshly poured champagne, she also realized how rarely a man had ever gained her notice this way.

Lotte Leone had apparently experienced a similar reaction, since she lost her brusqueness almost immediately. She shook her finger at him. "If you didn't look so dignified in that tux, I'd take you over my knee!"

At that he laughed, throwing his head back a bit. His eyes glistened and his teeth were very white, the incisors curiously sharp. Alexandra didn't know why, but he gave her an odd feeling suddenly, bringing goose bumps to her bared shoulders.

"I'd better go around and protect the rest of my treasures

before that bell rings, or I may lose them, too!" Lotte said. She nodded to both of them and hurried off.

This left Alexandra alone with the stranger and suddenly she found herself feeling ill at ease, which she hadn't up until now. Remembering they hadn't exchanged names yet, she said, "I'm Alexandra Peters." She held out her hand toward him.

"You're the violin maker." As he took her hand, she felt an unusual, steel-like strength in his fingers. But his voice held an interest that bordered on awe. She suddenly found herself the focus of his full attention, which overwhelmed her so, she almost took a step back. His eyes warmed, and he was all deference as his long fingers enclosed hers. For some reason only the fates knew, the goose bumps chilled her shoulders again and made their way down her back.

"I noticed you looking at my instrument," she said with a smile, though her voice came out slightly breathless. This was ridiculous. She hadn't reacted like a teenager to a male since . . . since she was a teenager! She withdrew her hand from his.

At that moment Edith came up to her again. "Excuse me," she said, giving Alexandra's dark-haired companion a courteous smile. Eyes alight, she said to Alexandra, "I found out. He's Number 101. They say he came in about twenty minutes ago."

Heat came to Alexandra's face as she realized Edith had put them all in a situation that was a trifle embarrassing. "He's right here," she told her friend, not knowing if she should bother to whisper. "Edith," she said, taking her friend's elbow to make her turn again to the man standing with them, "this is Number 101. I mean . . ." She looked at him in confusion. "You're—"

"Mr. de Morrissey," Edith said, drawing out each syllable with churchlike reverence. "I can't express to you how pleased, how honored we are that you came tonight. Have the photographers found you yet? We must get your picture!"

"Not yet," he said, smiling down at Edith, who wasn't terribly tall even in her three-inch heels. "I hope you'll understand, but I don't care to have the photographers find me."

"Oh, but—oh, well, of course, whatever you want, Mr. de Morrissey. Can I at least point you out to people? Half the people here came hoping to see you. I must have you recognized at dinner, too."

"Certainly," he said, though Alexandra could see the reluctance in his eyes. She felt sympathy for him. She wasn't looking forward to being introduced at dinner either. And to her violin solo, even less.

At that point, someone called Edith away and Alexandra was left with David de Morrissey again. So this was Chicago's famous playwright, Alexandra thought as she glanced up at him. Why would a man like him be so shy of the public? she wondered. His looks and manner could only help his career. Was he like her—preferring his own company to anyone else's? She thought of asking, but she didn't know him well enough.

"I'm impressed with your violin," he said, apparently resuming where they'd left off before Edith came. "I can't imagine how you can make something so delicate and flawless. The other day I was trying to glue a broken desk drawer together, and I was all thumbs. The rich color of your instrument seemed especially rare. And the grain of the wood fascinated me. It seemed to radiate with little flames of fire."

Alexandra felt honored by his compliment. "You're right—that characteristic is called the flame or figure of the wood. But I can't take credit for it. That's nature's work. As for the varnish, it's a variation I invented of an old recipe handed down from the Italian masters."

"Truly? How many coats does it take?"

"Oh, nine or ten thin coats. It's a spirit base varnish."

"The patience you must have," he marveled. "How long did you study to learn to make violins?"

"Five years."

"And how—?" He smiled apologetically. "Sorry, I shouldn't be boring you with all these questions. You must have answered them a hundred times tonight."

She shook her head. "Not really. I've been keeping a low profile," she said conspiratorially, sensing he would empathize.

His eyes quickened and he raised his eyebrows. "Between you and me, I don't care for social events, either. But the cause is a worthy one."

"I hear you have a special interest in Shakespeare," she said. "Are you one of those who can recite long passages?"

He stroked his nose and his expression grew whimsical as she waited for his reply

> " 'Who will believe my verse in time to come,
>   If it were fill'd with your most high deserts?"

His eyes met hers as he recited the words. The blue of them, more blue than her own, was remarkably luminous.

> " 'Though yet, Heaven knows, it is but as a tomb
>   Which hides your life, and shows not half your parts.
>   If I could write the beauty of your eyes,
>   And in fresh numbers number all your graces,
>   The age to come would say, this poet lies,
>   Such heavenly touches ne'er touch'd earthly faces."

His voice lilted with an engaging, lighthearted warmth. He obviously loved words. The meaning of those words, which his gaze seemed to imply were written for her alone, made her heartbeat pick up a bit.

> " 'So should my papers, yellow'd with their age,
>   Be scorn'd, like old men of less truth than tongue;
>   And your true rights be term'd a poet's rage,
>   And stretched metre of an antique song:
>   But were some child of yours alive that time,
>   You should live twice;—in it, and in my rhyme.' "

Some child of yours. The words echoed in Alexandra's mind. How strange and ironic that he chose that particular sonnet to recite. She put on a smile. "How do you do that? Remember it all, I mean."

He tilted his head. "I don't know. When you revere something, you want to hold onto it. Make it a part of yourself to keep forever." His eyes appeared very pale now, almost hollow, as if he knew some deep inner sorrow.

"Does that sonnet have some personal meaning for you?" she asked.

His blue eyes seemed to refocus to the here and now. "No, not really. It came to my mind as I studied you," he said, the hue of his eyes growing rich again as his gaze held hers, "a woman of beauty and talent, whom a poet couldn't describe fairly without seeming to exaggerate."

"Thank you," she said, looking away, her mind reeling a bit. This man was too much. She'd received high-blown compliments from men before. But in de Morrissey's light and elegant manner, his words seemed understated and true. He made her want to believe him. And that was dangerous. And intoxicating!

Just as she was wondering what more to say after such a compliment, the bell rang. And then Edith was standing on a chair at the end of the room with a microphone that looked too big for her, asking everyone to leave and go into the dining room.

"Oh, good," Alexandra muttered, half to herself.

De Morrissey chuckled. "Glad this part of the evening's over? I am, too," he said as they began to move out with the crowd. "Would you mind if I sat at your table? I have a feeling I'll enjoy the rest of the evening a lot more if I have you to moan and grumble with."

"I'd be delighted!" she said, laughing, too.

They walked across the hall to the dining room, which was aglow with chandelier lights reflecting off white tablecloths. Alexandra was glad to see there were no reserved seats, and she and the playwright agreed on a table in one corner of the large room.

As they sat down facing the podium, Alexandra remembered that David de Morrissey had been with a blonde earlier in the evening. She looked over the room and eventually spotted the woman several tables away sitting with the blond Adonis. Alexandra couldn't help but wonder what de Morrissey thought about that.

Three married couples filled the remaining six seats at their table. Everyone introduced himself or herself in turn, though Alexandra promptly forgot all their names. The well-known playwright at her left introduced himself simply as "David." Since he spoke directly after Alexandra had told everyone her full name, the others probably assumed his last name was also Peters and that he was her husband. Clever of him. Well, for two hours or so, she could tolerate that, she thought with amusement.

The waiter came around and set a small dinner salad in

front of each person. As Alexandra picked up her fork, she noticed David pushing his plate away. He leaned back in his chair and turned a bit toward her. She saw that he was staring at her hand as she cut a piece of lettuce with her fork and knife.

"That's a striking ring," he said. "A ruby, isn't it?"

"Yes." She put the knife down and stretched out the fingers of her right hand so he could see it. "It was my mother's. She died when I was six. My father let me have it when I graduated high school."

"The deep shade is exquisite," he said, eyes glistening as he leaned forward to study the large stone set in silver. "It's the exact color of—" He clenched his teeth oddly, making his jaw muscles ripple. His eyes carried a strange, almost primeval look for a fraction of a second and then grew complacent. "It's beautiful," he said, leaning back, never finishing his earlier thought. "Do you also *play* the violin?" he asked as she resumed eating her salad.

She nodded, still chewing. After swallowing she explained, "I play with the Chicago Philharmonic."

"You do?" he said with surprise. He leaned his elbow on the back of his chair and turned in his seat to face her more directly. "I've been to several concerts over the last few years. I don't recall seeing you."

She smiled as she set her fork down. "I'm at the last stand of the second violins, sort of buried between the first violins and the wind section. I'm not surprised you didn't notice me."

"You must play very well to be in the Philharmonic at all."

"I play well enough for my purposes. Making violins is my first love. I enjoy performing classical music almost as a hobby. Though the Philharmonic provides me with a steady income, which gives me a nice sense of security."

"Who is your favorite composer?" he asked.

"Beethoven."

He studied her with admiring eyes. "You must have a well-developed musical taste. Why Beethoven?"

"Because his music seems to take on new meaning each time I hear it. I enjoy Beethoven's fondness for eruption. His music has sudden changes from pianissimo to fortissimo. Very emotional. And the magnificent pauses in his works are so full of meaning. It's as if the music continues through the momentary silence. There's a lot of symbolism in his style that I've grown to understand more and more as I get older. I don't know if I'm explaining myself well . . .," she said, feeling a bit muddled in her own words trying to express herself.

"You've explained it beautifully," David said in a reassuring tone. "I have a natural affinity for the symbolism of literature, and I know what you mean about appreciating it more as you mature. But I can't seem to grasp the symbolism in classical music. I've always felt I had an intellectual deficiency in that respect."

"Which composers do you like?" she asked, curious.

He hesitated, glancing at the tablecloth for a long moment. When he looked up, humor danced in his eyes. "Gershwin and Cole Porter."

She didn't know how to take him. "You're joking?"

"I'm afraid not. I wasn't sure if I should even admit my tastes to you."

Alexandra pondered this, not wanting to offend him, but nevertheless perplexed. "I like *Rhapsody in Blue,*" she told him. "But Cole Porter? Show tunes?"

"Now," he said, raising his index finger, "before you chalk up his work as simple pop songs, remember he had musical training and understood classical composition. His rhythms are unique and complex. And his lyrics are so ingenious." David scratched his nostril. "You see, that's the problem I have with classical music. No words to accompany it. Other than opera, which I confess I sometimes find tedious—so grand and overblown. I like a compelling melody with clever, well-expressed lyrics. I can see you're disappointed in me now," he said with amusement.

"No," Alexandra said, shaking her head, though she was rather. "But even if you prefer words to express emotion, how can a man who rattles off passages of Shakespeare be impressed with Cole Porter lyrics?" And then she remembered that David wrote vampire plays.

"But his lyrics are almost miraculous to me," David said, his face growing more and more animated. "He loved *le mot juste.* He enjoyed wordplay and invented dense, delightful rhymes."

Alexandra paused, thinking it over. She recalled an ingenious line from one song about voodoo and another lyric she

had always liked about authors who only used four-letter
words. "Okay, so Porter was clever with lyrics," she conceded.
"But where's the emotion you were talking about?"

"Where? He composed songs about romance constantly,"
David said. "He saw the huge gap between idealized romantic
love and most people's ordinary domestic situations. But instead of the ironic despair that I tend to find, he found ironic
celebration. He found whimsy and humor. And if you want
passion, consider the words to 'Night and Day.' "

She chuckled. "I barely remember them. Recite them for
me."

"I don't dare," David said, eyes sparkling, almost devilish.
"Who knows where it might lead us?"

Alexandra's shoulders shook as she laughed. She might not
admire his taste in music, but his conversation charmed her.
He'd almost made her forget that she had to perform a solo
in a little while. As the thought suddenly reentered her mind,
she felt the salad she'd eaten churn slightly in her stomach.
Oh, God, she thought, here come the butterflies.

The waiters arrived then, each carrying plates of chicken
cordon bleu. David waved away his plate, saying he wasn't
hungry. Alexandra decided that was a good idea for her to
follow and told the waiter the same thing.

"Have I made you lose your appetite?" David asked.

"Not at all," she said. "I have to play a solo tonight to show
off my violin. I'm too nervous right now to eat."

"I'm sorry you're nervous, but I'm anxious to hear you
perform. What will you play?"

" 'Timbourin Chinois' by Fritz Kreisler."

"Is it difficult?"

She shrugged. "I was always good at fast fingerwork. And
I'm using music. I'm not brave enough anymore to try performing by memory."

"I think the audience will forgive you."

She smiled. The sincere reassurance in his voice felt comforting to her right now, though at another moment it might
have made her highly uncomfortable. He was an emotional
person, she intuited, and she never quite knew how to handle
those types.

"You know," she said, her jitters increasing as she spoke,

"I'd better go get my violin and see if I can find a quiet place somewhere to warm up. Will you excuse me?"

"Of course," David said, standing to help pull back her chair. When she had risen, he reached out to lightly touch her forearm. "And don't be nervous. You've already impressed everyone by having built the violin. However you play it is simply icing on the cake. So have fun with it."

"Thank you," she said, a little surprised that his advice was already lowering her anxiety level. "I'll try."

David sat down again and watched Alexandra glide out of the dining room, tall and serene in her shining pink dress. She'd said she felt nervous, but she certainly didn't look it. She appeared more like a graceful, haute couture mannequin who had magically come to life.

He'd never met anyone quite like her. Beautiful, intelligent, she had a fine appreciation for the arts, and she made violins to boot! He'd thought he'd be either annoyed or bored tonight; but thanks to her, he was actually enjoying himself. She was a breath of spring air, a woman who could make intelligent conversation, someone on his intellectual plane, perhaps even above it. After all, she knew how to appreciate Beethoven.

David had heard performances of Beethoven's works for centuries and had never learned to properly understand the composer's music. He could enjoy the performances, but never pull from them that profound satisfaction others seemed to find. It was the same with most of the other classical composers. Mozart, in fact, often bored him with musical themes that seemed to run in endless circles.

Two centuries ago, David had come to the conclusion that music couldn't move him deeply. But eventually there came the 1920s, '30s, and '40s, when George Gershwin and Cole Porter made their mark on the music world. Once David had heard the restless rhythms and felt the obsessive passions expressed in their works, he knew he'd finally found music that spoke on his level, to his needs.

This discovery was perhaps the one benefit he'd ever received from becoming a vampire. If he'd ceased to exist in the 1600s as he ought to have, he'd never have heard "An American in Paris" or "Night and Day." And further, he would have never seen Kelly or Astaire dance, inspired by such music.

But to David, such benefits hardly outweighed the endless guilt and stark feeling of banishment he'd experienced ever since becoming a vampire. Music and dance only helped him pass the long nights. They didn't take away the pain.

"What are you looking so sad about?" Darienne said, taking the seat Alexandra had vacated. "Lost your new lady friend?"

Her voice intruded on his thoughts. "She's not lost," he said. "She's gone to warm up her violin. She's playing a solo later."

"Is that why you're so glum?" Darienne's eyes sparkled with amusement. "You'd rather she were warming you up?"

David glanced at the others at the table. They were busy talking. "Darienne, why are we having this conversation?"

"I saw you all alone and wanted to see if you're happy."

"I am."

"And I wanted to ask a favor of you."

David looked into her cheerful eyes and recalled the plan afoot to distract her with Merle's nephew. "What favor?"

"You remember the emerald broach on display? They're going to auction it off after dinner. Will you bid on it and acquire it for me?"

"Why don't you bid on it yourself?"

"Because I'm leaving in a few minutes with Chad."

Secretly pleased, David rubbed his forehead, pretending disapproval. "I don't believe your nerve," he said. He looked into her expectant green eyes. "You expect me to bid on a broach for you, leaving me to pay for it, so you can go off with another man?"

"I'll pay you back—in money or some other way. It's such a lovely emerald." Her full lips formed a pretty pout.

"You already have more jewels than the Tower of London!"

Darienne perked her shoulders up, making her bosom quiver. "And some of them rescued *The Scarlet Shadow*. But never mind. I'll let someone else have the emerald," she said with equanimity. She studied David's face with obvious curiosity. "So, what's she like? She looks attractive, from a distance anyway. What's her name?"

"Alexandra. She's very attractive."

"And she makes violins? That's unusual. Is she?"

"Unusual?" David said. "I find her quite remarkable."

"Seduce her, then."

"Darienne!"

"Why not? You need a fling with a mortal. Maybe it will make you realize what you've thrown away for no good reason."

"What? You?"

"Veronica, you idiot."

He stared at her, a frozen feeling overtaking him. His voice came out a harsh whisper. "Don't mention her to me. Not here. Not now."

"All right," she said in an airy voice. "I just thought this Alexandra might help you forget. You need to forget. In order to remember."

"Your wisdom escapes me," he said with impatience.

"I know, *cheri,*" she said, rising from her seat. "You're only a man, poor thing." She leaned over him to kiss his forehead, but stopped halfway. Something seemed to have caught her eye. "Is that Matthew over there? I didn't notice him come in, did you?"

David glanced in the direction Darienne was looking and after some searching found Matthew sitting at a table toward the front. A small cluster of people had gathered around his chair and he appeared to be signing autographs. "Merle mentioned he was going to attend, but I didn't notice him come in. I've been talking to Alexandra for quite a while."

"Yes, I've been preoccupied with Chad, too." Darienne straightened to get a better view. "He looks rather handsome in a tux, doesn't he?"

"Chad?" David said in a hopeful voice.

"Matthew. Striking, actually. The lights pick up the silver streaks in his hair. He looks elegant and mature."

David experienced a sinking feeling. "Since when do you admire mature men?"

She glanced down at him as she stood next to him, one hand on his shoulder. Eyes sparkling, she said, "You're mature."

"Yes, and look how boring you find me."

"Not on your Aubusson, *cheri.*"

"Shh!" He glanced at the others at the table, who were still talking and eating.

She laughed. "You're adorable when you're outraged."

David paused to get his bearings. "Be that as it may, I think you ought to get back to Chad. He seems like an appropriate companion for you."

"Appropriate! Are you my father now, approving of my boyfriends?" Her eyes grew suspicious. "You aren't trying to keep me away from Matthew, by any chance?"

"Why would you think that?"

"Just reading your anxiety level. It's been on the rise ever since I noticed him."

David wished he weren't so transparent. "Leave him alone, Darienne. For the sake of the show. Involvements between investors and cast members are never a good idea."

"Always so practical," she cooed.

"You keep saying you don't think he's attractive."

She tilted her chin in a reflective attitude. "He strikes me differently moment by moment. I read those magazine articles you gave me and found others, too. According to them, some women have become infatuated with him. But I also rented an old movie of his and I wasn't impressed. On his old TV show, he's only a clown. Backstage he seemed ordinary. But," her bosom rose as she drew in a breath and stared off in Matthew's direction, "he's got something that surfaces now and then. Look at him now!"

"You've read articles and rented his movie?" David repeated in surprise. Darienne was studying him like some starstruck fan?

"I was curious."

"Curiosity killed the cat," David muttered.

"Nothing can kill me," she said, raising her brows, "as you well know. I'm going over to say hello to him."

"No, Darienne—"

"It's only polite."

"Polite! Next you'll be following him home."

"I'm hoping he'll invite me," she said in a sly, sensual voice.

David grabbed hold of her hand. "Leave him be," he said in an expressive whisper. "For the sake of the show."

"You worry too much," she replied blithely. "What harm

can I do? A little conversation, a little dalliance, if he's interested. Matthew's an adult, David. Other men have survived their interludes with me—and been that much happier for having met me!"

"I just hope he has more sense than you."

She clicked her tongue in the French way. "Men forget about being sensible when I'm around. Forget about him and worry about your evening. You ought to be making plans of your own. Night-night, *cheri.*"

She swirled away and moved toward Matthew's table on the other side of the room.

Don't let her get to you, David instructed himself. He didn't know if it was possible for a vampire to suffer from high blood pressure. But if it was, then Darienne was sure to give him the affliction.

The waiters were collecting plates and passing out dessert. David decided to leave the table. He didn't want to watch helplessly while Darienne weaved her web around Matthew. A brief walk in the night air might be soothing. He left the hotel and walked around the block. The temperature was cooler now than when they'd entered the hotel. Apparently it had been a hot day. The moist breeze off the lake felt good on his face.

Maybe Darienne was right, he started thinking. Maybe he was taking all this too seriously. Matthew was a grown man, after all.

When he entered the dining room again, he felt calmer. But when he looked at the place where Matthew had been sitting, he saw that the actor's chair was empty. Darienne was nowhere to be seen either. Chad seemed to be searching for her. David closed his eyes momentarily. He, Merle, and Chad had done their best. It was up to Matthew now. In his life as a celebrity, Matthew had probably met many women who might fit the appellation *vamp*. But the poor fellow didn't know he had a real one on his hands tonight.

As David distractedly took his seat, Edith Cornwall was introducing Alexandra. She walked up to the podium carrying her violin. Edith asked Alexandra to say a few words about the instrument and to "play something for us."

Alexandra approached the microphone looking self-contained and calm, as if she did this every day. Unsettled himself, David had to marvel at her outward composure, knowing she, too, was nervous.

"This instrument is made from two-hundred-year-old spruce grown in the Swiss Alps, and from Bosnian maple. It's patterned after the Stradivarius design." Holding the violin up, she pointed to the top of the instrument. "The soundboard has a high arch, giving this violin a sweet resonance. The f-holes are cut to give a bright, sharp timbre."

She put the violin under her arm, smiled at the audience, and said, "I'll give you a taste of its sound now. Please remember, I'm more skilled at making violins than playing them."

The audience chuckled as she walked to the music stand Edith had set up for her. Edith, meanwhile, had taken a seat at a piano placed nearby to accompany her. Alexandra opened up the music, put the violin under her chin, and began to play. The sound was clean, clear, and sweet as her fingers flew over the strings.

David admired not only her musicianship, but her doll-like appearance. Her back was ramrod straight, her graceful bow arm held well away from her body so that the bow moved at a perfect right angle over the violin strings. She played with authority and rapierlike fluidity, each note almost military in its crispness. As she played, the notes coming faster and faster in more complex patterns, David began to feel lightheaded trying to keep up with her. She ended with a flourish, and the audience applauded heartily. David felt so pleased for her. What on earth was she ever nervous about? She was perfection itself!

After a bow, she graciously gave the violin to Edith, who placed it on a display table while the professional auctioneer, a man in his sixties, began asking for bids. As they sprang from various parts of the audience, David watched Alexandra walk quietly back to her seat next to his.

"Marvelous!" he whispered to her as she sat down.

"Thanks," she whispered back. "I'm glad it's over."

They watched the auctioning procedure for the next minute or so, until the violin was officially sold to the highest bidder at $3,500.

Alexandra nodded as she applauded with everyone else. "That's a fair price. Well," she said, leaning back in her seat in a relaxed attitude. "Now that that's all over, I feel like going home."

Her words took him by surprise. He hadn't expected his time with her to end so soon. Other than his concern about Darienne's designs on Matthew, he'd been enjoying the evening. "Are you really leaving?"

She shrugged, as if ambivalent. "I wouldn't mind. Though talking to you has been a pleasure. Maybe . . . I hope you'll come and visit my workshop sometime. I'll show you the process of making a violin, if you're interested."

"I'd like that very much." David couldn't help but compare the intellectual quality of their new friendship with Darienne's mode of operation. He liked being on a higher plane with a woman, instead of worrying about if and when and how he would have sex with her. Alexandra was above all that, and what a relief it was to be with her! He realized he wanted to continue this new and different relationship.

"If you're leaving, then I'd just as soon leave, too," he said. "Would you like to go for a walk? Or have a glass of port in the hotel bar?"

Alexandra smiled. She had a regal sort of smile, but gentle. "That sounds nice," she said, absently touching the side of her neck, just below her jaw.

When she drew her hand away, David noticed for the first time a red spot, about an inch round, beneath her chin. He leaned his head to one side to see it better. "You have a mark on your neck," he said.

The raw color of the spot suddenly drew out his sensory impulses. He could almost taste the rich blood flowing so close to the surface of her skin. He found himself reaching out to test the abrasion with his fingertips as his mouth began to water.

"It's from the chin rest," she said. Her shoulders came up slightly when his fingers touched her neck. "I . . . it's a permanent mark. All violinists have it. It gets red and sore after playing." Her blue eyes grew still, the pupils widening as she stared at him, her mouth remaining slightly parted after she'd finished speaking.

Though the cognizant part of David's mind told him he should draw his hand away, somehow he couldn't. Her throat was so slender, strong, and white. And the red mark, slightly pulsing, looked so fresh, so tantalizing. His heart began to beat faster as the desire for blood heated his senses.

"I . . .," she began to say, her eyes still fixed on his, as if she, too, could not break the spell, "I came in a limousine."

"You did?" he replied, barely aware of what she'd said. And then, somehow, the fact that she was carrying on a conversation made him focus fully on her face. Her eyes, he saw now as he looked directly into them, were expectant, sensual, and a little frightened. He realized all at once that she mistook his touching her neck as something of a sexual overture. He ought to be glad she didn't understand what it really was, David thought, coming to his senses now.

And yet, the curious and rather delightful thing was, she was responding to him. A limousine, she'd said. Good Lord, a limousine? Was she suggesting—?

"Edith arranged it for me," she said, sounding breathless, blinking her eyes as she looked away from him. "Because I donated the violin, she wanted to do something nice for me. If you like, we can—" She looked into his eyes again and stopped speaking, as if she'd lost the thought.

"Can what?" he asked, growing mesmerized by this new side of her. He put the longing for her blood out of his mind, and applied himself to study her revealed sensuality, which he found equally tantalizing. Drawing his fingers away from the red mark, he moved his hand slowly down the length of her throat to her graceful collarbone.

"We can go see my workshop now," she said, "if you want to." David watched fascinated as she tried to pull herself together, only to flow back again into sensual reverie while he stroked her soft skin. Even her eyes seemed to lose focus as he held her gaze. "And . . . the driver . . . he can take you to your home . . . afterward."

David smiled at her. "That sounds wonderful. What do you think—would you like to leave now?"

She straightened her back a bit when he drew his hand away. "The problem is," she said, glancing toward the po-dium, where the fur coat was being modeled, "Edith wants to introduce you to the audience when your manuscript comes up for auction."

"All the more reason to leave immediately!" David said.

She laughed, eyes dancing into his. Her voice grew soft and sure. "Let's go."

6

In your eyes, I can see fire

THE ATMOSPHERE inside the limousine grew soft, rich, and silent as the long car seemed to float along Chicago's streets. Lights from vehicles and department stores streaked by outside Alexandra's window. The city at night looked surreal and beautiful.

Alexandra couldn't ever remember feeling so sublime and yet so reckless. What was she doing taking this suave, sensual stranger home with her? It wasn't at all like her to extend such an open invitation to a man within two hours of meeting him. But no man had ever made such an impact on her. If she had any sense, she'd rethink what she was doing. But she felt as if she'd lost her senses, and the loss came as a thrill!

Alexandra turned from the side window and glanced at David sitting next to her. In the darkness his eyes met hers, startling and luminous. Perhaps dangerous. He seemed to study her as if she were the only woman on the surface of the earth. Passing lights from outside played over his angular face, highlighting his high forehead, his flared nostrils and stern jaw, the broad set of his shoulders. She felt weak remembering how he'd touched her neck earlier. One touch, one fiery flare of sexuality from those still, lazerlike eyes, and he'd rendered her almost helpless. All she could think was that she wanted to experience him, wanted to know how a man like him would be with a woman.

He smiled now, the appealing vertical lines appearing in his cheeks, his eyes warm and glittering. Suddenly he seemed easy and full of humor, his good-natured expression masking for the moment the imposing masculinity that had held her prisoner a half second ago. Perhaps he thought things were moving too fast between them, too.

On the empty seat across from them lay the Kelly poster he'd stopped to pay for before they hurried out of the hotel. "Where will you hang it?" she asked, trying to start a conversation to cool the heady atmosphere between them.

"I thought I'd give it to you," he said.

"After paying a thousand dollars for it? Why?"

"You were correct when you pointed out I wasn't very sporting. I didn't know you then and I didn't care. But now I do and I feel I've taken unfair advantage."

How could a man who was so sexually charged also be courtly and polite? His mercurial personality kept her so pleasantly off-balance she began to feel giddy. "No," she said with a little laugh. "Anyone willing to pay that much for an autographed poster should have it. I'm sure you'll value it more than Susan ever would."

"Susan?"

"She's a college student who helps out in my shop. She likes old musicals and I was going to give it to her as a gift."

"Then please do give it to her," David insisted.

"No," Alexandra said, touching his white cuff below the edge of his tuxedo sleeve. "Next year she'll be on some other kick, put the poster in a closet, and replace it with one of Madonna or some other celebrity. She's still young—you know what I mean?"

"And you're so old," he teased, sliding his hand over hers at his wrist.

Alexandra liked the feeling, but prudently drew her hand away after a moment. "I'm thirty-eight," she told him in a matter-of-fact tone. No use beating about the bush. She didn't believe in lying about age. If he was younger than she, he'd have to deal with that. "How old are you?"

He hesitated.

Must be younger, she concluded.

"Thirty-four," he told her in a soft, clipped manner that seemed to hide a discomfort.

Well, you can't win 'em all, Alexandra thought. "You don't like older women?" she said, using an amused tone to cover her sinking spirits.

He laughed, as if at some joke she wouldn't understand. "I

never think about age. That is," he corrected himself as his
smile disappeared, "unless a woman is too young." His eyes
settled on Alexandra's, unmoving, their marvelous light growing more intense. "But *you* are not too young. You have
experience and maturity, which form the basis for your keen
artistic intellect. And you're beautiful and creative, too. With
such a unique combination of gifts, you shall always be age-
less."

"Oh, I wish *that* were true!" she said with a chuckle.

"Does your age bother you?"

"Not until I meet someone younger than me."

"So my saying that I'm thirty-four has made you uneasy?"
She nodded reluctantly. "A little."

"Then forget I said it."

"How can I?"

"I *feel* older than you. Does that ease your misgivings?"

"You feel older to me, too," Alexandra said, studying him.
"I wonder why that is"

"One should never waste time wondering about something
that pleases rather than offends."

His tutorial tone made her smile. Usually she didn't care for
men who took an instructive attitude. Her father's authoritative manner had permanently stained her personality with
resentment at such behavior. But David spoke to her as if he
were some wise, spiritually evolved guru, nurturing and kind.
He struck her as odd, almost ingenuous in his wisdom. She'd
never met anyone who thought or talked like him. But what
a novel and complex personality! One moment overpower-
ingly sensual; the next, a reassuring Confucius. God, what
would he be like in bed?

Alexandra pushed that thought aside by asking a more
innocuous question she'd wondered about earlier. "You're
basically an introvert, aren't you? I am, too."

"I sensed that," he said with interest, "though you cover it
well. Yes, I'm an introvert—and proud of it!"

"Do you get lots of compliments on being a good listener?
I do. I don't even consider it a compliment anymore."

David laughed. "Not lately, because I avoid people. But I
know exactly what you mean. People will carry on a dialogue
all by themselves and then thank you afterward for the interesting conversation."

"Oh, it drives me crazy!" Alexandra said. She couldn't resist venting her grievances to a sympathetic ear. "And I get so frustrated talking to people who finish my sentences for me. And those who flit from one topic to another. I've met so many shallow men, I've given up."

"I have a woman friend who's exactly like that."

Alexandra remembered the blonde on his arm at the beginning of the evening. "I saw you walk in with a woman in a black-and-white dress. And then she—"

"Went off with someone else. Yes, that's exactly to whom I'm referring."

"Is she—are you involved with her?"

"Nothing serious, believe me," he replied, raising one brow in an ironic, arch expression. "I've known her for a long while. She uses me as an escort when she's between men. Like the people you described, she's effervescent and shallow."

"Well, she and that blond boy toy she left you for should be having a great time right now," Alexandra said.

"Actually, she left the auction with a third man," David said in a dour tone.

Alexandra was astonished.

"But let's forget about her," he said in a brighter voice. "You and I are enjoying a much more meaningful time together."

"I'm glad you said that," Alexandra told him as the limousine driver pulled up in front of her home. "I was hoping I wasn't second choice in your mind."

"Not at all. Though I do owe Darienne something. She dragged me to the auction. If she hadn't, I wouldn't have met you."

Darienne, Alexandra thought as the young driver opened up the car door for her. What an unusual name. How did David know her? And why did he allow her to wheedle him into things? Somehow it didn't seem to fit his personality and it made her curious.

She asked the uniformed driver how long he could wait. He replied that he was paid until midnight, but a longer wait could be negotiated.

"I'll settle with him when I leave," David told Alexandra and took her elbow to hurry her along, as if not wanting her to worry about the expense.

Either that or he didn't want to waste any time. Now that they were approaching her doorstep, Alexandra was having second thoughts. Had she appeared too "easy" to him? Was he just another man in a hurry to reap his reward for being a pleasant dinner companion? Oh, God, what was she getting into just because she'd let herself be demolished by a pair of radiant blue eyes!

Unsettled and questioning herself, she opened her beaded evening purse to get out her key. He waited quietly beside her while she unlocked the door to her small, old, wood frame home. The lights were run on a timer and were already on as they entered.

David noticed Alexandra seemed nervous when they walked into her house. He supposed she was having misgivings about inviting him in. "Is it too late for you?" he asked. "I can leave and come another time, if you're tired."

She'd been putting her key back in her purse and looked up. Her blue eyes seemed startled as they met his. "No, it's not too late," she said with a self-conscious smile.

"I'm anxious to see your shop," he went on, "but only if you're comfortable with my being here. It occurs to me that we've only just met, and perhaps we let our newfound rapport get ahead of us."

She shook her head and tossed her glittering purse onto a nearby chair. "I'm sorry if I seem a little uptight. I *want* you to stay. It's just that it's been a long time since—" She stopped mid-sentence and seemed to regroup her thoughts. She gestured toward the kitchen off to the right. "I can make us some coffee, if you like."

"No thanks," David replied, relaxing. "I don't drink coffee."

"You suggested having a glass of port when we were at the hotel. I think I have some, if you'd prefer that."

"That would be fine, thank you."

As she walked into the other room, David looked about him. The wood floor was worn and uncarpeted, but swept absolutely clean of dust, and waxed. He was standing in what would ordinarily have been the living room. A staircase at the far end led upstairs. She obviously used this room as her shop, judging by the two old, well-used worktables, both with partially made instruments lying on them. Shelves along one wall held a tidy assortment of boxes, each with its own label: Frogs, Pegs, Bridges, Strings, and so on. High above, on a shelf made of rails of wood, were piled raw slabs of timber. Bows of different sizes for various stringed instruments hung from hooks. Along one shelf sat a row of violins and violas, each with a tag indicating to whom it belonged. Below, three cellos lay on their sides on the floor with similar tags.

"I do repairs, too," Alexandra said as she approached with two glasses of port. She handed him one.

"And these blocks of wood up here are—?"

"My stock. I bought those in Germany last year. I go about every three years to purchase my wood. They have to be kept well ventilated, so the shelf is made of wood strips with spaces in between so air can get in from underneath."

"Fascinating." David walked over to one of the worktables and Alexandra followed. He leaned over to study a half-made white violin shaped around what appeared to be a wooden mold.

"The back and sides have been formed. I'm working on the top now," she said, pointing to a thin, fragile-looking piece of wood in the shape of a violin top lying in a shallow bed of wood shavings. "Careful you don't get shavings on your clothes. I didn't have time to clean up today before getting ready for the auction."

"Don't apologize. Your shop looks immaculate." He gestured toward the first object. "Did you shape the sides around this block of wood?"

"Yes, that's the mold. I make that first."

"Make it first? You mean, you don't use the same mold over and over?"

"No," she said with a light shrug. "I give it to the client when I present them with their finished violin. They always seem to appreciate it."

"Isn't it extra work to make a new mold for each instrument?"

"Yes, but it's more of a challenge. Otherwise I'd feel I was making the same violin over and over. This way no two instruments are exactly alike."

David shook his head and chuckled. "If it were me, I'd take the shortcut."

"I bet you wouldn't," she replied. "You wouldn't write your plays according to the same formula over and over, would you?"

"There are some newspaper critics who think I do."

"Critics! They can't produce art themselves, but they pretend to be the delineators of artistic achievement." Alexandra looked self-conscious then. "I saw *A Tale at Twilight* years ago and enjoyed it, but I have to confess I haven't seen any of your later plays. Now that I've met you, I'll have to go see your musical when it opens."

"I never mind if people do or don't see my plays. I find it has little to do with my personal relationships—what few I have."

"I don't have a lot of friends, either," she said, her eyes matter-of-fact. "You must be like me; you like your solitude. I've never minded being alone for hours and hours, as long as I can work. Do you have a daily writing schedule you follow?"

"My hours are quite regimented," David had to agree, though in a different way than she meant. The sun dictated his schedule.

"People tell me I'm too rigid, but I think having a regular routine and sticking to it is the only way to accomplish anything." Alexandra set her glass on the corner of the table. "Are you also a perfectionist?"

David laughed. "Now you've really pegged me! I'll work over a line of dialogue for hours, trying to get the wording and rhythm just right."

Alexandra smiled with delight. "We're two peas in a pod. I'll work over the scroll of a violin for days trying to make every curve flawless. People tease me about my nitpick attitude. Even Edith, though she's sweet and I like her."

"I liked her, too. I hope she wasn't devastated not to find me in the audience when she wanted to introduce me."

"Well, if I tell her you left early with me, that will compensate. She's always trying to play matchmaker for me." Alexandra glanced up at him quickly. "Not that *I'm* trying to make a match here . . ."

"I understand," David said, sensing she felt just as he did. Apparently neither one of them was quite sure why they were here together or what to expect next. The heady sensuality that had reared its head earlier had mysteriously done a vanishing act, and now they were back to the more intellectual mode they'd begun with.

David took a last sip of his port and set the glass down. "How did you decide to become a violin maker?"

Alexandra sat on the stool in front of the worktable as David leaned against the table. "I loved violin and played it in my high school and college orchestras. My mother was a violinist and started to teach me at home when I was only five. I took lessons from professional teachers throughout my school years, after my mother died. They each said I was very good technically. I learned to play all the positions with ease, my sense of rhythm was steady, and I had a good ear for pitch."

She paused and gave him a modest smile. "My technique became so good because I was a perfectionist even then. But I never could get any emotion in my playing," she continued. "I don't know why. It wasn't that my teachers or I didn't try. Anyway, I knew my sawhorse style would prevent me from ever becoming a virtuoso. I liked working with my hands and gradually grew interested in the idea of making violins. I read every book I could find about it and went to talk with a violin maker downtown. He let me assist him, as Susan assists me now. I thought, if I couldn't play with emotion, at least I could make perfect instruments for others to emote with."

"And you apprenticed with this violin maker?"

"No. My mother had left some money in a trust for me. I used it to attend the violin-making schools in Cremona, Italy. You know, the home of Stradivarius? I studied there and learned the 'secrets' of the Italian masters, which aren't really so secret. Actually, I've developed some secrets of my own in the methods I use to mix my glues and varnishes, which I think makes them superior."

"Your father must be proud of what you've accomplished."

Her eyes flashed up at him. "My father practically disowned me for choosing this as a career. He's a military man. The Great Lakes Naval Station is his whole life. He's proud of my younger brother, who's off on an aircraft carrier somewhere in the Pacific. But me? No, I've always been his greatest disappointment; first, because I was born female, and second, because I chose a profession which he considers nonessential and makeshift. 'What kind of way is that to earn a living?' he asked me. 'You'll either starve or wind up married to some musician who drives a cab to make ends meet!' " Alexandra chuckled grimly. "What he didn't realize was that after knowing him, I doubted I'd ever want a husband. I vowed to run my own life."

David felt sad for her, seeing what effect her insensitive father had had on her. "Do you see him often?"

"Once a year at Christmas. My brother's usually in town, too. I'm either angry or depressed for days afterward. I've grown to hate Christmas."

"Your family aside, *you* should be proud of yourself," David said. "I'm deeply impressed with your craftsmanship and your knowledge."

As she looked up at him, David thought her eyes glazed slightly. But she smiled again, thanked him, and said, "Do you play any instrument?"

David shook his head. A few centuries ago, he'd tried learning the harpsichord, but wasn't about to mention that. "I told you before, I have more of an affinity for words than music."

She reached forward and took one of his hands in both of hers. Putting her fingertips beneath his, she made him extend his hand so she could study it. "Your fingers are extraordinarily long. You could reach an octave on a piano without even stretching!"

David already knew he could. "What about the violin? Are my hands also suitable for that?"

She turned his hand over. "I'm not sure. The length might slow your left-hand fingering. Though it would be an advantage in the higher positions. You'd be great at reaching the harmonics. They're played up near the bridge, you know."

"I haven't a clue what you're talking about," David said with humor. He noticed something curious and made her stretch out her left hand, palm up. The tips of all four of her delicate fingers were calloused, with slight grooves making small, permanent indentations in her skin. "Are these from the violin strings?" he asked, stroking her fingertips with his.

"Yes," Alexandra said, her voice slightly unsteady. "I . . . keep forgetting to put lotion on them when I go to bed at night. Calloused fingers are something a violinist has to accept, like the mark beneath my chin."

"It's a minor sacrifice for the sake of art," David said. Still bending over her, he folded her fingers tenderly and looked up at her face.

When their gazes met, their faces close together, he saw her lambent eyes studying his, quiet and yet expectant. All at once, before he could guess it, the sensuality they'd felt earlier hung between them again with all its previous intensity.

He gently let go and she withdrew her hand. She averted her eyes, apparently reacting to the situation just as cautiously as he. Neither he nor she seemed to know how to respond to the attraction that arced between them so instantaneously and without warning.

David straightened and glanced downward. Happy to find a small diversion, he saw that some bits of wood shavings had gotten onto his tuxedo from the table he'd leaned against. With the flat of his hand, he brushed the lower edge of his jacket, then stroked his palm swiftly downward over his thigh, twice.

He looked at Alexandra and noticed she'd been following the movement of his hand. Her lips were soft and parted. As she raised her eyes slowly up the length of his body to his face, he saw her pupils widen. Both remained breathless for a moment.

Alexandra wet her lips. "You're very attractive," she said as if trying to sound matter-of-fact.

"So are you."

She hesitated before speaking again. "I'm not looking for a long-term relationship. To me, sex is . . . is sort of a necessity for the body. Like water and oxygen." She tried to smile. "I don't mean to sound so clinical. Certainly, it can be a pleasant diversion. But I don't think sex means anything, really. I'm not possessive about men, and I don't want them to be possessive about me. Even after sex."

How strange, David thought. It seemed she was trying to keep something she obviously longed for at arm's length. Trying to be cool about passion, intellectualizing desire. He wondered if he could help her. But should he get involved? Now *he* was being analytical, too.

"I understand. No strings," David said.

"Do I sound cold?" she asked.

David took her hands and made her rise from her seat.

"You *do* sound cold. But I don't think you mean to be. In your eyes, I can see fire."

He also saw a hint of anxiety in her face now. She was afraid of her own inner fires. He'd love to help her free herself. Yes, he was sure he could help her.

David drew her closer to him. She ran her hands up his white shirt beneath his jacket and rose up on her toes. He met her halfway and kissed her mouth. Her lips were urgent and moist, and her breath felt warm on his cheek. The pink dress and her breasts crushed softly against his chest as he encircled her in his arms.

After a prolonged, heady kiss, she drew her mouth from his. Her eyes, bright with desire, moved back and forth over his face, unblinking. "My bedroom's upstairs," she whispered.

"Are you sure? We aren't moving too fast?"

"No! Maybe. I don't know," she replied in a tumble of words. "I just know I want you. I've never wanted someone so much before."

Her words made him reel. This beautiful, gifted, unique woman wanted *him*. "Then lead the way."

Alexandra took his hand and turned toward the staircase.

As David followed, Veronica's face appeared in his mind's eye, unbidden, her large brown eyes sad and tearful. David shut the image away, knowing it was an illusion. Veronica was with Rob now, and she despised David. She was better off.

This is insane, Alexandra kept telling herself, but she wouldn't listen. Images had invaded her intellect. The glow of desire in David's eyes. His long fingers reaching toward her neck. His hand stroking his muscular thigh. His ardent face just before he'd kissed her. Her heart pounded so hard, she wondered if she could climb the steps.

When she reached her bedroom, she turned her back to him so he could unzip her dress. She had it off in moments, along with the rest of her clothes. She curled up on the quilted bedspread her mother had made years ago and watched David. He had removed his jacket and cummerbund and was taking the studs out of his shirtfront. He pulled the shirt apart, revealing his well-developed pectoral muscles and flat, hard abdomen. The white of the shirt contrasted in a dazzling way with his dark skin and hair. She watched, transfixed as his lean hands unfastened the waistband of his pants.

When he'd undressed, she pulled him onto the bed with her and lay back as he stretched his length beside her. He slid his hand along her upper arm, the smoothness of his touch giving her a sensual frisson. His hand rounded her shoulder and then moved downward onto her breast. His fingers seemed unbelievably sensitive to her desires as he squeezed and fondled her nipple and stroked the soft mound of flesh.

Eyes closing in sensual delight, she reached for him, slipping her arms around his rib cage, her mouth seeking his. His lips fastened onto hers eagerly as his torso moved over hers. She allowed herself to be lost in the feel of him, the weight of him, the strength of him.

His breaths were becoming uneven and his mouth grew hot as he deepened the kiss. It pleased her no end to know she could arouse a man like him. He was the most desirable male, in intelligence and physique, that she'd ever met. This would be more than an evening's diversion, she knew it already.

She'd forgotten a few things she always discussed first before reaching this point, and she decided she'd better bring them up even if it did break the mood. "David," she said, pulling her lips from his, "we don't have to worry about pregnancy. I can't have children."

"Neither can I."

His admission surprised her. "So we have even that in common," she said, running her hands through his thick hair. "What about—you know—diseases?"

"No problems."

She smiled, relieved. "I've had my blood tested. I'm all right, too."

"I'll bet your blood is exquisite," he murmured. "Like everything else about you."

Her body shook as she laughed. "You give unusual compliments."

"But well meant."

"Kiss me again." She raised her lips toward him and he covered her mouth with his.

He spent a long, languid time caressing her body, arousing her to ever-spiraling heights. He didn't handle her the way most men did, stimulating her body as a means to obtain a desired end. No, his manner was craftsmanlike, enjoying the process, using an artistic sensitivity to her female form, reminding her of the way she lovingly sculpted a violin from raw wood.

Soon her breasts were swollen with desire, their skin taut, almost shining, her nipples reddened from his lips, contracted. Tears crept from the corners of her eyes at the beauty of his touch, the intimacy that enveloped them. Sex had always been a sort of enjoyable exercise with other men. But now, with David, she was beginning to experience sex as something quite different, tenderly hypnotic, emotional, a little frightening.

As David ran his hand down her smooth abdomen and soft stomach, Alexandra braced herself. When his fingers found the slick, moist center of her desire, she gasped and almost sobbed. His touch was sheer ecstasy. As he stroked her deftly, she held onto him more tightly, as if looking to him for strength to see her through this uncharted adventure. It wasn't that she'd never experienced an orgasm before. She had them easily. But her body's building reactions were telling her that this would be an experience beyond anything she'd known.

"God, you're a wonderful lover!" she whispered, her cheek against his shoulder.

"Sometimes I'm stronger than I realize," David told her in a restrained voice. "You must tell me if I hurt you."

"You're too sensitive to ever hurt me."

"I hope I am. Tell me what pleases you and what doesn't."

"You seem to know better than I," she said, kissing his chest. As his gentle fingers suddenly sent a sensual spasm through her, she gasped hotly. "Ohh, God. God! David, now!"

He moved over her as she settled back and parted her thighs. She moaned softly at the feel of him entering her, the magnificent intrusion of his body into hers. As he started slow, back and forth thrusts, she almost cried with the satisfaction of it. The closeness, the oneness she felt with him was unlike anything she'd experienced with any other human being.

As he continued with more powerful thrusts, commanding equally powerful sensations from her body, she sensed that, even so, he was holding himself back. She wondered how strong, how overpowering he could be. But she dared not ask for more, because she could barely cope with him as it was.

At last her body reached that point where she knew fulfillment was near. As she felt the final level of tension building, she wanted to look at him, to share the moment. Even that was unusual. Ordinarily, she preferred to enjoy the moment on her own, trying to forget a man was with her. But she needed to see David's face, wanted to communicate with him on a mental level as well as physical.

She pushed at his shoulders and made him rise up on his elbows. As he did, his thrusts within her took on a new, even more acute sensation. All at once her body exploded with pleasure, and as she cried out, she looked into his eyes. The blue of them transfixed her. They were a glowing, cobalt hue, and they mesmerized her so completely, somehow her physical reaction became almost secondary. She felt transported, floating, as if to another realm just beyond the earth's atmosphere.

And then all at once he closed his eyes as his own climax came. She felt him throbbing within her, and then he settled his body onto hers. She slipped her arms around him, just wanting to hold him, feeling such an intense closeness, that it almost pained her. And all at once, tears flooded her eyes, and she began to sob.

Immediately he lifted himself away and leaned over her. "What's wrong?"

She wiped her eyes, trying to stop the tears. "I feel so odd, so emotional."

He sat up against the headboard and drew her into his arms, holding her like a child as she continued to cry. "Did I hurt you?"

"No!" she said in the midst of her tears. "You're the most incredible lover! I feel as if you opened up something in me—" She paused, trying to examine her own mind and emotions. "I'm just realizing how lonely I've been. I feel so sad. And . . . and scared somehow."

"Scared?" he said, stroking her hair. "Of me?"

"No." But then she drew away. "Well, maybe."

"You looked in my eyes when—"

She met his gaze and found the blue of his eyes rich and deep, but normal. It must have been the intensity of her physical sensations that had altered her perception somehow. "I needed to be connected with you, personality to personality.

I wasn't looking for a relationship. Now I wonder if I'm already in one with you."

David smiled, his eyes warm on her, full of wisdom. He took her in his arms again. "I'm happy that we've shared more than just a sexual coming together. I think sex should be meaningful. Maybe that's new to you." He kissed her forehead. "But I think you'll get used to it."

All at once she found herself asking something a part of her strongly warned not to ask. "Will you come and see me again?"

David sat alone in the quiet of the limousine, watching the lights of the night pass by outside the windows as the driver sped him home. He wondered how Alexandra could appear so strong and yet be so vulnerable when he'd made love to her. What an extraordinary woman—enchanting, scintilating, and yet so frightened of affection.

David knew in his heart that he could help her. He already had. How she'd blossomed for him, giving herself so fully while confessing fears she barely understood herself. He would be good for her and she for him.

David liked the idea of being needed, of being the catalyst to enable a woman to become a whole person, her true self, unburdened of fears and self-doubt. Of course, in a different, nonsexual way, he'd like to think he could help men, too. But men were no challenge. He could read them like a manual. Women, on the other hand, were such mysteries.

Veronica would always be his most darling, most ephemeral, most wistful mystery. But trying to help Veronica had been a great mistake, for which both he and she were now suffering. David was certain Veronica would recover, even if he never would. But now he had Alexandra, for the moment anyway, to occupy his mind, to make him feel needed. This new, exciting relationship, he felt sure, was *not* a mistake.

7

The nerve of him

SITTING LOW in her seat, Darienne watched from the end of the front row in the first balcony. Matthew stood on the stage below singing by, and apparently for, himself. At one side of the stage three electricians worked overtime installing cables and wiring. "Mind if I caterwaul while you work?" Matthew had asked them when he'd first arrived.

Earlier at the auction, Darienne had approached Matthew at his table to say hello. The actor had been cordial, made small talk with her for half a minute, then announced with the proper amount of regret that he'd been just about to leave. When she'd pointed out that he hadn't finished dinner yet, he'd replied with a grin, "Don't want to look fat in my costume." Before she could say any more, he was out of his chair and waving goodbye.

Darienne had waited a few moments, until he reached the exit door, and then she followed. Unknown to him, she'd trailed a block behind him as he walked down Michigan Avenue to the theater.

Now as he stood on the empty stage, he still didn't know she was there watching and listening. He'd taken off his dinner jacket, set it on a ladder, and moved across the half-darkened stage in his black vest and white shirt. The bow tie had also been undone.

He stood at center stage and sang without the accompaniment of an orchestra or even a piano. The song was the same one David had played for her on his tape recorder, the one she'd later heard referred to by the title "She Can Never Be Mine." When Loni had shown them around the theater,

Merle had mentioned that Matthew would record this song and another from the show in a few days. They would be released as singles before a cast album was produced. Everyone hoped the songs would be played on local radio stations.

As he sang with the slow, eerie effect he'd developed for his vampire character, Darienne couldn't help but admire how well he managed to capture the anguish of David's lyrics. She'd seen David suffer for years over his guilt about loving a mortal woman and involving her in his night world. Matthew knew nothing about the truth on which the song had been based. Yet, watching him now, his tortured expression, his emotional outpouring of despair, she could just as easily see David.

And then all at once Matthew stopped in the middle of a lyric. He grimaced and seemed provoked with himself. He began walking along the stage, looking about him, as if getting his bearings. The electricians glanced up briefly, apparently wondering about the sudden silence, and then went back to their work.

Darienne looked on with curiosity, sitting very still, hoping to remain unnoticed. Matthew seemed too wrapped up in his own creativity to bother about his surroundings, however. She wondered what troubled him. He'd been singing so beautifully, she didn't see what could have dissatisfied him. In fact, he sounded better than on the tape David had played for her; his voice seemed even more pure, more tender, more heartfelt. He possessed a voice that could soften steel.

He stopped walking then, closed his eyes, and stood as if transfixed by some inner thought, as if he were hypnotizing himself. When he opened his eyes and stepped forward, it was as if he'd become a new person. He moved like Sir Percy, with the strange, slow, gliding steps he'd used when she'd seen him rehearse in costume. Like fog, she thought, remembering his own description. Every move contained poignant grace, from the mystical positions of his hands to the tragic inclination of his head. Every eerie step, toe-heel, toe-heel, gave a sense of some inherent danger lurking deep within him, and yet appeared effortless and natural. She was amazed he could project such power and sensuality without the aid of his costume and makeup.

Bending his knees, he slowly swiveled toward the empty

theater. She saw the material of his vest grow taut when he took in a deep breath. He rose up on his toes a bit as he began to sing again, giving a visual appearance of buoyancy as his voice floated out into the empty hall.

Darienne sat mesmerized at the magic he was creating all alone. He appeared beautiful to her now; she wondered how she could have ever thought him ordinary. She thought it a shame he needed to wear so much makeup on stage. Perhaps his curly hair, healthy complexion, and round eyes did not fit the image mortals had invented of how a pale, aristocratic vampire should look. But somehow he transcended his face and less than heroic stature with his voice and stage presence. He deftly channeled and projected his inner energy so that he became more than he was, more than most mortals could be. He became a living female fantasy. He became something sublime.

He sang the song through as if inspired by some hidden force. When he finished, the three electricians stopped to applaud. Matthew didn't seem to hear them. As he came down from singing the last high note, he remained in character, closing his eyes, savoring the feeling, as if he were enjoying the exquisite sadness of the song.

And then suddenly he opened his eyes, his body went back to a normal stance, and he looked about him as if he'd heard something he couldn't identify. He spotted the electricians, one of whom touched his thumb to his forefinger in a "perfect" gesture. Matthew grinned, his face suddenly all teeth and appreciative, beaming eyes. He waved at the men as he walked off stage, picking up his tuxedo jacket along the way.

The spell broken with his disappearance off the stage, Darienne scrambled out of her seat and down the steps. It was her intention to keep on following Matthew. She wanted to see where he went next. And if he went home, then she wanted to see where he lived.

In minutes, she was back on Michigan Avenue, following a block behind, watching Matthew's broad-shouldered figure walking at an easy pace ahead of her. He turned west near the Wrigley Building and walked down a street that led to the round, twin high-rise buildings by the Chicago River known as Marina Towers. Darienne picked up her pace, wondering what to do. She didn't know if there were security guards in the building, if she'd be able to follow him in to see which apartment he went to.

And then something happened that made her catch her breath. Matthew turned around. There was no reason for him to have turned. The street was empty and she hadn't made any noise. It was as if he'd sensed someone was following him. He studied her for a moment and then turned and kept walking. Darienne decided to brazen it out and kept following. Maybe it was lucky he'd noticed her. She'd have to think of some excuse for being there, however.

When he reached the glass entrance doors, he paused outside and turned again in her direction. She smiled as she walked faster to catch up.

"Hello, Matthew," she said, using exactly the breathy, expensive tone that a man might expect from a tall, glossy blonde.

"I thought I recognized you." If there was a trace of reluctance in his voice, he camouflaged it well. "How did the auction go?"

"Someone else got the emerald I wanted," she said, improvising. "I was just riding home from there in a limo when I saw you. So I asked the driver to stop so I could catch up with you."

"Oh," he said with studied enthusiasm. "Did you need to see me about something?"

Darienne found his reserved yet cordial manner attractive. It fit his careful way of speaking, his subdued tenor voice. "Well," she said in explanation, "you rushed out of the auction before I could tell you. I wanted you to know that I've been a fan of yours for years. Ever since I saw *The Boy from Savannah.*"

"Thank you," he said with a little smile. "I don't like to remember how long ago I did that film. You must have been a child when you saw it. Aren't you French? I didn't realize it had been released in France."

"I was a child," she said, smiling as she lied. "American films are seen everywhere. I'm also a fan of 'Rick and Rosie.' But I saw that in this country. I travel a lot."

Matthew nodded slowly, politely taking in what she said but with waning interest. "What do you think of *Shadow?*"

"I've only seen bits of a couple of rehearsals," she said.

"You're developing your role marvelously well. I love the way you move, the way you sing." Darienne would have said more, but she stopped herself. She grew self-conscious for some reason and felt uneasy giving him further compliments.

"I appreciate that," he replied.

Both were silent for a second. Darienne couldn't think of anything to say, which wasn't like her.

"Well . . ." he said, still facing her but taking a step backward toward the entrance door.

She realized that was meant as a cue for their conversation to end. Her mind regeared. "You know," she said, dropping her long lashes, "that I have a big investment in *The Scarlet Shadow.*"

He paused in his backward stride. "Merle mentioned you rescued the show. We're all very grateful for your faith in us."

"Well, I wonder if my faith has been misplaced. There are many problems, *n'est-ce pas?* I'd like to hear your opinions about a few things."

Matthew pursed his lips. "All right. How about tomorrow morning at the theater?"

"I'm not free then."

"I'll be rehearsing all day, probably into the evening. How about tomorrow night while I'm getting my makeup off?"

"I'd rather speak to you in private," she said, maintaining a cool poise befitting an influential financier.

"When would you suggest?"

"Are you doing anything now?"

"Now." He stated the word, studying her with eyes that appeared darker in the night atmosphere. "You'd like me to invite you in?" he asked calmly, as if for clarification.

"If it's convenient," she said, smiling with a touch of humility. "If you have someone waiting for you, then of course, I'll understand. But if you have nothing to do now, I don't either, and . . ."

"No, I have no one waiting and nothing to do. Except sleep. I was hoping to catch up on my sleep," he said, glancing at his watch.

"It's only around eleven. I'll stay no later than midnight."

He nodded, his actor's face curiously devoid of expression. "All right. Let's do it, now. The sooner the better, right?" He made a perfunctory smile.

Darienne walked with him into the building, feeling a bit undone. Most men were eager to invite her anywhere. What was with this . . . this polite mannequin with his marvelous chest, delving eyes, and curly hair? Suddenly he had the look and all the personality of the cold marble statues she'd seen in Greece. Perhaps his misadventures with women in his past had made him wary. She would have to be careful in her approach.

When they reached his apartment on one of the top floors, she walked into a place that was nicely decorated with traditional furniture in subdued shades of green, gray, and peach. The place was clean, but not quite neat. There was a grand piano with music strewn over its curved top. The matched pillows on the sofa were in disarray and some shirts were lying over one armrest. These Matthew picked up and took into the bedroom.

"I haven't gotten to my laundry yet," he explained when he returned.

"How long have you been here?" she asked.

"Three months. It's sublet from some people who are living in Europe for an extended time. I may be able to keep it—if the show lasts, that is."

Darienne sat down on the couch, straightening the throw pillows. "I think the show will be a huge success," she said.

"You do?" He took a chair opposite her. A glass-topped coffee table lay between them. On it stood a large green candle, which had been used often by the look of it, and some hardcover books and magazines. "What about the problems you wanted to discuss?" he asked.

"That's what I meant to say," she corrected herself. "The show will be a success if all the problems are solved."

"What problems do you see?"

"I hear the computer still isn't behaving."

Matthew laughed. "I know. I was too close to that guillotine this afternoon when it suddenly came down for no reason. I almost lost a shoulder."

Darienne was astonished. She didn't know the set was dangerous. "Are you all right?"

"Sure. Just a bruise. The shoulder pad in my costume saved me. The blade's not sharp, fortunately. But the coat needed repair."

"Which brings up another problem," she said, maintaining her business air while waiting for the right moment to switch gears on him. "I understand the costumes aren't being produced fast enough for opening night."

"Yes. But I'm afraid I haven't got much to do with either the running of the computer or the costumes."

"But you're very meticulous about your costume," she quickly pointed out. "Making them tailor it over and over because it doesn't fit the way you'd like. That may be part of the reason the costume department is running behind schedule."

He bowed his head for a moment. Darienne couldn't help but admire his delightfully tousled head of hair. When he looked up, she was sure he caught her admiring expression before she could hide it, but he ignored it. "The costume has to move just as I move, with me, not against me. It takes a lot of adjustments to fit it so that I feel right in it. I try not to be demanding in most matters, but my costume and makeup are critical to my performance. I'm sometimes accused of being a fussbudget."

"I didn't mean to accuse you," she said.

"I understand. You're concerned about your investment."

"It's more than the money," Darienne corrected, not wanting him to think she was mercenary. In truth, money had always been what she had the most of and what was last on her mind. "David is a friend of mine, and I want the show to be a success for his sake."

"How long have you known him?" Matthew asked, his eyes showing a hint of curiosity.

"Many years. Since we were teenagers in France."

"Really? He's always a gentleman and I respect his talent, but I haven't gotten to know him. He's a very private man."

Darienne perked up at the opening he'd given her. "That's interesting," she said with a chuckle. "That's exactly how he speaks of you. He admires you immensely, but says he doesn't know much about you."

Matthew seemed pleased and a little surprised. "We ought to do something about that."

"Perhaps I can help," she said, energized by the way he was playing into her hands. "I can tell you a few things about

David, and I can pass along some news about you to him. What would you like to know?"

"About David?" Matthew grew thoughtful, pressing his fingertips in front of his ear, deepening the long lines which radiated below the corner of his eye. "I'd like to know how he got his fascination for vampires, why he connects with that folklore so strongly and with such insight."

Darienne hesitated. "He visited Transylvania once. I think that started it. And David has strong feelings about ethics and morality. Writing about vampires gives him a chance to work out his angst."

Matthew listened intently, his eyes shining with interest.

"How about you?" she asked. "Why did you want to play a vampire?"

"It was a chance to sing and do a serious role. I've enjoyed doing comedy all these years. But I've found that an actor doesn't get much respect for comedy, even though it's more difficult to do than drama. *Shadow* was a way to demonstrate that I can play a different sort of character and sing, too."

"You really enjoy acting, don't you?"

"It's my life," he said.

"What do you prefer, movies, TV, or theater?"

"Theater."

"Why?"

He smiled, as if to himself. "The silence."

"Silence?"

"Of the audience. If you've played your part right, when you come to a pivotal scene, the audience grows absolutely silent. You can almost feel them holding their breaths, and you know you've got them in the palm of your hand. It's similar to the high you get when you're doing live comedy and you get a big laugh. Only more profound."

Darienne was fascinated, both by what he said and by the energy in his eyes as he spoke about his work.

"Have you been singing long? Do you enjoy that, too?"

"Yes. I've been taking lessons all my life. I've never worked so hard as in the last six months, though, preparing for this role. I had to extend my range to do justice to the music. I've even increased my chest expansion so I can hold notes longer."

"I noticed," she said, her eyes dropping to his vest. "It's very sensual."

Matthew's placid expression changed. He seemed startled.

"The way your stomach goes in and your chest comes out when you take a big breath," she explained. "That undulation of your body is exciting for a woman to watch." In a casual, languid movement, she leaned forward as she spoke. Her legs were crossed and she pretended to smooth her nylon from the knee downward, making sure her cleavage showed.

"My breathing is that noticeable when I'm on stage?"

She stopped and looked up. "Oh, God, yes."

He seemed to grow wary again. "Thanks. I'm . . . glad to know that."

"How do you psyche yourself to bring out all that sensuality? David explained the idea of casting against type."

Matthew's forehead crinkled, making vertical lines between his eyebrows. "I'm not sure what David means. As for sensuality, I don't think about that. I just try to understand the character, to express what Sir Percy is feeling."

"Well, what's he feeling?"

"Inner torment because of his great love for Marguerite."

Darienne sat up straight. "Oh, come on. You don't know what you're doing when you're on stage?"

"Of course I know what I'm doing."

"Then you must know how sexy you look," she said, tired of careful words.

She was surprised to see his ruddy complexion grow ruddier.

"I appreciate that you think so," he said in a smooth tone, "but I'm trying to aim a bit higher than just looking sexy—if that's how I look."

Darienne smiled, wondering whether to take his ingenuousness seriously. "Matthew, I predict that every woman who sees this play is going to want to run off with you. Including me."

He paused, studying her, his gray-green eyes looking mystic in the low lamplight. "Then it's a good thing I run off with Marguerite at the end of the show."

"What about the actress who plays Marguerite?" Darienne asked, bringing up something she'd wondered about. "Is life imitating art? Is she falling in love with you?"

"Elaine is engaged to be married."

"That doesn't answer my question."

"I have no idea. You'd have to ask her." He seemed to rethink his abrupt response, perhaps reminding himself it wasn't a good idea to seem rude to the show's top investor. "I can assure you, I've worked with many actresses, and they haven't treated me any differently than they treat anyone else."

Darienne knew from the old articles she'd read that this wasn't quite true. But she humored him, saying, "Perhaps you never showed them the side you keep hidden, that you're hiding even now."

"What side?"

"Your sensual side."

"Oh," he said, smiling now. "We're still on that."

"You aren't taking me seriously," she chided him, pouting a bit. She lifted her shoulders and breathed in so her collarbone would protrude and her breasts would jut out more. "We French women may seem frivolous, but underneath, we know exactly where we stand."

Matthew raised his eyebrows and looked down. "I'll bet you do," he said softly, suddenly sounding a lot like that "boy" from Savannah.

"Where were you born?" she asked.

"Atlanta."

"You're really from the South then."

He nodded. "I dropped the accent to get more roles."

"I've always heard about the charm and hospitality of Southern gentlemen," she purred, casually bringing her fingertips to the top of her low-cut dress.

"I left the South before I was twenty," he said in an accent that was pure Midwestern again.

What did it take to get him going? Darienne wondered. He must have read her signals by now. How woman-wary could he be?

"Are you married?" she asked.

"No."

"Engaged?"

"No."

"Involved?"

"No."

"A misogynist?"

"No."

"What are you?"

"I'm not a 'what.' I'm just me."

Darienne sat dumbfounded for a moment. Other than David, she'd never been told off before, however lightly Matthew had done it. Usually she could wind a man around her finger, but Matthew wouldn't twist.

"No wonder no one knows much about you," she said. "You don't talk."

"I thought you wanted to discuss the show with me," he said with a patient air.

"We are discussing the show."

"No, we've been discussing me mostly."

"You *are* the show," she said, using her most winning smile, giving him one more chance. "At least, to me you're the whole show. I'd like to get to know you better—on a more intimate basis."

He employed his own dazzling grin. "I appreciate the trouble you've taken. Not many investors want to get involved on a personal level. I believe you when you say your interest isn't monetary." He made a charming little glance at his watch and then rose from his chair. "I'm afraid it's almost midnight. I know for the sake of the show you wouldn't want to keep me from getting the rest I need. But thank you for taking this time with me. Your limo is waiting?"

Darienne knew now how smooth an actor he could be. She decided to take his cues, at a loss for the time being to know how to press his buttons, or even know where he kept them hidden.

"Yes, thank you. I appreciate your time, too," she said, imitating his manner as he walked with her to the door.

When they reached it, he opened it in an unhurried way, keeping his businesslike air. "Good-night, Darienne. See you at the theater?"

"Yes, you will," she said, turning to him after she crossed the threshold into the hall.

"I'm glad," he said and softly shut the door on her.

Darienne felt numb for a moment as she walked toward the elevator. By the time she entered it, she was incensed. The nerve of him to sidestep her every hint, even her most unsubtle ones! He was like a castle with no drawbridge over his moat.

Well, he wouldn't get away with it. She would experience that rarified sexuality of his one way or another. Neither a stage nor a theater full of people were going to seduce more out of him than she!

8

Now that you've made her love you

WITH HASTE, for he was running late, David fastened his gold cuff links. In a little while, he'd be with Alexandra, and he didn't want to lose a moment with her.

He'd seen Alexandra every night since they'd met. Though less than a week had passed, their relationship had spiraled into an extravagant, whirlwind affair—a mad ecstasy that made him blissfully numb to all the problems the show presented. With Alexandra, he entered a higher plane of artistic intellect combined with heated sensuality. She almost vied with Darienne in her physical need for him. But unlike Darienne, Alexandra cherished his mind, too. He wondered how he'd ever gotten along without someone to challenge him on so many levels as this beautiful violin maker could.

Within the hour, he met Alexandra at the Opera House. She smiled at him, tickets in hand, when he spotted her by the box office, where they'd agreed to meet.

She wore a strapless flowered cotton dress, with a slim skirt that ended above her knees, showing her graceful shoulders and long, slender legs. Even her manner of dress was becoming more free and youthful, David noted with pride, for he felt he could take credit for her lessening inhibitions. Her blond hair hung loose and bright around her shoulders. She made a dazzling sight, sophisticated, lively, and sensual.

She rushed up and kissed him, right there on the street. It wasn't something David would ordinarily have felt comfortable doing, but he never gave it a thought. All he could do was admire her glass-blue eyes staring mischievously up at him.

"What are you thinking?" he asked as they walked toward the entrance doors.

"That, much as I love Verdi, I can't wait until this opera's over, so we can be alone."

David smiled, pleased with her thoughts. "Shall we skip *La Traviata?*"

Her eyes slanted in mysterious amusement. "No. Our seats are very good, and the soprano is supposed to be out of this world. We might feel guilty afterward for substituting one lovely experience for another, when, if we're diligent, we can do both."

"Spoken with your usual attention to precision," David said, putting his arm around her. They entered, found their seats, and talked of Verdi and the much-touted diva until the performance started.

The French production, part of a visiting tour company, seemed to enchant Alexandra. Though David enjoyed the first half, he knew he did not have the musical sophistication to derive from it the same level of pleasure Alexandra did. But it was enough for David just to observe her close at hand, to see the passing expressions on her beautiful profile; her eyes, especially, now closing dreamily, now intent and analytic, now sparkling with delight.

When intermission came and the houselights went on, she turned to him with a smile and warmly took hold of his arm. "I'm glad we stayed."

"So am I," he replied. "Watching you is more exciting than the music."

"David," she said, laughing. Then she kissed him again on the mouth. "Shall we go into the lobby? I'd like a glass of champagne."

After David had obtained the champagne for Alexandra, they stood near a wall talking while crowds of well-heeled people milled about. All at once, they were interrupted when David heard a throaty, feminine voice call his name. He turned.

Darienne approached, dressed in her usual splendor. She wore a sequined white gown, low-cut to reveal her voluptuous curves. Diamonds twinkled at her neck and her hair, caught in a clip at one side of her head, draped over her left shoulder coyly. She pronounced his name in her most French manner, Dah-veed, prolonging the second syllable for all it was worth. "David, I didn't know you would be here tonight!"

"How would you know?" David said, dryly. "I haven't seen you lately. I don't even have your phone number to leave a message." He leaned close and whispered in her ear. "I want to talk to you."

Wariness entered Darienne's green eyes briefly. But they grew radiant again as she glanced at Alexandra. "Introduce me to your friend."

Alexandra's face had acquired a rather cold expression, which surprised David. But then David realized she had seen him whispering to Darienne.

"Alexandra, this is Darienne Victoire. We grew up together in Paris. Darienne, Alexandra Peters. She's the excellent craftswoman who made the violin sold at the auction."

"David is so impressed with you," Darienne said. "He's spoken of you often."

"Thank you," Alexandra murmured, barely smiling. "What do you do?"

"Do?"

"For a living."

Darienne looked up at David, her manner ingenuous. "I don't know. What do I do, David?"

David made a wry expression. "You're a connoisseur of the world."

"Yes, that's it!" Darienne laughed with delight, settling her hand on David's chest. "I knew you would find a way to explain what I do."

"But what do you *contribute?*" Alexandra asked, seeming to grow impatient.

Darienne's smile grew languid. She stared at the other blonde and said, "Why, *myself.* What better thing to contribute? I provide gaiety and *joie de vivre.* There are people who don't know the meaning of those words until they meet me." She turned as a man approached and joined the group. "Chad, of course, was not one of them."

David smiled at Chad and shook hands. "Nice to see you again," he said with genuine enthusiasm. He hadn't realized the young man was still pursuing her—successfully, it appeared. Good! Maybe Chad could distract Darienne from Matthew after all. David wondered what had happened after the auction, to what extent Darienne had managed to pursue the actor. It was why he wanted to talk to her.

Chad looked confused at Darienne's remark, and she explained to him what she'd just said. The young man smiled at her compliment. Darienne introduced Chad to Alexandra, who again was markedly cool. Alexandra had been in such a lovely mood; David wondered what had put her off. Now that Darienne was clinging to Chad, David thought she had no reason to feel jealous.

"Well, how does everyone like the performance?" Chad asked, taking on a convivial air.

"Excellent," David said.

"The costumes are *magnifique,*" Darienne gushed. At this, Alexandra subtly rolled her eyes to the ceiling.

"The soprano's all they say she is, don't you think?" Chad asked of no one in particular.

"She's quite good," Alexandra took it upon herself to reply. Her tone had grown clipped, authoritative. "Her voice is superior to most, though not perfect. Crystalline, but inflexible, I'd say."

David listened with interest, but felt he lacked the musical sensitivity to really understand Alexandra's critique. Chad looked puzzled and impressed.

Only Darienne seemed unfazed. " 'Crystalline, but inflexible,' " she repeated blithely. "Are you describing the soprano—or yourself?"

Alexandra's mouth dropped open. Before she could say anything, David rushed to her defense. "Darienne, that was uncalled for! What's gotten into you?"

"Moi?" Darienne said, eyes all innocence. Her French accent suddenly grew thicker. "I ask only a *petite question,* to understand what she say. I mean no harm."

The lights flashed, indicating that the audience should take their seats again. Of one accord, all four of them began walking toward the doors. Chad fell in step next to David, separating the two women.

He leaned toward David. "Any idea what that was all about? Did I miss something?"

"I don't have a clue," David replied.

Chad shook his head. "If I live to be a hundred, I'll never understand women completely."

"Not even if you live to be four hundred," David muttered.

"I just couldn't stomach her," Alexandra said as she drove David to his home after the opera. "What a shallow woman!"

"I've said that myself about her," David agreed, though he still sounded perplexed at the intermission incident.

"I know you've said that. Yet you allow her to fawn all over you."

"That's her personality. I can't change her. She made a fuss over Chad, too."

"Yes, she obviously prefers men!"

"Alexandra," David said with a chuckle, "you're letting yourself get disturbed over nothing. Let Darienne play out her little *femme fatale* role. You're above all that."

"I thought you'd be above it, too. Why do you associate with her?"

"I've known her all my life. I won't discard a lifelong friend, however irritating she can be."

Darienne's flagrant sexuality and calculated effervescence had irked Alexandra to the core. Not to mention her insulting behavior! Women like that always seemed to have to hold the spotlight, to ooze sex from every pore, to turn every male head in their direction. Narcissistic and egotistical! A glittering, plastic butterfly! Why did a cultured, intellectual man like David have anything to do with a woman like that?

"No doubt you were lovers at one time." Alexandra couldn't keep the words from coming out of her mouth.

"Whether we were or not has nothing to do with you."

Next he would point out that Alexandra had had previous lovers, too. How could she argue? She had to drop the subject, though she longed to find out what hold Darienne had on him. He'd whispered something in her ear, he'd allowed her to touch him—in fact, he'd seemed used to her touch. And he'd once said Darienne had talked him into going to the auction. Obviously the woman had influence with him. And that made Alexandra uncomfortable. How could she compete with this eager, shimmering, ball of fluff? Darienne seemed so relaxed about sex her mere smile formed an open invitation to every male in sight!

She'd have to find a way to keep David *out* of Darienne's path, Alexandra told herself as she turned the car down Oak Street. And then she realized she was taking a possessive attitude about him, which she'd promised wouldn't happen. What was wrong with her? Was she falling in love with David? She must be, she acknowledged with a sense of wonder. Why else would she feel so unsettled and insecure?

She was silly to be jealous of Darienne, Alexandra told herself. Alexandra was intelligent, attractive—and blond, too. David had told her over and over how he admired her. He'd ably demonstrated his admiration in bed. Why should Darienne suddenly make her feel inadequate?

Because Darienne knew how to live her life with exuberance and give herself without hesitation. Men would always be drawn to such a woman. Would Alexandra ever be that free?

"What are you thinking?" David asked, studying her.

Alexandra chuckled self-consciously. "I'm just thinking I've made a mountain out of a molehill." She pulled the car to a stop in front of his home. "Why should I let Darienne get to me? She is what she is, and I am what I am. Live and let live, right?"

"Absolutely!" David said with a grin, as if relieved she'd come to that conclusion.

Alexandra hoped she could correct the bad image of herself she'd given David tonight. The way to eliminate Darienne from David's mind wasn't to keep talking about the other woman and tearing her down, making him want to defend his "lifelong friend." How stupidly she'd behaved the last couple of hours! She'd better show him a different side of herself before the evening was over.

"So this is your home?" she said, leaning to look out the car window. Until now, they'd always met at her place. "It's magnificent."

"Would you like to come in and see it?"

"Yes," she said, flashing him a warm smile. His invitation reassured her that their relationship was still on track despite the way she'd behaved.

They walked into his home, and immediately she was impressed with the architecture of the oval entry hall, with its high dome and spiral staircase. The sculptured molding and columns of the doorways also caught her eye. "This is Romanesque, isn't it?"

"Yes. I loved the house immediately the first time I saw it."

"It's so unusual."

She listened while David gave her a brief history of the home as he led her up the carpeted, spiral steps. She was a bit surprised to find that he'd chosen the third floor to install his living room on, but she decided not to ask why. When they entered his living quarters, she found herself equally impressed with the decor he'd chosen, the odd insect-and-flower pattern of the drapes and furniture, the way the pattern blended and complimented the large Aubusson rug that covered the entire living room floor, the exquisitely carved oak furniture. Over their heads hung a wonderful antique chandelier. She'd have thought the chandelier would be more suitably hung in a hallway or dining room, though in some peculiar way it blended into the living room.

She'd expected David to have good taste in his selection of decor, and he did. This room even showed an artistic eccentricity she found intriguing. However, it was not quite the style she would choose for herself, if she had the money.

He showed her his small office, which Alexandra thought quaint and serviceable. To her surprise, she noticed that he'd hung the *Singin' in the Rain* poster there—side by side with Shakespeare's portrait!

Next, he led her down a hallway, at the end of which were double doors of carved oak. He opened the doors and took her into the vast expanse of a large ballroom with a beautiful wood floor, more chandeliers, and three high, grand bay windows, complete with heavy gold drapery and velvet-cushioned windowseats. The only thing that marred the delightful ambiance was the wide-screen television in one corner. Alexandra couldn't help but laugh.

"David, this is magnificent! But isn't there some other room in this big house where you could put your television?"

He laughed, too. "I know it's incongruous here. But I like to watch tapes of Gene Kelly and Fred Astaire and imitate their dance steps. So I like to have a lot of space around me."

Alexandra remembered his conversation with Lotte Leone, the dance instructor at the auction. She supposed dancing was his form of exercise; he had such an athletic build. The

thought of his body led Alexandra's mind down another path.
Her eyes strayed to the nearest bay window—and the velvety
windowseat beneath, just the right length to stretch out on.

She walked toward the window, saying she'd like to see the
view. David followed, though he seemed reluctant. She sat
down on the seat and twisted to look out the windowpanes on
either side and in back of her. When she looked up, she
noticed glass above her head, too, and could see the stars
shining down on her. "David," she said, reaching out to take
one of his hands. He'd remained standing a couple of feet
away. "Let's make love here?"

Immediately a troubled expression crossed his face. His jaw
muscles clenched and his brows drew together darkly. "No!"
He pulled her up firmly by the hand. "Not here."

"But why?" she asked, finding her balance as she stood.
"It's a wonderful, romantic place."

"Right in front of the window? Someone might see."

"But we're on the third floor. And we can turn out the
lights."

"Come downstairs." He smiled now, looking eager. "I
haven't shown you my library yet."

"All right." With reluctance, she allowed him to pull her
back toward the double doors. She hadn't thought he'd be
prudish, but perhaps he was one of those who were uncomfortable doing "it" anywhere but in a bedroom. Though, if
he'd tangled in the past with Darienne, he couldn't be that
awfully conservative. Oh, don't start thinking about *her*
again, Alexandra admonished herself.

When they had descended the stairs to the second floor, she
was surprised to see him unlock the door to the library, just
as he'd unlocked the door to his living room. Most people, in
her experience, locked only their home's front door. Why was
David so preoccupied with security? Well, she'd sensed he was
a bit offbeat. After all, he wrote plays about vampires. Perhaps locks and bolts revealed a compulsive behavior pattern.
She wondered what that indicated about him psychologically.

These thoughts were forgotten when she walked through
the door and saw nothing but shelves and shelves of books.
She wandered with him from one room to the next, astonished
at the enormity of his personal library. Books of all types,
from philosophy to art to history, were represented. His col-

lection of great fiction writers, historic and current, was equally massive. He had an incredible collection of rare, out-of-print books, many looking as though they were two or three hundred years old.

David took pride in showing her many individual books, and he even loaned her a couple which had to do with violins, one on Stradivari and Guarneri written at the turn of the century, and another about the history of violins which was written in Italian. Alexandra confessed her Italian had grown rusty, but she was eager to take it home and peruse it.

"Thank you, David," she said as they retraced some of their steps. They came to a corner where a leather couch and an easy chair were placed. David had lit the lamp on a table between the seats when they'd passed by earlier. The area was surrounded by book shelves, though the shelves were interrupted on the far wall by a curtained window. The coziness of the place appealed to Alexandra. Taking David's arm, she walked with him toward the couch. "Do you sit here and read sometimes?" she asked.

"Often," he said. "It's why I put some furniture here, so I wouldn't have to carry books all the way upstairs."

"The couch looks comfortable," she said, pressing her knee into the soft leather cushion. "Would you consider making love to me here?"

He slipped his hands around her waist and smiled. "You mean shatter this quiet corner of enlightenment with mad cries of passion?"

She slid her hands up around his neck. "Do you think your intellectual self could tolerate such a sacrilege?"

"I think so," he murmured. "How about you?"

"To dally amidst Dante and Dickens? I can't think of anything more delicious."

"Well, that settles it," David said, easing her onto the couch. "How can I resist a woman who alliterates so ably?"

Darienne climbed up the side wall of David's mansion, taking care not to scrape her dress or her hose. Toe- and finger-holds were easy to find between the rough-hewn blocks, but the sandstone was hard on her finer fabrics.

When she reached the second floor, she noticed a dim light coming from a window about five feet to the left. Should she look for David in his library? She edged herself over with careful sidesteps. When she reached the window, she bent and looked in. What she saw riveted her attention.

There on David's brown leather couch lay Alexandra and David in the midst of coupling. Both were naked, their clothes thrown on the floor. David lay on top of her, the strong V of his back angled as he supported himself on his elbows. His small, tightly rounded buttocks rose and fell with an urgent, pulsing rhythm that made Darienne's breaths come fast. So that was how he looked. Watching him was almost more erotic than being with him. Almost. It made Darienne wish *she* were there beneath David instead of the musical Lorelei he'd become enamored with.

What on earth did he see in Alexandra? Look at her lying there, appearing to be more in pain than enjoying earthly delights! Her twisting and writhing seemed to come from panic more than pleasure. She gripped him and then let go, then gripped him again, as if not knowing whether to be frightened of him or to give in to her raging need. How fascinating!

Darienne found a more stable footing so she could continue to watch, feeling only a trifle guilty. She was doing it for David, she rationalized. If it were Veronica he was with, Darienne wouldn't invade their privacy. She adored and respected Veronica. But Darienne hoped to make David see the light about his new paramour, and she needed ammunition. And the panting, neurotic woman in his embrace was giving her some ammunition, though she couldn't know it.

Darienne peered closer to the window, for she had to see them through the thin curtain. What luck they'd left the light on! Alexandra was reaching her climax now. Darienne could tell by the way she arched her chest and neck. But again, she wasn't reaching her moment with anticipation and joy; fear contorted her face.

What on earth did the woman have to fear, Darienne wondered. Losing control? She'd heard some mortal women suffered from that anxiety. But then why did Alexandra get involved with a man like David? Ah, of course. Because he *could* make her lose control. Poor Alexandra, Darienne mused as she watched. She'd found a man who could give her the profound sexual release she'd longed for, and yet being over-taken scared her witless.

Alexandra was crying now in his arms, her climax over. Darienne almost felt some sympathy for her. Any mortal woman would have a challenge coping with David's lovemaking. But it seemed to tear Alexandra apart.

And there was David, comforting her.

So that was it: He thought he could *help* her. Darienne should have guessed that in the first place.

Having seen enough—Darienne was feeling slightly sick to her stomach now—she continued her upward climb and entered the side window of David's living room. She sat on his couch to wait.

David walked up the stairs after seeing Alexandra to her car. It troubled him that she still seemed to have some anxiety regarding their increasingly close relationship. She wanted him, wanted sex, and yet couldn't relax. How could he break down that formidable barrier she carried in her mind to protect herself from being hurt, that kept her from enjoying true intimacy? He knew a way, but . . .

As he entered his living room, he stopped short when he saw Darienne sitting on his couch. "What are you doing here?" he asked.

"You said you needed to talk to me," she replied, smoothing the skirt of her white dress.

"Alexandra was here with me," he said, moving farther into the room. "What if she'd seen you?"

"I took care that she didn't."

David began to feel uncomfortable. "How long have you been here?"

"A half hour. I saw you two in the library as I climbed up. So I waited here."

"*Saw* us?"

"Quite a sight it was, too. She survived, I take it?"

David came to a halt in front of her. "I'm not going to listen to sarcasm from a female Peeping Tom! How could you have the gall to watch us?"

"David," Darienne replied with patience, "I might remind you that I gave up the remainder of my night with Chad so that I could talk to you, *as you asked.* If I happened to see something as I came in, it's as much your fault as mine."

"Do I ask you to climb my wall instead of coming in by the front door like any normal person would?"

"Normal? I relish the fact that I'm not!"

"Did I ask you to come *tonight,* when you might have guessed I'd be with Alexandra?"

"I'd guess you've been with her every night," Darienne said, her tone cool. "I haven't seen you at the theater since you met her. You asked to see me, so I've come. Let's quit this useless bickering."

"You push my patience to the limit!"

Darienne rose from the couch and stood squarely in front of him, green eyes fiery. "And you try mine! Seeing you with that woman has made me positively ill. When I think of poor Veronica! How truly and purely she loved you. How cruelly you cut her away from you and left her to suffer alone. And now you replace her with this oh-so-talented, oh-so-cultured *ice*-bitch who's incapable of returning any emotion you invest in her!"

David felt so shocked he could barely think. "Don't speak to me about Veronica! And don't call Alexandra names!"

"Why shouldn't I mention Veronica? Someone ought to speak on her behalf since you seem to have forgotten her."

David turned away, his breath caught in his throat. "Do you think she's ever out of my thoughts?" He looked at Darienne again. "Have *you* forgotten it was you who suggested I have an affair with Alexandra?"

Darienne paused, as if recalling her own words. "Then I admit it's the most stupid advice I've ever given you. I thought you'd have only a brief little fling. I thought the experience would be such a disappointment, it would make you realize what you've lost. I hoped you'd long so much to be with Veronica again that you'd go back to her. I never imagined you'd fall in love with Alexandra."

"I'm not in love with her," David said. "At least, not the way I love Veronica. I'm impressed, I'm dazzled, I'm challenged by Alexandra. And she needs someone. She's lonely, doesn't know how to have an intimate relationship. I think I can show her."

"And then what?" Darienne asked. "What if you're successful? Then she'll be in love with you. What will you do with her?"

Darienne's barrage irritated David. "I don't know! I wasn't looking for a relationship when I met her. Neither was she. All of a sudden, we're in one. I don't know what the consequences will be. But I think I can help her, and for the time being that's most important."

"Why do you always think you can *help* women?" Darienne asked, pacing around him, looking and sounding exasperated. "You set out to help Veronica, and look what came of it. Don't you ever think ahead? Alexandra doesn't need your help. The woman needs a psychiatrist! You'll only confuse her more. And what happens when she finds out you're a vampire? Veronica figured it out, and so will she. And that knowledge in Alexandra's hands could be dangerous."

"Alexandra would never be a danger to me. I've been considering telling her myself, so she won't suffer the shock Veronica did when she discovered the truth accidentally."

"And what happens after you tell her? Will you initiate her?"

David exhaled. "I don't know, Darienne. I *don't know.* I'm taking it a step at a time."

"And what about Veronica?"

He spread his hands, feeling drained of energy all at once. "We're abiding by our pact. She's with Rob now."

"No she's not. He left her."

David studied Darienne for a moment. "How do you know that? You haven't been spying on her, too!"

"Of course not. I know she's miserable because I know how much she loves you."

"But how do you know Rob left her? You haven't seen Veronica, have you? I forbid you to communicate with her."

Darienne laughed. "Forbid? After four hundred years, you still haven't learned that I don't take orders?"

"Have you?"

"What?"

"Seen her?"

"My friends are *my* concern."

David stared at her, his heart beating faster. "You have, haven't you?"

Darienne glanced away. "What did you want to talk to me about? Matthew?"

"How dare you see her! You knew it would be against my wishes."

She pivoted to stare into the empty fireplace. "I came here to talk about your musical, David."

David had the urge to make her look at him again. But he kept himself from taking her by the shoulders and making her turn around. In a quieter voice he asked, "How was she? How did she look?"

Darienne kept her silence.

"What did she say?" David persisted. "Tell me. Please."

Darienne turned to him. "I'm relieved to see some sign that you do still love her. I'm not going to tell you if I've seen her, or if I'll see her in the future. And should I do so, I refuse to report back to you about her. It's up to you to break your pact. You chose to separate from her, and you must live with that choice. I'm not going to make you feel better by telling you if she looks well. And if I had to report that she'd fallen madly in love with some mortal, it would destroy you. Either way, it defeats my purposes."

"But is she in love with Rob? Why did he leave her?"

Darienne sighed. "David, I just explained that I have nothing to tell you concerning Veronica."

"Can't you answer even one question?" David said, angry with her impervious attitude.

"Ask her yourself!" Darienne spat at him. "Either break your pact, or abide by it. Don't cheat by putting me in the middle. I won't be your go-between."

David felt chastised. She was right, he'd attempted to circumvent his own pact. He hadn't heard or felt or sensed Veronica's presence for years now, leaving him in deep despair that he would ever have her for his own again. He missed her desperately.

David was almost certain Darienne had seen Veronica. What agony to be with someone who'd spoken to her and not be able to ask about her! Darienne wouldn't talk, and now he despised her for her strength of conviction. She was on Veronica's side and was keeping her confidences. Veronica had done the same for Darienne in the past. David knew they used to have secret discussions about him. He wished he could have been a fly on the wall and overheard them. How odd that Veronica would form such a friendship, a sisterhood, with Darienne, whose disposition differed so from Veronica's sweet innocence. And that Darienne would keep her loyalty to Veronica, when it was David she'd known for hundreds of years. David felt like the odd man out, simply because he *was* a man.

David's thoughts scattered when he realized Darienne was studying him, her eyes keen with humor now.

"You look a little lost," she said in an empathetic tone. "I'm sorry to take such a strong stance, but I'm on your side, believe it or not. Because I know the best thing for you is to be with her. And once you realize that yourself, and you go back to her, everything will be fine."

"You're so simplistic," David said with a long sigh.

Darienne tilted her head, diamond earrings glistening. "My ideas are simple, but correct. Go back to her and you'll see."

David pinched the bridge of his nose and leaned tiredly against the mantel. There was no use pursuing this any further. Darienne lived by emotion, not logic.

"Now what did you want to talk to me about?" she asked.

He pulled himself together. "I want to know if you seduced poor Matthew."

" 'Poor' Matthew?" she said, laughing. "He knows how to take care of himself, believe me!"

"So you didn't?"

"That's none of your business," she said, a subtle flash of hostility in her eyes. Then her attitude changed. She seemed worried. "Am I losing my touch, David? Have I grown less attractive somehow?"

"You're as attractive as ever. What happened?"

"He threw me out. Politely, of course. He's infuriatingly polite. I couldn't so much as light a spark."

David smiled to himself. "I'm glad to know Matthew's as sensible as I imagined he would be. I'm very relieved. I hope you'll take his cue and leave him alone."

"Oh, no," she said, shaking her head. "I don't give up that easily." She closed her eyes sensually. "On stage he's so mysterious. He's sexual in a way I've never seen before. I have to experience him. I have to! That's all there is to it."

"But don't you see how that could increase tensions at the

theater? We already have enough problems without our main investor trying to make a conquest out of the show's leading man. It could cause a scandal. Don't you care about my musical at all?"

"I'll handle it delicately," Darienne said.

David had to laugh. "You come on like a dazzling roller-coaster."

"I'll change my tactics. I'll try to appeal to his intellect next time."

"That I'd pay money to see!"

"You think I can't seduce him?" she taunted.

"Whether you can or not is beside the point. I think you *shouldn't*, Darienne. You're placing him in the awkward situation of trying to avoid you without offending you. He already has enough on his plate just getting prepared for opening night. I've spent two years creating this musical. Can't you put the show first for my sake?"

"Are *you* putting your show first?" she retorted. "Problems at the theater are getting worse, but you haven't been near there since the auction. You've let Alexandra distract you from your work. If you don't care, why should I?"

David felt self-conscious, his line of argument shattered by Darienne's observation. "I need someone," he said quietly. "Why do you dislike her so?"

"She's not good for you. She's cold and self-involved. And neurotic."

"You don't know her at all," David said. "She's brilliant. Delightful. She has *lots* of warmth. If anyone's self-involved, it's you. You always do just as you please."

"Yes, but I don't make any emotional claim on anyone. Alexandra is claiming your emotions, David. You saw how jealous she was of me. Why would she be jealous if she didn't want you all for herself? I may be lustful, but she's tenacious. What will she want from you, now that you've made her love you?"

9

Curiosity can be a dangerous thing

AS THE cab turned a corner, David leaned back and closed his eyes for a moment. He should be on his way to the theater, not Alexandra's, his conscience told him. But Merle and the others could handle things, he rationalized. He needed Alexandra's company. Being with her lifted him out of his shaded existence, made him feel human, needed, admired just for himself.

The way Veronica used to make him feel.

So Rob had left her. He wondered how she felt, if she'd loved Rob, if she missed him. Or perhaps she'd met someone else. As always, David wondered if she still had any remaining love for him. Much time had passed. She was young and beautiful. She must have lots of men wanting her. No doubt Rob had left because she'd found someone new.

For several long, deep minutes David brooded over the inevitability of losing Veronica. He came back to reality only when the cab driver screeched to a halt to avoid a collision with a car that had cut him off. The driver honked and yelled obscenities out the window. David pressed his fingers to his eyes and could only feel the ugliness of his world without Veronica. His sole comfort was the thought that her world would be much more wholesome without him in it.

David remembered then that he was riding in this cab because he was on his way to Alexandra's house. Alexandra—would he be equally bad for her? He knew she was growing more and more attached to him. More and more possessive. This surprised him, after her no-strings declaration the night they'd met. He'd hoped to free her emotionally, and apparently he had. Now she felt free enough to want a relationship with him, perhaps even love him.

And what did David want? He wished he knew. Veronica might forget him, reject him when they finally met again. Alexandra could be a comfort to help him through the loss. But how would a relationship with a vampire impact Alexandra's life? She didn't know his secret yet. What would the consequences be if he told her?

When David reached her home, Alexandra opened the door before he could ring the bell. Her golden hair hung sleekly about her shoulders and her eyes glistened with happiness. She wore a short skirt and a gauze peasant blouse pulled down to bare her shoulders. "David!" she said with an eager smile and opened the door wide.

To be welcomed so warmly served as a balm to David's melancholy. He took her into his arms and they embraced for a long moment.

"I miss you during the day," she said, sliding her hands beneath his jacket. "Let's make love first tonight."

David spent the next hour in Alexandra's passionate embrace, trying not to think of Veronica. But tonight Veronica stuck in his mind and would not go away. He couldn't help but recall how joyfully and tenderly she used to make love, how her innocent sweetness enveloped him, transported him, made him feel whole, alive.

Alexandra offered experience and a peculiar vulnerability that made sex with her something of a challenge. He could sense that with each coming together, she grew more fulfilled. He felt he was bringing her out of a cocoon and into life. That alone made their relationship a satisfaction. But tonight, even so, he sorely missed Veronica.

"God, David," Alexandra whispered afterward, still breathing fast from her climax. She wiped tears away and smiled at him as he held her close. "I think I may get used to you yet. You're overpowering. All day long I think about you, think about being in bed with you. But then, when you finally arrive and you take me upstairs, I start to feel uneasy and frightened. I hate myself for it, but I can't seem to help it."

"You make love beautifully," David said, stroking her hair away from her moist forehead.

"I think I build you up in my mind too much because we're

apart all day long. Do you think—could we spend a weekend together? All day and all night? I know you write during the day, but surely you could take off a weekend. I think if I were with you constantly, you wouldn't overwhelm me so. I wouldn't get anxious about seeing you, because you'd already be here with me. Could we try it?" She looked at him, her clear blue eyes winsome and expectant.

"I'm afraid we can't," David said with regret.

Her face slackened in disappointment. "Is it so much to ask?"

"No, it's not a lot to ask, if I were an ordinary man," David said, choosing his words. "But, you see . . . I'm not."

"I don't understand."

"I exist at night and sleep during the day."

"You write during the day," she said, drawing her brows together.

"No. That's the story I tell people to hide the truth. I must rest when the sun is in the sky or else I would perish."

"This is . . . I don't understand what you're saying."

David let go of her and straightened up against the head-board of the bed. He looked into her perplexed eyes.

"Alexandra," he said in as calm a voice as he could find, "I am a vampire."

Alexandra started laughing. "That's a good one!" she said, touching her fingertips to her nose as her shoulders shook. She felt embarrassed at her gullibility. "You almost had me going there."

David continued to look grave. "This isn't a joke. I *am* a vampire."

Alexandra's laughter trailed off. "What do you mean?" She stared into his pale blue eyes. Somehow they looked paler now than they ever had before. "There's no such thing as a vampire."

"You're wrong," he said in the same calm tone that was beginning to unnerve her. "Vampires do exist."

A dire thought came to her. She knew *Street Shadows* and his new musical were both about vampires. Had he gotten too wrapped up in his characters? Was he delusional? Yet, David had always impressed her as being more steady and insightful than any other man she'd met.

"David, you're carrying this too far. Vampires are fictional creatures and you know it!"

"Have you noticed an odd light in my eyes when we're making love?"

Alexandra had always thought the cobalt glow was a product of her imagination, brought on by the high level of arousal David could give her. She felt cold pinpricks break out on her forehead and shoulders. "I've noticed . . . something."

"And my teeth. Don't my incisors look longer and sharper than the average person's?"

Her eyes lowered to his mouth. She remembered the eerie feeling she'd had moments after she'd first met him, when he'd thrown his head back slightly as he laughed. "They may be a little different, but not . . . not abnormal."

"It's true, most people don't seem to notice," David agreed, looking downward for a moment. "I've tried to be gentle, so you wouldn't have noticed my unusual strength, either. How can I convince you?" he asked, as if pondering aloud. "Other than by doing the obvious."

"What do you mean by 'the obvious'?"

He raised his eyes and suddenly they were a deeper hue. A hint of cobalt flickered in their depths. "I could take your blood. I imagine you'd believe me then."

Instinctively she backed away, feeling vulnerable being naked and having just made love with him. She grabbed the edge of the bedspread and pulled it over her breasts, up to her throat. "Don't talk like this, David. You're beginning to frighten me."

"You *should* be frightened. Though I'd never harm you."

Did he have some sort of fetish? "You don't actually drink . . . b-blood, do you?"

"I must," he said, his tone earnest and grave. "To survive."

He had to be suffering from delusions, Alexandra thought. It was the only explanation. Some men went around thinking they were Hitler or the Messiah. David believed he was a vampire. "How do you—?" She couldn't even finish the sentence.

"Do it? Usually I get my blood supply from medical sources. Occasionally I drink from the artery in a person's neck. But only with their permission."

He was downright looney! Alexandra couldn't stand it anymore. She jumped off the bed, away from him, and grabbed a terry robe out of her closet. As she wrapped it closely around her, she said, "David, I don't understand why you're saying these things. Either you're crazy, or you're taunting me because I asked you to spend more time with me. If you can't stop this nonsense, then please leave!"

David stared at her in a peculiar, still way for a moment, then got off the bed and began to dress. "I must say, Alexandra, you're rather resistent to new ideas. In the past, most women I've become intimate with had noticed differences between me and other men by this point in the relationship. Some of them even deduced I was a vampire before I could tell them. But you seem to discredit the supernatural, and you disregard the evidence that your senses show you."

David began to buckle his belt as he spoke. Then he stopped and pulled the belt out of his trouser loops. He held it up by the metal buckle. "Take this," he said, holding it out to her. "Try to squeeze the sides of the buckle together between your fingers."

"I'm not going to play silly games."

"Please. Humor me for a few moments. Take it and try to bend the metal."

With an audible exhale, she reached out to take the belt. She pressed on the metal, tried to twist or bend it. "Okay, I can't do it," she said, handing it back. "What is this, some magic trick? Do you have a deck of cards for me to pick from, too?"

David stepped closer and held the buckle at her eye level. With no apparent exertion, he pressed his fingers together so that the two sides of the buckle touched in the middle. He gave her the squashed ring of metal to examine.

Alexandra felt her nerves begin to jump unsteadily. "Okay, I'm impressed. So you're unusually strong. It doesn't mean you're supernatural."

David took the belt back and straightened the buckle to its original shape. "What would convince you?" he asked as he smoothed the metal between his fingers. "Shall I show you my coffin?"

"Coffin!"

"Vampires must sleep by day in a coffin."

"Sorry, I'm not up on my vampire lore," she said in a sarcastic tone. "You could show me a coffin, cobwebs and chains, spiders, anything you want. All it would prove is that you're a little nuts!"

David eyed her as if becoming disillusioned. "I didn't realize how narrow-minded you are. You really need to open up to all the possibilities of the universe."

But Alexandra told herself she needed to keep a scientific attitude about what was possible and what wasn't. "You may be a terrific lover, David, but you spend too much time indulging your imagination. Writing those plays has warped your mind."

As she said the words, David took her by the hand and went to her antique dresser. "Look in the mirror," he said, standing beside her in front of it. Alexandra blinked in disbelief. She could see herself in the mirror, but not David. Instead she saw the mussed bed behind him. Her mouth went dry. "I don't understand . . ."

David opened her sewing basket on the dresser, fingered through her spools of thread and bits of lace until he drew out a pair of scissors.

"What are you going to do with those?" she asked, backing away.

She watched in horror as he calmly stabbed the point of the scissors into the palm of his hand.

"David!" she shrieked.

But then he pulled the scissors out, his jaw clenching as he withstood the pain. He put the scissors down and held up his hand. A tiny drop of blood ran down to his wrist, and he reached for a tissue from the box on her dresser to blot it before it could stain his shirt cuff. "Look," he said, holding out his hand so she could examine it. He no longer seemed in pain. "You see that it's healing already. In less than a minute there will only be a pink scar. And after ten minutes or so, the skin will be unblemished as it was before."

Alexandra couldn't believe her eyes. The deep wound healed as time-lapse photography would show it. In seconds it closed and formed a thin scar, which began to fade even as she watched.

"Do you believe now that I'm not like mortal men?"

She swallowed. This was all too unreal. "Yes." She looked up into his face, so strong and steadfast. "Why do you use the word 'mortal'?"

"Because I'm *immortal.*"

And then, vaguely, she remembered—probably from some old movie she'd seen as a child—that vampires lived for hundreds of years. "Immortal," she repeated. She'd heard the word before, but it felt new to her. "You can't die?"

"I died in 1616. Now I *exist*—by night, nourished by blood, for as long as the world lasts, if I choose."

Alexandra stared at him in astonishment. 1616! Was she dreaming this? Was she really looking at a man who had walked the earth for the last four hundred years? She felt faint suddenly and lifted her hand to her spinning head. David gripped her shoulders to steady her, then picked her up in his arms. Even in her daze she could feel how easily he carried her, as if she were a doll stuffed with tissue paper.

He layed her on the bed and gently massaged her shoulders until the spots of black in front of her eyes began to disappear and her head and vision cleared. He sat at her side and held her hand.

"What people have you known?" she asked, when she could speak. "Where have you lived?"

"I've lived in many places. Mostly in Europe." He smiled as if eager to impress her. "I met Mozart once in Vienna. I saw him conduct one of his own works." He looked self-conscious now. "I'm afraid I can't remember which one. I never could get into his music. Half a century later, I heard Paganini play. Now *that* was an experience!"

"Paganini? What was he like?"

"He was tall and terribly thin. He wore his hair long, had piercing eyes and a haggard, strange face. But when he played his violin, the sounds he created were so breathtaking, people in the audience wept. Even me, I have to admit. He was a genius. So much so that people whispered he'd made a pact with the devil." David chuckled in a bemused way. "How times have changed."

Alexandra studied him in wonder. "Tell me more. I mean, about yourself."

"I studied under Shakespeare. He was my beloved teacher. That is my fondest memory. I was still a mortal at that time. And when he died, I traveled to Transylvania to become a vampire, so that I could protect his works. I'd feared that future generations would forget him." David's expression grew muted. "Obviously my efforts were unnecessary."

"You knew Shakespeare!" Alexandra marveled. She sat up against the headboard, feeling stronger now, even energized. Now that she believed David, he no longer frightened her. She could only look at him in awe and amazement. This modest man had lived for centuries and known famous people. This explained how he'd compiled his vast library of rare books. This explained his odd habits. "Why have you told me these things?"

"You wanted our relationship to grow. I had to tell you before we carried things any further. I didn't want you to find out by accident and run from me. Though now I have the feeling you might never have guessed," he said with a smile.

"Narrow-minded," she said, repeating his description of her. "Maybe you're right. I've always believed in concrete things, what I could see and touch."

"Except for the mirror, you can see and touch me."

"That's just it. You behave so normally, I had no reason to believe you could ever be anything other than what you appeared to be. I never believed in vampires or ghosts. I can barely believe now. You mean all those vampire movies were based on truth?"

"The movies were based on Victorian literature, which in turn was based on the folklore of Eastern Europe. But the folklore *did* stem from truth, which is often the case with folktales."

"I'm afraid I never paid much attention to vampire stories. What else should I know about you?"

David's eyes warmed. "Only that I won't harm you. I'm relieved you're accepting this so well."

"I'm fascinated. No wonder you're so remarkable. How will this affect us?"

"It needn't affect our relationship at all," David replied. "We can go on as we have been. You understand now why we can only see one another after the sun has set. I can't spend weekends with you."

Alexandra nodded. A question became prominent in her mind and made her nervous. "What about— Vampires are always supposed to be biting people on the neck, right? Are you going to . . . ?"

"As I said, I only take a person's blood with their permission. And, I might add, after much consideration."

Alexandra drew her brows together. "What's there to consider? Isn't it just a matter of your need and my willingness to donate?"

David made a sad sort of smile. "I wish it were that simple."

"Why do vampires need blood anyway?"

"The Bible tells us that the life is in the blood. Though a vampire technically is dead, he can continue to exist through that mysterious life force that blood contains."

Alexandra tried to cut through his rather metaphysical explanation and discern what the biological process must be. It must be some type of biochemical reaction that scientists either weren't aware of or hadn't yet investigated.

"How did you become a vampire?"

"When I went to Transylvania, I sought out a vampire. He was a crude, uneducated fellow who only thought of blood. I didn't speak the language well, so I merely bared my neck and offered him money. He seemed to understand that I wanted immortality, not assisted suicide. I felt very much at risk, though, believe me. He performed the blood ceremony. I died and in a few moments awoke as a vampire. My teeth elongated a bit and my strength grew over the next few days. And I felt the degrading lust for blood. But I learned to deal with it, subdue it, so that I could go about my purpose for becoming immortal—to carry on for William Shakespeare."

"What's the blood ceremony?"

"It's the comingling of blood between a vampire and a mortal, the only path by which a normal person becomes transformed." David's eyes scanned her face. "You've just had a fainting spell. I don't really think you're up for a detailed description of how it takes place."

Alexandra swallowed convulsively and accepted his advice, but planted the subject away in her mind for further investigation later. Just the idea that such a thing could be done sent a feeling of electricity through her. She'd never imagined immortality to be a real alternative, not just a human longing. And apparantly it was an alternative open to anyone! At least, anyone who knew where to find a vampire. And *she knew* David—in all senses of the word. My God, she'd been having sex with a man who could live forever!

"What would happen if you took blood from me? Is it life-threatening?"

"Only if I took too much." He paled a bit and seemed to be distracted by some memory. "I almost did once, with someone I loved," he continued. "I would be very careful not to repeat that mistake."

"Do you need blood now?"

David's mouth twisted in an expression of self-loathing. "I always feel the need for blood. But, no, I have a supply for the moment. You've read in the papers about occasional blood bank robberies?"

"That was you?"

"Yes." He looked at her with a vulnerability she found winsome. "You see how much I trust you to make such an admission, in addition to telling you my darkest secret. You must reveal what I've told you to no one."

Alexandra shook her head and reached for his hand. "I won't," she told him with heartfelt assurance. "I would never betray you. I . . ." She chewed her lip for a moment, a trembling feeling coming over her for what she was about to say. "I think I must be in love with you. I've needed to be with you ever since I met you. I've never felt this way before about anyone."

David's eyes warmed and he squeezed her hand. "I care for and admire you, Alexandra. In all the hundreds of years I've existed, I've never met a woman who was so accomplished, so bright, so talented, and beautiful as you are. Every moment I spend with you is an honor."

"Thank you." Her words came out as a whisper, she was so enchanted with his compliment. "Would you . . ." Alexandra could hardly believe what she was saying. "Would you like to take my blood? You've given me so much. You make me feel like a new person. I want to give to you in return. I want you to need me for something the way I need you."

David smiled and leaned down to kiss her. "I'm sorry I called you 'narrow-minded' before. You're so open and giving. There's a simple sweetness about you I hadn't appreciated until now. I *do* need you, but not for your blood."

She ran her hand up his chest. "But I want to. I guess I'm curious. Is it pleasurable? I want to know what it's like."

"Curiosity can be a dangerous thing. It *is* pleasurable. However, as I told you before, there's a lot to consider."

"What?"

"If I took your blood, I would have power over you."

She chuckled at his melodramatic statement. "You already have *that.*"

"The power isn't only sexual, Alexandra." His expression grew stern. "We would have a mental bond. I could force you to come to me, to do anything I wanted, merely by willing you to do so. I would try not to misuse the power. I've never felt right about taking away a person's free will. That's why I have to warn you that you would be giving yourself over to me entirely, more than you can even imagine now."

Alexandra stared at him, thinking this was preposterous. He must have an inflated idea of his sway over women. Yes, he was sexy, persuasive, overwhelming. And maybe the act of taking blood had a kinky pleasure to it that women liked. She found that idea very intriguing. But that he would have some kind of mental power over her—oh, come on!

"How does this power happen?" she asked him. "How would taking some of my blood give you any power over me? It doesn't make sense."

David thought a moment, as if mystified. "I don't know," he said. "I've never tried to analyze it. I just know that it happens. You might as well ask me to explain gravity."

His lack of logic made Alexandra even more dubious about his claims. She could believe vampirism and immortality to be some biological secret that hadn't been discovered yet, except by vampires, who perhaps had stumbled on the secret accidentally and had kept the knowledge to themselves. But mind control? Loss of free will? No, there was no scientific basis for that, she didn't think.

"Do you get mental control over all the people whose blood you drink from the blood bags?" she asked.

"Apparently not," David said. "That's a good question. I don't know why it only happens with people who are bitten. Perhaps there's something that's transmitted orally during initiation. Or perhaps it's all psychological. I really have no idea. But the power exists, Alexandra. I have the feeling you're doubting me again. Don't make that mistake."

"I won't," she said, humoring him.

For the moment she decided not to pursue this any further. Instead she asked him to tell her more about his past. He described the various names and changes of location he'd taken to protect himself. He couldn't remain in the same place for more than twenty or twenty-five years, looking the same age, he explained. He had lived in many countries and cities. In most decades he had continued his long career as a playwright, often writing under a pseudonym. But he had tried other careers here and there—a museum curator in Italy in the late 1800s, a theater critic in New York in the 1930s and '40s. "My days as a turncoat," he joked.

She found all that he said fascinating. When he left in the early morning hours, she remained awake until dawn thinking of it and marveling over all the possibilities vampirism could provide. To never age. To live forever. She could carry on her craft. She wouldn't have to find some young violin maker to pass on her secrets to. She could keep them to herself and go on improving her skills. With hundreds of years ahead of her, she could even one day realize her most profound dream: To make the perfect violin.

When the first rays of sunlight came through her bedroom window, she still lay wide awake, having gotten not a moment of sleep. She thought of David. He must be in his coffin now, at rest. The thought chilled her. Not everything he'd told her about the vampire existence enraptured her. But still, it wasn't such a bad trade-off, giving up daylight for immortality.

Alexandra got out of bed and went to her dresser mirror. She'd always been too preoccupied with making love with David to ever notice that he couldn't be seen in the glass. Looking at her own reflection now, she ran her fingers lightly over the thin lines forming around her eyes, across her forehead, and at the corners of her mouth. The skin over her jaw and under her chin was beginning to slacken. None of these flaws were terribly noticeable yet, but she couldn't help but be aware she was aging, that these signs would not improve, but worsen with each passing year.

She had always been considered beautiful. Even her father would on occasion speak proudly of his daughter's beauty, though he could find little else to praise. She liked the idea that she could have her choice of men, when she wanted one around. And David had awakened a new pride in her appearance, in her choice of clothes. She liked looking good for him, because the way he appreciated her efforts gratified her and affirmed her in such a positive, enriching way. When she'd told him she felt like a new person, she meant it. Now at age thirty-eight she felt more attractive and sure of herself than she ever had in her life. But how long would it last? Her reflection in the mirror guaranteed this new image she'd achieved would be short-lived.

But not if she became immortal. Then she would stay just as she was. And she could go on being with David, just as she was. She couldn't bear the thought that he would go on looking young and handsome while she aged. How would he feel about her only two years from now when she turned forty? Or in ten years when she was pushing fifty? Even if he didn't mind, her pride couldn't tolerate the thought. No, if she wanted her exhilarating affair with David to continue, she would need to stop aging, and soon.

But to ask David for immortality was a big step. The very thought made her mind reel. She still didn't know enough about the process, or about how she would adapt to such a profound change. There was the lust for blood he had described. He'd called it degrading. The idea caused a shiver across her back. Drinking blood decidedly wasn't Alexandra's style, either. Still, David had managed to adjust and retain his civilized, courtly manner. If he could do it, shouldn't she be able to, also?

She had better approach all this carefully. Some instinct told her she'd better not tell David right away that she was interested in becoming what he was. He had said he only took a person's blood after much consideration. He'd even gotten stern with her when she'd asked him to take hers. She had the feeling that if she requested him to perform the blood ceremony and transform her, he'd be even less pleased.

No, she had to take this slowly and use the right psychology to get him to do it. She'd start by coaxing him to take her blood. From Alexandra's point of view, it was a good way to begin anyway. She'd wet her toes, so to speak, in the supernatural realm, to understand better what a vampire's existence would be like. Yes, she'd start working on David right away

to carry out this first step. What had he called it? He'd used
some quaint term—

Oh, yes. Initiation.

The next evening David expected Alexandra to behave differently with him. Women usually did once they found out he
was a vampire. But he hadn't expected the reaction he got.
There was a businesslike quality about her, an attitude of
negotiation. What's more, he'd been there almost an hour,
and she hadn't even mentioned going to bed yet. Though on
that score, he found himself feeling a bit relieved, he was
surprised to admit.

"I don't understand why you're so reluctant to initiate me,"
she said, continuing her argument. They sat on her wooden
stools facing each other by one of the work tables. "If I'm
willing, what's the big deal?"

David shook his head. "I've tried to explain about the
bond. You gloss over it as if it were nothing."

She pulled the hem of her short skirt downward over her
slender thighs and smoothed the material. "Maybe because it
still doesn't make sense to me. Sometimes you talk about loss
of free will and sometimes you call it a bond. It sounds like
two different things."

This puzzled David. He thought he had just finished explaining it thoroughly. She wasn't usually so obtuse. But perhaps he still hadn't made himself clear. "By bond I mean that
we'd be on the same mental wavelength. You'd be able to feel
what I felt, and I'd be able to feel what you felt. We would be
extremely close, a psychic intimacy between us. You would
feel an intense need to please me, to be with me. In addition,
if I chose, I would be able to impose my will on you, and you
would automatically obey me. That's what I mean by loss of
free will."

"And would I be able to impose my will on you?"

"No."

"Why?"

"Because I'm the vampire. You would be something of a
slave to me, I'm afraid. That's why initiation isn't something
to fool with just for the experience. It changes you forever."

He studied her face for her reaction. She seemed careful not to let her expression reveal anything and kept a placid exterior.

Then she smiled. "You've already changed me forever, David. I can't see anything so awful about being your 'slave.' It sounds romantic, even erotic. As for having a psychic bond with you, that intrigues me even more. Won't we understand one another better if we have a bond? Maybe we wouldn't have to waste time trying to get through to one another as we are right now."

He had to admire her agile mind. He moved his elbow to the table at his side and leaned on it. "You're right, we would understand one another better."

"Well, don't you want that?" she asked, eyes widening brightly. "I do. I want to be close to you. I love you and I want to understand you better, how you exist, what you feel. You're very complex. I want to really *know* you. And what's wonderful is that I could know you that way, better than I could ever know a mortal man, because you can form this unusual bond with me. You try to paint it in such scary, negative terms, but I see it as a positive thing."

David leaned forward. "Alexandra, you're very independent. I'm telling you you would lose your free will to me. That should upset you."

She pointed her forefinger at him. "But you said you wouldn't take advantage of that power. Well, I trust you."

"But once I initiated you, there would be no going back. You would have that attachment to me as long as you lived. If we separated, it might fade, but it would never go away."

"I can live with that," she replied. She took his hand in both of hers. "David, I want you to do it. Initiate me. I want to enhance and deepen our relationship. I'll feel very hurt if you deny me that closeness. Why did you tell me about it, unless you wanted to present it to me as a choice? Well, I choose initiation."

David had to question himself. Had he told her because he wanted her to have the choice? He didn't know, couldn't think it through just now. She argued so intelligently, with such sincerity, she took him off-balance. "I need to consider this yet, and you should, too."

Disappointment clouded Alexandra's expression, but she covered it quickly. "All right. I will. You're sweet to be so careful about what you do. I know you hesitate in order to protect me, and I love you all the more for thinking of my welfare first. But the more you think about it, I know the more you'll see that this step is right for us. We both love the arts, we enjoy our discussions about music and literature, we're already so much on the same wavelength. I can't see any harm in forming this bond with you, because it will only enhance what we already cherish."

David couldn't help but be moved by her argument. To understand her sense of craftsmanship, to be able to take on her love of classical music, to feel what she felt when listening to Beethoven—how it would broaden his cultural sensitivity, his intellect! Through her he could pull himself into an artistic sphere he'd never been able to enter before.

"Ah, I can see I've begun to make you understand the advantages I see," she said. She got up from the stool and placed her hands on his shoulders. He looked up at her beautiful face as she smiled down. "But I won't push you. I want you to be sure, too, David. We've talked about this enough for now. Shall we go to bed?" She bent and kissed him, her mouth warm and loving, almost worshipful. "At least give me that closeness now, until we can share a stronger bond."

She unbuttoned her blouse and opened it, revealing her bare breasts. David felt in a pleasant spin and brought his hands up from her waist to caress her. He leaned forward to kiss her nipple. The soft pink nub hardened beneath his lips and David grew aroused. He stood and took her roughly in his arms to kiss her mouth. She clung to him, warm and pliant.

"David, David," she murmured, drawing her lips away. She grazed his cheek with hers, moving her hand up his shoulder to the back of his head. She ruffled his hair with her fingers. Then she tilted her head to one side and put pressure on the back of his head, urging him to lower his mouth to her bare neck.

Instinctively David's mouth hit her pulse point. He could feel the pulse, the blood vibrating through her. He could almost smell her blood. Opening his mouth slightly, he put the tip of his tongue at her artery. The urge to bite, to taste, threatened to overwhelm him.

"Do it, David," she said in an urgent whisper. "Drink from me."

Instantly David drew away and looked at her. He could see fear in her stunned face. Probably from the strong vampiric glow he knew must be in his eyes from his desire.

"Don't try to trick me into initiating you, Alexandra." He felt angry and his voice showed it. "I won't be seduced!"

She looked thunderstruck. "No, I— I wasn't trying to trick you. I just can't stop thinking about how it would feel to have you drink from me. What it would mean for us. And I want to give you sustenance. I forgot myself, that's all. I'm sorry, David. I'm sorry. Please don't be angry."

There were tears in her eyes. David's sudden wrath subsided and he took her back into his arms. He wasn't sure what to think. He wanted to believe her. He'd never seen her in tears, other than after sex, and he knew she felt badly. He decided it must have been an act of desire on her part. Clearly he had to keep better control of himself from now on. He'd almost taken her blood. Only her eagerness had stopped him.

"It's all right," he said, running his hand up her back. He slipped her blouse down her arms and removed it. He cupped her breasts with his hands and massaged her nipples with his thumbs. She closed her eyes with pleasure as a tear ran down her cheek.

"I'll make love with you now," he told her with a little kiss. "But nothing more."

She opened her blue eyes, bright with wetness, shining with gratitude. "Anything you give me of yourself, I cherish," she whispered, earnest and heartfelt. "I love you. I need to be with you. As close as you'll allow. That's all I want—You."

10

Sex, wits, or willpower

DARIENNE SAT in the tenth row watching as Matthew, his leading lady, and other performers walked through an elaborate ballroom scene in makeup and costumes. Tonight they were finishing up a technical rehearsal to work out the pattern in which the actors moved onstage as they sang, to make sure costumes didn't get caught on props, to see if the computer and the lighting still needed adjusting. Darienne had gleaned this information from listening to Merle, Loni, the choreographer, and the director. They all sat together, consulting with one another and making suggestions to the actors and computer technicians.

Darienne was staying out of the way tonight. She'd decided it best not to interfere. She was eager to watch Matthew, and thinking about anything else became a distraction. He'd become her constant focal point. Dressed in lavender, playing the fop complete with lace handkerchief and raised eyebrow, he was reciting an inane rhyme Sir Percy had written. According to the story line, Sir Percy behaved this way in aristocratic circles to camouflage his secret identity as the Scarlet Shadow.

Matthew played the scene to the hilt, using his comedic talents, yet never losing his underlying intensity, the sense of vampiric danger in his stage presence, in the mysterious way he moved. The more Darienne saw of Matthew, the more fascinated she grew.

After her fiasco with him the night of the auction, Darienne had kept some distance the last few nights. But she'd decided that it was time she had another go at him, and she grew impatient for the rehearsal to be over. Already she was planning her strategy.

She'd learned that he usually walked home. He owned a car but liked to get exercise walking. Tonight she would stop by his dressing room while Wendy removed his makeup and engage him in a discussion about acting or some safe topic. When he was ready to leave, she'd walk out with him, keeping him wrapped up in conversation. Before he realized it they'd arrive at his apartment. There, she'd get him to invite her in again . . .

Or—why not pretend to be dumbfounded that she'd walked all that way with him, when she'd meant to go home? A gentleman, especially a Southern gentleman, wouldn't allow a lady to walk home after dark. He'd offer to drive her. When they got to her place, she'd coax him to come up, see where she lived. Oh, this was definitely a better plan. On her territory, he'd be trapped . . .

"Darienne."

She was engrossed watching Matthew as she contemplated her tactics and barely heard her name at first.

"Darienne?"

She turned to find David taking the aisle seat next to hers. "Well, you're here! Does Alexandra have a headache tonight?"

David's dark brows drew together. "I decided it best if we were apart for a bit. How's the show going?"

Darienne looked up at the stage. "Matthew's wonderful."

"What about the computer, the lighting?"

"I haven't noticed anything wrong. But then I haven't really been paying attention."

"You've been here every night, haven't you?"

"Yes." She barely took her gaze from Matthew for a half second to glance at David's confused face. "You told me, *cheri,* that I know nothing about the theater. I've discovered you were right. It looks fine to me, but all I look at is Matthew."

"Are you still pestering him?"

"Are you still involved with Alexandra?"

When she didn't get any retort, Darienne turned to look at David more fully. She saw a troubled aspect in his face, but such an expression was not unusual for him. She wasn't in the mood to listen to his angst.

"I told Alexandra," he said, keeping his voice low.

"Told her what?" she asked, looking at the stage again.

"About me."

"Did you," she muttered.

"She wants me to initiate her."

"Oh." Darienne watched Matthew approach his leading lady. While outwardly portraying foppish boredom and disinterest, he revealed Sir Percy's underlying passion for her by his subtle hand movements and a certain sensual, liquid quality he instilled in his singing voice. Their duet was exquisite, her lovely voice blending perfectly with his.

The director stopped them, however, shouting that Elaine, the actress playing Marguerite, was showing too much interest in Sir Percy. In this scene she was supposed to show disdain. Darienne smiled to herself. If she were playing Marguerite, she'd have the same problem.

"Did you hear what I said?" David asked.

"What?" Darienne said, annoyed.

"Alexandra—"

"David, I don't give a damn about Alexandra. If you have to keep seeing her, then do what you want. I have no more advice to give you. You never listen anyway."

"All right," he replied in a tight voice.

At that point, Merle, in the front row, turned around and spotted David. Immediately, the producer rose from his seat and hurried up the aisle to where they were sitting.

"Have you been sick again?" he asked with concern.

"No," David replied. "Preoccupied with personal business. Sorry. How are things going?"

Merle lifted his hands in a helpless gesture. "We get one thing solved, something else happens. Listen," he said, squatting next to David's seat. "Matthew met a disk jockey from a local radio station at the auction. The guy invited him on his talk show. It's tonight."

Darienne's ears perked up. Tonight?

"Matthew remembered the stipulations you put in his contract about permission and asked where he could find you," Merle continued. "I told him I didn't know. We waited a few days. You never showed up and you never answered my phone messages. So I took the responsibility and gave him permission. He was anxious to do it, and I think it's great publicity. He's going to bring the tapes he just recorded."

Darienne had heard something about the tapes. They wanted to release both Matthew's songs from the show quickly, hoping they would become popular with the Chicago stations and increase interest in the musical. But David traditionally discouraged media interviews with actors in his shows, always fearing his secret might eventually be revealed if too many questions were asked.

David remained silent for a moment. "Yes, that's fine," he said at last. "If I remind Matthew not to talk about me, I know I can trust him."

"I already did," Merle said. "He understood. There are questions about himself he's going to insist they don't ask, too."

"Then I trust Matthew completely."

Merle exhaled, visibly relieved, and ran his hand over his fuzzy gray head.

"How's your ulcer?" David asked.

"In a holding pattern."

All at once there were shouts, a few screams, and laughter coming from the front of the theater. Darienne's eyes were glued to Matthew, and she didn't see what was wrong at first. She opened her mouth in astonishment.

The guillotine had suddenly come on stage in the wrong scene. More than that, its shiny blade was moving up and down nonstop. On the other side of the stage, a brick building had appeared and was moving back and forth. Both these incongruous objects from the previous scene intruded on the glamorous ballroom set. The actors had all stopped singing and everyone looked around in amazement, including Matthew.

"The computer's gone crazy!" Merle said.

"Shut the damn thing off!" Charlie, the director, was shouting at the top of his lungs. "What the hell's the matter?"

"Oh, jeez," Merle sighed. "Come on, David. We'd better calm him down."

"Right," David replied. The two men left Darienne and joined the chaos. In moments the actors were asked to leave the stage. When they couldn't get the guillotine and building to move back off stage, they dismissed everyone, since the rehearsal was nearly finished anyway.

Glad for the early dismissal, Darienne hurried toward Matthew's dressing room. There she found not only Wendy, but Elaine with Matthew. They were still in costume, laughing at what had happened. Darienne stepped back, remaining near the doorway but out of their sight, waiting and listening.

"Gosh!" Elaine exclaimed in her delicate, high voice. "I don't believe what happened. Will this show come together?"

"Sure it will," Matthew replied.

"Our duet was going so well, too, when the guillotine went berserk."

"It has an ego of its own," Matthew joked. "Doesn't want to be upstaged."

"Will you rehearse with me again tomorrow morning? I still need to work at matching my style to yours. I love what you showed me about the breathing and phrasing, but I haven't got it down yet."

"Sure. I enjoy singing with you."

"You've been so helpful." Elaine's voice sounded shy now. "I really appreciate it."

"I know what it's like to prepare for your first big role, Elaine. Just remember that they chose you because they knew you could do it."

"Charlie keeps saying I need to look stronger in my scenes with you. I'm not sure what he means."

"You do avoid my face sometimes. James Cagney once said, plant your feet on the ground, look 'em in the eye, and tell the truth. It's good advice. Maybe if you keep that in mind—"

Elaine's voice changed and grew hurried. "I don't think I could do that. Look, I'd better go. You've got to change and get to that radio station. See you tomorrow, okay?"

"Good-night," Matthew said, sounding a bit surprised.

Elaine almost ran into Darienne as she turned out of the open doorway. "Oh, sorry," she said, pushing the wide skirts of her ornate, pale blue, low-cut gown out of the way. Her doe-like eyes looked startled and skittish beneath the heavy black eyeliner and false eyelashes applied for the stage.

"It's all right," Darienne said with a smile. "I'm Darienne Victoire, one of the show's investors. You're Elaine?"

"Elaine Seaton. I noticed you around. Nice to meet you." She put out her small hand and Darienne shook it cordially. She was glad to have a chance to talk to the actress.

"You have a beautiful singing voice."

"Thank you," Elaine said. "I'm just thrilled to have this part."

"And a little petrified, too, I'll bet," Darienne said in a sympathetic tone. She seemed quite a guileless, almost naive young woman. Her manner reminded Darienne of Veronica, when she'd first met David.

"I admit I'm scared to death. But Matthew says you never stop being scared."

"How old are you?"

"Twenty-three. I understand David de Morrissey wanted someone young for the role. Is that what you're wondering? Why they picked me? I have a good voice range. I know I don't have that much stage experience, but—"

Darienne touched her wrist. "I'm not questioning their choice in the least. But I have the feeling *you're* wondering why they picked you. Have confidence in yourself. You're a perfect Marguerite. You look lovely onstage with Matthew, too."

The young woman's eyes brightened. "Thank you. He's been so sweet. He's just . . . well, I've never met anyone like him."

"I haven't gotten to know him yet," Darienne said carefully. "What makes him special?"

Elaine glanced downward, inclining her head in a sensitive manner. "He's so caring and gentle. When he gives advice, there's so much warmth and reassurance in his voice. He really wants you to do your best, and he makes you feel it's for your sake, more than for the show." She looked up. "He has a lot of depth and philosophy and things like that," she said, unconsciously twisting her fingers. "I don't even know how to describe . . . he's sort of spiritual, you know?" Elaine's golden brown eyes searched Darienne's, alive and questioning.

"Spiritual," Darienne repeated.

"Well, maybe that's not the word. I don't know. He's wise and mature and knows things."

"Like a father?"

"Yes . . ." Elaine's eyes grew troubled. "No, I don't think of him as a father."

No, you couldn't, Darienne thought. She smiled. "He doesn't look like a father, does he?"

Elaine laughed. "No. He looks younger than he is . . ." Her smile faded.

"I heard someone say that you're engaged." Darienne injected excitement in her tone. "Are you getting married soon?"

The frail actress looked lost for a moment beneath her thick makeup and elaborate wig. "We haven't set a date. I've been tied up with the show."

"You've been working very hard," Darienne agreed. "Well, I didn't mean to keep you. You must be anxious to change and go home. I've enjoyed talking with you."

"I have, too," Elaine said with a sincere smile. "Bye. See you again, I hope." She walked down the hall to her dressing room, slender, graceful, and shy in the way she moved.

She'd given Darienne a few things to contemplate, but Darienne put their conversation aside to think about later. She had something more immediate to consider: how to handle Matthew. She knew she wanted to go to the radio station with him. How fascinating it would be to observe him being interviewed. But would he let her?

When she walked into his dressing room, he was out of costume, sitting in his chair, and Wendy was busy rubbing off his makeup. The door to his inner room was open; in the subdued lighting, the green candle burned brightly. Darienne quickly walked over to her position to one side of his mirror, facing his chair.

He looked up, startled. "I didn't see you come through the door."

Darienne knew it was because the only way he could see the door was through the mirror. "I move fast. I hear you're going to be on the radio tonight."

"Yes." He closed his eyes as Wendy carefully wiped the makeup off his lids.

"Are you nervous?"

"Oh, a little."

"Want some moral support?"

His eyes opened and grew sharp. "You want to come?"

Where was the nurturing warmth Elaine had described? "I've never been to a radio station. Would I be in your way?" Darienne asked in as meek a voice as her stomach would allow.

"No, I suppose not," he said, his tone polite and measured. "Of course. Come along."

In a little while the makeup was off. Matthew showered and changed while Darienne waited, chatting with Wendy. He came out of the inner room, then paused and turned back again to blow out his candle.

"What's the candle for?" Darienne asked as she walked out of the theater with him.

"Just a superstition," he said. "Actors get that way after a while."

"What sort of superstition? What does the candle mean?"

He smiled as if mildly embarrassed. "My co-star on 'Rick and Rosie' once told me green is the color of health. She believed that if you light a green candle it draws health to you. I was getting injured a lot doing stunts back then."

"Did it work?"

"Sometimes it seemed to. I don't know if it helped me draw on a higher power, or just helped me rely on my body's ability to heal itself. But it got to be a habit. I'm afraid to stop."

"So you keep one lit all the time?"

"When I'm at the theater."

"You have one at home, too," Darienne said as they reached the underground parking area reserved for actors.

"Yes, sometimes I light it in the evening and meditate— pray, if you like. It makes me feel more whole, more focused. I'll start going through that ritual in my dressing room before each performance, now, I think."

Darienne was reminded of Elaine's word for him—spiritual. Matthew had so many facets, she didn't know where to begin to figure him out. But what a fascinating puzzle!

She sat in the passenger seat of his Jaguar as he drove to the station. Darienne discovered that his spiritual side disappeared behind the wheel. He drove fast, racing yellow lights, zooming from lane to lane and whipping around corners. This was a man who worried about his health? She grabbed her armrest more than once during the ten-minute ride.

When they reached the station, they were ushered into a glass-walled cubicle and introduced, while a record played, to the host of the late-night show, Sid Dorset. He was a young man, tall and overweight, with blue eyes and a baby face, his brown hair mussed beneath his headset. He wore a plain short-sleeved shirt and pants. When he spoke, his voice came as a shock; it was low, resonant, and calm.

"Pleased to meet you both. Darienne, you can sit here and watch," he said, pointing to an upholstered metal chair. "Matthew, you'll have to sit at the table with me. Here's a headset. You'll be on from ten to ten-thirty. Got the tapes of your songs?"

"Here," Matthew said, pulling two small cassettes out of his shirt pocket. "And we agreed—no personal questions about David de Morrissey or myself."

"Agreed."

Darienne settled herself in her chair. She eyed with fascination the microphones, the large wall clock, and all the broadcasting equipment. Soon 10 P.M. arrived. After a few commercials, Sid introduced Matthew to the radio audience. Sid's show combined music with a talk-show format, and he smoothly plunged Matthew into an interview. After asking some general questions about the upcoming musical, he asked Matthew to explain the show's unusual story line.

"It's taken after *The Scarlet Pimpernel* by Baroness Orczy," Matthew said, "the story of an Englishman who helps rescue innocent French aristocrats from going to the guillotine during the French Revolution. But in our show he's called the Scarlet Shadow, and he's a vampire."

"I know David de Morrissey has written other vampire plays, but why did he choose to put a vampire in this?" Sid asked.

"It adds to the story and character," Matthew replied. "The Scarlet Shadow—his real name is Sir Percy Blackeney—uses his vampiric strength and special powers in his nighttime rescues. And he atones for being a vampire by saving lives. Sir Percy suffers huge guilt about what he is."

"Now, you're known, of course, for your comedy roles. 'Rick and Rosie' made you a household name a few years ago," Sid said, leaning into his microphone. "Why did you decide to play a vampire at this point in your career? Were you afraid of typecasting?"

"Typecasting is always a problem. But I wanted a chance to sing. Not many people know I can. And I haven't done many dramatic roles, either."

"Isn't it quite a jump from comedy to drama?"

"Not really. They're closely related. Rick, for example, was actually a rather sad character. He was lonely, shy, in need of love. And he was hopelessly clumsy. Because he was so inept, in social situations he felt like an outsider. He couldn't fit in. The vampire is also an outsider, different from everyone else, alone."

Darienne listened quietly, aware as she hadn't been before of the vast difference between herself and Matthew. David always pondered over his sense of alienation, but Darienne usually didn't give it much thought. She'd always enjoyed her vampire existence. But for some reason, Matthew made her unusually conscious now that she was unlike any other woman he'd ever known.

"Isn't there a difference in how you play comedy vs. drama?" Sid asked.

"I had to play Rick as though everything that happened to him was real. Rick never knew the humor of his situations because every time he fell off a chair or over a coffee table, he was truly hurt and embarrassed. I play Sir Percy the same way. He may be a melodramatic character, but I play him as if his situation and pain were completely real."

"Just for the record, do you believe in vampires?" Sid asked with a smile.

Matthew's broad grin appeared. "No. But I've nailed a few cloves of garlic around my door, just in case."

Unobserved, Darienne looked askance while Sid laughed. Mortals had invented such silly ideas. Their ignorance sometimes took away her sense of dignity.

"Now about all those file cabinets that fell on Rick, and the library ladders and moving escalators he tumbled down," Sid continued. "I've read you insist on doing your own stunts all the time. Your co-star once said you'd do anything for the show even if it killed you."

"I get possessive about my characters. I can't stand to see a stuntman pretending to be me. Especially when I feel I can do the thing myself. I've never minded a few bruises."

"What about broken bones and pulled tendons? You've had a few of those, too."

"Yes, it's true."

"I get the feeling—tell me if I'm wrong—that you're an intense man. You focus on things to a high degree."

"I have a high energy level, if that's what you mean. Yes, I do focus. A one-track mind, that's me," Matthew said with a chuckle.

"Well, let's hear one of your songs." He asked Matthew to explain what was happening in the story line when Sir Percy sings "She Can Never Be Mine" and then played the tape. As Matthew's singing voice came on, the two men leaned back in their seats and relaxed.

"Interview's going well," Sid said.

Matthew nodded and glanced at Darienne. She was glad to see he remembered she was there. She smiled at him.

"Bored?" he asked.

"Not at all," she replied. "This is exciting!"

"But you already know all my answers."

How she wished that were true. "Not about 'Rick and Rosie,' " she replied. She leaned toward Sid and gave the young man a mischievous *entre nous* look. "Why don't you ask Matthew about his rib cage?"

"Excuse me?"

"In *The Boy from Savannah* he was thin from head to toe. Now he's got a large chest cavity. I think it has to do with his singing."

Sid looked thoughtful but hesitant. As Matthew put his chin in the palm of his hand and leaned on the table, Sid turned to him and said, "It's a great question. Too personal?"

"No, you can ask me that," Matthew replied with equanimity. "She's not the first to wonder about it."

"Okay. I'm going to ask you to do the weather report first though." Sid handed Matthew some copy to read. "I always ask my guests to do this. It makes the weather more interesting for the audience. Mind?"

Matthew made the most stunning grin Darienne had yet seen as he took the paper. "It'll bring back old times. I used to be a disc jockey."

Darienne was amazed. Sid's eyes brightened, too. When the song and the commercials were over, he introduced Matthew's weather report.

Matthew read tomorrow's forecast smoothly in his gentle voice, talking about warm fronts and humidity and overcast skies clearing by afternoon. Darienne thought he was adorable.

When he'd finished, Sid said, "You read that like a pro."

"I worked as a disc jockey for a year at a small station in Atlanta. I was seventeen."

"After school?"

"Yes. The family needed money."

"How did you get the part for *The Boy from Savannah?*"

"They'd sent a casting agent to Georgia to find someone who had the right look and accent. I was in a school play and he spotted me. It was the easiest role I ever got."

"Did that give you the idea of making your living as an actor?"

"Yes, I was hooked after that."

"Now, someone wanted me to ask you about your chest size. She mentioned, correctly, that in your first film you looked thin, but now you have a stout rib cage. Is it from singing?"

"Exactly. Many singers develop it from singing and breathing exercises. As the lung capacity expands, the cartilage of the rib cage stretches to accommodate the lungs. The result is, I can hold a note forever, but I have trouble finding shirts that fit. The buttons tend to burst when I breathe."

Darienne smiled and averted her face.

The disc jockey chuckled. "Do you have to do a warm-up before you perform?"

"I'm trying to decide what my schedule will be before performances. I'll need at least forty minutes of vocal warm-up. Maybe a half hour of physical warm-up. And that's in addition to getting my makeup on."

"I hear you're going to be a blond vampire."

"Yes, we felt Sir Percy should look pale, English, and aristocratic. Very handsome, except for his paleness. So they had to change my face, you see."

"Can you do the vocal exercises while they put on your makeup?"

"No, no. I have to sit very still. Or I might get blown away."

"What do you mean?"

"Wendy, my makeup artist, gets annoyed with me if I start to fidget. If I don't watch myself, she'll get back at me by dabbing too much powder on my nose and making me sneeze. Never argue with a woman who has a powder puff in her hand."

Darienne's eyes widened. She'd never heard *this* before.

Sid was laughing. "I'll remember that. What about vampire teeth? I know Sam Taglia wore long incisors in *Street Shadows.*"

"I couldn't if I was going to sing properly. We decided to overlook that, let the audience use their imagination."

"Speaking of singing properly, let's play your second song." He asked Matthew to introduce it, and they relaxed again as the music played.

Matthew checked his watch. "Aren't we almost done?"

"I'll wrap up after the song ends. Anything you'd like to add?"

Matthew glanced at Darienne, then shook his head. "Just remind them when the show opens. But don't mention the price of the tickets. They're a little steep."

"You bet."

The show wound up smoothly. Sid thanked Matthew on the air, said goodbye to Darienne off the air, and soon they were racing home in Matthew's car.

"Can I drop you somewhere?" Matthew asked as he swung around a corner.

"Yes," she said, holding on. "The John Hancock."

"You live in the Hancock? What floor?"

"The ninety-first."

Matthew chuckled. "I think my nose would bleed living that high up."

The thought of his blood made Darienne's pulse jump. Her mouth watered. Clutching the armrest, she made an effort to get hold of herself. He was far too tempting for her to even entertain the thought. Sex was all she could allow herself—if she could get even that from him.

She put her fingers to her mouth and closed her eyes for a moment.

"You all right?"

"Yes," she said, trying to sound calm though her pulse was still irregular. "The interview went well. You were charming."

"Thanks. Sid's a good interviewer, though I have to say it was your question that made it 'up close and personal.' "

"I thought listeners would want to know what I wanted to know."

"You think everyone is fascinated with my chest measurement?"

Darienne smiled. *"Mais oui.* The ladies, anyway. It's a natural feminine thought pattern. Just as, if your hormones are in working order, I imagine you would be equally fascinated with my chest."

There, she thought, let him deal with that one! She stared at him as he drove, daring him to respond.

Matthew remained expressionless, his eyes on the road. "I think *your* hormones may be overworked."

"You haven't answered my question," she persisted.

"You didn't ask one. You made a statement."

"Do you agree with my statement?"

He drew in his breath silently. "You're beautiful, Darienne. And you have an astonishing structure. Why do you need so much male affirmation?"

"Affirmation isn't what I'm looking for," she told him in a straightforward voice.

"You can't always have what you want."

"Oh, yes, I can," she replied, simply stating a fact.

He peered out the window. "That's the Hancock up ahead, isn't it?"

"Yes. I'll direct you where to park."

He shot a glance at her. "I'm just dropping you off."

"You don't walk a lady to her door?"

He pulled up in front of the black skyscraper, but kept the motor running. "I'll watch to make sure you get inside the building safely."

She looked at him, miffed. "Your fans would be disappointed if they knew how ill-mannered you can be."

His eyes remained tranquil as they connected with hers. "I don't live for my fans."

"Be careful what you say. I'm a fan, too, remember."

"I'm always careful what I say to you."

Darienne stared back at him. "Do you dislike me?"

"No. In fact, it's fascinating to watch you operate."

"What a crass choice of words," she exclaimed. "I'm getting to know you, not 'operating.' "

"Well, then, the way you 'get to know' a person is interesting to observe. And observe is all I want to do."

"So passive!"

"As I said on the radio, I have a one-track mind. I don't like complications when I'm involved in an important project."

"And you think I would be a complication? Why?"

"Gut feeling."

She nodded. "So you trust caution more than impulse. Yet onstage, you tap into your hidden impulses. And you come alive in a way you aren't offstage."

"Real life is different than theater."

"I disagree," she said, leaning toward him. "I live as if I were onstage all the time."

He chuckled as if genuinely amused. "That's a good way to describe yourself!"

"You ought to try it," she said. "Be the sensual Shadow in reality. I'd love to see some passion in you, off the stage."

He calmly stared at her again. "Why?"

"I like variety and experiences. You're different. I want to understand your personality."

"Why?"

"Because you're complicated. You're a human chameleon. I want to see all your colors."

"But why?"

Darienne inhaled, keeping her patience. She knew what he was doing. Short-circuiting her with a broken-record tactic. And it was working. She was stumped, couldn't keep the upper hand with him. He was the first man she couldn't override by using sex, wits, or willpower.

"Maybe you should go up to your apartment and think about why you do what you do, Darienne. You're single-minded and purposeful, but underneath I think you're mixed up." He added in a soft, but authoritative tone, "Now, say good-night and go home."

He spoke to her as if she were a child. What's more he made her *feel* like a child. Thoroughly undone, she could think of no retort. Not one. What was it about him?

Trying to retain her dignity, she said, "Good-night" and got out of the car. As she walked toward the glass entrance doors, her temper grew. She realized he'd more or less humiliated her. Again. Her, Darienne!

Well, she wasn't done with him. She'd find the drawbridge across his moat yet. There must be one somewhere!

* * *

The next evening, David rose from his coffin, went to the third floor, and began getting ready to see Alexandra. As he bathed and dressed he pondered whether or not he should initiate her. Part of him warned that it wouldn't be wise to do so. From past experience, he knew the bond had a different effect on each woman. Some became so clinging, so obsessed with him that he lost respect for them. Some became confused and lost touch with their own personalities. On the other hand, some blossomed with the positive reinforcement of his personality bonded to theirs. Veronica had reacted this way, though she was also plagued with confusion about herself. She'd been too young to deal with his impact on her life.

But, as he'd noted before, Alexandra was not too young. She was a woman who knew who she was and what she wanted. He could be quite certain she wouldn't cling to him excessively or become confused about her place in the world. In fact, it intrigued David to find out just how she would react. It might not affect her much at all.

And what she could offer him! A new window to the world from a female who appreciated art and culture better than he in many ways. Wasn't it like Alexandra to know just what she could offer him, too!

Only, it bothered him that she seemed so eager, that she'd tried to coax him into taking her blood. Well, perhaps he'd overreacted. Alexandra was in love with him and she probably got carried away with emotion. Her tears were genuine enough when she'd apologized. Darienne would probably form a different opinion, but that didn't matter. She didn't care anyway.

David chuckled as he buttoned his white shirt. It confounded him to imagine why the two remarkable blondes had formed such a mindset against each other. He supposed it was jealousy. Not over him so much as over territory. Neither could tolerate another star as bright as she in the same sky.

Still, it seemed beneath Alexandra's intellect to hold such contempt. And until now, Darienne had always been quite generous about allowing another beauty to intrude her sphere. Well, it was no use trying to analyze the female mind. If their mutual mistrust made sense to them, there was nothing he could do about it. Except be amused.

* * *

"You will?" Alexandra felt at once so jubilant, and at the same time so suddenly filled with anxiety, that she braced herself against her worktable for support.

"Are you all right?" David asked, putting a hand on her shoulder.

"Fine! Just surprised, that's all. You were so hesitant about it before."

"I decided you were right. Initiation can only enhance our relationship." He gazed at her with empathy. *"You* look a little hesitant now. Are you afraid?"

"No," she said quickly. "I want to do this. It's just . . . will it hurt?"

"Only briefly. A little pinprick. We can do it while we make love, and you won't even notice."

Alexandra shook her head. Pain or no pain, she wanted to be aware of what he was doing every second. "I'd like to experience the initiation by itself, without any distraction."

His brows drew together and he brushed some tendrils of hair away from her face. "You're sure?"

"Positive," she said, touched by his caring manner. Gentleness was so much a part of his nature, she sensed she had nothing to fear. "How do we go about this? Should we be sitting? Standing? Lying down?"

"Sitting or lying down," David replied. "There's a chance you might become light-headed for a few moments."

"Let's go upstairs then," she said, and they climbed the staircase to her bedroom, arms around each other. Alexandra's heart began to beat with anticipation. She was embarking on an adventure, an adventure that could lead to immortality. What would this first step be like?

She wore a knit top with a boat-shaped neckline. As they sat down on the edge of the bed, David turned to her and ran his fingertips along her neck. His touch gave her a soft, hot, shimmering feeling, and she began to breathe faster.

"Should I take this off?"

"No need to."

His fingers stopped at her pulse point. She looked up and saw the keen, cobalt glow in his eyes, growing more vibrant even as she watched. She'd never seen his eyes quite so fearsome. "David," she said, edging away slightly despite her

eagerness to go through with the vampiric act. "Your eyes
. . ."

"I'm sorry. I'm not trying to frighten you. It's an involun-
tary reaction. Whenever I'm emotional. Or aroused. Close
your eyes, if you feel more comfortable."

"No, I want to see. I'm not afraid," she said, leaning closer
to him. He tilted his head to the side and began to slowly bend
toward her. She could feel his breath on her neck as his fingers
left her pulse point. He slipped his arms around her and pulled
her closer, until her breasts met his chest. She raised her chin
and arched her neck to the back and side, leaving herself
completely vulnerable to him.

She did close her eyes then, while her chest began to rise and
fall with each anticipatory breath. Suddenly she felt his burning lips against her pulse point and she gasped aloud. And
then there was a deft, sharp little pain which made her inhale
deeply. She held her breath for a long moment.

All at once she began to feel so sensually giddy and euphoric that tears filled her eyes. She exhaled slowly, with such
longing that the moment never end, that she felt as if she were
melting into David. Moving her arms around him, she held on
tightly, wanting her body never again to be extricated from
his. She felt the sucking motions of his mouth, felt the lick of
his tongue now and then, heard him swallow. And it gave her
such pleasure beyond belief that she was nourishing him, that
he craved her to this extent, that he could feed from her.

And now she felt herself growing deliciously languid and
cherished the strength of his arms supporting her. She felt as
if she were whirling slowly downward, downward, until something soft came up to meet her back and head. And David's
body pressed against hers now, its weight so comforting and
fulfilling that if she had died right then she would have had no
regrets. And now her arms were growing limp, and they
slipped from his body and floated on either side of her. And
all she was aware of was his suckling mouth and his weight
and the peaceful oneness she felt. Oneness with David, whom
she adored with all her body, intellect, and heart . . . whom she
could never again be separated from. For if she were, she
would surely vanish.

Her brows constricted in torment when his mouth left her
throat. "No," she whimpered, trying to pull him back to her.

But he resisted and lifted his weight off of her. She felt so bereft it pained her.

"Are you all right?" he asked.

She opened her eyes and saw his face hovering over hers. She realized she was lying back on her bed, her head on her pillow. He was sitting beside her. It startled her that she couldn't remember moving to this position.

"How do you feel?" he asked. He'd taken out his handkerchief to wipe his mouth. He pressed the cloth to her throat.

"All right, I guess," she murmured with some confusion. "It's not over already—"

"It's over, Alexandra. I dare not take any more from you."

She noticed now how rich a blue his eyes were and how his lids were pink-rimmed and how the color of his cheeks brimmed with health. And then she realized that while her body felt limp and languid, she could also feel a profound energy which seemed a part of herself, yet outside herself. She reached out to him.

"Hold me, David. I need you to be close to me."

He bent over her and lifted her off the bed. She put her arms around him and began to cry again. Somehow it wasn't good enough. "Drink from me again. Please, David."

"No, I would be taking too much. I know it's difficult right now, but you'll adjust. Our bond is brand new and it will seem overwhelming at first."

Even as he said the words, she could feel a comforting energy coming from him, calming her, as if he were imposing his feelings onto her.

And yet this thought alarmed her. How could it be? How could he—? She remembered his warnings about the loss of free will. Panicking, she pushed away from him. But as she did so, she felt the acute pain of separation from him. "No!" she cried out, trying to impose her will against the inevitable. "No! You can't have done this to me!"

"Alexandra," David said, rising and placing his hands on her shoulders. "Calm down. I've done what you wanted me to do. I told you the consequences and you accepted them."

She stared at him in alarm and his expression changed. "You didn't believe me?" he asked, as if she'd said the words out loud. "I warned you! These are the consequences. There's no going back."

He took his hands from her shoulders. And as he did, she felt again the acute anxiety of separation. She felt so helpless, so completely helpless. She was inextricably tied to him, craving him, subject to his will.

"I won't impose my will on you," he said in a reassuring tone. "I only used my power a moment ago to calm you because you seemed in such a state. Your feelings of insecurity, your desire for me will grow less acute with time. Right now you need patience and trust."

And it appeared he could read her mind, too!

"I can feel your feelings, Alexandra. You can also feel mine, if you try. We have a closer bond now than mortals can ever know. I believe you'll grow to appreciate that." He began to rise from the edge of the bed. "I'm going to get you some water. You need to drink liquids. I'll be back in only a moment. Try to be calm and rest."

She nodded and watched him go. But despite his words of assurance, she felt such a frenzy of panic when he disappeared out the bedroom door, that her rib cage seemed to contract and she felt cold and wretched and alone. And then again she felt an imposed calmness come over her. He was doing it again! He'd just promised not to! She felt as if she were in a prison with David forming the invisible walls and holding the keys. Who was she? She was no longer herself, not if David could control her feelings!

In a moment he was back with a filled glass. He frowned as he handed her the water. "You're still agitated."

"Can you read my every thought?" she asked, angry.

"Only if you consciously send one, just as I can transfer a thought to you. I've only tried to calm you, now in these early moments of our new bond. But if it upsets you, I'll refrain from doing even that."

"Don't *I* have any power?" she asked. "Have you taken everything from me?"

"You have your free will—I won't go back on my promise. You can summon me from a great distance now, just as I can summon you with my mind."

"And if I summoned you, you would have to come?"

"No, I would not have to come. But if I knew you wanted me, I would."

"But if you summon me . . . ?" Alexandra began, afraid of the answer.

"It depends. I could ask you to come or I could will you to come to me. But I will only use the power to ask."

Alexandra found his answer only somewhat reassuring. "How do I use this mental power to call you?"

"Merely envision me and think it."

Feeling dazed, she brought the glass of water to her mouth and took several sips before setting it down. She realized she was thirsty.

"You still haven't told me how you feel," David said. "I sense your strength is good, that you aren't too weak, but I'd like to hear it from you."

"I feel fine," Alexandra said. "Maybe a little tired, that's all." But there was something else she felt and it both excited and troubled her. "I have such a need for you. It's beyond desire."

"Would it help if we—"

"Yes! Please," she said, squeezing his hands. She pulled her knit top over her head then, her body urging her to hurry. As she did, the handkerchief David had placed at her neck fell away and landed in her lap. She was taken aback when she saw the bright red stains. Dizziness threatened to overcome her.

"Don't think about it," David said, grabbing the handkerchief and pushing it into his pocket. "The bleeding has stopped. You're all right." He slid his hand over her bared breast. "We'll make love now. Think about that."

Once she felt his fingers graze over her nipple, she could think of nothing else. A raging need overtook her, an ache in the lower part of her stomach that craved gratification. She tugged at her skirt. "Hurry, David."

He adjusted his clothing and moved over her. She shut her eyes at the intense pleasure of feeling him enter her. As he started sensual, rhythmic thrusts, she moved along with him, deliriously happy. But as his movements grew stronger, more dominating, her old anxieties returned and a part of her did not want to give in to the feeling, while her body begged her to.

"Attach your mind to mine," he whispered. "Dream my

dream with me. You can now. Allow your feelings to bond with mine."

She felt his mind imposing itself on hers. Acute desire weakened her stamina to fight. She relaxed and felt as though she were cutting her mind loose, just as one would cut the rope of a boat to free it from the shore. And she floated with him on her bed, feeling as if it had become a quiet, rippling lake beneath the heat of the sun. Birds chirped, and insects, butterflies, and bees lilted on the warm, rising air.

In the soft, vaporous atmosphere, she lay back with David inside her and felt only the obsessive rhythm of their bodies. All she wanted was to respond to him and give to him. And soon the rhythm and heat began to close in on her, so that she had to gasp for each breath, her chest heaving, her heart pounding against her rib cage. But the sensation didn't frighten her. The heady feeling of sensual claustrophobia became a mental and physical challenge. She felt eager to master and tame it, and she took on the challenge with vibrant energy.

Grasping onto David more tightly, she reveled in every surge of his body, while her mind reeled with ecstatic fervor at the ever-mounting tension. And finally her body reached the brink, the huge precipice before blissful oblivion. But rather than being frightened this time, she felt only that she wanted to jump off the precipice and go with the exploding release.

The experience came like a glorious starburst, with colors dancing all around her while her body convulsed in ecstasy. She cried out with the joy of it, the cataclysmic release of pent-up energy that had waited so long to be free.

Her climaxes continued for several minutes, until, exhausted, she lay back on the pillow smiling.

"Oh, David, you were right," she breathed.

David stroked the hair back from her face and looked down at her lovingly. "Now you know the full experience. You'll never have to go back again."

She kissed his shoulder in a worshipful way, then his mouth. "I love you. I love you," she whispered. "Will we always be together? Will you always be here to give me this gift?"

"If you want me to."

"I'll die if I don't have you with me."

He shook his head. "You won't die without me. You'll be your own person. I'll only support you."

She kissed him again with reverence and felt her eyes grow heavy. She felt so drowsy she could barely move and sank back onto the pillow.

"Rest now. Go to sleep," he said, moving his fingers gently over her eyelids to close them.

The next thing she knew, she opened her eyes to a bright, empty room. Panic overwhelmed her. Where was David? And then she saw the sun was up, and knew where he must be. Instinctively, she focused her mind on him. When she made contact, she felt his profound lethargy and disengaged her mind completely for fear she would fall into it herself, the pull was so strong.

She touched her neck and got up to look in the mirror. A dried smudge of red discolored her throat. Two small wounds, about an inch and a half apart, one above the other, left evidence that all that had happened last night had been true and not a dream. The reality of it excited her. She'd been initiated! She belonged to David. And one day, she might even become immortal, like him. But that could wait. She had enough to deal with just getting used to this experience, for it encompassed her entire being, physically, emotionally, and mentally.

Physically, she felt fine this morning, strong as ever. Emotionally, she felt both ecstatic and anxious. After the profound sexual experience David had given her, her ecstasy was easy to explain. She wasn't sure where the anxiety came from. Perhaps because she still wasn't sure of all the ground rules in the vampiric world she'd entered.

And mentally? Well she wasn't sure she could even define her mental state. She wasn't even sure she owned her own mind anymore. What had David told her? *You'll be your own person. I'll only support you.* Last night the words had comforted her. But now as she thought of them again, she couldn't understand why they had reassured her. How could she truly be her own person if he was supporting her with his psychic influence?

She thought back on their lovemaking. She had reached such heights only because he had fused her feelings to his through their bond. *He* had controlled the situation, not she!

Alexandra felt terrified suddenly. Where was her cherished self-sufficiency? He'd made her dependent on him! Just as he'd warned, she'd become his slave. Even now she felt the longing for him, to be near him, to feel his body on fire with hers, to nourish him with her lifeblood. Why hadn't she listened to his warning?

Sex with David used to lure her and frighten her because losing control was such a shimmering roadblock, beckoning and yet too awful to contemplate. Now he'd brought her through the roadblock on a wave of supernatural ecstasy generated from the core of his own being. And now that she was on the other side, her *whole life* was out of control.

She sank to the floor and curled up against the dresser in confusion and fear. What was she to do? How was she to cope?

Her mind rattled in chaos now, an orchestra gone wild without its conductor. Her mind's new leader lay in a deep, lethargic sleep, leaving her to find her way blindly through the ruins of her overturned life.

She hated David now, even as she craved his presence. Why did she ever want to be immortal? If it weren't for her selfish yearning to live forever, she would still have her quiet, productive little life. Now she behaved like a bereft orphan when David wasn't near, a sensual beggar when he was near. She'd demeaned herself and lost herself.

Nothing, nothing would ever be the same.

11

God, he was stupid!

AT DUSK the next day, David rose from his coffin and went upstairs. He was getting ready to see Alexandra when he heard a noise. Pulling on his shirt, he hurried into the living room.

"There you are," Darienne said, coming from his office, where she'd apparently looked for him. She wore a yellow cotton dress and seemed agitated.

"Is something wrong?" David asked, wondering how long this would take.

"Yes! I'm very upset." She stood in front of him, her blond eyebrows knitted in a worried expression. "It's Matthew. He treats me like a child."

Good for him, David thought, still buttoning his shirt.

"And I go along with it," Darienne continued, starting to pace around him in a fitful manner. "Last night he told me to say good-night and go home. And do you know what I did?"

"What?"

"I said good-night and left. Do you see what I mean, David? I'm behaving like that comedienne on that old TV program . . . oh, you know, it follows 'Rick and Rosie.'"

David shrugged, growing impatient. "I have no idea."

"Gracie Allen," Darienne said. "Her husband says 'Say good-night, Gracie' and she says good-night. Me! I'm behaving like that."

David spread his hands. "What do you want me to do about it? I'm rooting for Matthew."

She looked at him, apparently dumbfounded. "That's all you can say?" Her beautiful eyes grew impatient, injured. "I thought you were my friend! I've come here to confide in you, to tell you I seem to be losing my sense of myself and I don't know why. And all you can say is, 'What do you want me to do about it'? When I think of all the times I've comforted you—"

"All right, all right," David said, settling his hands on her shoulders. Impatient with her though he was, she'd made him feel guilty. "Calm down. It doesn't seem like such a monumental thing to me. You've met a man who's your equal, that's all."

Her eyes flashed. "There are no men who are my equal!"

David's mouth dropped open. She'd been a feminist before the concept was invented, but he'd never seen her this vehement before. "Why are you asking me, a lowly male, for advice then?"

She seemed chastened. "I'm sorry. I didn't mean that the way it sounded. It just shows I'm not my usual self."

"The answer is simple. If Matthew upsets you, then stay away from him."

Darienne gave him an impatient glare. "I thought you would help me analyze this instead of making jokes."

"It wasn't a joke."

"I'm losing my finesse somehow," she went on. "Have you noticed it? Do you see any change in me?"

David studied her. "You look the same to me."

"I don't mean only looks—"

"I don't know, Darienne. You're as independent as ever around me. There must be something about Matthew's personality. Why get so overwrought about it?"

"Here you go again. I come to you for advice, and you minimize my problems!"

"You didn't give me much attention last night when I wanted to talk about Alexandra," he countered.

"Oh, her." Darienne's tone became weary. "What was there to say that I hadn't already said? So what happened?"

"I initiated her."

"What!"

"I initiated her. I told you, she'd asked me to."

"Is that what you—? I wasn't listening."

"I know. You only had eyes and ears for Matthew."

"You initiated her! My God, why, David?"

"Because she loves me," David said, annoyed with Darienne's negative reaction.

"Loves you! She's not capable of the emotion."

"Oh, she isn't?" he taunted. "And love is something you know all about?"

Darienne didn't seem to hear. "What about Veronica?"

"Veronica has begun a life without me."

"At your insistence! What happens when your pact is finished? Have you forgotten your promise to summon her?"

"Of course I haven't forgotten! I just know how it will end. She'll choose mortality. She despises me."

"What if she doesn't?"

David turned away. "That's too much to hope for," he said with quiet sadness.

"But what if she *does* choose you? Don't you see Alexandra will be in the way?"

"How can I say what will happen years from now? I don't anticipate my relationship with Alexandra will last that long."

"David," Darienne said, walking around him to face him, her voice incredulous. "You have a bond with her now."

"The bond will fade."

"How can you say that?" Darienne sounded as if she couldn't believe her ears.

"Veronica has forgotten me," David said, trying to keep his voice steady. "She must have. The bond between us is still in place, but she has managed to go on without me. If she can do it, so can Alexandra, who's a much stronger woman."

"Oh, David, David," Darienne said, shaking her head. "It's because you've never experienced the initiated state. You went from mortal to vampire in one giant leap. You don't know the in-between stage at all."

"I've observed it enough. I know how strong the bond is at first. But it fades if ignored. And Veronica is the proof of that."

"Are you saying this to assuage your guilt about Veronica?"

"Guilt?" David paused to question himself. "I did the correct, the moral thing for Veronica. I'm sorry that she had to suffer our separation, but she's over it now. What have I to feel guilty about? I did the honorable thing and let her go."

Darienne put a hand to each temple, as if his logic made her head swim. "This is all my fault," he heard her whisper. "If I hadn't been so distracted . . ."

She seemed to pull herself together and she looked him in the eye. "What about Alexandra? Did you do the moral thing in initiating her?"

"I don't know," David admitted. "But she convinced me that a bond with me could only benefit both of us."

Darienne nodded, the wise look in her eye seeming to say that she knew better. "When did you initiate her?"

"Last night."

"How did she react?"

"The strong need for me upset her at first, but she was calm and asleep by the time I left."

"How is she today? Have you tuned your mind to hers?"

David paused. "I hadn't thought of it, frankly," he said, surprised at himself. "I'm seeing her in a little while."

Darienne's eyes quickened. "What time is she expecting you?"

"I usually get there about eight. I'm sure she'll be fine, Darienne. In fact, I'm amazed at your concern about her."

"It's not her I'm concerned about, believe me. I'll go now and let you get ready."

"Sorry. I don't mean to rush you. I know you wanted to talk."

"No, no, *cheri,*" she said, taking his hand. "My problem is only temporary, I'm sure. I shouldn't have troubled you. Go finish dressing."

"Good, all right," he said, squeezing her hand. "You see, you're back to your usual, plucky self already. So don't get into a dither about Matthew. And don't worry about Alexandra, either."

"No, I won't worry about her," Darienne said, smiling with assurance now. "Thank you, David," she added sweetly and kissed him on the cheek. Then she headed for the window.

The doorbell surprised Alexandra. She was upstairs trying on a new silk dress to wear for David tonight, aching to see him. Was he early? Her heart leapt at the thought. She zipped the dress up the back, then grabbed a scarf to wrap around her neck in case it was someone else at the door. Though she couldn't imagine who.

When she opened the door, she found herself staring into bright green eyes and a crocodile smile.

"Alexandra," Darienne said, extending her hand as if they were friends. "What a lovely dress. May I come in? I just want to see you for a moment."

"How did you know where I live?"

"I looked in the yellow pages under violin makers." Darienne proceeded to walk in without permission.

Alexandra closed the door behind Darienne and followed her in, annoyed and puzzled. What was this all about? An attempt to make her break up with David, so Darienne could get him back? Fat chance of that now, Alexandra thought, touching her scarf. She might feel deeply unsettled about their new bond, but one thing was certain: She and David were united in a way he couldn't be with Darienne. And then she wondered. Quickly she eyed Darienne's bared throat, devoid of jewelry tonight. She saw no marks that matched her own.

"What could we have to talk about?" Alexandra asked in a dry tone. "David, perhaps?"

Darienne had been looking over the studio, but her eyes alighted on Alexandra's face at the question. "David, perhaps. You, most certainly. Are you happy?"

"With David? Blissfully."

"You enjoy being under his power? Some women do."

"Power?" Alexandra hesitated at the question. Did Darienne know?

"You're not so independent as you used to be, are you?"

"I'm sure I don't know—"

"But I do," Darienne interrupted. "You see, I was in your situation myself once. Many years ago, David initiated me."

Alexandra stared at her, astonished.

"I know what your scarf hides," Darienne said.

"But you don't have any marks."

"Mine healed."

"Healed? But I thought he continued to . . . to . . ."

"Drink from the initiated? Yes, he does, if he chooses. But my situation changed."

Alexandra didn't understand. And then she noticed Darienne's continuing smile, her sharp incisors. She backed away. "You're—?"

"Yes, *oui,*" Darienne said with blithe pride. "You *are* clever."

Alexandra studied her with new eyes. Darienne had immortality, too. "How did you become one?"

"Did David tell you about the blood ceremony?"

"He mentioned it, but wouldn't explain."

"Yes, that's just like him," Darienne said with a chuckle. "What is it?"

"I'd better not tell you either. He'd be angry. Call it interfering and so on. He's very protective of his women. He was that way with me, too, when I was under his power."

"You aren't under his power anymore?" Alexandra asked, wanting beyond anything to know the secret.

"I have power of my own, now. Equal to his."

"Equal?" Alexandra said, breathless.

"Mais oui. I do as I please. I own myself. But I still couple with David. And that is more delicious than you can even imagine."

By coupling, Alexandra assumed she meant sex. For some reason, the news that Darienne still slept with David didn't bother her much. She had more important things to learn.

"How can I find out about the blood ceremony?"

"Did you ever see his play, *Street Shadows?"*

"No."

"Get a copy of it from the library and read it. I'd better go now. David is on his way, and I don't think he'd understand our little visit, *Comprenez-vous?"*

Alexandra nodded. "I understand. But why did you come to see me at all? What's in it for you? You want David all to yourself?"

Darienne turned at the door. "Oh, David doesn't belong to me. I wouldn't want him to. If I were you, I wouldn't waste time worrying about my motivations. We're both clever women. You know how to take care of yourself, and so do I. Enough said. The rest is up to you. By the way," Darienne said, taking Alexandra's hand to look at her ring, "I noticed your beautiful ruby that night at the opera." She fingered the red stone. "I collect gems, you know. This is one of the finest jewels I've seen."

"Thank you," Alexandra said, confused by the change in subject. She pulled her hand away. "It was my mother's."

"Ah, an heirloom. I don't suppose you'd want to part with it then. But if you ever should, call me first, will you? I'll give you my phone number." She took out of her purse a slip of paper on which her number was already written and handed it to Alexandra. "I have an answering machine. You won't be able to reach me during the day, and I'm usually out at night."

"Yes, of course," Alexandra muttered, still astonished at the thought that she now knew *two* vampires. "I have no plans to sell my ring, though."

Darienne smiled and pulled open the door. "Plans sometimes change. Goodbye."

"Goodbye," Alexandra said as the door shut. She looked down at the phone number in her hand, baffled.

The next morning, Alexandra called Susan and gave her the day off, then went to the library and got a copy of *Street Shadows*. She set her work aside, though there were customers waiting for their instruments, and read the play.

In the second half she found the scene she'd been looking for, the blood ceremony: The Vampire and Claudine, whom he'd initiated in the first half, kneeled facing each other on a bed. The Vampire told her he would make her his immortal bride, that they would be together through all the coming ages. He took her into his arms, opened her neck wounds, and drank from her as she clung to him in adoration.

Alexandra's heart pounded like a drum as she read. Claudine soon grew limp in his arms as he drained her of blood. When she was all but unconscious, he drew his mouth away and cut a slit in his chest with his fingernail. He forced her mouth to his wound, saying, "Drink from me, my beloved. Our blood comingled will give you to me for eternity."

So that was it, Alexandra thought as she read on in horror and fascination. David would take a great deal of her blood, and when she drank from him, her own blood would be comingled with his. And then? Eagerly she continued reading.

Claudine took a few swallows and died in his arms. He kept a loving vigil with her as she lay still on the bed for a long, long moment. All at once Claudine's eyes fluttered and opened. The Vampire held out his hand to her, and she took it, sat up, and gazed at him with a serene smile. As her smile widened, her incisors were revealed, to prove she had become the same type of creature as he.

Alexandra put her hand to her face and had to tell herself to breathe slowly and deeply, because she'd begun to feel dizzy.

Nevertheless, she continued to read. In the last scene, the play took a twist she hadn't expected. Instead of remaining with the Vampire as his immortal bride, Claudine left him. Now equal to him, she wanted to go off on her own to explore all her new vampiric powers. Alexandra couldn't help but think of Darienne. Had he patterned Claudine's character after Darienne, who had once been under his power but now enjoyed being his equal?

The very end of the play took Alexandra completely off-guard. The Vampire, desolated at having lost Claudine, chose not to return to his coffin the next sunrise. Instead, in what must have been a stunning stage effect, he disappeared before the audience's eyes in a puff of white dust at the first light of dawn.

Alexandra knew *that* wasn't based on David's own experience. Darienne may have become independent of him, but he hadn't chosen self-destruction because she'd gone her own way. In fact, they were still lovers. A tragic hero required a tragic ending in a play, she supposed. Real life could provide a much better ending, Alexandra decided. She had to be grateful to Darienne for indicating the path she should take. Now all she needed was to get David to cooperate.

That night David took a cab to Alexandra's home. On the way he kept hearing her voice calling to him. "David, hurry to me. I love you." She was using their mental bond for the first time.

This pleased David. Perhaps she was less uneasy about their bond now that she'd discovered her new power to communicate with him. Last night she'd been eager to see him, but curiously preoccupied somehow, and he'd worried about it. Tonight, he knew, would be different.

When he arrived at her home, she answered the door speedily. She stood there smiling at him with eagerness in a stunning black lace dress, and he thought her even more beautiful than he'd ever seen her before.

"David," she said, wrapping her arms around him and kissing him. "It worked, didn't it? I called to you, and somehow I knew you heard me."

"What a lovely experience to hear you in my mind," he said.

She laughed, a sound like a flight of notes on the E string of a violin. "Guess what. I read *Street Shadows* today," she said, closing the door behind him.

"You did? What did you think?"

"I adored it. I wish I'd seen it when it was playing in Chicago," she said, taking his arm. "I thought of us the whole time I was reading it. You're brilliant to have re-created your supernatural existence into a stage play."

"The special effects made it work."

"You're too modest," she said, running her hands over his shirt. "You should have played the part yourself."

"Couldn't make the matinees," David said, trying to keep his equilibrium. Lord, Alexandra was simmering tonight. Her hands were running down his chest now, down his hips to his thighs. The white skin of her breasts beneath the black lace tantalized him, too. What had set her on fire? He smiled. "Has reading my play energized you somehow?"

"Read my mind," she replied in a coquettish tone.

"I can't read your mind unless you consciously plant a thought there." She was running a finger along his swollen masculinity now. "Though I think I'm getting your drift."

She chuckled wickedly. "I can tell you are. Let's go upstairs."

When they reached her bedroom, she pushed him down onto the bed and unfastened his clothes. David found himself enjoying her unexpected aggressiveness. She slipped out of her dress then and threw herself naked astride him. The feel of her soft body against his aroused him thoroughly. With a thrust of his hips he made them one.

"Oh, God, this is wonderful!" she breathed and leaned over him to kiss his mouth, her nipples grazing his chest softly. David lay in a sensual daze, enjoying her eagerness, anticipating their fulfillment now that she'd lost all her former inhibitions. She moved her mouth up along his cheek to his eyes, his forehead, then to the side so that his mouth was near her throat. He pressed his lips against her skin, feeling the delicious throb of her pulse point . . .

Suddenly she used their mental bond again. *Drink from me. Let me take from you. The blood ceremony. Drink from me. Let me drink from you . . .*

In one swift move, he grabbed her upper arms and flipped her over onto her back. Still breathing hard from his arousal, he loomed over her face-to-face. "What are you trying with me?"

Alexandra looked totally frightened. David realized he was gripping her tightly and loosened his hold, but kept her pinned beneath him. "You're trying to seduce me into the blood ceremony. I won't allow it!"

"David, no. Don't be angry. It's just that I read the play and—"

"And instead of asking me, you try seduction instead! I don't like your tactics."

"I— I just wasn't thinking. I love you. I want to be with you forever. Your play showed me how. I want you, that's all."

David got up from her and stood beside the bed, fastening his clothing back into place. "I don't know what to think about you. When you tried to trick me into initiating you, I decided to forgive you. But this is far more consequential. I don't admire women who use sex to get what they want. I'm very disappointed in you!"

Alexandra got up and threw herself weeping on his chest. Her tears were genuine; David could feel her inner anguish. He just wasn't quite sure what the anguish was from—fear of his wrath or disappointment that she'd been unsuccessful.

"Please, David, I just want to be with you. I'm sorry I went about this wrong. I was afraid you wouldn't agree to the blood ceremony. I didn't want to wait." She sank to her knees and looked up at him with pleading eyes. "I want to be certain that I'll be with you always. I love you so. Make me like you, David. Make me your immortal bride, like the Vampire in the play. I want to be with you forever."

Feeling some empathy now, though not sure if he should, he made her rise and sat with her on the edge of the bed. "You don't understand what you're asking," he told her. "The play glamorizes something that goes against nature. Once you are transformed, you'll be separated from humanity and God.

The loneliness is shattering. You can never again be a part of the real world, the daylight world. You can never again be normal."

He bowed his head gravely. "And God will turn His face from you, as surely as if you'd never existed. I know. I feel the void every day. And I had once felt so close to God that I contemplated becoming a priest. To exist feeling unloved and alienated is so demoralizing you may find yourself wanting to do what the Vampire in my play did—destroy yourself."

"But *you* haven't," Alexandra pointed out, drying her tears. "You've gone on."

"I haven't always wanted to."

"But you would have me. We would be together. How could we be lonely? Make me your immortal bride!"

The words sent an uncomfortable coldness through him. Veronica was to be his companion for eternity. But he was sure he'd lost Veronica. And at this moment, Alexandra's seductive tricks made him realize just what he'd lost.

"What are you thinking? You're thinking of another woman, I can sense it!" Alexandra said, her blue eyes widening in jealousy.

"Someone I once knew," David said, turning away. Veronica was none of her business.

"It's Darienne, isn't it? You still have sex with her! Are you still in love with her, all this time you've been coming here to me?"

David faced her again. "I wasn't thinking of Darienne," he said coldly. "And how do you know if I still have sex with her?"

"It's . . . it's obvious by the way she hung all over you that night at the opera."

"Why do you want me if you think I'm in love with another woman?"

"Because *I* love you," she said, her voice returning to its pleading tone. "No matter what, I need you. I want to continue making love with you."

"We can continue. You don't need to become an immortal."

"But I'll grow old. And you won't. I'll die, and you'll go on," she said, the words coming out as a taunt.

"And what else do you want, Alexandra? Besides me and eternal youth."

She studied him for a moment. "I . . . I want to carry on with my craft. I have secrets for my varnishes and so on. I don't want to give them to someone young and hope they won't disappear. I want to continue honing my skills and knowledge. I want to make the perfect violin. You're artistic. You wanted to carry on where Shakespeare left off. You, of all people, should understand."

Her words touched him. He did understand. "Yes, I had noble reasons, too. But after I was transformed, all my mortal logic seemed only the quicksand into which I'd fallen. I'd become a prisoner in a cage of my own making. Don't make my mistake. Selfish egoism is not a reason to live forever."

"But you *have* gone on," Alexandra argued. "Look how brilliant your plays are. To me, you're an inspiration."

David winced. "Don't say that. I'm no inspiration. I could live a thousand years and never reach Shakespeare's genius. We have only the intellect that God gave us, and it's useful only for a lifetime. Eternity requires a greater awareness which comes, I believe, only after natural death. You won't acquire it by becoming a vampire."

Alexandra put her hands to her face. He could feel her anguish.

"Don't say that," she said, shaking her head. "I don't believe you. I don't believe you can live four hundred years and not learn anything."

"I didn't say I haven't learned anything. But what I've learned is only the same painful lesson over and over: I made a mistake, and I will spend eternity paying for it. So I say to you, don't make my mistake. Not for knowledge. Not for eternal youth. Perhaps not even for love."

"Why not for love?"

David fought to keep control of his voice. "I've lost two great loves because of what I am."

"Two?"

He adjusted his sitting position, leaning forward, elbows on his knees, buying a bit of time to prepare himself mentally to tell her the story. "When I was still mortal," he began, "I lived in London while I studied with Shakespeare. I rented rooms at an inn. I fell in love with the daughter of the innkeeper. Her

name was Cecilia. She was quite beautiful. Dark-haired, green
eyes. Slender and delicate. A shy, sweet, delightful personality."

He could still picture her as fresh as yesterday in his mind's
eye. "We were planning to be married. But then Will died and
I felt bereft. He'd been the most wonderful teacher, so brilliant, so full of knowledge. I grew obsessed with the idea of
carrying on for him, protecting his works and improving my
own skills. I've already told you I sought out a vampire in
Transylvania. I returned to England, transformed, already
aware of my separation from God, of the difference between
me and the rest of humanity."

He paused to catch his breath before going on. "I appeared
to Cecilia one night. At first she was thrilled to see me. I'd
gone away without telling anyone my plans. I tried to explain
to her what I'd done, how I wanted her to become like me, so
that she and I could be together forever. She backed away,
terrified as she noticed my teeth had changed. She was quite
religious, as I'd been. She called me evil, said I'd become one
of the Devil's demons and wanted no part of me. I tried to
explain that I had no connection with Satan. I was still me,
just changed. She wouldn't listen. I decided the only thing to
do was to take her by force, transform her, and then she would
understand and everything would be fine. But she seemed to
intuit my plan as I came towards her. She backed away from
me again and picked up a knife that lay on the table. I knew
the knife wouldn't hurt me, so I kept approaching her."

David stopped to collect himself. Tears already stung his
eyes at the memory. "When I reached her, she raised the knife
to strike. Only—she didn't strike me. She plunged the blade
into her own heart. She died in my arms. Natural death, you
see, was the only way she could escape me." He paused to
brush away a tear from his cheek. His voice was calm as he
finished. "But I don't grieve for her anymore. I remind myself
that she's at peace. She's with her Maker now."

"How awful," Alexandra said in a hushed voice. "No wonder you carry a sense of sadness about you. Who was the
other?"

"Other?"

"You said you'd lost two great loves."

A spasm tightened his jaw for a moment. "I can't talk about

her. I've lost her and that's all anyone needs to know. My point is, the blood ceremony, even the contemplation of it, only brings heartache and destruction."

"But David, I could make you happy. I could replace those you've lost." Alexandra inched toward him on the bed until her thigh leaned against his. She ran the palm of her hand along his leg, her fingertips digging into his inner thigh. "We're alike in intellect. We're good sexually. We have the same sense of artistic purpose. Eternity together would be wonderful. I won't back away from you in fear, like Cecilia. I want to share your existence. Make me like you," she whispered, biting his earlobe. "I'll give you everything you need. I'll make you happy."

Just as her fingertips reached his groin, he stood up and stepped away. He looked down at her in disgust. "You haven't heard anything I've said! All you want is immortality, just like I did four hundred years ago. At least I was forthright enough to offer money for my transformation. I'd have thought you'd be more honest than to use your body to get what you want. I would have thought you'd give me more credit than to fall for it!"

"It's only because I love you and I want you," Alexandra cried, grabbing his hand. "This bond has made me sick with love for you. I don't know how else to approach you. Don't go. Stay and make love with me, please. Please!"

David pulled his hand out of her grasp and paused on his way out her bedroom door. "And be seduced into making you a vampiress? No thank you! Enough is enough."

"No," she pleaded as he sped down the steps, three at a time. "Please don't go. What'll I do? I need you—"

David slammed the front door and headed down the street, angry and humiliated at the way she'd behaved, at what their relationship had become. He'd thought so highly of her. How could she have tried to use him, trick him? And through sex, the most vulgar way of all. She'd turned their stylish, impulsive relationship into something that resembled a sordid night in a brothel. All for immortality. She'd said it was because she loved him. But he wondered now if that was all part of the grand seduction, too.

God, he was stupid!

12

It's just a superstition

DAVID SAT on his couch feeling cold inside, gazing into his empty fireplace. He wished it were winter so he could build a fire and have something cheerful to look at. But the heat and humidity of the late-summer Chicago climate held deep into the night.

The windows were open and a soft breeze wafted over him. The gentleness of it reminded him of Veronica.

David closed his eyes and leaned back. When it came to women, he didn't have much luck. Or perhaps he should rephrase that: He didn't have much sense. The ones who were truly worthy, he injured or destroyed. The ones who weren't worthy, well, they demolished *him*. He ought to stay away from the female gender altogether.

But he couldn't. He'd always adored women. Vampirism hadn't dampened his libido, unfortunately.

Now he found himself wondering if he'd been unfair to Alexandra. Yet, at the same time, he wondered why he was such a fool to think of giving her another chance. He had a right to be angry and disillusioned with her.

But a small corner of his brain argued that he'd put her under his power. She wasn't entirely responsible for her desires and actions, because he'd put her in a state that made her crave him. Perhaps she'd been justified when she said that she was so sick with love she didn't know how else to approach him.

He heard a noise at his open side window. When he turned, he found Darienne climbing into the room. She wore a green, polka-dot dress with bared shoulders and a low back. Her hair

192

hung gloriously about her face, like a radiant halo. The satisfied smile in her eyes and on her lips made her look like a pampered Pekingese. David wished he could be that contented for even an hour.

"Hello!" David said, rising as she approached him. "It's past two. I figured you were occupied tonight."

"I was," she said with a sleek smile. "With Chad. But I came to check on you."

"Chad?" David repeated in a hopeful voice. "You've given up on Matthew?"

"I'm regrouping, getting my momentum back," she replied, eyes alight with pride. She must have had quite a successful evening with Chad, David concluded. "How is Alexandra?" Darienne asked, changing the subject. "How is she reacting to her bond with you?"

David hesitated. "She wants immortality. She tried to seduce me into the blood ceremony."

"Aha! You see her true colors now."

"You suspected her all along, I suppose," he said, sitting down again.

"It doesn't surprise me. Her actions sound perfectly natural—for her. She doesn't deserve your concern. She's a cold, grasping, neurotic shrew. She'd be happier as a vampiress. And you'd be rid of her."

David felt insulted. "If she were all you say, I'd never have been attracted to her! I just didn't expect her to react to our bond the way she has."

"I warned you."

"You warn me about everything!"

"Because I know better than you," she said sweetly.

David narrowed his eyes at her. "Except when it comes to Matthew."

"We're discussing Alexandra."

"Not anymore," he said, crossing his legs. "Your uncharitable opinion of her has convinced me I should give her another chance." He watched Darienne's shoulders fall in disappointment. "Maybe we shouldn't advise each other about relationships."

"Perhaps not."

They were silent for a while. Suddenly there was nothing to talk about. Darienne paced around the loveseat where he sat.

"Did you go to the theater tonight?" he asked.

"No. Did you?"

"No," David replied, his conscience bothering him. "Well, the show is really out of my hands at this point anyway. The lyrics are set. It's up to the director and the actors now. And the computer," he added in a gallows tone.

"The preview performance is only a week away," Darienne said, sitting on the armrest. "It seems so soon."

"I know."

"I wonder if Matthew is worried," she said as if thinking aloud.

David gave her a wry look. "He doesn't confide in you, I see."

"Not yet," Darienne replied, keeping her pride. "I was going to stay away until opening night. Give him time to overlook our last encounter. But maybe I shouldn't. He might need me."

"Need you?"

"For support. As I've given you so often and so well."

"Yes, sometimes you have," David agreed. "But your support may be more than a mortal man can handle. Especially when you turn it into sexual comfort."

"No, I'll wait for that." Darienne's eyes glowed with an inner sense of purpose. "I'll show Matthew I have more to offer than he thinks."

David inhaled and then sighed. Vampires were precluded from enjoying normal relationships. Darienne used to instinctively understand that—much better than he, in fact. He wondered what blinded her now.

"What about Chad?" he asked out of curiosity. "Why do you still see him?"

"Chad is window-dressing, *cheri.* But very sexy window dressing. Men who want money are always so much more charming than anyone else, *n'est-ce pas?"*

Early the next evening, David rang Alexandra's doorbell. She answered in moments, wearing jeans and a T-shirt, her hair disheveled, a frantic aspect in her eyes.

"David!" A smiled trembled on her lips. "I didn't expect—I tried to call you with my mind, but—"

"I blocked you," he explained, walking in. "I was still angry. But I've reconsidered. Maybe I've been unfair."

"Oh, David," she said, sliding her arms around him, her cheek on his shoulder as they walked into her workshop. "I've been out of my mind thinking you'd gone forever, that you'd never come to me again. I love you. I can't live without you."

David wondered if that was her true feeling, or if it was the power of their bond. "Do you love me?"

"Of course, I do! Drink from me, David," she begged, stopping to look up at him. "I want to give to you."

"No." He sat down on a wood stool and drew her onto his lap. "But there's something else you could do for me. Would you, if I asked?"

"Anything. What?"

"Let our relationship continue as before. Ask for nothing more."

"But I want more. I want to be with you forever. Give me that, David! It's only fair."

"This isn't a question of fairness."

"It is!" she said, her hands on his shoulders. "I can't go on like this, needing you this way, unable to think of anything but you. My old life is over. I need you to give me a new kind of life. You owe me!"

"You begged me to initiate you," he said. "I told you how it would be. It's not my fault you didn't believe me. Immortality is a far worse mistake. You must believe me this time. Be happy in your mortal life. Be happy with our relationship as it is. I won't give you more."

She stared at him, her eyes like blue, cold fire. Her body began to tremble. David realized her shaking was from rage.

"I hate you!" She got up from his lap. "You've bonded my emotions to you, you make me crave you, and yet you won't give me the one thing that could free me. You're selfish and cruel!" She began beating her hands on his shoulders. "I loathe you for what you've done to me! You've made me love you too much! I want to be myself again. I want to be free!"

He fought with her hands, gripped them, and willed her to be still. "Immortality is an unending prison. You wouldn't be free."

She was crying now, like a tragic child. "You're controlling me even now," she sobbed, sinking to her knees in front of him. "You have no heart! How can I hate you so much, and still need you?" She wrapped her arms around his legs.

David closed his eyes in pain. This was his fault. He should have foreseen this. Why had he thought Alexandra would be strong enough to deal with the bond? In reality, she was weaker than most. He didn't know women at all.

He gripped her by her arms and made her stand up as he stood himself. "Alexandra, the bond will fade if we stop using it. Then maybe you can be yourself again. Perhaps we should stop seeing each other."

"No!" she cried, horror-stricken.

"It's the only way."

"No, don't leave me. I love you!"

"You don't," David said, his voice hoarse as he realized the truth. "I wonder if you ever did."

"I do! Don't leave me! I'll be good. I won't pester you for immortality. I'll let you choose my destiny."

"Will you? Are you being honest with me?"

"Of course, I am!" she insisted, her red-rimmed eyes wounded. "I love you. I love you! I'll be whatever you want me to be. Only don't leave me. Please, David. I'm begging you. Please don't leave me."

David felt a tear slide down his cheek. That he could have caused any mortal this much anguish! He had to give her another chance. "All right," he said, smoothing her hair back with his fingers. "Don't cry. I won't leave you. I won't leave."

A few nights later Darienne sat in the theater watching the last rehearsal before the preview performance the next night. The computer seemed to have been straightened out; at least the guillotine confined itself to the scenes in which it was supposed to appear. The costumes were almost finished, but there were still arguments about the lighting. An orchestra now occupied the dark pit beneath the stage, supporting the singers with its full musical sound.

Darienne might have had hopes that everything would finally come together by opening night, except for an ominous new problem: Merle told her a summer flu had invaded the cast and seemed to be spreading quickly. Tonight a few of the supporting actors were out sick, replaced by nervous, inadequately prepared understudies. Worse yet, Elaine seemed ill;

she was not singing well and appeared exhausted. Darienne noted with relief that Matthew looked and sounded as wonderful as always.

When the rehearsal finally ended late that evening, she spent several minutes talking with Merle and Loni before heading for Matthew's dressing room. She didn't want to look too anxious to see him. Her new strategy, she'd decided, would be to play it cool for a while, hoping he would trust her more if she were less aggressive. Once he began to be more easy and less guarded with her, she'd make her move. For now, as she'd told David, she'd try to show Matthew her other qualities.

When she reached his dressing room, Wendy was cleaning up and Matthew had already showered and changed into jeans and a light blue sport shirt. His curly hair was still damp and fell over his forehead in short, haphazard locks, as though it were towel-dried and not combed. He looked cuddly, a thin, broad-chested teddy bear—not at all the type of man she usually gravitated toward. But as she gazed at him after not seeing him for several days, she felt an odd sensation in her stomach. Her limbs seemed to weaken.

Had she forgotten to feed? she asked herself. She had consumed an entire blood bag just yesterday. She ought to be fine.

Was she nervous? She, having jitters because of a man? She'd been above all that since she was a sixteen-year-old mortal, since the day she'd discovered her ability to make a man—a priest, no less—helpless with a look and an ingenuous flaunt of her body. Men were her playthings.

There was nothing wrong with her, Darienne told herself as she entered the room. Wendy was on her way out, and they exchanged greetings as they passed one another. Once she was in his dressing room, she realized Elaine was also there. She'd been hidden from Darienne's view by the door frame. The actress, dressed in light summer pants and a T-shirt, was in the midst of a conversation with Matthew.

"Excuse me," Darienne said when Matthew gave her a sharp look. "I didn't mean to interrupt."

Elaine smiled, though her eyes were glassy and her face was pale. "It's all right. How are you, Darienne?"

Matthew seemed surprised that Elaine greeted Darienne so cordially. Men never realized that most women liked her, too.

"I'm worried about you," Darienne told her. "You haven't caught the flu that's going around?"

"I think I have," Elaine said. "My throat's sore and it's affecting my voice. I'm so worried."

"I think you have a fever, too," Matthew said. He gently placed his hand on her forehead. "Yes, you do. I felt it when you kissed me during the rehearsal."

Watching him touch her and hearing him refer to their stage kiss made Darienne stiffen and grow quiet. She envied Elaine for his tenderness toward her. They reminded Darienne of David and Veronica. But she'd never been jealous of Veronica or wanted that tenderness from David for herself. And she didn't think Matthew was even in love with Elaine.

"It's probably my fault that I'm getting sick, too," Elaine said, bowing her head as she confided in them. She glanced up at Darienne. "Remember you asked if I'd set a wedding date?"

Darienne nodded.

"Well, I broke off the engagement yesterday."

"What?" Matthew said, drawing his brows together.

Elaine turned her eyes to him. "I couldn't marry him. Not once I realized he didn't have all the qualities I want in a husband. He's too young. He's immature in some ways. It was you who made me realize it," she said, looking down. She didn't see Matthew's astonished reaction.

"Anyway," Elaine rushed on, "he's very hurt, and I'm upset because I know I've hurt him. And I suppose that's why I came down with the flu. I always get sick when I'm upset."

"You couldn't have waited till after opening night to tell him?" Matthew asked.

"He was pressing me to set a wedding date."

Matthew nodded, though his broad shoulders seemed to have slackened. "What will you do? Do you have someone to take care of you?"

"I'm staying at my mother's. She said she'd make me chicken soup," Elaine replied with a wan smile. "Maybe I'll be okay by tomorrow."

"They say it's a three-day flu." Matthew appeared worried. "Maybe if you take tomorrow off, you'll be okay for opening night."

"But I hate to miss the pre-performance. One of the critics is supposed to be there."

"If you're sick and your voice is affected, there's no other choice. I'm afraid you've already stressed yourself more than you should have tonight. Your understudy isn't nearly as talented, but she's good enough. These things happen, Elaine. The show always manages to go on. The important thing is that you get well and don't make yourself worse. If you're still feverish tomorrow, you must stay home."

Elaine looked up at him earnestly, as if she were receiving advice from her private guru. Darienne didn't think anything he was saying was that remarkable. But his tone sounded so supportive and nurturing, even Darienne could understand the young actress's clinging to his every word.

Elaine nodded with reluctance as tears filled her eyes. "Okay," she whispered.

Matthew took her in his arms then and hugged her. As she shed tears onto his shoulder, he said, "I know it's tough to miss a show when you've been working so hard. Don't blame yourself. Any one of us can get sick. It's part of being human."

Darienne found herself backing away from them, though she couldn't take her eyes off the couple.

Elaine looked up at him tearfully. "I hope you don't catch it, too. You work so closely with me."

"Don't worry about me," he said, placing his hands on her upper arms. He kissed her forehead. "I never get sick. Go home now and get some rest."

She nodded, wiping her eyes. As the actress walked toward the door to leave, Darienne noticed a party of people waiting for her in the hall: Merle, the stage manager, and the theater owner were among them. Elaine hesitated at seeing them. Matthew put his arm around her and walked out with her to speak to them.

Darienne stayed behind for the moment. If Elaine needed further support informing the powers-that-be that she was too ill to go on tomorrow, she would lend it. But she knew Matthew would perform that role better. She gazed about his empty dressing room and noticed his candle burning in the adjoining inner room. As she turned, she realized she'd been standing in front of the mirror. Quickly she moved to the side of the mirror, wondering how she could have made such a slip. Fortunately, everyone had been too distracted to notice.

Matthew returned looking grim.

"What did they say?" Darienne asked.

"What could they say? She's obviously sick. They're hoping she can be back for opening night."

"What do you think?"

He pushed his chair to one side in an agitated manner. "The virus going around congests the chest. If you can't get enough breath support, you can't sing. It usually takes a while to get over that. I think she'll be really sick tomorrow. Whether she can recover fast enough for the next night—who knows?"

Darienne nodded, her concern increasing. She happened to glance at the wood counter beneath his mirror and noticed something she'd never seen there before. There were small tins of throat lozenges, the kind that advertised they could ease sore throat pain.

"Matthew," she said, pointing to the tins, "do you have a sore throat?"

He looked up suddenly, but didn't answer.

"Do you?" she asked again.

"It may be because I've been singing too strenuously. Just like if you shout too much, your throat gets hoarse."

"But singers know how to take care of their voices, don't they?"

"We're supposed to," he said, looking down pensively.

"Are you sure you haven't caught what's going around? You look a little pale."

"As I told Elaine, I never get sick."

"But you also told her that everyone gets sick."

"I was trying to comfort her," he said, sitting down in the chair as if he were tired.

Darienne smiled. "Yes. You're very good at it, too. No wonder she's fallen in love with you."

His head came up. "Don't say that," he told her with annoyance.

"The truth bothers you? You should be flattered."

"It's not true. I haven't done anything to give her the idea that—"

"I imagine she knows her feelings aren't returned quite the way she'd like them to be. But she is in love with you."

"I'm old enough to be her father."

"Perhaps she never got the emotional support she needed from her own father. Mine was like that." Darienne's mind skipped backward centuries to her childhood. Her aristocratic father had ignored her, treated her as if she were part of the expensive furniture that decorated their grand Parisian mansion.

"So she looks to me for that?" Matthew asked.

"Yes," Darienne said, shaking away her ancient memories. "You nurture very well."

"If I'm replacing her father, why would she fall in love with me? She wouldn't view me as a lover."

"Yes, she would. She was satisfied with her fiancé until she met you. You supply more of what she's missed in her life. Father, lover—it all gets mixed up in a woman's psyche somehow." Darienne grew self-conscious, remembering Matthew had told her she was mixed up.

But he was wrong, of course. Darienne had always felt she understood very clearly what she wanted from a man and why.

"I hope you're mistaken," Matthew said, rising from his chair. He reached for a tin of throat lozenges. "I never know what to do with women." He opened it and put one in his mouth. "They need support, so I give it to them. The next thing I know, they're around me all the time." He looked up. "Even you."

Darienne felt heat rise to her face. "You've never given me support."

"But you're here all the time."

"I am not! I've stayed away from you for several days."

"Gathering strength, probably."

"Sorry if I'm a nuisance," she said, feeling warm again.

He shifted the lozenge in his mouth and studied her thoughtfully, standing only a few feet from her. "You're an unusual woman. I might like your visits more if I didn't always have the feeling you're ready to tug at my zipper."

"No, you keep a lock on that, don't you?" she said sarcastically. "Or you save it all for the stage. Nothing left over for real life."

He said nothing, but gazed at her for a long, suspended moment. His gray-green eyes grew clear and sharp with his intense inner energy, probing her as if she were a hidden pool whose depth he was trying to fathom.

All at once he turned away, crunching on his lozenge. "I'd better get going."

"Yes, you'd better," she said, breathless from his gaze. He might play hard to get, but when he looked at a woman—he looked!

As he walked to the counter to pick up one of the lozenge tins and put it in his pocket, Darienne regained her equilibrium. "Tell me truthfully, are you coming down with the flu?"

He tilted his head slightly. "I'm afraid I may be."

Darienne had a sinking feeling. "Oh, Matthew. What will you do?"

"What I always do. Think positively and will myself not to get sick."

"Is that possible? Does it work?"

"You bet!" he said.

She fell in step with him as he headed toward the door. Then he paused and turned, muttering, "Forgot to blow out my candle."

He stepped back to the door of the inner room and stopped short in the doorway.

"What's wrong?" Darienne peered into the room over his shoulder.

The candle had gone out.

"Did you blow it out?" he asked.

"No, of course not."

Matthew stared quietly at the cylinder of green wax with its black, dead wick. "Well, it's just a superstition."

13

How ill is he?

"HOW ARE you?" Darienne asked Matthew as Wendy was finishing applying his stage makeup. It was seven-thirty, a half hour before the preview performance would begin.

Matthew didn't answer. Darienne wasn't sure if it was because he didn't want to reply or because he didn't want to move while Wendy dusted powder over his face. She glanced up at Wendy, who shot her an ominous look.

"Matthew?" Darienne persisted. She'd seen the audience pouring into the theater as she'd arrived and couldn't help but feel a sense of urgency about his performance.

All at once David walked in. "Matthew?" he said, taking a place next to Darienne at one side of the mirror. "Merle told me Elaine's out sick and you're not feeling well."

Matthew stirred in his chair as Wendy turned to put the powder back on the counter. "I can sing through a cold," he said in a subdued but testy voice. "I rested all day. I've done my warm-ups. Don't worry, David. Sir Percy will be born tonight as planned."

"Are you sure?" David asked with concern. "You might make yourself worse. You could wait till tomorrow and let the understudy go on."

"Too late now to get him into makeup. Besides, what kind of performance would it be with understudies doing the two lead roles? *I'll* play Sir Percy. He's mine. I wanted the role and I'll do it well. A little flu bug won't stop me."

His decisive manner made everyone silent for a moment. Darienne glanced at David, wondering what he would do.

David seemed to cover his concern and stepped forward to

shake hands with Matthew. "I'm not worried. I'll be watching
from the wings." He looked surprised as he drew his hand
from Matthew's grasp, but said nothing further.

"Thanks," Matthew told him as Wendy stepped away, apparently finished. He looked at himself in the mirror, inspect-
ing her makeup job. His eyes had a sharpness and quickness
which showed his tension. "Now, if you don't mind," he said,
leaning back in his chair, "I don't want anyone to speak to me
until the show starts. I have to get into character."

Wendy looked up at them and nodded. Darienne complied
and walked out of the room with David. Wendy followed,
softly closing the door to the dressing room behind her. "He
always takes time to get into character," the attractive redhead told them in a whispered voice. "His dresser will come in
shortly, but she won't say anything to him as she works with
him. He's had us follow this pattern the last few rehearsals. I
think he takes time to meditate, too."

"Is his candle burning?" Darienne asked, realizing she'd
forgotten to look.

"He lit it as soon as he came in."

"How ill is he?" David asked, stepping forward as actors in
costumes passed behind him in the hall. "His hand felt hot. He
has a fever, doesn't he?"

Wendy nodded, glancing downward at her own hands
which had makeup streaks on them. "When he came in late
this afternoon he looked terrible. Worse than Elaine was yesterday. Merle told him to go home, but he refused. Mr.
McDowall's driven, you know. That's his reputation, and
now that I've been working with him, I see it's true."

David nodded gravely. "Then he must do what he must do.
I'd better see how Merle is holding up under the tension." He
turned to Darienne. "Are you sitting in the audience?"

"Yes," she said. "Merle gave me a ticket yesterday. You
said you'll watch from the wings?"

"I prefer it to being in the crowds. Besides," David added
in a monotone, "I'm taking Alexandra to opening night tomorrow. I'll have to sit in the balcony then."

"How is she?" Darienne asked.

"Fine," David said without conviction. Darienne knew he
couldn't say much with Wendy present. "Perhaps I'll see you
after the show?"

"I'll come backstage to congratulate Matthew," Darienne said. Her eager tone faded as she grew conscious again of his illness.

"We have to think positively," Wendy said as David left them.

"Yes, we do," Darienne agreed. "What's it like to work with Matthew? You seem pretty cool considering his situation."

"Oh, often I've wanted to tell him not to work so hard, to rest. But he's obsessive, and advice from me or anyone else would only annoy him. I learned early on not to get emotionally attached to the actors I work on." She rubbed at the makeup smudges on her hands as she spoke. "They usually prefer a friendly but businesslike attitude, and that works best for me. Actors come and go. If you get attached to each one, it's too painful. So I just paint their faces, and wipe it off when the show's over."

"But Matthew's different than most actors, isn't he?"

Wendy smiled. "All the more reason not to get attached. He'd be a heartbreaker."

David stood at a spot in the wings the stage manager had directed him to, where he would be out of the way of the actors and crew. He couldn't view the entire stage, but he could see enough.

The show was nearing intermission and so far was going well, considering the circumstances. Elaine's understudy performed adequately in her role. Matthew sang as if out of breath at times, but otherwise his portrayal seemed inspired. David might almost think he'd made an instant recovery, he projected such energy on the stage.

But when intermission came, David saw the truth. Matthew walked off the stage exhausted, nearly wilting under his running makeup, for he was sweating profusely. His dresser accompanied him to his dressing room, where Wendy was waiting. David saw the door close and made no effort to pry. He only hoped Matthew could recover before his cue in the second half.

After intermission, David saw the actor as he went on again, looking refreshed and determined. His makeup had been retouched and he'd had a change in costume for the ballroom scene. As the play progressed, Matthew's performance continued to be so mesmerizing and poignant that David again felt a kinship with the actor. He made a reality of David's personal vision. He communicated to the audience all that David had felt as he wrote the lyrics. Again David wondered how a mortal could understand so well the vampire's lonely view of the world. His portrayal brought tears to David's eyes several times during the show.

Matthew performed marvelously straight through the happy ending, the reprise of the love duet between Sir Percy and Marguerite. The curtain came down to huge applause, which sounded better than any music could to David's ears. Smiling broadly, he congratulated a few of the actors as they came off stage and regrouped in a predetermined order to go on again and take their bows.

Matthew came off smiling, looking strong, though again he was sweating through his costume. His dresser came up to straighten his clothing and Wendy approached with a hair dryer to dry the sweat off his face before he went out again to take his bow. David hurried over as the women worked and clapped the actor on the back. "Extraordinary!" he said, his voice choked with triumphant emotion. "Thank you!"

"I hope I did your work justice," Matthew managed to say, though he was completely out of breath. "I think I did."

"You were brilliant—" David began, but then stopped when Matthew put his hand to his head.

"What's wrong?" Wendy asked, turning off her machine.

Matthew's hand was shaking and he stepped backward in a clumsy manner. All at once his knees buckled.

With his agility and superior strength, David was able to easily catch the actor before he hit the floor. The women stood back in alarm. Immediately the stage manager grabbed a nearby folding chair and assisted David. They tried to help Matthew into it, but he appeared to be nearly unconscious.

"I'll carry him," David said, picking up Matthew's limp body beneath his broad back and knees.

"Can you manage?" the stage manager asked with surprise.

David didn't answer, but moved off toward Matthew's dressing room.

"What about his bow? He's on now!" one of the others yelled.

"He'll have to miss it tonight," David called back.

* * *

"What happened?" Darienne asked David as she and Merle, whom she'd sat next to in the audience, rushed backstage. David was standing in the hall while actors and stagehands scurried about.

"He collapsed," David told them.

"Oh, God," Merle said. "I knew he shouldn't do it. He was so sick, he hadn't eaten all day. How did he make it through the performance? He was magnificent!"

"Willpower," Darienne said, feeling unsettled, helpless.

She'd been so excited by his performance, that she'd been waiting eagerly in the audience to give him a standing ovation. And then he never came out to take a bow. The audience had been confused and continued applauding long after the curtain came down. Finally the applause stopped but there were murmurs throughout the audience. Darienne knew something must have happened.

"Did anyone call a doctor?" Merle asked.

"They called paramedics," David said. "They're with him now."

"It couldn't be a heart attack, could it?" Merle said. "He's what? Forty-four? Some people start having them at that age."

"No," Darienne whispered. "He might die?" Her throat closed and her head swam as tears filled her eyes.

"I think he just grew faint," David said, studying Darienne. "He's sick and he pushed himself too far." He put his hands on Darienne's shoulders. "Pull yourself together. We haven't heard any bad news yet. This isn't like you."

Darienne blinked and tried to compose herself. She knew it wasn't like her. Usually she was the one calming down everyone else.

In a little while three paramedics came out of Matthew's dressing room. Merle caught them as they walked by. "How is he?"

"He's okay," one of the uniformed young men said. "Probably dehydration because of his fever and sweating during his performance. We told him to go in for a checkup, but his heart and blood pressure were good. Chest's a little congested from the respiratory flu he's got. I don't know how he sang through a two-hour show."

"We don't either," Merle said, smiling now, shaking his head. "Thanks."

Darienne sighed with relief. "I want to see him," she said, moving toward the open dressing room door.

"Darienne," David called after her, "let him rest."

She paid no heed and walked in. She found Matthew sitting on the couch in his inner room, a glass of water in his hand. The candle on the small table next to the couch was still burning. His wig had been removed, but he was still in costume. Wendy was hovering over him, wiping makeup off his face with a cloth.

"How do you feel?" Darienne asked when he glanced up.

"Shoot me now and put me out of my misery," he said in an exhausted voice.

"I don't know how you did it," Merle told him, coming up beside Darienne. She noticed that David, too, had reluctantly followed her in.

"There was no question that I was going to do it," Matthew said. "Hope I can get my bow tomorrow night."

"You ought to stay home tomorrow," David said.

"Opening night? No way!" Matthew replied. He took a sip of water.

"But after tonight, how can you go on again until you're well?" Darienne asked, her voice revealing her concern.

"If I did it tonight, I can do it tomorrow."

"You'll only get worse," Darienne said.

"You might get pneumonia or something," Merle added.

"No, I'll be all right tomorrow." Matthew told them this as if it were a predetermined fact.

"That's what you said yesterday," Darienne pointed out.

"Well, I was all right on stage, wasn't I?"

"Yes," she admitted as her vision blurred with moisture again. "You were wonderful."

"Thanks." He looked at Darienne curiously as Wendy made him tilt his chin. "Are you crying?"

"No!" Darienne grew annoyed with herself, unused to feeling tears continually welling in her eyes. "They called the paramedics for you," she explained lamely.

"Totally unnecessary. I forgot to drink enough water, that's all. Maybe I should take salt pills."

Merle looked exasperated. "You need to get your fever

down first. Why don't you come home with me? My wife and I can take care of you until you're well."

"Thanks, but I'll sleep better in my own bed."

"But you live alone. Who'll look after you?"

"I'm not helpless."

"You're not sensible either," Merle said. "You don't have anyone to fix meals for you. You didn't eat all day."

"I can cook. I didn't feel like eating."

Merle ran his hand over his gray crew cut. "Okay, I can have food sent up to your place tomorrow. Right now we have to get you home. Did you drive or walk today?"

"Drive."

"I'll drive you home in your car and catch a cab back."

"I'll come along," Darienne said. "I can stay with him tonight in case he gets worse."

She noticed David lifting his eyes to the ceiling, but Merle seemed to jump on the idea. "Would you?" the producer said. "I'd feel a lot better if he had someone with him."

"Does the patient have anything to say about this?" Matthew asked.

"No!" Merle replied.

"Just thought I'd ask," the actor muttered.

Merle seemed to think better of his high-handed manner. "Do you mind?"

"Darienne would make an interesting nurse, all right," Matthew said, eyeing her.

Darienne bowed her head. "I'll try not to intrude on your privacy."

"If you get worse in the night, someone would be there to call a doctor," Merle told him.

"Okay," Matthew said in an indulgent tone. "If it'll make you feel better."

"It'll make my ulcer feel better."

While Matthew changed out of his costume, Darienne said good-night to David, who didn't look happy about the situation. She accompanied Merle and the actor to his car in the garage below the theater. Soon they arrived at Marina Towers.

When they reached Matthew's apartment, Merle said he'd run out and try to find a fast-food place to get him something to eat.

"There's canned soup in my kitchen. Heat up some of that," Matthew suggested.

"Okay. Darienne, you do that while I get Matthew into bed."

Matthew shot her an amused look as Merle pushed him toward the bedroom.

Darienne knew he thought the idea of her being in a kitchen was a joke. It was, of course, but he didn't have to needle her about it. Miffed, she walked into his small, tiled kitchen and looked through the cupboards to find his canned goods. Eventually, she found several cans of soup and picked out chicken noodle. She remembered Elaine saying her mother would fix her chicken soup.

The problem was Darienne had never opened a can in her existence. She saw an electric gadget that she guessed was a can opener, but couldn't figure out how to get it to work.

Merle came in and showed her how to use it. With a grin, he said, "You're not the type of woman who cooks, are you?"

"No."

"Well, why should you, if you can pay someone else to do it?"

Darienne couldn't explain that she didn't cook because she didn't eat. "What do we do now that the can's open?"

"Put it in a pan and heat it up."

She looked through more cupboards and pulled out a small saucepan. "This?"

"Perfect," he said, pouring the contents in. He turned a knob on the stove and a flame erupted. "There. When it comes to a boil, we're done."

"Good," Darienne said, relaxing now that her assignment was completed.

"You're an all right lady," Merle said.

"I am?"

"At first I had my doubts about you, but you've turned out to be okay."

"I know, I made you nervous," Darienne said. "I'm sorry. I was enjoying being influential. Now I'm enjoying just being a part of it all. The theater is fun."

"Yeah, especially if the show's a hit. And it looks like we've got one!"

Darienne grinned. "Wasn't it exciting to see the audience

react! If Matthew had just been able to take his bow, I think he would have gotten a standing ovation."

"Me, too. He sure makes me nervous, though. What if he'd passed out while he was swinging on the rope from the proscenium to the stage? I don't know what to do with him."

"I don't think you can do anything," she said, feeling proud of Matthew and worried for him at the same time. "I never met anyone so intense and strong minded."

"He's a great actor and a lousy patient."

Darienne watched as Merle brought the soup in to Matthew. He was propped up in the king-sized bed in pale blue pajamas, looking worse than ever. He couldn't finish the soup. When Merle suggested he take aspirin for the fever, Matthew replied, "I've already taken every drugstore remedy I could find. I just need some sleep."

"Okay, I'll leave then," Merle said. "I'll call you in the morning. Darienne will be here if you need anything."

"Oh, good," Matthew said in a sardonic, nasal tone.

"Make sure he drinks his liquids," Merle told Darienne as she walked with him to the door.

"I will. I . . . have to leave very early in the morning."

"I'll check on him as soon as I get up then," Merle said. "Night. And thanks."

She closed and locked the door after Merle left, then hesitated about going back into Matthew's bedroom. Perhaps he'd just as soon not have her hover over him. But she wanted to put a pitcher of water by his bed.

Deciding she had no choice, she went into the kitchen, took down a pitcher she'd seen earlier, filled it, and brought it with a glass into the large bedroom. Like the living room, it was done in greens and grays.

Matthew had slid down beneath the light blanket, his head on the pillow, his eyes closed. He looked fatigued, pale, and ill. Compared to the stunning vampire figure he created onstage, now he looked very much like a mortal, frail and limited. She worried he might not have the stamina to recover at all.

Quietly she approached his bedside and set the pitcher and glass beneath the lamp on the table next to him. His eyes opened and he looked up at her.

"Sorry, I didn't mean to wake you."

"I wasn't asleep." He pulled aside the covers. "I'm too hot and my head aches."

"Won't you get chills if you don't have a blanket?" she asked, trying to remember what it was like to be sick.

"Probably." He began rubbing his temples.

"Let me," she said. "I used to be good at this." She sat at his side and pressed her fingertips into the sides of his head with a small, circular motion.

"You have strong fingers."

"Too hard?" she asked, lightening the pressure. With her vampiric strength, it was difficult to tell.

"No, it's all right. It feels good." He closed his eyes and relaxed.

After a while, she brought her hands down to the bottom of his head and massaged her fingers into the hair at the back of his neck. His chin came up and his neck arched a bit. She saw the pulse at the side of his throat. Her lips parted as the desire for his blood came upon her.

And then it occurred to her that it was in her power to cure him. Not only cure him, but give him superior strength. His strenuous stage role as a vampire would not be the least bit taxing for him if he actually were a vampire.

"Matthew?" she said softly. "Have you ever thought what it would be like to be a vampire?"

"Hmmm?" His eyes remained closed and he seemed to be enjoying her massage.

"You would never be sick like this. You would be stronger than you can imagine. You could play any role."

"I could go for that," he murmured.

Her hands stopped and she stared at him, her breaths coming faster. Should she tell him what she was? Should she explain what she could do for him?

His eyelids opened as if he sensed something amiss. He looked into her eyes and she quickly lowered them, realizing he might have glimpsed their vampiric glow. And in a flash she realized she didn't want to tell him that she was so different from him. She didn't want him to know. He might not even believe her. He'd told the disc jockey he didn't think vampires existed. Perhaps it would be better for them both if he went on disbelieving.

"What's wrong?" he asked.

"Nothing." She made herself smile. "My fingers are getting tired," she said, pulling her hands away from his head.

"Thanks. That helped."

"Did it?"

"You make a fine nurse after all."

She smiled, though tears came to her eyes. She didn't know why, and began blinking hard again.

"What is it with you lately?" he asked. "I didn't peg you as a weepy sort of woman."

"I'm not," she insisted, wiping the corner of one eye. "I'm just not used to seeing you so ill. I feel helpless."

To her surprise, he took one of her hands in his. "That's nice. I appreciate that. But I'll be all right in the morning. All I need is a good night's sleep."

Her heart sank as she listened to him. She admired his tenacity, but feared his mortal's body would disappoint him. He couldn't be this ill and be well tomorrow. He'd either miss opening night, which would make him hate himself, or he'd play his role tomorrow and perhaps kill himself doing it. His hand touching hers was still burning with fever.

"I'll let you sleep then," she said, gently pulling her hand away. "There's water here. You should drink some."

"Yes, ma'am."

"Good-night."

"Going to sleep on the couch?"

"I'll find something to read," she said. How could she explain that she never slept at night? "Call me if you need something."

He nodded and closed his eyes. "Thanks."

She turned out the lamp and left the room.

As she walked into his living room, she noticed the green candle on the coffee table. She picked up the matches nearby and lit the candle for Matthew.

Darienne leafed through the latest copy of *Variety*, which she'd found on the coffee table. It was about two-thirty in the morning. All at once she heard a groan from the bedroom, and then Matthew's voice. She rushed in and found him with the covers still thrown off, bathed in sweat. He seemed to be having a nightmare.

"Don't take him," he murmured. "Don't—"

"Matthew," she said, shaking him. "Wake up."

"No—"

"Matthew."

He opened his eyes and looked about.

"You're at home. You were dreaming."

"Oh . . ." His head sank back onto the pillow.

"You said, 'Don't take him.' Who were you dreaming about?"

"Larry," he murmured, eyes staring at the ceiling. "I haven't seen him in years."

"Who is that?"

"My son."

Darienne had no idea Matthew had a son. Then she recalled seeing a photo of a boy in his dressing room. "Someone took him?"

"My wife."

"Your wife?"

He ran his hands over his perspiring face and began to sit up. "She left me years ago. God, I'm soaked."

"I'll get you a towel."

Darienne hurried to his bathroom, grabbed a towel, and came back to him. She wiped his face, then unbuttoned his pajama top and ran the towel over his deep chest.

"Do you dream about your wife and son often?"

"No."

"Did she really take him? Or was that just in the dream?"

His chest beneath her hands shook as he chuckled grimly. "A nightmare based on a nightmare."

Darienne decided not to pry any more for the time being. "You'd better drink some water," she said, stopping to pour him a glass.

As he drank it, she asked, "Do you want me to call a doctor?"

"No." He put the empty glass on the table.

"Do you have a thermometer?" She knew mortals used them nowadays to measure body temperature.

"No. I don't believe in knowing how sick I am. Besides, I'll be okay now."

"Matthew—"

"No, I will. I feel better now. The fever's broken."

"Really?" she said, doubtful.

"Sure. Haven't you ever broken out in a sweat when you're sick?"

"I haven't been sick lately," she said.

"You'll see. I'll be fine."

She smiled, though her heart wasn't in it. "I hope so."

Darienne left him so he could sleep and went back to the living room. She checked now and then and he seemed to sleep peacefully through the next few hours. Shortly before dawn she wrote him a note, rather than wake him, to say she was leaving and would see him at the theater. She pretended as she wrote that she was as optimistic as he was about his condition. But inside she knew he was too sick to recover in time.

She rushed home and reached her coffin minutes before dawn.

The next evening, Darienne left for the theater as soon as she rose at sundown. When she arrived she headed straight to Matthew's dressing room. She wondered if he would be there, almost hoped he wouldn't for his health's sake.

She looked in and saw him sitting in front of the mirror in his undershirt as Wendy spread a thin coating of some substance over his face. Darienne caught Wendy's eye, and the redhead smiled at her. She walked in and stood in her usual spot to one side of the mirror, facing Matthew.

He looked up and grinned. "You always appear without warning. How are you?"

She didn't answer as she studied him in wonder. He appeared perfectly fine. "You look so well!"

"I told you."

"But how could you recover so quickly?"

"After the fever broke I slept until Merle phoned me at seven this morning. After that I fell asleep again until noon. I took an antihistamine to dry up my nose and relaxed the rest of the day."

"But you must feel weak."

"Adrenalin will fix that when I go on stage."

Darienne shook her head. "You shouldn't push yourself so hard. You're not Sir Percy."

"You reminded me of that last night, didn't you?" he said, looking pensive and yet amused as Wendy continued to apply brush strokes to his face. "Do you have a thing about vampires?"

"A . . . a thing?" Darienne asked, confused by the question.

"American slang," he said, chuckling. "Does the vampire fantasy excite you? Some women are turned on by the overpowering-male image. That's why I wanted Sir Percy to look powerful, to tap into that myth."

Darienne found his analysis amusing. "Oh," she said in an ingenuous voice, "you mean it's *only* a myth?"

He laughed, showing his broad grin.

"Does the female vampire have the same effect on men?" she asked.

"Oh-ho," he said in an arch tone. "I'm afraid to even contemplate that."

Too bad, Darienne thought, losing her smile. She wished he could treat it as more than a joke. But he never would. He saw his vampire role as completely separate from real life, even though he could empathize with his stage character so completely—just as he'd been able to empathize with Rick, his clumsy, comic character, with whom he also had nothing in common in reality. He was an actor.

It was just as well she hadn't told him anything last night. He'd have thought she was a lunatic. It would have ended whatever tenuous, little relationship she'd been able to form with him.

Matthew was still amused. "You think up the most unusual comebacks," he said. "I like your sense of humor."

This took Darienne off-guard. "I'm glad you've finally found something about me you like!" she quipped.

He twisted his mouth in one of his comic expressions. "No, I'm not getting myself into another verbal fencing match with you. There are reporters and a TV news crew coming any minute to interview me. I don't want them inventing any gossip if they overhear some choice remark. You'll be at the opening night party, won't you?"

"Yes."

"I'll see you there."

"You won't be too tired to go?" she said, worried again.

"I'll be all wound up after the show," he replied. "But I probably won't stay long."

"And whom are you escorting?" Darienne asked, purposely putting hope into her voice.

"My leading lady. It seemed appropriate."

"Elaine's recovered, too?" Darienne asked with surprise.

"Well enough to go on tonight. All the actors who were sick are back, except one. It should be a terrific opening. Assuming the computer hasn't caught some bug."

In a few minutes the TV crew arrived with their equipment. Darienne watched from the door while they interviewed Matthew, taping as Wendy applied his makeup. A half hour before curtain time, Wendy asked everyone to leave, so Matthew could begin getting into character. Darienne left and took her seat in the audience, row eight, center, and waited anxiously.

An hour later, Darienne found herself riveted once again by Matthew's magnificent voice and the sensuality he infused into every move he made. So did the rest of the full-house audience, judging by their rapt silence. When he sang "She Can Never Be Mine," there wasn't so much as a cough to break the spell he wove over them. And she could tell he was enjoying himself up there. Last night he'd performed beautifully, but she could see the effort he put into it. Tonight he seemed to move effortlessly, gliding in his slow, sensual manner while singing as if it were no strain at all. He put energy into every move. Later when he swung to the stage on a rope, she could almost think of him as a highly skilled, enviably talented, precocious youngster having fun, enjoying the time of his life. He lived to perform, she realized. He'd said once that acting was his life, but she hadn't fully understood what he'd meant until now. She wished she could share it with him somehow. But it was so personal an experience, others could only observe it, not experience it with him. Except perhaps another actor. Elaine, maybe?

Darienne inhaled and let the breath out in a sigh. He was singing to the actress now in the first scene Darienne had seen him do, when he stood behind her and skimmed her breasts with his hands, showing his desire. Oh, what Darienne wouldn't give to be Elaine, to experience that stunning sensuality! There must be a way. But he was never like this offstage, not with anyone, including Elaine. His deep sexuality only surfaced while he was in character.

That must be the key she was looking for, Darienne thought, her breaths coming faster as she watched Matthew's magical hands covet Elaine's body. Perhaps if she could see him directly after a show, before he'd had a chance to come out of character, before he reverted into his cautious self again. Darienne had to give it a try. Not tonight, not with the gala opening night celebration afterward. But another night, after another performance. She could wait.

During intermission, Darienne stayed in her seat and solidified her plans while others left to order drinks or stayed and talked. Even from her seat, she couldn't help but overhear breathless female voices commenting on Sir Percy, and asking how Matthew McDowall, whom they all knew as the bumbling Rick, could ever become so sexy?

As Darienne turned to see who belonged to the voice of one particularly vocal female behind her, her eyes drifted across a familiar face. It was Veronica! She was sitting in a seat in row ten, but farther to the right. She was dressed in a lacy, Victorian-style dress and looked lovely, but she appeared to be alone. The couples on either side of her did not seem to know her.

Just as Darienne thought of going over to talk to Veronica, the houselights flashed, indicating that the second half was about to begin. The people next to her took their seats, and she decided it would be too difficult to try to see Veronica now.

And then another thought hit Darienne like a thunderbolt. David was in the audience. She turned and looked up at the first balcony behind and above her. Immediately she spotted him in the front row, center, talking to Alexandra. Darienne clutched her beaded purse with anxiety as she faced forward again. She hoped Veronica wouldn't spot them. To see David with another woman might crush the vulnerable young woman who loved David with all her heart. Oh, David! Darienne thought, growing angry now. Why did he have to bring Alexandra? The icy blonde sitting next to him might ruin everything for him. Getting rid of her was a matter Darienne had been meaning to attend to.

But Matthew had constantly occupied her mind. How strange it was that the quiet, unassuming actor had taken over her thoughts and imaginings so entirely. She couldn't remem-

ber another man ever affecting her to this extent. Not in four
hundred years. Not even David.

When the musical ended, David watched Matthew come
down the center of the stage to take his bow. The applause
grew thunderous. Suddenly everyone around them in the balcony and on the floor below rose to their feet. David and
Alexandra followed suit. What a triumph for Matthew! David
thought. How well deserved!

"You should be down there taking a bow," Alexandra said
to him with a smile.

"No, I don't wish to be," he said while still applauding.
"I'm just glad it all worked." Even the computer.

After several minutes of continued applause, Matthew put
up his hands to ask the audience to grow quiet. When they did
he said, "There are many people behind the scenes who made
this production happen. Merle Larson, our producer, Charles
Macy, our director, Loni Gustafson, our set designer, and of
course, Leonard Southfield who wrote the music. But there is
one man whose profound inner vision created both the idea
and the lyrics, David de Morrissey."

Matthew pointed up toward the balcony as the audience
broke into energetic applause once again. David felt stunned
by the attention he did not wish, like an insect pinned to a
block of wood for everyone to inspect. He was touched that
Matthew had paid him tribute, but wished to the bones that
the actor had forgotten him.

Finally the applause ended after the curtain came down.
People began filing out.

"Let's wait until the aisles clear a bit," he said to Alexandra.

She smiled and took hold of his arm. "I'm so proud of
you."

"Thank you. That means a lot to me." He glanced at her.
She'd been a pleasant companion this evening. Looking beautiful in the pink dress she'd worn when he met her, she reminded him of all the qualities he'd admired in her when he
first saw her. Perhaps their affair would be on a more even keel
as time went on. She might be getting used to their bond after
all. Perhaps tonight would be the first of many pleasant nights
together, sharing their new relationship.

As the audience thinned, David rose from his seat to leave.

Alexandra followed suit. Somehow—something shifting in
the atmosphere, an unexpected tug on his mind—he was
drawn to look over the balcony railing at the half-empty seats
below. His eyes followed the middle aisle and he saw Darienne
there with Merle. She was looking up at David, but when he
waved, she didn't wave back. Her face carried an apprehensive expression, and he couldn't imagine why.

And then his gaze was drawn to another woman standing
in the middle aisle almost directly below the edge of the balcony. She stared straight up at him, her brown hair falling
over her shoulders, her large brown eyes bright with tears.

Veronica!

David looked down at her, transfixed, feeling faint. She
looked lovely, so incredibly beautiful to him. Instantly, without trying, without thinking, his mind connected with hers.
Though much time had passed, their dormant, unused bond
suddenly regained full strength, as if they had never been
apart. The sudden mental fusion of their beings enraptured
David, made him feel free and whole. He could sense the throb
of her heart pounding, her joy at seeing him. Though she
wasn't speaking, he could hear her clear, feminine voice in his
mind.

I love you, David.

Tears sprang to his eyes. Placing his hands on the railing, he
leaned forward to see her better. He answered her with his
mind, telling her urgently, *I love you! I need you!*

"Oh, Veronica," he whispered, looking down at her with
longing.

Veronica smiled, dark eyes shining and sweet. If he could
see a sunrise again, it couldn't be so beautiful to him as her
smile. He wanted to jump down to her from the balcony,
which he was perfectly capable of doing. He wanted to enfold
her in his arms, to talk to her, to bring her home to make love
with her again in the ballroom on the windowseat, their special place.

And with a heartrending thud he realized he could do none
of those things. He'd made a solemn agreement with her, and
for her sake he must keep it. He was breaking their pact just
by looking at her and communing with her now.

We must wait the allotted time, he told her with his mind,
even as his chest shuddered with a renewed sense of loss. *I'll*

summon you to me. Forever, if you wish. But we must wait until then. Goodbye, my Angel. He watched as she put her hands to her face and began to weep. She looked up once more, tears streaming down her face, and mouthed the words, "I love you!" then ran beneath the balcony and out of David's sight.

David remained for a long moment looking at the spot where she'd stood, then closed his eyes tightly in despair. The moments seeing her, hearing her voice in his mind, brought back every memory, every feeling he'd ever had for her. What torment to be so close, and yet have to send her away. But this he had to do, he insisted to himself. For her sake.

"David!"

Alexandra's voice intruded on his thoughts, just as her personality suddenly intruded on him through his bond with her. He turned and looked at her. Her blue eyes were bitter, like fiery ice. "David, who was that woman you were staring at?" she demanded in an infuriated whisper. "Who was she?"

14

A vampire has no honor

DAVID HADN'T really wanted to attend the opening night party, held at a French restaurant off Michigan Avenue. But he'd wanted to be left alone with Alexandra even less. So he'd escorted her there, as planned. Here Merle, Loni, and others he'd worked with on the show had come up to him to share congratulations.

Now he sat with Alexandra in a booth by the wall, sipping port and still recovering from seeing his beloved Veronica. Alexandra leaned back against the red velvet of the booth seat and looked coldly at the excited crowd of theater people which filled the restaurant. She finished her glass of champagne, her third in the half hour they'd been there. A waiter came by to refill her glass. David sent him away before he could pour any for her.

"David, how dare you!"

"You've had enough."

"That's not for you to decide."

"It isn't?"

"Are you taking away my free will?" she asked with sarcasm.

"Go ahead and get drunk, then," David said, looking away. "You can stay here and seethe as long as you like. I'm leaving in a few minutes."

"You wouldn't leave without me." Her tone changed to one of anxiety.

"No? I have free will, too. I don't have to stay with a woman who makes a spectacle of herself."

"And what about you? Staring at that . . . that girl like you were some lovesick calf! Right in front of me and everyone!"

"Are we back on that?"

"You haven't made any explanation."

"I don't intend to," David said, glaring at her now. "She is none of your business."

"Everything about you is my business," Alexandra said, her voice quivering with anger. "You made it that way when you initiated me." She touched the thick ribbon that held a cameo at her neck.

"It was what you wanted," David said in a tired voice.

"I wanted you," she said. "You never told me you were in love with someone else."

David grew silent and leaned back in his seat. It was true, he hadn't told her. He'd thought he'd lost Veronica. Not until tonight did he realize that Veronica did still love him, incredible as that seemed. Not only could he read it in her transmitted thoughts and see it in her eyes, but she'd even told him with her lips. A part of him was filled with joy. He had hope again!

But he also had Alexandra. Why had he ever thought initiation would do her or him any good? Why hadn't he had enough faith in Veronica to be true to her and not allow another woman into his world? What on earth would he do with Alexandra? She would always be there, wanting him. Just as Veronica's bond hadn't disappeared, neither would Alexandra's. Oh, God, what could he do?

"Don't look so glum, *cheri!* You should be celebrating like everyone else."

David looked up to find Darienne, draped in a sequined lavender gown, standing by their table. She smiled, but there was accusation in her eyes and a hint of chastisement in her voice. Darienne had seen what had happened with Veronica. He glanced away, feeling guilty all the more, for, indeed, Darienne had predicted his acute problems.

"Where's Chad?" he asked, to make conversation.

"I preferred to come on my own tonight." Darienne turned her eyes to the tight-lipped woman beside him. *"Bonsoir,* Alexandra. How are you?"

"Fine."

Darienne tilted her head and lowered her eyes at Alexandra's clipped response. "Good. Well, our stars aren't here yet."

"It takes Matthew a while to get his makeup off," David said, keeping up their idle chatter, not knowing what else to do or say. "They'll make a grand entrance soon, I imagine."

"Careful," Darienne said as Alexandra reached to grab another glass of champagne from a passing waiter. "Champagne isn't good for the complexion."

"I didn't know you worried about such things," Alexandra said in a waspish tone.

Darienne gave her a glittering smile. "You're right. *I* don't have to anymore."

Alexandra stared back at the other blonde, her eyes wide, her breathing becoming uneasy.

David grew impatient. Alexandra was upset enough over Veronica without Darienne baiting her, too. "Darienne, isn't there some attractive man here you can attach yourself to, since you didn't have the foresight to bring Chad along?"

Darienne shifted her gaze to him with amusement. She clicked her tongue in the French manner. "The man I intend to attach myself to hasn't arrived yet. So I decided to come over here to be polite and say hello. But I'll leave now so you and Alexandra can be alone, which I know is just what you'd like."

He stared at her for a moment, shifting his jaw. Exasperating female! He loosened up enough to say, "Good-night, Darienne."

After giving him another upbraiding look, Darienne glanced at Alexandra and walked off into the crowd at the center of the restaurant.

"How can you stand that horrid woman!" Alexandra said before polishing off her new glass of champagne.

"Who? You?"

She turned on him. "I won't be spoken to like that!"

"Sorry," he said coldly.

"I'll bet! I'll bet you're sorry for everything. Especially for meeting me, when you already had so many other females in your life." Her speech was growing a bit slurred.

With deliberation David placed the palms of his hands on the tablecloth and studied his spread fingers. "You know, when I met you, I thought you were the most elegant, cultured, most refined woman I'd ever met. I'd never have imagined you could turn yourself into a drunken shrew."

"You're making me this way!"

He coolly glared at her. "I? If I chose to make you anything, it wouldn't be this!" he said, gesturing toward her.

Tears welled in her eyes. "It's only because I love you, David. I can't stand the idea of another woman. Who was that girl? Maybe if you explain, I'll understand."

"She has nothing to do with you."

"Did you initiate her, too? You were communicating with her, I could tell. Do you have a bond with her?"

David glanced over the crowded room. "This isn't the place to speak of these things."

She grabbed hold of his arm and shook him. "Oh, God, I hate you for being so secretive! I have a right to know!"

He took hold of her hands gripping him. "Stop it," he said with a soft but authoritative voice. "You're getting hysterical."

"I don't care!" she cried in a voice loud enough that a few people nearby turned to look. "I have a right. You owe me!"

Growing angry and exhausted from arguing with her, David fixed her with his eyes. He implanted a thought in her mind, and while he was at it, seized mental hold of her will and twisted it to his own. He let go of her and in a gentler voice he asked, "What do you want to say to me?"

"Nothing, David," she replied meekly, a tear sliding down her face. "This isn't the time or the place."

"That's right." David could barely find his voice as he realized he'd just broken his promise. Dazed and ashamed, he sat still for a long moment. Then he rose, took her by the hand, and quietly led her through the celebrating crowd and out of the restaurant.

Since she was in no state to drive her car, he hailed a cab and took her to her home. After seeing her into her house, he turned to leave.

"Where are you going?" she asked.

"Home."

"No, stay," she said, pulling at his arm.

"I've had enough, Alexandra. I'm leaving."

"Please don't go! I'm sorry. I'm sorry. I know I haven't

behaved well. Please stay. Let me make it up to you. We haven't made love for days. I need you, David."

David knew he would never make love to her again. He took hold of her hands and unclasped them from his arm, just as he had at the restaurant. "We must stop seeing each other."

"No!" The word sounded like a wail.

"Alexandra, it's the only way. This is no good. Let's separate before we hate each other."

"You say that as if it were so simple! I *can't* leave you."

"You can and you will. I'll make you forget me if I have to. I can, you know. Just as I forced you into obedience at the party."

"You said you wouldn't take away my free will."

David looked down at the cold wood floor. "I've done it already, so what difference would it make? It would save us both a lot of needless grief."

"But what would I do without you?" She sank to the floor weeping, clinging to his hand.

She looked so pitiful, he was close to despising her. "If you don't remember me, you won't miss me."

"You can't do that to me. You promised me my free will. You promised. I thought you were a man of honor."

"A vampire has no honor."

She looked up, eyes flashing. "Make me like you, David. Free me through the blood ceremony."

"Free you to drive me crazy, as Darienne does? No, I'd rather have you like this. Disgusting as you've become, at least I can control you."

She looked up at him with harrowed eyes. Letting go of his hand, as if it singed hers, she said, "I never thought you could be so heartless. I've become a disgrace and you've become so cruel. How could this have happened? We were once so good together."

He shook his head. "It only seemed good, and for the wrong reasons. I used you to escape loneliness. And you used me because your feelings frightened you and I eased you through your fears."

"You helped me."

"That's the folly," he said. "How could I help you? I'm not human anymore. How could I help anyone?"

Even Veronica, David thought, overcome with a hopeless

feeling. When their pact ended and Veronica came to him, would their renewed relationship end as sadly as this? Veronica would do best not to choose to be with him. In his darkest, most truthful moments, he'd always known this.

"You're thinking of her again—that girl! Even now, while I'm pleading with you for my sanity, you're thinking of her."

David looked at the disheveled blonde at his feet. "If I'd been true to her, all this would never have happened."

"But what about me? I needed you to happen to me."

"No."

"Yes! Don't make me forget you, David. My life was so empty without you."

"But now it's miserable *with* me."

"It doesn't have to be." She rose to her feet. "Let's try again. I won't hold your other women against you. Not even Darienne. But let me be one of your women."

"You're too possessive for that."

"I can change."

"No," he said. "I know you now. The only way you'll change is if I change you. The only way we can possibly continue this sick relationship is if I control your mind." He grasped her hands. "Is that what you want? Shall I take away your free will? Or would you rather I took away your memory of me?"

"Make me a vampiress!" she said, eyes bright.

He shook his head grimly. "I have enough morality left not to condemn you to be what I am."

"I *want* to be a vampiress!"

"You don't know what you're asking. I explained to you what an alienated creature you would become. But you refuse to listen. And I'm tired of trying to reason with you. So, shall I make you my slave? Shall I make you forget me? Or shall I leave you as you are and never see you again? These are your choices."

She looked up at him in agitation. "I . . . I need time to think."

"No stalling, Alexandra. I have no more patience with you, my dear."

He could feel the turmoil in her soul, but it garnered no sympathy from him. He really didn't care much what she chose, though he supposed making her forget would be the best from his point of view. God, she was right: How cold-hearted he'd become!

"Leave me be," she said at last, looking at him with some hesitation and fear.

He nodded. "If that's what you wish, then so be it. I will not see you again."

"W-what about . . . ?"

"The bond? That, unfortunately, will stay with us. But we won't employ it. There is nothing other than the bond to pull us together."

"Except the love I have for you!" she said with new tears. "That was there before you initiated me."

He smiled. "Sorry. I question what you call love. I managed to help you find your sexuality, Alexandra. And we're both cultural eggheads. We had that in common. But neither of those things can be equated with love."

"You never even cared for me, did you?"

"You're wrong. I did care, though I admit I never loved you. I still care enough to try to do what's right for you. Now you've made your choice, and I am out of your life. Forget me and go on making your beautiful violins. Pursue your dreams, but don't make me one of them. Good-night." He turned and opened her front door.

"David—"

"Good-night!" He walked out and shut her door behind him, then hurried down the steps and up the street, moving as far from her as fast as he could.

Darienne accompanied Matthew as he walked down the sidewalk toward Marina Towers. Earlier he'd dismissed the limousine provided him for opening night. It was almost 2 A.M. now, the city streets were quiet and the night air was delightfully cool with a strong breeze off Lake Michigan.

Getting access to him at the boisterous, crowded opening night party had been easier than Darienne had expected. Matthew had cooperated, though not for the reason she might have hoped. Elaine had firmly attached herself to his arm as they arrived amidst the glitter of flashbulbs, and they were loudly welcomed with another standing ovation at the restaurant. After that, Elaine made every effort to keep her place at his side. When Darienne came up to congratulate him, Matthew had congenially encouraged her to stay nearby, as he did with Loni and some of the show's dancers.

Darienne had understood this was his method of keeping Elaine from getting too close without hurting her feelings. However, Darienne had also noticed, somewhat to her surprise, that Matthew did not look the tiniest bit uncomfortable surrounded by females. Indeed, he seemed on top of the world and flashed his huge smile, made jokes, and flirted with them all. When he turned his eyes full force on Darienne for a brief moment, she experienced again that stunned, inebriated feeling he'd given her once before with just a look.

Leaving the party with him had also not been difficult. Elaine hadn't recovered from the flu as well as Matthew. When her mother, who was at the party, insisted she leave early to rest, Matthew had earnestly concurred and sent her away with an affectionate hug and kiss on the cheek. Darienne again had felt unfamiliar pangs of jealousy.

With Elaine gone, winnowing Matthew out from the crowd and leaving with him had been child's play for Darienne, partly because Matthew hadn't put up any fight. Darienne might have hoped it was because he was suddenly succumbing to her charms, but she suspected it was because she'd stayed with him when he was ill and he did not want to offend her. This more or less put her in the same boat with Elaine, she realized with a sense of irony.

Well, she was here with him at the entrance to his building, not Elaine, and she intended to make the most of her opportunity.

"Shall I drive you home?" he asked. "If I'd thought of it, I'd have asked the limo driver to stay for you."

Darienne thought quickly. If he drove her home, she wouldn't be able to coax him up to her place, because it was so late. A better plan was to ask to call a cab, because he'd have to invite her up in order to make the call.

She smiled at him. "I don't want to keep you up. I'll call a cab."

He nodded with equanimity. They went up in the elevator and soon were in his living room. Darienne, of course, did not rush to the phone.

"Elaine performed well, didn't she?"

"She's a little trooper," Matthew agreed, putting his keys into his pants pocket.

"What will you do about her?"

Matthew's expression grew sober. "She does kind of cling to me, doesn't she? I don't know. I have to work with her and I don't want to mar our good relationship. But I don't want to lead her on—though it doesn't seem to me that that's what I do."

"You have this trouble often, don't you?"

"It's not the first time it's happened," he agreed.

"You're warm and supportive. Lots of women wish they could find those qualities in a man."

"The father thing you mentioned."

"Yes." She smiled and moved closer to him. "That's not what I see in you, though."

As she smoothed the lapels of his tuxedo, he took hold of her hands. "I think I'd better call you that cab."

"Now, Matthew, don't get nervous. I know you need your rest. I nursed you, remember? Shall I tuck you into bed? Rub your temples?"

"I don't have a headache. But I do need sleep. There's a matinee tomorrow."

"I know. But this is your opening night triumph. You should celebrate by giving yourself an extra treat—me." She took his hands and placed them at her waist.

He kept them there for a second, but then pulled away and slid his hands into his pockets. His eyes took on a firm, knowing expression. "Elaine's looking for a father, and you're looking for—"

"A passionate lover."

He ignored her interruption and finished his sentence. "An overpowering male to mesmerize you. That's what you want—the image I portray on stage, not me."

"But you are Sir Percy."

"Sir Percy, as you've often reminded me, is a vampire. You bring that up all the time because that's your fixation."

She looked at him with surprise. "You think I'm fixated?"

"It's a psychological thing. I've mentioned it before. Women who have inhibitions about sex get hooked on the idea of a man who can mesmerize and overpower them. Unconsciously, they feel they could enjoy total sexual abandon with such a man because they would have no guilt. No guilt because he overpowered her and there was nothing she could do about it. I read it in a psychology magazine."

Darienne laughed, stroked his cheek with her fingertips, and said, "You're cute."

"You're not taking this very seriously."

"If only I could!" she said. "You don't know me yet. I have no sexual hang-ups, *cheri*. I love men and I love sex. I don't need a man to mesmerize me and make me forget to feel guilty, because I never feel guilty to begin with."

"You're sure?"

"Try me."

He looked askance and took a long, deep breath.

"Oh, do that again."

"What?"

"Make your chest come out." She slid her hands up his white shirt as he exhaled. "You have the most sensual way of breathing."

"I still think it's Sir Percy you're after."

"And I still say, you are he." She lifted her hands to his temples. "Somewhere in here is where Sir Percy dwells, though you keep him well hidden when you're offstage."

"But you have this thing about vampires, Darienne. You seem to think about them more than most people."

For reasons he would never know, Darienne thought, lowering her eyes. She decided it was a good time to change the subject a bit. "What sort of relationship did you have with your wife?"

He blinked. "Where did that question come from?"

"You mentioned her when you talked in your sleep last night. I'm just curious."

He left her and walked into the middle of his living room. "That's a long story."

"I'd like to hear it."

"It's not something I like to think about."

"You have nightmares. It might do you good to talk about it."

He sat down in an easy chair and rubbed his eyes. "I met her in New York when I was doing a play. It was a few years after I filmed *The Boy from Savannah,* and I was making a pretty good living as an actor. There was a cast party and she was the sister of another actor. I was twenty-two and she was eighteen. We fell head over heels. When she got pregnant, I rushed her to Las Vegas to marry her. I was so happy. I thought, 'I've got it all now—a career I love and the girl I love.' "

He paused and Darienne sat in front of him on the floor, at his feet, wanting to watch him closely as he spoke. "What happened?" she prompted when he hesitated to continue.

"Our son was born. Everything was great for a while. In fact, we stayed married for five years. But my career began to get in the way. I had to go to Europe to make a couple of films. When I had another stage play in New York, I spent hours rehearsing at the theater, so even when I was home, I wasn't 'home' as much as she wanted. We both grew disappointed. She thought I was obsessed with acting, and I thought she should have understood that a man needs to pursue his career. I argued that she knew I was an actor when she married me. She said she thought I would change my priorities because I *was* married."

He spread his hands. "It was hopeless. Really, she was right. I should have changed. But I couldn't. I have to perform. I need to perform. I'm an insatiable actor. There's nothing else I want to do."

He sighed and looked down. "Losing her was hard. I still loved her. Because of that a custody fight developed over my son. I thought I saw a way to keep her near, maybe win her back, if I had care of the child she loved. I argued that I could support him best. She insisted she would give him more love and attention. I said I could give him that, too—but that was a bluff, of course. If I couldn't give her what she needed, what attention would I have given him? Since I could afford a better lawyer, I won custody. By then the fight had gotten so hostile, I was afraid to allow her visiting privileges because I feared she might take him. As it turned out, she managed to do it anyway. He disappeared after school one day. Later I got a note from her saying she'd taken him and was leaving for a foreign country where I would never find them. A private detective discovered she'd taken him to Scotland, where she had relatives. I let it be since I'd finally begun to realize all the arguing wasn't good for the boy."

"You said you haven't seen him in years?"

Matthew shook his head. "Not since he was five. He's grown now. My wife gave me an old photo of him, but even she hasn't seen him for three years. She thinks he's still in Great Britain, maybe London. Apparently he feels bitter towards me. I don't blame him."

"You've seen your wife?"

"When she returned from Scotland a few years ago to live in New York again." His expression changed as he spoke. His eyes took on a vulnerable quality Darienne had never seen in them before.

"What happened?" she asked.

"I'm not sure. It was an odd reunion. I don't want to talk about it."

Darienne nodded silently, feeling unsettled. "You refer to her as your wife. Didn't you ever divorce?"

He looked up. "Yes, we did. I should call her my ex, shouldn't I?"

"Are you still being true to her? Is that why you don't allow yourself to be with other women?"

His head went back a bit. "Who says I don't?"

"Oh." Darienne felt put in her place again. He allowed himself women, just not her. "Have you seen your wife since she first returned?"

"No."

"Why?"

"Busy working."

"You use that excuse a lot."

He leaned back in his chair. "Maybe it is an excuse. But I'm intense about my work. Since that trait ended my marriage, I've avoided commitments with women ever since. Being busy working is the best excuse I have, because it's true."

"Yet you find time to be so nurturing toward women."

He chuckled. "Maybe I'm trying to make up for my failure to give my wife what she needed. And my son."

"But it's just that quality that makes women like Elaine long for a commitment from you. You'll always wind up in a double bind."

He rested his head on his hand. "You may have something there."

She rose slightly and leaned her arm across his knees as she smiled at him. "And you have something here," she said, pointing to herself. "A woman who isn't looking for a commitment and doesn't need to be nurtured. Maybe I'm just what *you* ought to be looking for."

He reached out and touched his forefinger to the tip of her nose. "Maybe. But what you don't realize is that you'll be disappointed. I know what you're expecting. And I can't give you what you imagine I can, Darienne. I'm not Sir Percy Blackeney. I'm only me."

"Matthew—"

"Shhh." He took her by her arms and stood up, making her rise, too. "I think it's time I phoned for your cab."

15

This would be a night of nights

A FEW days after opening night, David walked down Oak Street toward Lake Michigan in the cooling night air. It was about nine o'clock. As he passed the renovated brownstones, he hoped the noise of the city or the sound of the waves when he reached the lake would obliterate Alexandra's voice from his mind. She'd been mentally calling him constantly ever since he'd risen. *Forgive me. Come to me. I need you!*

David ought to have been able to block her out, but guilt prevented him. As he tried again to push her out of his mind, he heard the sound of high heels coming up the sidewalk behind him. He began to walk faster, afraid to look in back of him and find Alexandra.

All at once the footsteps were beside him and someone took his arm. He glimpsed blond hair and smelled French perfume.

"Bonsoir, cheri."

David relaxed at the familiar throaty voice. He turned and looked at Darienne. "Where did you come from?"

"Your home. When you weren't there, I looked up the street and saw you."

He glanced at the clothes she wore: a pink, slim skirt that crossed in front and fastened at the waist, leaving a center opening that revealed her long legs as she walked. With this she wore a sheer pink blouse that buttoned down the front, the highest button being between her breasts, which were covered by big, well-placed pockets. As she moved, her flesh softly bounced and cleavage begged to be glimpsed.

"I don't quite understand this costume," David said. "Innocent pink. A conservative ensemble. Yet you're managing to show off everything you've got."

Darienne grinned like a sleek Mona Lisa. "Then I've accomplished what I set out to do."

"This, I deduce, is for Matthew's benefit?"

"Oui."

David glanced at his watch. "Why are you here? He's beginning his performance now."

"He'll be giving me a special performance afterward, if I do my part right," she said, eyes sensual and glittering.

David shook his head. "Can't you leave that poor man alone?"

"But he *won't be* poor or unhappy after I leave him tonight. It's just a matter of catching him at the correct moment."

David inhaled as if trying to breathe in patience from the moist night air. "So why have you come to see me instead of drooling over Matthew on stage?"

"One must make some sacrifices for one's friends," she said. "I'm worried about Veronica. And about your relationship with Alexandra."

"I've ended the affair with Alexandra," he said, not ready yet to talk about Veronica.

"How?"

"Told her I'll never see her again."

Darienne lifted her eyes to the moonlit sky. "She'll never let you be, David."

He nodded with reluctance. "I'm afraid you're right. She's been calling to me all evening. I can't make myself block her out."

"Try harder."

"I feel too guilty. It *is* my fault that she's in this situation."

"Don't start feeling sorry for her," Darienne said in a warning tone.

"I was very cold and harsh with her last night."

"I'm glad to hear it!"

He glanced at her impatiently. "You never had a heart, so how can you know?"

Light from a street lamp illuminated her shining hair falling over her shoulders as she walked beside him in silence. "You really think I have no heart?" she said after a few moments.

"I don't mean that you're cold," David said, trying to be

more tactful. "You care about me, and I try to appreciate that. But you've cared for very few mortals. Veronica is one of the exceptions."

Darienne's eyes quickened. "What happened when you saw her?"

He swallowed before he could speak. "She told me she loved me," he said in a broken voice, smiling. "It gave me so much joy."

She made David stop walking by tugging on his arm. "Go back to her then! It's the only way you or she will ever be happy."

He shook his head adamantly and continued his pace. "I told her we must wait the full ten years. She wept, but I believe she understood."

Darienne lifted her hand to her forehead and closed her eyes, obviously exasperated. She would never understand the concept of moral obligation, David reminded himself while gearing for her response.

"What about Alexandra?" Darienne asked. "Wasn't Veronica upset to see her with you?"

The question surprised David. "I don't know. Her eyes were focused on me alone. She may not even have noticed Alexandra beside me."

"I hope you're right," Darienne said in a vehement whisper. "I don't know what she would do if she knew you'd found someone else."

David bowed his head. "I was sure I'd lost her," he tried to explain, though it seemed a weak excuse now.

"It's my fault, too," Darienne said with a sigh. "I gave you the stupid advice to have a quick fling with Alexandra."

"I didn't do it because you told me to," David insisted. "I was lonely. I needed someone to replace the woman I was sure I'd never have. As if anyone could ever replace Veronica."

"Particularly not Alexandra," Darienne said with disgust as they paused before crossing a street. "Get rid of her, David."

David looked at her with alarm. Darienne's tone sounded murderous. "What do you mean?"

"Make her a vampiress. She'll leave you alone then."

David relaxed a bit. "You know I can't do that."

"You'd put an injured animal out of its misery, wouldn't

you? She'll pine for you all her life unless you transform her life."

David thought this over for a moment. "No," he finally said. "If anything, I should give her another chance."

Darienne's mouth dropped open. "You've given her too many chances already! That woman will never redeem herself."

"Maybe she just needs more time. She said I owe her, and my conscience tells me she's right."

"Owe her what?"

"My emotional support. I put her in this situation. Yes, she wanted it, but she couldn't have understood the consequences. No mortal could. I knew that and I initiated her anyway. I should repay her for my mistake by resuming our relationship. Not sexually, of course. But I should be there to help her through her dilemma. I should do right by her somehow."

Darienne shook her head, her expression impatient, agitated. "Look, David, I know how strongly you feel your obligations. But will you agree to one suggestion from me?"

"What?"

"Let it rest for a few more days—till the end of the week, say. Don't see her. Don't give in to her calls to you. You told her you wouldn't see her again, so don't cave in yet. You don't want her to think you can give in to her that easily, do you?"

David looked down at the sidewalk. For once Darienne had a good point. "No, I wouldn't want to appear to have feet of clay. All right, I'll wait before I see her again. Thank you for pointing that out to me," he added, feeling he must give credit where it was due, even to Darienne.

She smiled and seemed to relax. "You're welcome," she said as they neared the traffic of North Michigan Avenue. "Ah, it's nice to have that off my mind for the moment. I have much more important things to attend to tonight."

David pinched the bridge of his nose. "Darienne, leave the man alone. You'll only embarrass him and yourself."

She grinned as she began to turn south down Michigan Avenue. "Matthew's adorable when he blushes," she told him blithely. *"Bonsoir, cheri,"* she called, blowing him a kiss as she hurried off in the direction of the theater.

* * *

Darienne reached the theater during intermission, entering by the stage door. She stayed out of the way and made no attempt to speak to Matthew while Wendy touched up his makeup after his costume change. When he left his dressing room and walked with his dresser to his entrance point in the wings, Darienne didn't think he even saw her standing in the hall. He appeared to be in deep concentration, and she'd heard that the bright blue contact lenses he wore diffused his vision a bit. But seeing him in makeup as Sir Percy made her pulse race, knowing what plan she had in store for him.

After he left, she walked into his dressing room, where Wendy was putting some makeup brushes into a protective case. Darienne took her usual position beside the mirror. The redhead looked up and smiled.

"Hi! I didn't know you were here."

"I just arrived," Darienne said. "How's the performance going?"

"Fine, so I hear. Everyone's calmed down since opening night."

"The rave reviews from the critics probably soothed everyone's nerves," Darienne said.

"Better than that, Matthew's starting to get loads of fan mail. Most of it from women, of course," Wendy said with a chuckle. "They've started gathering at the stage door after each show to get his autograph. Some even bring him gifts." She pointed to a nearby shelf where a teddy bear sat which someone had dressed in black with a red vest and cape. Next to it was an enlarged copy of a photo someone had taken of Matthew waving to crowds as he got into his limousine to attend the opening night party. There were plants and balloons and also dozens of congratulations cards arranged on an upper shelf.

Looking at them, Darienne had a slight feeling of apprehension. Other women were beginning to admire him and no doubt imagine themselves with him just as she did. It wasn't fair, Darienne thought. She'd seen him first.

She'd have him first, too. And maybe last, while she was at it. Why should she give him up to these parasites, these stage door Jills? "Has he been signing autographs for them?" she asked Wendy.

"Oh, yeah. Last night he must have been out there at least

twenty minutes. He stays until everyone has what they want."

He does, does he? Darienne thought. Well, he'd better give her what she wanted, too. She smiled at Wendy, who was wiping up powder that had been spilled on the counter. "What's Matthew's procedure after a performance?" she asked as if from idle curiosity. "Does he change and then get his makeup off like he did after rehearsals?"

"His routine hasn't changed much. First he takes out his contact lenses. He gives those to me and then he goes in there," Wendy said, pointing to the adjoining room with the couch, "and changes. Then he comes out and gets his makeup off."

Perfect, Darienne thought. "What about you? What do you do while the show is on?"

"Me?" The redhead shrugged. "After I clean up and arrange my tools, I go have a Coke and talk with some of the women from wardrobe. Or I read until I hear the applause at the end of the show."

"You almost sound bored."

Wendy chuckled. "It gets to be old hat pretty quickly."

"I'm glad it hasn't reached that point for me yet. I still think it's exciting," Darienne said with a smile. "In fact, I think I'll watch the rest of the show from the wings. It was nice to talk to you again."

"Sure. Maybe I'll see you afterward."

"It's possible," Darienne said, trying to sound noncommittal. She hoped Wendy wouldn't see her. At least not before she'd executed her plan.

Darienne left and walked to the wings. The stage manager pointed her to a spot where she would be out of the way. She looked toward the stage then, and her eyes settled greedily on Matthew.

Watching him, she was quickly drawn into the momentum of the musical. And just as quickly, she fell once again under his spell. The elegant poignance of his hands, his passionate singing voice, the masculine sensuality his body exuded with each breath and step, all made Darienne as high as if she'd been inhaling too long from an open bottle of French perfume.

When they came to the final scene, Darienne watched as he sang a love song to Elaine. In this scene, Sir Percy initiated

Marguerite, though the bite was done in a somewhat symbolic manner, not with the realism David had achieved in *Street Shadows*. For this reason, Darienne had always been a bit disappointed in the way it was staged, though she'd never voiced her opinion on the matter.

But tonight, as she watched it from such a different vantage point, the scene had a much more powerful effect. The audience saw Matthew and Elaine in profile as they stood facing each other. But from the wings, Darienne saw Elaine's back and Matthew's face as he sang to her. When he drew her to him and bent her backward for the symbolic bite at her neck, Darienne could see him physically enveloping Elaine, overpowering her. And when, as the script required, Marguerite grew faint and he swept her up in his arms, carrying her limp body across the stage in a triumphant manner while singing of his passion for her, Darienne could barely breathe.

Perhaps Matthew's theory of the overpowering male had some merit after all. At any rate, she could guess that it was more than his kind, caring manner offstage that had made Elaine fall for him. To be the actress responding to his sensual embrace each night—well, poor little Elaine didn't stand a chance. No wonder she'd dumped her fiancé! Who could compare to her stage lover?

Too bad for Elaine that I'll get him first, Darienne thought with a smug smile. But it stood to reason that a man like this would need a full-bodied woman to satisfy him, not a sweet, slender, young thing. When it came to pulchritude combined with experience, no woman living could hope to compete with Darienne. She wasn't being immodest. She was just reminding herself of the facts.

Darienne remembered suddenly that if her plan was to be a success, she'd better leave the wings before the show ended. She was already cutting it close. Tearing herself from Matthew's spell, she quietly walked out of the stage area, down the empty hallway to Matthew's dressing room. Heart beating with excitement, she peeked in, but no one was inside. She glanced both ways down the hall, but other than the security people by the stage door, who were reading, there was no one about.

Quickly she slipped into Matthew's dressing room, then

entered the adjoining rectangular room. Here she passed the long couch and the candle burning on the small table. On the floor stood a large bouquet of balloons and another of roses, probably sent to him opening night. She passed these and went to the door at the far end, his bathroom, complete with a shower. She closed the door and waited.

Several minutes later, in the distance, she could hear the long, thunderous ovation from the audience as the actors took their bows. A couple of minutes later, she heard voices, Matthew's and Wendy's, in the mirror room. She held her breath in anticipation. She had to move quickly to approach him before he mentally disengaged from his stage character.

All at once she heard the door to the rectangular room shut and footsteps outside the bathroom door. Inhaling deeply to calm herself, Darienne opened the door she'd been listening at and walked out. Matthew, still in costume except for his blue contact lenses, looked up. Beads of sweat dotted his makeup and his breathing was still somewhat labored from his exertion onstage. His broad chest expanded beneath his scarlet vest as he took off his black cape.

"Darienne?" he said, eyes questioning.

"Sir Percy?" she said. She walked up and took the cape from him, tossing it onto the couch. "I've been waiting for you."

"What's wrong?"

"Nothing, *cheri*. Nothing at all." She stepped around him to lock the door to the other room. He watched in puzzlement, as though his mind were at sea. Good, she thought. He hadn't completely reverted to Matthew yet. She moved close and ran her hands up his vest, feeling his heart beating beneath his expanding and contracting rib cage. "You show so much passion onstage," she whispered. "It must be frustrating to never carry that passion to its logical conclusion. But I'm here tonight. Fulfill yourself with me. Pretend I'm Marguerite." She began unbuttoning her blouse. "I'll make a good Marguerite. I'll match your sensuality and then some." She pulled apart her blouse, exposing her bare breasts.

As she ran her fingertips slowly and provocatively over her nipples, she studied Matthew and was encouraged by what she saw. His lips parted and his misty eyes carried a dazed look as he followed the movement of her hands. It almost disappointed her to see that, like any other male, he turned into a wide-eyed child at the sight of her undraped body. But that was all right. Now she had total control.

She pushed the waistcoat off his shoulders and down his arms until it fell to the floor. "Wouldn't want to muss your expensive clothes," she whispered as she went to work on his vest. As a bead of sweat poured down his face, he lifted his hands to her shoulders. Slowly he moved them down her large breasts, not quite touching her, yet savoring every inch he crossed. She could feel the heat of his fingers, which trembled slightly. Darienne's breaths began to grow as ragged as his. Oh, this would be a night of nights. Finally, finally she would experience him!

In no time, for she worked with lightning speed, she'd unbuttoned his vest and then his shirt. But when she tried to pull the shirt out of his breeches, it wouldn't budge. It had never occurred to her that his stage clothes would be sewn differently. But in an instant she realized that his shirt must be fastened underneath, so that it wouldn't ride up. No wonder he always looked so impeccably groomed onstage.

There was nothing to do but unfasten the breeches, if she could figure out how. They didn't have a zipper. As she groped about his waistband, trying to find where they fastened, he suddenly caught her hands in his. She looked up.

"Darienne, that's enough." He sounded like the old Matthew now.

"No, don't stop me," she said. She took the hands that held hers and pressed them onto her breasts. "You want me. I know you do."

She saw heat in his eyes and sensed possessiveness in his warm hands on her flesh. But nevertheless, he pulled his hands away from her body. "This is ridiculous," he said in an angry undertone. "Sneaking in here, waiting for me, tearing off my clothes! How can you debase yourself this way?"

"Debase myself! I'm just going after what I want."

"I thought even you would have more class than to do it this way," he said, stepping away to pick up the cape. He put it over her, covering her. "Now please leave."

Furious, she began buttoning her blouse beneath the cape.

"Why won't you give in?" she asked. "There's nothing wrong with having desires and appeasing them. Are you trying to be a saint? Are you still in love with your wife? Or Elaine? What's the problem?"

"It has nothing to do with other women. And I'm no saint. I just think people ought to conduct themselves with a little more dignity than this! Wendy's in the next room ready to take my makeup off. I have fans waiting for me at the stage door. You expect me to indulge in a quick lay while all these people are waiting for me to come out of this room?"

"Why not, if it's what you want?"

"It isn't."

She threw the cape aside and walked up to him. Her breasts were covered again, but she pushed herself against him, knowing he could still feel their round firmness pressing into his chest. "Isn't it?" she whispered. She brought her lips close to his and slid her hand downward over his breeches. Soon she found proof positive that she'd aroused his desire. "You say one thing," she told him with a smile, "and your body says another."

Closing his eyes tightly in a grimace, he took her by the shoulders and pushed her away from him. "You'd better go home now."

"Why, Matthew?" she asked, her tone showing her severe disappointment.

"I don't want to have you arrested for attempted rape," he muttered. "Now go, before I yell for security."

"Matthew!" she said, incensed.

"I'm warning you. I'm not putting up with people sneaking into my private quarters. This is my sanctuary and you've intruded it. So get out."

"Ooohh!" she fumed. "You must wear a chastity belt on those breeches! No wonder no one can get them off. You seem to have lost the key!"

"Darienne—"

"All right! Yes! I'm leaving!" She reached for the door-knob, then turned back for a parting tirade. "I feel sorry for you! You're so frustrated, you've forgotten what real satisfaction feels like. The adulation of an audience can't take the place of good old-fashioned sex. But when you finally recognize that, don't come to me. I don't give second chances!"

With that she pulled open the door. She breezed past a startled Wendy with all the dignity Matthew had said she lacked.

16

For I have sworn thee fair

A FEW days after he'd last seen Darienne, David sat in his office at about 8 P.M. cleaning up his desk. He was filing newspaper clippings, the glowing reviews of *The Scarlet Shadow*, in a folder and deciding whether to discard or save his notes and rough drafts of the libretto. Minute by minute as he worked, he grew more aware of an odd feeling. His home seemed too quiet. He could hear the ticking of his wall clock and his wristwatch and a dog barking down the street. Somehow something, a sound, seemed to be missing, but he couldn't pinpoint it.

And all at once the realization flashed into his mind: Alexandra wasn't calling to him tonight. Ever since he'd walked out on her, he'd heard her voice calling him through their bond. But tonight—silence. He ought to have been grateful, relieved. Yet he couldn't help but wonder why she'd suddenly stopped. What had happened?

Reluctantly he tuned his mind to hers. He needed to know if she was all right. As he mentally searched, projecting his thoughts to her, he grew increasingly alarmed. He couldn't find that special wavelength that tied her to him. It was as if their bond had been broken, or had evaporated. David turned cold and stopped breathing for a moment. Was she dead? Had she killed herself out of desperation because he hadn't responded to her pleas?

David rose from his chair in a panic. This was all his fault. She may have taken her own life, but he had created the despair that had caused her to do it!

Wait, he told himself, gripping the back of his office chair.

Calm down. He didn't know yet what had happened. He ought to find out the facts before he condemned himself.

Immediately he left for her home. He hailed a cab on nearby Rush Street and arrived at her house within a half hour. With trepidation, he climbed her front steps. The house lights were on. All of them. Every room was lit. David felt relieved. She must not be dead. Unless—unless her body had just been discovered and police were searching the house.

He looked up and down the street. No police cars in sight. What was going on? He peeked through the curtained window beside the door. Her shop was cluttered with boxes lying on the wood floor and on her worktables. The shelves in the back had been cleared and stood empty, except for the stockpile of wood on the highest shelf.

He gave a start when all at once Alexandra entered the room. Thank God she was alive! Dressed in a black blouse and pants, she carried a short stepladder. She pulled the ladder apart and set it below the shelf with the wood.

David drew away from the window. Was she packing? Moving? Wonderful, he thought. He could go home and rest easy. Except—what about the bond? How could it have been erased? He didn't sense the open channel lying dormant as he should. He felt an absolute void in that place in his mind where he had used to communicate with her, even now when he was in close proximity to her. There was something very odd here, and he had to know what. He rang her doorbell.

In a moment Alexandra opened the door. She stood there looking collected, purposeful, and only mildly surprised as she gazed at him. She said nothing, but calmly raised a questioning eyebrow.

"Something's changed," he said.

She smiled a bit and opened the door wider, inviting him in. When he'd entered, she shut the door and leaned against it, eyeing him in a cool, triumphant manner. "Yes, David, something's different." She smiled again—a radiant, full smile.

In an instant David saw what had changed: Her incisors were slightly elongated and sharp. Like his.

"No!" he exclaimed, reaching out to her with one hand. "Oh, no!"

"Oh, yes!" she said, bright self-possession infusing her eyes.

"Now I am what you are. It's what I've wanted ever since you told me it was possible."

He stopped short of touching her. "How?" he asked, his anguish revealed in his voice.

"Darienne," she replied.

David shut his eyes in pain and inclined his head. Why hadn't he foreseen this? He might have stopped Darienne before it was too late. Darienne may have been trying to protect him, but she'd gone too far!

"Don't look so grieved. I *asked* her to do it," Alexandra said. "I'm glad Darienne isn't burdened with all your hang-ups. She was perfectly willing to perform the blood ceremony. For a price, of course."

He looked up in alarm. "A price?"

"My ruby."

"Your mother's ring?" Darienne did this for a paltry jewel? And Alexandra went along with it? "How could you part with something your mother gave you?"

Alexandra shrugged. "She would have wanted me to be happy and independent. And I am—now. More independent than I ever was. Because I don't belong to the mortal world anymore, and that's fine with me. Mother's long gone and my father and brother can go to hell, for all I care. I don't need or want any ties to my past. That's why I'm leaving."

David shook his head, feeling dazed. He sat down on a nearby stool. "Where are you going?"

"Cremona, Italy," she said with a smile. "I liked living there when I studied violin making. I'm going to set up my shop there. I'd have to leave Chicago anyway. Too many people know me here and might notice a change in me. I couldn't continue with the Philharmonic. The rehearsals are during the day."

David slumped with a feeling of heaviness and regret. This cultured woman now had to live by night in the sordid way he did. All because she'd had the misfortune to meet him. "How can you be happy about this?" he asked, wretchedly distressed for her. "Don't you feel the chasm between yourself and the rest of humanity? Certainly you must feel your separation from God! We're outside His laws of nature. We're outcasts as surely as He cast Adam and Eve out of Eden."

Alexandra looked at him and laughed. "You really believe

all that nonsense, don't you?" She composed herself a bit and shook her head. "I never did," she said with a superior pride in her tone. "I couldn't believe in the deity presented in Old Testament mythology. It blames the The Fall of Man on Eve! Just because Adam had no willpower to resist the apple she offered him, why should that make it all *her* fault? I could never find comfort in a religion that blames the world's problems on women."

David shook his head. "Genesis has another version of the story where both sexes are blamed equally. Read it for yourself."

Her eyes flashed with amusement. "Why? If I'm supposed to be banished from God now anyway, I don't care to be convinced that He exists."

"But where did your talent and intellect come from, if not from a higher power?"

"The genes I inherited from my parents," she said with a shrug. "Except for my bond with you, I never felt zapped by any force outside myself. Have you?"

"You never prayed?" he asked.

"To what? Or whom?"

David sighed with a sense of hopelessness for her. In the late 1500s, when he had grown up, God was looked upon as unquestioned fact. At least, none of his family or friends doubted His existence. Even Darienne, though she never spent much time thinking on the matter. When he was a mortal, he used to feel very strongly the presence of the Creator when he prayed, so much so that he had wanted to make religion his life's work. It was difficult for David to understand someone who had no belief. He began to feel a little less guilty about Alexandra.

He thought of something else and grew amused with irony. "I remember that during sex you always used to call on God."

She stared at him, brows drawn together.

"You'd always cry out, 'Oh, God! Oh, God!'" David said. "I suppose that's why I assumed . . ."

Alexandra's face reddened. "It's only a manner of speech," she said with a hint of hostility.

"Yes, I see." He lost his amusement as he changed the subject. "What about the bloodlust? Surely you feel *that* now.

Doesn't it fill you with self-loathing, make you feel more animal than human?"

Her expression changed and she looked away. "I'll learn to deal with it," she said, her voice probably not sounding quite as firm as she wished it to.

"Well, then, I guess you have what you wanted," David said, spreading his hands outward in a fait accompli gesture. "Darienne explained the parameters of your new existence?"

"Yes!" Alexandra replied, regaining her equanimity more easily than David would have imagined anyone in her situation could. "I have to give Darienne credit. She explained everything, even went with me to the nearest mortuary to pick out my coffin. She dug up earth in my backyard and inserted it beneath the bottom lining. I know about blood banks now, how to sense dawn approaching, how to travel to other countries." Alexandra lifted her shoulders in a satisfied way. "I don't think there's anything she left out. I wrote my letter of resignation to the Philharmonic last night. I'll be on my way to Italy by the end of the week."

David felt appalled by her composure. He also couldn't help but feel sad, even if she didn't. "What about Edith? Wasn't she your friend? You must have other friends, too. Susan, your assistant? Don't you feel cut off from them now?"

"I'm not a people person, David. Never have been. Music is the only thing I truly love."

He raised his eyebrows. "You always insisted you loved me."

She quirked her mouth. "And all the while you were in love with that girl."

David felt suitably chastised and lowered his eyes. "So what will you do, now that you no longer have to be bothered with relationships?"

"Now I can actually hope to perfect my art," she replied with new enthusiasm. "I'll have all the time I need to learn how to create a flawless violin. That will be my contribution to humanity. Though humanity has never given much of anything to me," she added in an undertone. "No, I'll do it for myself."

"Then I suppose I shouldn't feel sorry for you," he said, still feeling some guilt nonetheless.

She smiled with confidence. "Absolutely not! I'm happy,

David. Happy to be free of you. Just happy to be free. If you'd performed the blood ceremony when I first asked you to, you would have spared yourself and me those last ugly scenes."

He nodded. "But I'm still compelled to ask, what about love? It's a human need. Even for you, I suspect. You're thrilled to be free of our bond, but you used to say you wouldn't leave me if I made you what I was."

Alexandra shrugged. "Well, you didn't transform me. Darienne did. So I don't have to worry about my promises."

"Would you have kept them if I had been the one to perform the blood ceremony for you?"

She looked at him whimsically. "Probably not. This sense of vampiric freedom is too infectious."

David studied his knuckles, feeling sarcastic. "It seems to infect females more than males," he muttered. "You and Darienne adore being what you are, while I loathe myself."

"In this world it may be the only way a woman can be truly free. You never experienced being a member of the 'second sex.'"

He tilted his head. "It's true, I don't know the female life experience. So—I suppose you and Darienne are fast friends now? Sisters?"

Alexandra laughed in a disparaging way. "I still think she's a preening ball of fluff. We have nothing in common except blond hair—and now, long incisors. But," she said, changing her tone a bit, "I'm grateful to her for rescuing me out of my bondage to you. And for setting me up in my new existence. She also told me . . ." Alexandra studied David a moment, a hint of cobalt entering her blue eyes. "She said sex between vampires is even better than sex between mortals. She bragged about her relationship with you, how she always comes back to you because only you can satisfy her vampiric need."

David's hair almost stood on end as Alexandra began approaching him. She slid her hand over his shoulder. "It was good between us before, David. I'd like to know how it would be now." Her eyes were big and brilliant. "Do for me what you do for Darienne," she whispered.

David stood up and quickly moved past her, toward her front door. "One of you begging for my services is enough, thank you! You'll have to find some other male vampire to appease you."

"Where?" she asked, coming after him as he took hold of the doorknob.

"I don't know," he replied. "Darienne's much better at finding others of our kind than I am. There aren't many of us. We're spread out, and we mix into the communities about us in as unobtrusive a way as possible. In the old days, there used to be more of our kind. Darienne and I have survived longer than most of the others we knew."

"What happened to them?"

"Accidents. Such as fires. Or being caught outside their coffin after the sun rose. Some chose suicide. Living forever can become boring. Some were sought out and destroyed by mortals—you know, a stake through the heart."

Alexandra shuddered.

"Don't worry," he said. "It doesn't happen much anymore. Nowadays mortals think we exist only in old movies. So we're safer, but fewer in number. We don't add to our numbers often, either, because blood supplies are limited and none of us wants to go back to the old ways."

"Old ways?"

"Surviving off of animals or people."

"Yes, I see," she murmured, her lip curling with distaste.

He leaned on the doorknob and looked in her eyes. "You avoided my question before. Maybe you'll answer me now. How do you like the bloodlust?"

She swallowed. "I don't much. Darienne got me a supply and it tastes surprisingly good. But I don't like that feeling of need, of looking at people as objects of prey. You were right about that. It is degrading."

"It never goes away."

Alexandra's eyes hardened. "I still say it's worth it. My freedom and my craft mean more to me than anything." Her blue eyes lost their brittle glitter and softened as she looked up at him. "You still mean something to me, though. Despite everything, I still remember how we were when we first met. You challenged my intelligence and you showed me how wonderful sex can be. I'm sure I can learn to compete with Darienne in pleasing you."

"That's what I'm afraid of." He began turning the doorknob.

She stopped him by putting her hand over his. "I can come

back from Cremona regularly to see you. It would be nice for us, David. Maybe we can get back what we had when we first met. Make it even better."

"You'll have to channel your energies into making violins, Alexandra. Because I don't want to see you again. At least not for several centuries, minimum."

"Why?" she asked, her eyes storming with injury and anger as he opened the door. "You do it for Darienne! Why not me? I'm just as attractive as she is. You used to admire me."

As he studied for the last time her beautiful, intelligent face and fire-and-ice eyes, he remembered some words from Shakespeare. He hesitated, but then went ahead and recited them to her. " 'For I have sworn thee fair, and thought thee bright, who art black as hell, and dark as night.' "

He watched with sadness as she took in the meaning of the quote, the confusion in her eyes, the disbelief about her mouth. Clever as she was, she possessed too cold, too unsympathetic a disposition to understand how far she'd fallen in his esteem and why. She only understood herself from her own point of view. Other people's perspectives didn't matter to her, because she didn't care about anyone else.

"Goodbye, Alexandra," he said as he walked out the door. "Godspeed!" he added, under his breath.

David returned home quickly that night. As he entered his living room on the third floor, he found Darienne sitting on the loveseat, waiting for him. Immediately, his anger at what she'd done for Alexandra resurfaced. He fixed his eyes on her accusingly.

But when she barely looked up, he studied her more closely. She wore a navy blue pants suit with a white sailor's collar. Her hair was tied back simply at the nape of her neck, held by a ribbon. She almost looked like a schoolgirl—a surprisingly downcast schoolgirl by the brooding aspect in her usually bright green eyes. On the little finger of her right hand, David spotted Alexandra's ruby ring. Could it be that Darienne was feeling guilty?

"I know what you've done," he said, keeping his tone low, waiting to see what her response would be.

Her face colored slightly. It surprised him. He couldn't remember if he'd ever seen her blush.

"I'm glad to see you're suitably ashamed," he said in a strict, parental manner.

"Yes," she said, pushing back a stray strand of hair from her face with a rather limp hand. "First I was angry, but now . . . yes, I'm ashamed."

"I'm glad you can feel some guilt, because it shows you do have a sense of morality underneath. What you need to do in the future is stop and think before you act. I know you probably did it for my sake, but we must respect the vulnerability of mortals who don't understand the consequences."

Her eyes narrowed and she finally looked up at him with full attention. "What do you mean, I did it for you? You were the last thing on my mind. And as for vulnerability, Matthew seems quite invulnerable. He understands consequences very well—though I can't figure out what he thinks they might be."

David stared at her. "What are you blithering about Matthew for? I'm speaking about Alexandra."

Darienne sat still for an instant, then made an exasperated face and rolled her eyes. "Oh, *her*. Someday you'll thank me."

"How can you be so blasé about what you've done? Transforming her into a vampiress so you could get her ruby in return!" He pointed to the red stone on her hand.

"This? I earned it!" Darienne said, her shoulders squaring as she sat up straight in her seat. "Mixing my blood with that woman's was downright distasteful. I think she has antifreeze in her veins to keep from frosting over. I still feel ill from the experience. But I *did* do it for you. She was poisoning your existence and your future with Veronica. And anyway, she *wanted* to be like us. And she's happy now. She's grateful to me, even if you're not."

"I know she's happy," David said, pacing. "I've just come from her home. But I'm astonished that you can be so mercenary as to take payment for such a vile act!"

"She offered me the ring without regret, and I accepted it for services rendered. It was strictly a business transaction between us women, and frankly it's none of your concern. As I said, someday you'll look back on this and be glad I did what I did."

David sat next to her on the loveseat, lacking the energy to argue any further. "I have to admit," he said in a slow, tired voice, "that I'm already glad you did it. I've never been so relieved to be rid of someone."

"You're free to be with Veronica now."

"I know," he said with feeling. "I am truly grateful for that. I wish I *could* be with her now."

"Give up the pact, David. Summon her to your side. She needs you and you need her."

He winced at the painful truth of her statement. "I can't. She's still too young. We must wait."

Darienne sighed, apparently giving up the argument without her usual fight. "I just hope you don't let another woman get in your way again. What you ever saw in Alexandra is beyond me."

David ruminated for a moment. "I saw a woman of distinction and culture, a maker of fine instruments, a musician. We discovered a rapport on such a high plane, that I never anticipated we could fall from it. We seemed to have so much in common that I never saw the one huge difference between us. I cherish human relationships while she places no value on them at all. Perhaps she even disdains them." He turned to Darienne. "You knew that all along, I suppose."

Darienne nodded, though she seemed to take none of her usual pleasure in her superior understanding. She sat quietly, eyes downcast, and listened.

"I was so lonely, I failed to sense that in her," David continued. "I craved her mind, so compatible with mine in the arts. I forgot what I once told Veronica, that culture can be learned, but a loving, generous heart is innate. Alexandra either wasn't born with that trait, or she lost it at an early age because of her mother's death and her father's insensitivity."

David ran his hands through his hair, breathed deeply, and relaxed. "Well, she has what she wants now. She's happy as she can ever be. Though I don't know how anyone can be truly happy existing as a vampire."

He looked at Darienne, waiting for her to tell him not to have such a pessimistic attitude. But she said nothing. She was examining her polished fingernails now in a disinterested, almost somber way. David began to grow uneasy. She wasn't her usual self at all tonight.

"You said a few minutes ago that you felt ill after the blood ceremony with Alexandra. Do you still not feel well?" he asked.

She looked up. "Oh, I was exaggerating," she said with a halfhearted shrug. "I feel all right."

David studied her, remembering she'd mentioned Matthew earlier. "What were you talking about when you said you were ashamed for what you'd done? I thought you meant transforming Alexandra, but you were talking about something else."

"You haven't heard?"

"Heard what?"

"You haven't been to the theater, have you?" she said.

"No. Once a show is under way, I don't go anymore. Why? Did something happen?"

"I'm sure by now everyone's talking about it. Wendy saw me coming out of Matthew's inner dressing room."

All at once David remembered her plan to seduce him several nights ago, when she was dressed all in pink. "And what were you doing in his dressing room?" David asked, his voice lowering to a doomsday pitch.

"Hiding."

"Lying in wait for the poor man?"

Her gaze shot up to his. "Why do you always call him the 'poor' man? He seems to have the resources he needs to keep himself in splendid isolation!"

David was relieved to see a spark of insouciance in Darienne's eyes. "So you were lying in wait for him?"

"I hid there so I could catch him before he came out of character, so I could tap into that sensuality he saves for the stage."

"And?"

"It didn't work. At first he responded as I expected—"

"Responded to what?" David asked, curious about her tactics.

"My bared chest," she said, lifting her shoulders in the matter-of-fact Gallic way.

"You mean he managed to fend off your heavy artillery?" David said with amazement and humor. "He's a better man than I!"

Darienne glared at him, not amused. "Well, I would have kept his interest and doubled it, except for that stupid, stupid costume of his! It's so buckled and buttoned and fastened down on him, he must be Houdini to get out of it. I lost the momentum I had going. He got his bearings back. And then he ordered me to leave. Wendy saw me walk out. She must have guessed what I was doing there. I've been too embarrassed to go backstage ever since."

David chuckled. "You have indeed met your match."

"You may think it's funny, but I feel like I've lost all my femininity."

David took her hand and kissed it. "Now, now, you certainly haven't. He just has more strength of character than most of us. Perhaps he has a woman in his life already and wants to be true to her."

"I don't think so. He may still love his ex-wife, but they rarely see each other. And I know he's been involved with other women. They seem to gather to him like moths to a flame."

"Maybe that's why he's gotten so experienced at fending them off."

Her green eyes challenged his statement. "I'm not your average woman! I don't expect to be fended off." She slumped a bit then. "Or maybe I'm more average than I thought."

"Not at all," David said in a comforting tone. "You're unique. There's not another like you on the planet. But maybe you come on too strong to suit him. He probably has a sense of propriety."

She tilted her head back and forth like a child. "He said I'd invaded his privacy. I guess I did. I just want him so much."

"But why him?" David asked, shifting his position on the sofa to face her more. "You can get most any man you want. You manage to seduce *me* every time," he said with a sense of amusement and respect. "Why do you need Matthew?"

She sat very still for a moment, her eyes pensive and sad. "I seem to have succumbed to what all the other women who gaze at him from the audience see—that thrilling, ephemeral sensuality he projects from the stage. The other women don't expect to experience it on a one-to-one basis with him. But I do. Because I know him, and I have access to him. And I have the gumption to go after him. Only he won't respond! And I'll go on feeling deprived until I do experience him."

She paused and sighed. "I feel like the wine connoisseur

who's tasted every wine but the finest, most rare, most expensive one. And that bottle keeps being snatched out of my hands. Somehow I have to break open what Matthew keeps so tightly corked!"

David took her hand again. "Are you sure that's all it is? Just a rare sexual adventure you don't want to miss?"

"What else would it be?"

"Something to do with Matthew himself? Not just his artistic sensuality, but his personal qualities. Perhaps you've found something in him you've never found in anyone else."

Darienne rubbed her nose as she pondered a moment. "Well, he's a puzzle. I suppose I find that intriguing. Most men are so simple."

"Maybe you're still missing a piece of that puzzle."

"I know just what piece, too!"

David laughed and couldn't stop laughing for a few moments. Darienne always got back down to basics faster than anyone.

"There you go laughing again," she said. "I'm feeling rejected and repudiated, my sense of myself as a woman threatened, and you think it's all a joke!"

"No, I don't," he said, squeezing her hand. "Honestly, I don't."

"Then try helping me. I give you advice all the time. Why don't you try finding some for me? You're a male. What am I doing wrong? How can I make a dent in Matthew's armor?"

"Don't try so hard."

She looked at him askance. "If I didn't try, I wouldn't get anywhere!"

"Look, why don't you start by going to him and apologizing for your behavior? And don't expect anything from him, other than an acceptance of your apology. If he's willing."

"And then what?"

"Then you leave it up to him. You've certainly made your designs on him clear. If he wants to respond, he will. Forcing the issue won't help. Give him time. It may take weeks. Months. Give up the temptress routine and try showing that you can also behave like a lady. You can, can't you?"

She shifted her jaw a bit. "With difficulty. I'm not an actress."

"You'll have to do something to counter the bad impression you must have made. What did he say to you as he threw you out?"

Darienne tilted her chin inward, as if trying to look innocent. "That he didn't want to have me arrested for attempted rape," she said in a small voice.

David clasped his fingers over his eyes, then slid his hands down his face. He shook his head, at a loss for words. Finally, he said, "This time you may have gone too far to redeem the situation, Darienne."

"Oh, don't say that, *cheri,*" she said, clutching his arm. "There must be some way to win him."

David could only sigh and repeat his previous advice. "Don't try so hard. Remember he's only a mortal. You compared him to a fine wine—give him time to breathe!"

17

No clue what was the matter

DARIENNE THOUGHT over David's advice, but waited several more days before she did anything about it. Frankly, she was afraid. Afraid Matthew might not even listen to an apology. She'd sat in the theater each night watching him from the balcony, where she hoped he would not notice her, longing for him, but without sufficient nerve to make any move.

Finally, taking herself to task for lack of courage, she at last formed a new plan. She'd go to his apartment early in the evening on his day off, hoping he'd be home, hoping to catch him away from the stress of the theater. There she would give him her apology and leave, just as David had suggested. After she had seen how he responded, she would decide what to do next based on that.

It wasn't much of a strategy by Darienne's standards. But after losing one battle, she was wary of mounting any great force to challenge him again.

As she rode the Marina Towers elevator up to his floor, she smoothed the chignon at the back of her neck and checked her green gabardine dress. She wanted to be sure she looked modest. Since he regarded green as a special color, she'd chosen to wear the shirtdress with its full skirt and buttons down the front. She'd buttoned it higher than usual, so that absolutely no cleavage showed.

When she reached his floor, she walked down the hallway and approached his door with trepidation. She almost hoped he wouldn't be home. But she could hear piano music coming

from inside. It sounded like Chopin. Mustering all her courage, she rang his doorbell. The music stopped.

In a moment the door opened, and Matthew stood in front
of her in faded jeans and an old shirt. Offstage, clothes certainly weren't his strong point. He must have gotten a haircut,
however, since she last saw him without wig and makeup. His
hair was clipped more closely over his ears, though it still fell
in gentle tendrils of brown and gray over his forehead. As he
stood facing her in his natural singer's stance—straight posture, robust chest out, broad shoulders held back—she felt a
bit faint.

Though he, of course, recognized her at once, his expression
remained calm and inscrutable. "Darienne," he said. "I
thought you must have left town."

"No such luck," she said, trying for a light approach. "I've
come to apologize."

He searched her face in that penetrating way of his, as if he
were pulling everything he could out of her brain. But he said
nothing.

"You don't have to worry," she told him. "This isn't another trick. You don't even have to invite me in. I can say
what I came to say from here."

At that, he promptly pulled the door further open and
stepped aside, allowing her in. Surprised, she hoped he hadn't
interpreted what she'd said as a tactic. She'd been sincere
about being content to speak to him from the hallway. Self-
conscious now, she stepped over his threshold.

She began fingering her white handbag nervously. "You
were right, Matthew. I behaved very badly. People ought to
conduct themselves with more dignity than I did." As she
spoke she saw his eyes grow even more sharp as they focused
on her face. She couldn't even try to guess what he was thinking. "I'm sorry if I embarrassed you. I hope someday you can
forgive me."

When she'd finished, she held her breath. Would he forgive
her? Or would it take months as David had predicted?

Matthew continued to stare at her a moment longer, as if
waiting to make certain she'd finished. Then he turned his
head pensively in the direction of the piano on the other side
of the room. She supposed he was considering how to respond.

But long moments went by, and he said nothing. She couldn't stand it. "I heard you playing before I rang the bell," she said, just to fill the silence, which seemed to give her more discomfort than him. "Chopin, wasn't it?"

He shifted his eyes back to her. "Yes."

"I didn't know you played," she chattered. "But then, you own a piano. I should have assumed—"

"Do you play?"

"Piano?"

A hint of something flickered in his mystical eyes. "Yes, piano."

"Sort of." As a child she'd learned the harpsichord. She and David had shared the same teacher, in fact.

"Sit down with me."

"W-what?"

"At the piano."

"Oh," she said, confused. "Sure."

As she followed him to the black enameled grand, he said, "I have to finish the piece I started. I'm obsessive that way. Whatever I commit to, I have to complete."

"Just as when you insisted on playing Sir Percy even though you were too sick to perform?"

He smiled as he sat down on the piano bench. "I never get sick." He glanced at her. "But, yes, that's an example."

The bench was just wide enough for two, and she would have to sit very close to him. She didn't trust herself. "I'll stand here and watch," she said, moving into the curve of the piano, facing him.

Matthew looked at her again, eyes round, as if surprised. "Suit yourself." He began playing, taking up where he had left off. He leaned back slightly, arms outstretched, his broad shoulders swaying with the movements of his hands up and down the keyboard. The music was fluid, romantic, and emotional. He played the way he sang, with feeling in each note and clarity of expression in each phrase. Darienne began to think that he expressed himself more perfectly through music than he did in real life. She never quite knew what he was thinking or feeling. Even now she didn't know whether he'd forgiven her or not. Though she supposed she could assume that since he'd asked her to stay, he must have decided to overlook her indiscretion in his dressing room. When it came to Matthew, however, she'd finally learned not to make any assumptions.

When he'd finished playing, she smiled and said, "That was beautiful! You should give concerts."

"I'd like to someday. I'm not good enough yet. I figure maybe about three more years of study, and I'll be ready."

"You're taking lessons?"

"Sure. I still take voice lessons, too."

"That's a lot of practicing, isn't it?"

"Yes. Though now that I'm singing almost nightly, I just do my vocal warm-ups before each show. On my day off I have to rest my voice."

She felt sad for him. "What do you do for fun?"

He studied the piano keys. "Not much since I went into rehearsals for *Shadow*. It's the biggest project I've taken on in a long time, and I needed to do it well. So it's been all work and no play."

"And are you becoming a dull boy?" she teased, raising an eyebrow.

He smiled again, that dazzling smile that made her knees grow weak. "I guess *you* think I am."

He'd said it lightly, almost as a joke, but it reminded her of the events in his dressing room, and she felt reprimanded. "No, I didn't mean to say—"

"I know that. I know you didn't mean to imply anything." His brows moved upward together over the bridge of his nose, and all at once he looked adorably sincere. "You seem to be on tenterhooks with me. Afraid to even sit by me. It's not like you and it makes me nervous."

"Really?" she said, eyes searching his. "I thought I always made you nervous."

"You did, but I was getting used to it."

She straightened a bit from leaning against the piano. "You didn't seem used to me when you accused me of attempted rape."

"Well, you were a bit out of bounds then."

"I'm sorry. I have no idea what your boundaries are."

He closed the lid over the piano keys and absently ran his hands over the shiny surface. "That's probably because my boundaries seem to change from day to day. I'm . . . moody,

I guess. And with women, things always get more complicated than I intend. I'm very careful about commitment."

"But I'm not looking for commitment."

"I know, Darienne. But sex without commitment, I've found over the years, is empty, confusing, even degrading sometimes by the time it's over. I like long-term relationships. As I've said, when I commit to anything, including women, I really commit. It's what I've found is most comfortable and works best for me."

"But you haven't been married for years."

"Marriage is the ultimate commitment and it went sour for me because it conflicted with my career commitment. So I don't think I'll ever marry again. But I've had a couple of long-term relationships. And those worked out—for a while, anyway. There have been flings here and there, too, which, as I've said, left me feeling drained and mixed-up. One woman even tried to marry me by claiming she was pregnant. I guess I need some sense of continuity with a woman I can trust."

"And that's why you always rebuffed me? You were protecting yourself?"

He stared at her, but in a distracted way, as if some thought process was going on in his mind. "Protecting the show, too. Another problem is getting involved with co-stars, or those who have some investment in a show. It's just not a good policy."

"I've been told that," she said, reminded of David's protestations. She also remembered that Matthew's TV show ended because of his co-star's emotional attachment to him. "I'm surprised you tolerated me as much as you did. You were worried about offending an investor, I suppose."

"I'd heard a rumor that you didn't approve of me for the part."

Darienne felt her face turn warm. "That was before I saw you perform. I quickly changed my mind."

"And then you got curious about me." Playful lights danced in his eyes.

The amusement in his face disconcerted her. "It was only natural. Every woman in the audience wonders."

"About what?"

"What you'd be like."

He lowered his eyes and inclined his head a bit. She assumed she'd embarrassed him again. "I didn't mean to be so blunt. But you asked."

He looked up. "I'm not offended."

"Oh." Now she was confused again.

"It's flattering, in fact. Though I've always been well-liked by women, I've never been thought of as . . . as a sex symbol before. It's a little surprising at my age." He paused, as if sorting out his thoughts. "But this acute curiosity I seem to have inspired in you— well, it's been hard for me to know how to deal with it."

"You don't appear to have much difficulty," she said. " 'Just say no' seems to be your motto."

"An actor can hide emotions as well as portray them."

Her brows drew together as she stared down at him in puzzlement. "So, you mean . . . you're saying . . . What are you saying?"

"That saying no has been difficult sometimes."

Darienne felt her cloud of confusion lift away and saw a new dawning of hope. "You do find me attractive then?"

"Since I first set eyes on you."

"Then why—?"

"Because you were an investor in the show. Because of the entanglements I seem to get into with women, without even trying. Because of what I hope is my common sense. I don't know much about you. You look too delightful not to have some darker side I haven't seen yet. Everyone has a dark side."

Darienne lowered her gaze to the black piano top. Yes, her dark side was more dark than he could even believe. But he needn't ever know about it. She gave him a smile. "Let me explain myself then. I like to have fun. Amuse myself. I have all the money I need. I'm not looking for a husband, or anyone permanent in my life. Sex is just sort of a hobby with me. Like my clothes and jewels are. You really wouldn't need to worry about entanglements with me."

His eyes were infused with light and energy as he listened. "You make my mouth water."

She looked at him, feeling breathless. "Then—"

"Now wait," he said, putting up one hand. "Before you rip your dress open again—"

"I'm sorry," she said quickly. "I'm not trying to seduce—"

"No, I—"

"I'm just explaining myself, as you explained yourself."

"Right." He sat still for a long moment, apparently keeping track of his racing thoughts.

She watched him with an intaken breath. Her fingers were beginning to tremble.

Slowly, he raised his eyes to hers again. He grasped hold of the edge of the piano in a careful manner. "If . . . if I sleep with you once, would it satisfy your curiosity about me? I think it would satisfy mine about you."

Heart leaping within her chest, she grinned down at him. "Yes. Oh, yes. Yes! I didn't know you were suffering from curiosity, too."

His eyes held a steady light. "After that night in my dressing room? I'd give half my earnings from the show to get another peek at what's beneath that green dress."

"Only half?" she said, leaning toward him. "I'm worth more than that! But of course, I don't charge."

He shook his head ever so slightly. "I never met a woman like you. You're so totally frivolous about sex."

"That's what makes you curious about me, isn't it? You wonder if it can really be that much fun—no strings, no hangups, no cloudy morning afters. It can, *cheri.*"

"If that were true . . . ," he whispered. His shining eyes grew wistful as he gazed at her. "You're like some dream woman. After working on the show all these months, I'm in the mood for a good fantasy. One I don't have to create myself on a stage."

She tilted her head, leaning closer to him as he stretched upward toward her. Her heart was pounding against her ribcage, she was so anxious. But she dared not say a word, afraid of breaking the moment. He must be the one to begin, not her.

"But I want to make an agreement with you," he said, backing away a bit.

"Yes?" *Oh, what now?*

"That we'll be together for tonight only. I want to keep this simple. No expectations. No repercussions."

Darienne nodded eagerly, impatient for the negotiations to be over.

"And by expectations," he said, looking at her carefully, "I mean not only afterward, but before."

She lifted her shoulders. "I don't have any."

His eyes narrowed a bit at her. "I still say you believe I can fulfill some fantasy *you* have that I'll be like my stage character. You'll have to accept me as me. Or you'll be disappointed."

"I'll risk it," she said. "I won't complain if I am." Her voice lowered to a husky whisper. "And I promise you that you won't be disappointed."

He rose up from the piano bench and pushed it back. "Somehow I know that." He reached over the piano and took her by the hand, pulling her around the corner of the instrument to stand next to him. Darienne felt so eager she could no longer speak.

He let go of her and raised both his hands to her face, running his fingers along her chin. "You're very beautiful," he said, his voice clear and gentle. "You always look like a pampered, expensive Persian cat, all soft and serene and knowing, impressed with yourself and sure of your place in the world." His eyes traveled over her face for a moment and then he made her turn and began unfastening the chignon at the back of her neck. He unwound her long hair and spread it with his fingers out from her neck and over her shoulders. He made her turn slightly to face him again. And then he did something unusual. With his large hands on either side of her head, he picked up gobs of her thick hair between his fingers, gathered it forward over her shoulders and brought his hands together in front of her neck. He pushed his hands up a bit just beneath her chin, making her hair puff outward to frame her face.

He gave her a pleased smile as his eyes roved over her face in a winsome examination of her features. There was such a tenderness and consideration about what he was doing that she could only stand there feeling stunned. His actions were so unexpected, and she didn't understand why he would take the time to study her this way. Most men were undressing her by now. Or if they were too shy, she was undressing herself. If she were with any other man, she would have thought time was awasting. But here she was, dazzled, made shy, because Matthew made her feel even more special than she already thought she was.

He let go of her hair and lowered his hands to her dress. Gently, slowly, he began unbuttoning each button with care.

The dress separated, revealing her smooth skin and cleavage, enhanced by her black lace bra. His eyes devoured her and his breaths grew labored. Darienne stopped breathing as he slipped his hands beneath both sides of the opened dress and pushed it apart, then over her shoulders.

She gasped, smiling as she felt the dress slip down her hips and legs to the floor. She stepped out of it and kicked it out of the way. Sliding her hands up his chest, she started at the top and began unbuttoning him. She worked much more quickly than he had and soon had his shirt undone and pulled free of his jeans.

Meanwhile he remained transfixed by her attributes. "You're exquisite," he murmured, his fingertips moving over the edge of the bra without quite touching her. "You're like the sensual hallucination of a man lost on a deserted island."

"Matthew?" she said, looking up at him. "Would you do something for me? Fulfill my fantasy?"

"If I can."

"You can," she whispered. "Do to me what you do with Elaine on stage. When you stand behind her and move your hands over her body. You don't have to sing."

He smiled. "It won't be the same without music. I warned you, I'm not Sir Percy."

"I'm not Marguerite," she said. "But let's try it anyway? Who needs music! I just want—I need—to know what it feels like."

Warm indulgence filled his eyes. "Then turn around."

Darienne did and soon felt the firm heat of his chest against her back. With his head pressed next to hers over her shoulder, he brought his arms around her. He stretched his fingers tautly, elongating them, and pushed his middle fingers inward a bit, so that the tips of those fingers almost touched her skin. Her breathing grew shallow, her heart skipping beats as he skimmed his hands slowly and smoothly, as if in slow motion, down her cleavage, down her midriff, pausing over her navel, then tantalizingly to the top of her bikini panties.

Darienne felt giddy as she experienced what she'd imagined for so long. "This is beautiful," she murmured, writhing against him with sensual joy.

He separated his hands outward, slowly coming up over the sides of her rib cage. Beneath her breasts, he turned his hands outward slightly so that the palms grazed the sides of her bra. His fingertips drew toward one another as each hand rounded over a breast. By this time, his hands were trembling.

"Marguerite always wears a cloak when I do this," he said with a chuckle. "I'm afraid I'm running out of resistance. Your body is so, so sexy!"

"So are you," Darienne said, pressing her hands over his, urging him to cup each breast. This he did readily, with possessive, caressing warmth. "Let's not wait?" she pleaded, and bent to slip her panties off.

When she turned to face him again, his eyes carried a mixture of pleased shock and the building energy of desire. "Here?" he asked.

"Why not?" Pushing her naked derriere onto the fallboard over the piano keys, she leaned toward him with outstretched hands. He moved to her without hesitation. Smiling with the anticipation of their pleasure, she leaned backward over the top of the piano. As he bent over her, his mouth eager for her cleavage, she curled her legs upward and around him.

"The piano doesn't hurt your back?" he asked, looking up as she brought her hands to his head.

"Nothing we do together can hurt me—or you."

Things seemed to be moving too fast for him. "What about—?"

"Darling, darling Matthew," she said, stroking his hair. "I can't get pregnant and I have no blood diseases. So enjoy me, and give me what I've craved for so long from you, *cheri.*"

He smiled at her. "I'm glad you're fixated on me for whatever reason!"

She laughed, then threw her head back in a swoon of pleasure as he pulled her bra down and squeezed and stroked her breasts. Gently, he nuzzled her hardening nipple with his lips. Closing her eyes in sweet delirium, she could barely take it in that this was finally happening, that she was with Matthew at last. Darienne began to feel the familiar, intense pressure of arousal gathering in her lower stomach, the wetness coming in heated anticipation of fulfillment. She murmured Matthew's name over and over with yearning, kneading her fingers into his thick shoulder muscles.

He stopped then, one hand at each swollen breast, and

looked at her face in wonder. "You really crave this, don't you! Your eyes are so glazed with desire, they're glowing."

Darienne smiled and closed her eyes. He'd better not observe their vampiric glow too closely, or he might notice that their brightness was too unearthly to be merely from sexual desire.

"I've never wanted anyone as much as I've wanted and waited for you," she told him, her voice so sincere it was on the verge of breaking.

He always seemed to bring some unusual emotion out of her, even now during sex. She had always looked upon sex as a splendid sort of physical workout with a marvelous, instant payoff, but not as an emotional thing. Never that.

But now tears sprang to her eyes as she felt his fingers move down her taut stomach toward the heated, moist center of her desire. Oh, was it really going to happen?

Her stomach contracted as she gasped with painful pleasure. He'd touched the quick of her, as if testing, and then she felt movement as he unzipped his jeans.

In the next instant, she felt him enter her. She brought her hands to her head, buried her fingers in her hair with the ecstatic joy of a wish finally come true. He felt large within her, filling her. Instinctively she reached to pull him close as he leaned forward over her body again. She wound her legs over his lower back and ran her fingers over his broad shoulders and into his curly hair, while he began heated thrusts within her.

"Matthew, Matthew, Matthew," she whispered, almost sobbing with happiness. "I've wanted this. I've needed you. Oh, you're so good, it's so good . . ."

"I could eat you up, you're so damned sexy!" he said between ragged breaths. "Am I hurting you?"

"No, no," she said, smiling through tears, running her fingers through his tousled hair. His roughness was invigorating, tantalizing, and yet gentle, partly because he was only mortal and partly because he was Matthew. Matthew, she felt sure, could never knowingly hurt a woman.

The beautiful tension within her suddenly reached its highest plateau, and each urgent thrust now brought her closer and closer. She arched her neck, throwing her head back in anticipation. She felt him hotly kissing her throat, her shoulders as his hand fondled her breast. His other hand came up beneath her head, and he tangled his fingers in her hair. When she opened her eyes in sensual agony, she found him watching her, as if he knew she was about to climax. He was breathing heavily, the chords in his neck straining, the veins standing out. His eyes seemed on fire, and yet at the same time there was such tenderness in them, such eager joy.

"This is better than any fantasy," he said. "You're exquisite! This is going to be better than anything in the world."

His words thrilled her, compounded her excitement, made her breath come in spasms as her body's mounting tension begged, pleaded for release. With his next thrust, she reached that quiet split second before the rush of fulfillment. And then all at once, her body jolted with profound, radiating throbs of satiation, over and over. She cried out with each one, clinging to him, as she felt his own final, climatic thrust within her. Now she knew the sublime fantasy of belonging to Matthew, of knowing him fully.

Both quieted down, holding each other as their breathing came back to a more normal level.

"I told you," he murmured, kissing her throat. "Better than anything."

Darienne felt dazed, even a bit disoriented. She had finally gotten what she longed for from him. But the fulfillment of her dream left her feeling so odd, so . . . so vulnerable somehow. "You're a wonderful lover," she told him, her voice weak with feeling. "I've . . . I've been with many men. I've never felt like this before, Matthew." She lifted his face from her collarbone, which he'd been kissing, so he would look at her. "You're special somehow. I don't know how or what it is, but you're different."

A playful tenderness enlivened his eyes. "The chemistry works. That's all we need to know." He pushed himself off of her, stood up, and took her hands to help her down. "I have to admit, I never thought of doing it at the piano. I won't feel the same after this when I sit down to play it. I'll always wish I were playing with you instead."

She laughed and he pressed his cheek to hers, then bit her earlobe. "You can play with me anytime," she said, trying to get back her usual, carefree attitude.

"Don't tempt me." He studied her face closely with

bemusement and curiosity. "How did you come to like sex so much?"

"Don't you like it, too?"

"Sure, but I try to be sensible. And most women are more inhibited than you."

"I was born one of the idle rich. And with this body. What else was there for me to do to pass the time?"

He laughed and ran his hands over her ears and down her hair. "You're a delight! How late can you stay?"

"Dawn."

"I'm afraid I have to be asleep by midnight."

"You have a show tomorrow, I know. Well, we have a few hours," she said, touching his lips with her fingertips. "I can make sure you sleep well tonight."

"I believe you," he said in a smooth, gentle tone as he leaned toward her. Despite all that had just happened between them, Darienne felt an unexpected moment of panic as his mouth connected with hers. He'd never kissed her before. She shut her eyes with apprehension, even shyness. His kiss felt so warm, so filled with affection that a wave of weakness came over her and made her limp and languid as any mortal female might be in his embrace.

He slipped his arms around her back and held her tightly, deepening the kiss, feeling the contours of her rounded derriere and narrow waist with his large, sensitive hands. Many men had handled her body, but Matthew's touch felt so tender, almost worshipful, as though she were some rare treasure only he had the capacity to fully appreciate.

She brought her arms up over his broad shoulders and around his neck, hanging on, for she'd begun to experience a swaying, slightly dizzy feeling. When he drew away from her mouth, he looked at her with contented eyes. "I'd better be careful," he told her. "I could get used to this."

Darienne felt her mouth trembling yet from his kiss and could not trust herself to say anything. Instead she smiled, trying to look coy. Her attempt at acting seemed to cover her unusual emotional state, for he smiled back and said in a low voice, "Let's try it in bed this time."

She nodded eagerly, though underneath she felt an odd conflict of emotions. Her body told her she would give her soul, if she still had one, to lie with him again. But her psyche gave her garbled messages that something was happening here she didn't understand, that any further intimacy with him would only sink her deeper in the quicksand of her own emotions.

But as she was used to doing, Darienne obeyed her body first, and she followed him into his bedroom without further consideration. There he quickly slipped out of his clothes, pulled aside the bedcovers and fell onto the bed with her. Sliding one arm under her, he held her close as he caressed her breasts once again. She buried her face in his shoulder and neck, kissing him, but also hiding her wayward emotions. Tears were springing to her eyes with the exquisite touch of his fondling hand over her sensitized skin. He made her feel precious and adored. She experienced a strange sensation in the pit of her stomach, like a hollow ache, that she could not explain.

And then he ran his hand slowly down her abdomen and stomach. She held onto him more tightly as his fingers slid into the core of her sexuality. "Oh, Matthew," she breathed, her voice almost a whimper, her need and her strange weakness at his physical touch was so great. She always took the lead with men, but she hadn't the wherewithal even to try now. She lay back, feeling languid and sensual, and told him with her eyes to do whatever he wished, that she would love anything he did.

And being a mortal and, at bottom, a conventional man, Matthew responded in a normal, conventional way. He moved over her, slid between her legs and allowed the weight of his chest to relax onto the soft cushion of her breasts. There was nothing new and different in his approach, no record to be set for sexual gymnastics as she might have achieved with David as her partner, no tantalizing new position tried out, none of the usual avenues that Darienne had eagerly explored in her centuries of sexual escapades.

And yet this experience was so strange, so new to her, she felt confused, even frightened. Yet she couldn't, wouldn't forgo the experience even if it meant her existence would be changed forever. And some little voice within her was telling her that was indeed happening.

But all this semi-conscious dialogue in her mind quickly blurred as the heated urgency of Matthew's thrusts within her took over her body. He gripped her closely. She tightened her arms about his back, while he kissed her neck, her face, and finally her mouth once again. And then she was lost in the sensual fantasy of his embrace, feeling surreal, beautiful within herself, her mind and body, beautiful with him, already fulfilled in spirit, though her body still strived toward that portal of bliss.

And when the final moment came, she sobbed with the painful joy of it, keeping the tears and sobs deep in her throat so that he wouldn't know.

He lay back then and held her close, smoothing back her hair, saying in his most tender, adoring voice, "You're an exquisite lover. You've renewed me. I can portray my role with more truth now, because you've reminded me how deeply desire can motivate a man. I'd gotten cerebral and abstract analyzing it. It would have been so much simpler and more enjoyable to let you seduce me. I'm sorry I didn't let you."

"I'm glad I didn't seduce you," she said. "I like knowing it was your choice to be with me tonight."

He stroked her cheek. "I'm glad you happened by."

"I am, too," she said, smiling back, keeping her emotions at bay. Wanting to get out of her mental whirl, she tried to behave like her usual self again, thinking she could pull herself back to normal that way. She ran her fingers over his deep rib cage to his nipple, and fondled it. "We have another hour before midnight. Would you like to research your role one more time?"

His eyes gleamed. "You have endless energy! But then, you're younger than me. No gray in this hair," he said as he twisted a lock of her blond hair in his fingers.

She reminded herself he was only a mortal, and no adolescent, either. But she'd learned that she could coax residual force out of any man. "Gray hair means wisdom, and in wisdom there's strength," she whispered in his ear, sliding her hand downward. In moments, he proved she was right.

She regrouped her unsettled emotions enough to regain her equilibrium for their last hour together. As if to prove to herself she was fine, just fine, she took on her familiar role as temptress again, though somehow it didn't feel quite right with Matthew. But she maintained it anyway, because she didn't know what else to do.

So she climbed upon him, astride him, leaning over him so that her breasts bounced and grazed his chest with the movement of her hips and pelvis over his. Her blond hair trailed over his shoulders, and he looked up at her with sensual fire in his eyes, as though she were some love goddess come down to earth to give him her gift of profound sexual bliss.

She realized, as she saw the erotic adoration in his eyes, that it wasn't at all what she wanted from him, though she'd always thought she wanted it. She wanted him to look at her with sensitivity and tenderness, as he had for a fleeting moment when he'd framed her face with her own hair. She wanted him to understand and comfort her, the way he had Elaine. She didn't want to be his sex goddess. She wanted to be his cherished woman, whom he would stand by and take care of, and not out of a sense of humanity and duty, as he seemed to feel toward Elaine, but because he wanted Darienne for herself, to be with her for herself, her spirit and personality more than her voluptuous body.

But he didn't want entanglements. And being what she was, what sort of relationship could she have with him anyway? So it was best to fill his fantasy for him, for tonight only as he'd made her agree, and then leave. She was sure that by tomorrow night, or the day after at the latest, she would have forgotten him. Now she'd experienced him and found his rarified sexuality onstage was not so rare in real life. He was only a man, just like all the others. In a day or two, he would be of no importance to her.

This she repeated to herself, almost as therapy, even while her body vibrated again with a pent-up, building need about to explode. When it did, he took hold of her and held her close while he cried out in the throes of his own fulfillment. Tears filled her eyes again.

"You're thrilling," he breathed, holding her tightly over his heaving chest. "I could get addicted to you so easily." He turned over with her, kissed her, and looked into her face. "I may not be able to keep my word about being together for only one night. I know I'm going to want you again."

She tried to smile as a tear streamed back into her hair. "Will you?" she whispered.

His expression softened, his eyes all solicitous. "You're crying?" he said, touching the wetness at her eyes. "That's sweet. Were you secretly afraid I wouldn't enjoy our time together?"

She half-laughed, half-cried. "I wasn't sure." Sexual insecurity wasn't why she was crying, but if that explained her emotion to him, then she would let him believe it. "It's late. I'd better go."

He looked at her with regret, his round eyes soulful. "I guess you'd better." He kissed her forehead and stroked her arm. "But I'm so glad you came here tonight."

She smiled, and then as quickly as she could without seeming to rush, she got up and walked into the living room to put on her discarded dress. When she turned, she found him standing by the door, wearing a silk robe.

"Do you need a cab? Or shall I drive you home?"

"No. I have a car," she lied.

She walked up to him, and he took her hands in his. "I'll never forget tonight," he said. "Whether we ever come together again or not, I'll always remember this time with you. You're charming and delightful, and so wonderfully uninhibited. I'll always admire that about you."

Darienne somehow managed to listen to this and not show emotion. But then he took her in his arms one last time, hugged her and then kissed her mouth. She kissed him back with all the feelings she'd been holding inside, impulsive and trembling, just wanting him to know. Then, self-conscious, she backed away, eyes unable to meet his, and said goodbye. She opened the door and got brave enough to look at him briefly when she heard him speak.

"Good-night, Darienne." His eyes and face were caring, puzzled, as if he knew there was something going on inside her, but he couldn't guess her feelings.

"Sleep well," she said and walked out before he could delve into her any further with his incisive eyes.

She rushed to the elevator, took it down, and was soon walking along the black, rippling Chicago River in the midst of the city night with its lights and distant sounds of traffic. The strange mixture of emotions she'd experienced earlier came forward again, now that she had no reason to quell them for Matthew's sake or her own. She still had no clue what was the matter with her, why Matthew had affected her this way, why she wanted him to be different toward her than she'd ever wished any other man to be. For weeks she'd been longing to experience him, and she thought once she had it would satisfy her. But being with him had only ignited other needs in her she hadn't fully realized she had. And why? She'd been perfectly content and happy before she'd ever seen Matthew. Why had she become so shaken and confused by him? By one uniquely gifted, but otherwise average, mortal?

Suddenly, as she walked across a bridge over the river, she realized she didn't even know where she was, or where she was going. She looked about and saw the black outline of the Hancock in the distance. She'd been heading in the wrong direction, south instead of north. What on earth? She was behaving more like David, who could sometimes become so distracted he didn't know where he was going. But one of the things Darienne had prided herself on was that she always knew exactly where she was—what city and street on the planet, on what footing with other people, and even more surely than those two, what was in her own mind.

But on this dark and starry midnight, she felt lost on all three counts.

David searched his wardrobe, looking for clothing that was easy to move in and that also had a flair—something that looked creative and artistic. He hadn't realized until now how conservative his clothing had become over the last several decades. Where was Darienne when he needed her?

He tried slipping a tie through the belt loops of his pants, as Fred Astaire used to do. But he didn't have Astaire's carefree, debonair manner to carry off the effect. So he pulled the tie out and replaced it with a belt, deciding blue pants and a striped shirt would have to do.

Last night he'd been reading and he happened on a line written by Alexander Pope that he'd forgotten: "True ease in writing comes from art, not chance, As those move easiest who have learned to dance." He was reminded that he'd put aside his efforts at learning to dance lately, due to all the turmoil with his musical and with Alexandra. But the musical was playing to a packed theater every performance, and Alexandra had probably left for Italy by now.

He'd recalled that on the same fateful night he met Alexandra, he also met another woman: Lotte Leone, the dance

instructor. He'd found the card she had given him and phoned
early in the evening yesterday. She'd told him she had a begin-
ner's tap dance class and it wasn't full. But David said he'd
prefer private lessons, letting her assume it was because he was
a reclusive celebrity. The truth was he couldn't go to a dance
studio because it would probably be lined with mirrors.

So in a half hour, Lotte would arrive for his first lesson.
David was so excited, he'd begun getting ready far sooner
than necessary.

As he considered his choice of clothes again, he wished he
owned a T-shirt or even a pair of jeans. Sweat pants maybe.
That was probably the type of thing men in her classes wore.
She'd think he was a hopeless stick-in-the-mud in his conservative clothes.

As he fretted, he heard the tap-tap of the brass knocker on
his front door. Now, who could that be! A fan? A neighbor?
A reporter? Exhaling with annoyance, he walked into the
living room and looked out the window. He couldn't see his
front door from the window, but he could view the sidewalk
and street. No car was parked in front of his home. The
sidewalk was empty.

Aggravated at the thought of being bothered by some stranger, he went down the steps, three at a time, to answer the
door on the ground floor. When he opened it, he was amazed
to find Darienne.

"You're using the door?" he said, opening it further to let
her in.

She was dressed simply in shorts and a knit top, her hair
flowing over her shoulders in a carefree fashion. But she
looked anything but carefree as she stepped into his oval
entryway. She seemed distracted, disconcerted, even distressed.

"I forgot about the window," she said. "That's odd, isn't it?
That I should forget that?"

David nodded, growing concerned by her manner. "Is
something the matter?"

"I don't know. I feel like I've been turned upside down and
spun around."

"You'd better come upstairs."

As they began climbing the steps together, she said, "This
has never happened to me before."

"What? Are you ill?" David asked, though he didn't think vampires could get sick. On the other hand, there were nights that he felt better than others, but that was usually a function of his mental state.

"I get a funny feeling in my stomach sometimes," she told him.

"When did this start?"

"With Matthew."

"Oh," David said, smiling to himself. Now things were getting clearer. "Did you go to him and apologize?"

"Yes," she said as they passed the second floor on the spiral staircase they were climbing.

"How did he react?"

"He didn't say anything at first. But . . ." She hesitated, as if what she was about to say was more than she could deal with.

"But?"

"He . . . we coupled."

"I see." David had suspected that was what had happened. "Well, that's what you've been yearning and scheming for, isn't it?"

"Yes," she said, lowering her eyes.

"So? How did it go? Did he measure up to your expectations?"

"That's the odd thing. He was like most mortal men—adequate. Nowhere near the stamina that you have. And he's much more creative onstage than in bed. But . . ." She paused on the steps and looked up at David, her green eyes confounded and troubled. "The strange thing is, I didn't care. I got all emotional. I wanted to cry because it was such a beautiful experience somehow. He was so caring, so sweet. You're that way, too. But somehow with him . . . it affected me differently . . ." Her shoulders lifted and she made an outward gesture with her hands, conveying in body language the confusion she couldn't put into words.

They continued up to David's living room, and he listened as Darienne resumed her story after a silence. "And it doesn't go away. After I left him, I got lost. You know me—I'm never lost! And tonight I still feel happy that I experienced him, and yet melancholy and . . . and I still don't know if I'm coming or going. What's wrong with me?"

As they walked across the living room to the small sofa, David wondered why she could so easily recognize other people's emotional situations, but not her own. He considered how to tell her and decided the best way was the most direct. "I think you've finally fallen in love, Darienne."

She turned and stared at him. "What do you mean?"

"You're in love with Matthew. You've got all the symptoms."

"But I've loved men before. I love you, for example."

"Like a consort-brother, if there is such a thing. That's how you love me. You love me because we've known each other for four hundred years. There's a connection between us that's special and can never be replaced."

"Yes—"

"But," David continued, "you're *in* love with Matthew. And that's a different thing. That explains the excitement and confusion, the melancholy mixed with joy, the odd pangs in the depths of your abdomen. Because you're such a spirited, self-sufficient woman it took centuries before you met a man who could cut through your all-for-fun and fun-for-all philosophy, who could penetrate to that central core of human feeling everyone has."

Darienne slowly sank onto the love seat, looking like a mortal who had just been knocked down by a truck. "What do I do?"

With a sad smile, David sat beside her and took her hand. "Welcome to the real world, Darienne. No one knows what to do when they're in love. All they know is that they want to be with the other person."

"Yes! But I can't. We promised each other, no strings. Even if he changed his mind, he's mortal, and I'm . . . what I am."

"Now perhaps you begin to understand my torment over Veronica. You always tell me I should just go back to her. But you see it's not that simple, is it?"

"No," she whispered. "Oh, Matthew . . ."

David felt himself growing distressed now. He still missed Veronica, anguished about any future they might have together, just as Darienne obviously grieved about her feelings for Matthew.

He squeezed her hand, knowing this time he must be the optimistic one and comfort her. "Be happy you've loved at

all," he told her. "It happens rarely, to you especially. Love is
a life-changing experience, whether it ends happily or sadly. It
helps us grow as individuals."

"Oh, don't stuff your elegant philosophy down my throat,"
she said unhappily, tilting her head sideways to lean against
his shoulder. "All I know is I want to be with Matthew. He
made me feel like no one else ever has."

"I know," David said softly. "All I've wanted is Veronica.
And I don't know what my future will be, with or without
her."

They sat in silence for a long while, brooding in their
thoughts. At last, David remembered Lotte Leone and looked
at his watch. "My dance instructor will be here soon," he said.

"Your what?" Darienne asked in a vacuous manner.

"I decided to take tap dancing lessons."

"Tap dancing."

"I can't get the technical precision I need from watching
tapes of Kelly and Astaire. I need to have some formal training."

"Are you out of your mind?"

"No. I'm just trying to go on with my existence in a positive
way. As you always used to advise me to do—before Cupid
did you in with his arrow. Why don't you stay and take the
lesson with me?"

"Oh, David!"

"Why not?"

"I'm not in the mood."

"That's exactly why you should. I know it's not what you
want to do right now. But it's better than moping. If you try
to put yourself into a better frame of mind, maybe you'll think
of some new idea to resolve your dilemma over Matthew. You
were always better at solutions than I. You mustn't let yourself down. You never let *me* down."

Darienne smiled halfheartedly. "I'll look silly trying to tap
dance."

"So will I at first. But we have the strength and agility to
master the steps faster than any of Lotte's other students.
We'll be her star pupils if we aren't careful."

Darienne chuckled a bit at that. She touched his chin.
"You're adorable. Why couldn't I have fallen in love with

you? And you with me? It would have all been so much simpler."

"Nothing in the world is simple, Darienne. Not even for vampires."

David's door knocker sounded then. Lotte was a few minutes early. He stood and pulled up on Darienne's hand to lift her out of her seat. "Come on, let's dance. What else is there for either of us to do right now? We'll always have tomorrow night to brood."

If you enjoyed *Possession,* then don't miss the third exciting book in the *Obsession* series by Lori Herter . . .

CONFESSION

Coming Soon.

Here is a sample
of this thrilling
new story . . .

1

Honor was the only thing a vampire could hold on to

STRONG, PALE moonlight streamed in through the huge ballroom windows on the third floor of the Oak Street mansion. In another part of the house, a clock struck four A.M. David de Morrissey barely heard the chimes over the music coming from his large screen television. Concentrating on his tap dance steps, he didn't concern himself about the time, since dawn was still a few hours away.

The varying gray and white light from the TV screen flickered over David's white shirt as he copied Fred Astaire's moves in the fireworks dance from *Holiday Inn*. He threw imaginary fireworks onto the floor and deftly jumped away from imaginary explosions, copying what Astaire had done. David smiled as he danced. The tap lessons he'd been taking were definitely helping him polish his technique. David's superior strength and agility gave him more energy than his two idols, Fred Astaire and Gene Kelly, combined could ever have possessed. But their rhythm, finesse, attitude—these were the subtleties David longed to master. He was satisfied with himself tonight.

When the dance was over, David stopped the video tape and turned off the TV. The silence of the night filled the empty, vast room, lit now only by the still brightness of the full moon. Its light bathed the polished wooden floor softly and reflected off the faceted crystals of the room's three opulent chandeliers.

David told himself he should go back to work on the screenplay he was rewriting, from which he'd taken a break. But instead he felt drawn to his favorite spot, the cushioned window seat of the nearest bay window. This was the place where he and Veronica used to make love every night, sometimes all night, while they were together. His memories of her—her dusky hair and sweet mortal's eyes so full of love for him— were clear and vivid, though years had passed since their affair had ended.

No, that was incorrect. Their affair hadn't ended. It was in suspension, David reminded himself. He must continue, always, to think positively, and not give in to his natural pessimism.

Shifting as he sat on the velvet cushion, David looked out at the dark skyscrapers of Chicago, discernible as they contrasted opaquely with the midnight blue of the clear, starry sky. Veronica was probably out there in the city somewhere, and much as he wanted to use their supernatural bond to pinpoint her with his mind, he forced himself not to. Though he longed to make love with her again and taste her blood, he had a promise to keep, a pact with her to honor. And honor was the only thing a vampire could hold on to, if he was still to consider himself at all human.

So David pushed his beloved Veronica from his mind and thought instead of Darienne. What on earth had happened to the diamond-laden, voluptuous blond vampiress, his intermittent companion for the past four centuries? Almost three years had passed since he'd seen or heard from her. She'd never gone this long without returning to him from some corner of the planet to taunt him and tease him—and seduce him.

David curved his lips with ironic amusement. He knew what had happened. Darienne, the sublimely independent, egocentric femme fatale, had fallen in love. He remembered how devastated she'd looked when he'd explained to her why she felt so lost and bewildered. David had understood her confused emotional state only too well, because just as he had fallen for Veronica, so Darienne had also fallen hopelessly in love with a mortal.

And for making that beguiling, irresponsible, irresistible mistake, both Darienne and David had hell to pay.

"I'm glad you like it so much," Harriet Dvorak responded. Her cousin Veronica had just given her an enthusiastic compliment on the dress of mauve rayon Harriet had sewn for herself. "It doesn't look too *Vogue* for me?" Harriet asked, still feeling uncertain about her appearance. "I usually use *Simplicity* patterns."

Veronica studied Harriet's dress again, with its cleverly detailed collar and padded shoulders, as they approached the entrance of the hotel conference room. "No, I don't think so," Veronica said. "It's fun to see you in something really stylish."

"Better than the sweat outfits I used to wear?" Harriet chuckled, but actually felt annoyed with herself for having allowed her appearance to get so frumpy.

Veronica shrugged. "You looked fine in sweats, too. You had kids to run after, so what else should you have worn? Does Ralph like your new wardrobe?"

The question deflated Harriet a bit. "I don't know. He hasn't said anything. Probably hasn't noticed."

"Hasn't noticed?" Veronica pushed her beautiful long dark brown hair back over her shoulder with impatience. She was a small-boned, willowy young woman who looked ultra-slim today in her navy skirt and patterned blouse. Harriet had always admired her cousin for her ethereal beauty and wished she had inherited some of the same genes. Instead, Harriet had her father's sturdy bones and his tendency to put on pounds.

"I don't know how you live with Ralph," Veronica was saying, her tone a mixture of sympathy and irritation. "It's no wonder you've started going to psychic fairs."

Harriet raised her eyebrows. "Now, let's keep an open mind about psychics," she instructed her younger cousin.

Veronica always used to respond to a directive manner. Harriet had discovered this while she was a young adolescent and Veronica was still a child. This trait of Veronica's had continued into adulthood. But in the last few years things had changed somehow, and Harriet found she could no longer influence her cousin the way she used to. Harriet could tell now by the set of Veronica's mouth that she'd merely done Harriet a favor when she'd complied with Harriet's arm-twisting to come with her to the fair.

"My mind is officially open," Veronica told her in an indulgent tone.

Harriet had to be satisfied with that.

They entered the large conference room at a modern hotel

in Oak Brook, a few suburbs west of Berwyn, where Harriet lived. Veronica, who lived on the north side of Chicago, had driven out this Saturday morning to visit Harriet.

Harriet had heard about the three day psychic fair being held this weekend and had awakened that morning with an odd feeling that she should go today, that she'd learn something significant about herself if she did. When Veronica had arrived at her house, she'd begged Veronica to go to the fair with her.

They signed in at the registration desk and were asked with whom they would like to make appointments for readings.

"You go ahead. I don't want to," Veronica said, her dark eyebrows furrowing as she backed away.

"Oh, come on. You're here. Why not?"

"I'll just watch while you talk to your palm reader."

Harriet shook her head. "I check in with her once a week. I want to hear what some of the others have to say." She was following her feeling that, much as she relied on Madame Layla, she would get a special insight from someone new.

"One psychic's not enough?"

"Well, they have different gifts. One might be good at advising about relationships. Another about money. Some read cards or tea leaves. Others use a crystal ball or psychometry. The more of them you go to, the more you find out."

Veronica scratched her eyelid above her long lashes. "How do you know they aren't all quacks?"

"If what they tell you turns out to be true, it seems to me that's pretty good evidence."

"Okay, you pick one and I'll watch."

"No, I want you to have a reading, too. My treat," Harriet insisted, turning to the sign-up sheets before Veronica could object further. After scanning them, she found a name, other than her palm reader's, that she'd heard of. The name seemed to have a nice ring to it, too. "My neighbor said Dorothy Cummings is really good. She's a psychometrist. I haven't been to one of them before," she told Veronica as she wrote both their names down for appointments and paid the fees to the woman behind the desk.

A chance palm reading three months ago at a school fund-raising carnival had opened up a whole new world to Harriet. There she'd met Madame Layla, a middle-aged, black-haired

palm reader adorned with Egyptian jewelry who was donating
her time and fees for readings to the school that evening.
Harriet was dubious about the colorful-looking psychic, but
decided to have a reading for fun and to support her daughter's high school, which needed new gym equipment.

Madame Layla had examined Harriet's hands with great
interest and—like fate, it later seemed to Harriet—had correctly ascertained Harriet's marital problems, while also of-
fering sympathy and suggestions. Madame Layla had seemed
to provide the direction Harriet needed in her life. In that one
evening she'd given Harriet the shove she'd needed to look
more attractive for her husband in the hope that this might
inspire him to be more attentive and romantic. Layla had also
advised her to stand up to him now and then, because Harriet
had confided that she'd begun to feel like a doormat at home.

So Harriet quietly began seeing Madame Layla every few
weeks, then every week, and soon came to look upon the
psychic as a close confidante. Finally she told her husband,
Ralph, how much she was paying the woman and how often
her visits were. Ralph had gotten angry, put his large foot
down and ordered her to stop seeing the palm reader. "No
way!" Harriet had retorted. And since then Ralph hadn't said
another word about it. Harriet was impressed. Madame Layla
had told her it would happen that way.

While waiting for their appointments, Harriet and Veronica
walked around the fair perusing the tables of goods for sale,
which included books on psychic phenomena, witchcraft, the
use of crystals, etc. Also for sale were crystal balls, tarot cards,
herbs and potions, astrological jewelry and pendants made
from crystals. In the other half of the large room, about
twenty psychics sat at separate booths, taking their customer's
appointments.

Harriet led Veronica to the table where she'd spotted Madame Layla sitting, giving a reading for a young woman. As
usual, Layla was dressed in a colorful, flowing caftan that
draped her large frame. Her hands were covered with silver
rings in the shapes of Egyptian symbols. Harriet had once
thought all those rings—two to a finger, and thumb rings,
also—looked tacky. But now she understood that they were
meaningful to Layla, who felt her psychic power was connected with ancient Egypt.

When Layla finished with her customer, Harriet walked up and said hello. She introduced Veronica, who approached with reluctance.

"Your cousin," Layla said, her dark brown eyes bright as she studied Veronica. "You should bring her in for a reading sometime."

"I've been telling her that for weeks," Harriet agreed. "She needs help with her love life. Hasn't gone on a date with a man in years." Harriet had been teasing Veronica about her nun-like lifestyle the last few years. But beneath the joking, Harriet was beginning to grow concerned about Veronica's increasingly solitary way of life.

"Some poor fellow is missing a wife," Layla said to Veronica, who was studying the carpeted floor with a grim half smile. "Maybe I can help you find him. Let me see your hands."

"No, I—I didn't make an appointment," Veronica hedged.

"For free, dear. Just a quick look."

"Go on," Harriet urged.

With a sigh, Veronica approached and held out her hands. Madame Layla examined one and then the other.

"You have delicate, poetic hands," the palm reader said with admiration.

"She's a writer," Harriet told her, proud of her beautiful, accomplished cousin.

"I see that," Layla said, tracing the lines in Veronica's palm with her fingertip. "You will write a book someday," she told Veronica.

"About what?" Veronica asked.

"That would come clearer to me over time," Layla said. "I'm clairvoyant, too, and the longer I know you and the more you trust me, the more I can see."

"She gets images in her mind," Harriet explained.

"Oh," Veronica said. "So what's the verdict on my love life?"

"You are a late bloomer," Layla told her, squeezing her hand in a comforting manner. "But all good things come to those who wait, don't they? You will meet the man of your dreams soon. But he will be a challenge. You must prepare yourself or you may be disappointed in love. You could wind up a spinster."

"Prepare myself? How?"

"That would take more time for me to tell you than I have at the moment. My next customer is waiting. Have Harriet bring you to my home and I'll give you a much more thorough reading. Then I can tell you what to do to win this man when you meet him."

"What if I meet him and don't want him?" Veronica asked, her tone quite ingenuous.

Harriet suspected her cousin was baiting Madame Layla. But the palm reader simply repeated that Veronica should come in for a complete reading and thanked them with a motherly smile for stopping by her table.

"Why did you ask that?" Harriet said when they were out of earshot.

"Because she was full of beans!" Veronica replied.

"How can you say that? She knew right off that you were a writer."

"You told her."

"*I* told her?" Harriet remembered then and felt confounded. "I guess I did. But I was only confirming what she'd said, that you had a poetic hand. Are you planning to write a book?"

"No," Veronica replied with a dry laugh.

"Well, you have lots of years ahead of you. Maybe you will."

Veronica shook her head. "I don't know what you see in her, except that she has a reassuring way about her. You're paying a lot of money for someone to hold your hand."

Harriet kept her patience. "You have to go to her over a period of time. She really gets in depth about things."

"She'll get you in debt, too."

After taking a long breath to keep her good humor, Harriet replied, "Look, I don't drink, I don't smoke, I don't gamble—not even bingo at church. I don't have any expensive hobbies, unless you count making seventeen loaves of bread in one night, which I wound up giving away because my freezer was already full of my baking." She'd found that baking lifted her spirits. "Can't I have one vice?"

"I just hate to see you put so much trust in someone who may be out to fleece you, Harriet. I think she's a con artist."

"Now you sound like Ralph."

Veronica looked chastened. "I'm sorry. I know you're un-happy. But you'd be better off seeing a marriage counselor."

"Ralph would never go to a marriage counselor. He says if I'm not happy it's *my* problem. But, you see, Layla under-stands all that. She says she has instincts and psychic knowl-edge about people that counselors with all their college degrees just don't have. She's great at predicting Ralph, for example, just from what I've told her, even though she's never met him."

"Well, *Ralph*—I could predict him, too. Tell me, honestly, has your marriage improved any, with all this psychic assis-tance?"

Harriet lifted her shoulders. "We don't argue as much." The fact was they barely talked at all anymore, but she didn't feel like admitting that just now.

"Well, okay, I've met the Madame. Can we leave now?"

"No. We have our appointments with the psychometrist," Harriet said, checking her watch. "I think I saw her table down in the far corner of the room. Come on."

Soon they approached Dorothy Cummings's table. A sign with her name on it was posted on the wall behind her. She was dressed in a pink and gray business suit. Her hair was smooth gray, almost white, in a simple short hairstyle. Her face had a youthful appearance and her light green eyes car-ried an air of quiet intelligence.

"She's pretty," Harriet whispered to Veronica as they waited for the person ahead of them to finish.

"She looks halfway normal, I'll say that."

Harriet laughed. "What's with this attitude you have? You don't believe people can have supernatural abilities?"

Veronica was quiet for a moment and her expression be-came grave. "Oh, I *know* there are people with supernatural powers," she said, as if thinking of some personal experience. This surprised Harriet, because she didn't know what her cousin was referring to. Veronica usually confided in her. They had been close for as long as Harriet could remember. But before Harriet could ask, Veronica continued. "It's just an area where it's so easy to take advantage of people who are having problems."

"*Gullible* people like me, you mean?" Harriet said, raising an eyebrow humorously.

"Well, you have fallen for this stuff hook, line and sinker."

"All I know is I feel better after seeing Madame Layla and her guidance has been valuable. Don't I look better lately?"

"Yes, you do," Veronica agreed.

"I'm still working on the weight issue, but I bet she can help me with that, too."

Veronica looked as though she thought otherwise. She glanced at Dorothy Cummings, whose customer had just left. "Look, she's motioning us to come over. Let's get this over with."

Harriet approached the table with Veronica, disappointed with her cousin's attitude. Veronica had changed from the sweet, shy, dreamy girl she used to be. She'd grown more mature, more forthright, but also inexplicably grim, impatient, and often melancholy. Harriet was still terribly fond of her younger cousin, but sometimes felt as if she didn't quite know her anymore.

"Hello," Dorothy said with a smile, as they approached. She introduced herself and asked their names. "Who's first?"

Veronica pointed to Harriet. "She is."

Harriet put aside her ruminations about her cousin and focused on the present. "You need something of mine to hold, right?"

"Yes," Dorothy said. "A watch, a ring. Anything you've had for a while."

Harriet took off her wedding ring. "Try this," she said with a sense of gallows humor.

"All right." Dorothy took the ring and held it tightly in her hand. She closed her eyes in concentration. When she opened them and began to speak, her gaze seemed to be focused on some point in her mind's eye. "You're very impressionable, Harriet. It's something you always need to be careful of. Your marriage is not going well. You married very young. So young!" Dorothy shook her head in sympathetic dismay. "You're religious," she continued in a more positive tone. "You love your home and your neighborhood. You have children—three. No, two. Two. They don't need you much anymore. And your husband has become distant. You feel all alone."

Harriet listened, her spirits sinking as she heard her life capsulized. She wanted to say, "Yes, that's right!" but Dorothy seemed in deep concentration, as if interrupting her would break the messages she seemed to be receiving.

"You're an exemplary homemaker. But your efforts aren't appreciated." Dorothy paused, as if waiting. "I'm getting something about the future now. I see some upheaval ahead. Your relationship with your husband will be tested even more. Whether the marriage lasts or not depends on you. I sense there will be another man who will have a profound effect on you, how you think, what you do. I see this man acting in the role of a counselor or priest for you."

The psychometrist relaxed her hand and looked at the wedding ring. She nodded her head. "Yes, all the ambivalence you've felt about your husband lately will disappear over the next few months. You'll make a decision about him, and the decision will be all yours, I feel. He won't have much choice in the matter."

"How come?" Harriet asked, doubtful but greatly intrigued. Her heart rate began to escalate. Was this the important information she'd had a feeling she'd learn today?

"Because you will be the stronger one."

"Me? Stronger than Ralph?" No, Harriet couldn't see how that could ever come about. "What about this priest? Have I met him? Is he at my church?"

"I don't know," Dorothy said with some puzzlement in her voice. She gave Harriet her ring back. "He may not actually *be* a priest. I saw a flash—a quick brightness—of sensuality around you. Be careful. He may become your lover. Nothing more than that came to me. Sorry."

"Thank you," Harriet said, feeling a little shocked as she slipped her wedding ring back onto her left hand. She wasn't sure what to make of the reading. Everything Dorothy had said about her past and present were right on the mark. But her predictions about the future seemed a little far out. Madame Layla had never told her anything about a new man in her life. It sounded exciting, all right. But for a plump, thirty-six-year-old housewife who rarely met anyone new except other women in crafts classes, this was highly unlikely. Besides, there hadn't been a new priest at her church in years, and none was expected. Good thing, too, if this man might become her lover!

Amused now, Harriet decided that she'd better put any

future prescient feelings of hers aside, forget other psychics, and rely on what Madame Layla told her. At least Layla made predictions that were grounded in reality.

"Shall I do your reading now?" Dorothy said to Veronica.

Harriet noticed Veronica's previous expression of passive disapproval had changed. Veronica looked a trifle dumbfounded, probably because she knew the facts Dorothy had stated about Harriet's past and present were true.

Veronica began to take off her watch, but then stopped and slipped it back on her wrist. Harriet wondered if Veronica had changed her mind. But her cousin opened her purse, then a zippered compartment inside it, and took out a knotted handkerchief. She untied the cloth and took out two keys, one larger one and one smaller one. Harriet wondered what these separate keys were for. She knew Veronica kept her everyday apartment and car keys on a metal chain.

Veronica studied the two keys as if questioning which one to give Dorothy. She picked up the smaller one. With some hesitation, apparently worried she was doing the right thing, she handed it to the psychometrist.

Dorothy took the key and, as she did with Harriet's ring, held it tightly in her hand and concentrated.

"I sense a large house, a mansion. The third floor is important. But most important is a small room below the house. It's hidden. Always dark. Secret." Dorothy seemed to shiver a bit.

She swallowed and continued in a firmer voice. "You're very attached to the house, more than to your own home. But you haven't been there for a long, long while and you miss it terribly. I sense a man who is overwhelming in his importance to you. You love him deeply. I can feel the love between you and him. It's . . . it's quite beautiful and profound."

Tears gathered in Dorothy's eyes. She spoke with feeling, as if taking on Veronica's emotions herself. "And terribly, terribly sad. Such a burden of love you carry! But it's made you strong. Everything you do, your whole life is lived for this man you love so deeply."

She paused and then uttered a sound of pain. "Ohh . . ." Dorothy's hand began to tremble. Her voice diminished to a whisper. "He's ill! He's . . . cursed. I see darkness, darkness, nothing but darkness around him."

Dorothy straightened and blinked the wetness from her

eyes. She seemed to try to pull herself together, concentrating on the key, as if to discern a new message that was coming to her. "There's a remedy—a cure. I see this clearly. He can be cured, Veronica. A woman . . . far from here, across an ocean. She knows the way. She lives near a forest. You know of her. You must find her soon because she's very old and frail."

Her hand still trembling, Dorothy held out the key to Veronica. "That's all I can tell you," she said in a strained voice. "I'm sorry, this has exhausted me." She looked earnestly at Veronica. "But you *must* use this information. You have a great love to save."

Harriet glanced at Veronica as she took back her key. Her cousin was biting her lower lip to keep back a sob. A tear slid down her cheek. "Thank you," Veronica said in a hushed voice. "But I don't know who this old woman is. I've never been out of the States. How do I find her?"

Dorothy shook her head, her expression troubled. "I sensed some connection between you. I don't know any more than that. I'm sorry. I wish you well, Veronica."

Harriet and Veronica walked out of the conference room in silence. Veronica seemed distracted, almost dazed, and Harriet was afraid to say anything at first. Finally, when they left the hotel and were walking to the parking lot, Harriet said, "You never mentioned you had a man in your life. Who is he?"

Veronica, who had stopped crying, paused and stared at Harriet, eyes wide and unblinking, as if a thought had struck her. "Will you help me?"

"Me? How?"

"I need you to tell someone what the psychometrist told me—about the cure. You remember everything she said?"

"I think so. Who do I tell?"

"There's a house on Oak Street on the near north side. I'll write down the address. I need you to go there, but only after dark. Knock on the door and wait till he answers. Tell him—"

"Wait. Who's *he?*"

Veronica swallowed and a look shadowed her eyes that was at once tender and frightened. "His name is David."

"He's the man? The one the psychometrist mentioned, the one you love?"

Veronica nodded. "Tell him you're my cousin, that I sent

you to see him. Tell him what the psychic told us about the cure. Just say I wanted him to know. I . . ." She looked down. "I hope he won't be angry with me."

"Why? Does he have a bad temper?" Harriet asked, concerned for Veronica.

"Oh, he'd never hurt you," Veronica assured her. "Don't be afraid of him."

Somehow this unsettled Harriet even more. "Look, I want to help, but I don't understand. Why can't you visit him yourself? Or call him on the phone? I gathered that you and he broke up, but can't you write him a note at least?"

"No. We aren't to have any contact. I can't tell you why."

"Can't tell me because *you* don't know why, or because you aren't supposed to tell?"

"Whatever you may learn about David and me, *he* must tell you, Harriet. And he may choose not to tell you anything. I know this all must sound strange. But I need you to do this for me. Please? Will you?"

"Well, sure, I suppose," Harriet said with a shrug. It was a more interesting way to spend an evening than watching TV while Ralph sat behind his newspaper, she decided. Besides, she was curious about this David, this man Veronica had apparently been in love with for some time. She had to admit, Madame Layla's reading for Veronica had been all wrong. "But what about his illness?" Harriet asked. "Is it catching?"

Veronica looked at her as if she didn't know what Harriet was talking about.

"Whatever it is he's got that he needs the cure for," Harriet said.

"Oh, I see what you mean." Veronica almost smiled. "No, it's not catching. He won't give it to you." Her eyes grew sad. "He won't even give it to me."

Harriet was too confused to even ask what *that* might mean. Yes, she'd better check this man out to see what sort of relationship Veronica had gotten herself into. "When should I go?"

"Tonight? Can you?"

"Sure. I just ring the bell and ask for David? Does he have a last name?"

"Let him tell you his full name, if he wishes. And there's no bell. David's . . . old-fashioned. There's a brass door knocker.

Keep knocking until he answers. Sometimes he's in a far corner of the house and doesn't hear it right away."

"What if he's not home?"

"Then I'm afraid you'll have to go back again another night. You must keep trying until you see him," Veronica said earnestly.

"I will. You can count on me. I just wish I knew more about all this. Isn't there anything else you can tell me?"

Veronica hesitated and new tears shimmered in her eyes. Her voice grew husky with profound feeling. "Only that I love him more than life. I would die for him—if only he'd let me."